ANDROCLES IN THE ARENA

The
Animal Story Book

Edited by
Andrew Lang

with numerous illustrations by
H. J. Ford

DOVER PUBLICATIONS, INC.
Mineola, New York

Published in the United Kingdom by David & Charles, Brunel House, Forde Close, Newton Abbot, Devon TQ12 4PU.

Bibliographical Note

This Dover edition, first published in 2002, is an unabridged, unaltered republication of the work originally published in 1896 by Longmans, Green, & Co., London, New York, and Bombay.

Library of Congress Cataloging-in-Publication Data

Lang, Andrew, 1844–1912.
    The animal story book / Andrew Lang.
        p. cm.
    Summary: A collection of short stories, anecdotes, fables, and folktales involving animals from various authors and traditions.
    ISBN 0-486-42187-2 (pbk.)
      1. Animals—Literary collections. [1. Animals—Literary collections.] I. Title.

PZ5.L42 An 2002
810.8'0362—dc21

                                     2002019226

Manufactured in the United States of America
Dover Publications, Inc., 31 East 2nd Street, Mineola, N.Y. 11501

To

MASTER FREDERICK LONGMAN

This year our Book for Christmas varies,
Deals not with History nor Fairies
   (I can't help thinking, children, you
   Prefer a book which is not true).
We leave these intellectual feasts,
To talk of Fishes, Birds, and Beasts.
   These—though his aim is hardly steady—
   These are, I think, a theme for Freddy!
Trout, though he is not up to fly,
He soon will catch—as well as I!
   So, Freddy, take this artless rhyme,
   And be a Sportsman in your time!

PREFACE

CHILDREN who have read our Fairy Books may have noticed that there are not so very many fairies in the stories after all. The most common characters are birds, beasts, and fishes, who talk and act like Christians. The reason of this is that the first people who told the stories were not very clever, or, if they were clever, they had never been taught to read and write, or to distinguish between Vegetable, Animal, and Mineral. They took it that all things were 'much of a muchness:' they were not proud, and held that beast and bird could talk like themselves, only, of course, in a different language.

After offering, then, so many Fairy Books, (though the stories are not all told yet), we now present you (in return for a coin or two) with a book about the friends of children and of fairies—the beasts. The stories are all true, more or less, but it is possible that Monsieur Dumas and Monsieur Théophile Gautier rather improved upon their tales. I own that I have my doubts about the bears and serpents in the tales by the Baron Wogan. This gentleman's ancestors were famous Irish people. One of them held Cromwell's soldiers back when they were pursuing Charles II. after Worcester fight. He also led a troop of horse from Dover to the Highlands, where he died of a wound, after fighting for the King. The next Wogan was a friend of Pope and Swift; he escaped from prison after Preston fight, in 1715, and, later, rescued Prince Charlie's mother from confinement in Austria, and took her to marry King James. He next became Governor of Don Quixote's province, La Mancha, in Spain, and was still alive and merry in 1752. Baron Wogan, descended from these heroes, saw no longer any king to fight for, so he went to America and fought bears. No doubt he was as brave as his ancestors, but whether all his stories of serpents are absolutely correct I am not so certain. People have also been heard to express doubts about Mr. Waterton and the Cayman. The terrible tale of Mr. Gully and his deeds of war I *know* to be accurate, and the story of Oscar, the sentimental tyke, is believed in firmly by the lady who wrote it. As for the stories about Greek and Roman beasts, Pliny, who tells them, is a most respectable author. On the whole, then, this is more or less of a true story-book.

There ought to be a moral; if so, it probably is that we should be kind to all sorts of animals, and, above all, knock trout on the head when they are caught, and don't let the poor things jump about till they die. A chapter of a very learned sort was written about the cleverness of beasts, proving that there must have been great inventive geniuses among beasts long ago, and that now they have rather got into a habit (which I think a very good one) of being content with the discoveries of their ancestors. This led naturally to some observations on Instinct and Reason ; but there may be children who are glad that there was no room for this chapter.

The longer stories from Monsieur Dumas were translated from the French by Miss Cheape.

'A Rat Tale' is by Miss Evelyn Grieve, who knew the rats.

'Mr. Gully' is by Miss Elspeth Campbell, to whom Mr. Gully belonged.

'The Dog of Montargis,' 'More Faithful than Favoured,' and 'Androcles' are by Miss Eleanor Sellar.

Snakes, Bears, Ants, Wolves, Monkeys, and some Lions are by Miss Lang.

'Two Highland Dogs' is by Miss Goodrich Freer.

'Fido' and 'Oscar' and 'Patch' are by Miss A. M. Alleyne.

'Djijam' is by his master.

'The Starling of Segringen' and 'Grateful Dogs' are by Mr. Bartells.

'Tom the Bear,' 'The Frog,' 'Jacko the Monkey' and 'Gazelle' are from Dumas by Miss Blackley.

All the rest are by Mrs. Lang.

CONTENTS

LIST OF ILLUSTRATIONS

'TOM' [1]

AN ADVENTURE IN THE LIFE OF
A BEAR IN PARIS

Some sixty years ago and more, a well-known artist named Décamps lived in Paris. He was the intimate friend of some of the first authors, artists, and scientific men of the day, and was devotedly fond of animals of all sorts. He loved to paint them, and he kept quite a small ménagerie in his studio where a bear, a monkey, a tortoise, and a frog lived (more or less) in peace and harmony together.

The bear's name was 'Tom,' the monkey was called 'Jacko I.,' [2] the frog was 'Mademoiselle Camargo,' and the tortoise 'Gazelle.'

Here follows the story of Tom, the bear.

It was the night of Shrove Tuesday in the year 1832. Tom had as yet only spent six months in Paris, but he was really one of the most attractive bears you could wish to meet.

He ran to open the door when the bell rang, he mounted guard for hours together, halberd in hand, standing on his hind legs, and he danced a minuet with infinite grace, holding a broomstick behind his head.

He had spent the whole day in the exercise of these varied accomplishments, to the great delight of the frequenters of his master's studio, and had just retired to the

[1] From Alexandre Dumas.
[2] To distinguish him from Jacko II., a monkey belonging to Tony Johannot, the painter.

press which did duty as his hutch, to seek a little repose, when there was a knock at the street door. Jacko instantly showed such signs of joy that Décamps made a shrewd guess that the visitor could be no other than Fan, the self-elected tutor in chief to the two animals—nor was he mistaken. The door opened, Fan appeared, dressed as a clown, and Jacko flung himself in rapture into his arms.

'Very good, very good,' said Fan, placing the monkey on the table and handing him a cane. 'You're really a charming creature. Carry arms, present arms, make ready, fire! Capital!'

'I'll have a complete uniform made for you, and you shall mount guard instead of me. But I haven't come for you to-night; it's your friend Tom I want. Where may he be?'

'Why, in his hutch, I suppose,' said Décamps.

'Tom! here, Tom!' cried Fan.

Tom gave a low growl, just to show that he knew very well who they were talking of, but that he was in no hurry to show himself.

'Well!' exclaimed Fan, 'is this how my orders are obeyed? Tom, my friend, don't force me to resort to extreme measures.'

Tom stretched one great paw beyond the cupboard without allowing any more of his person to be seen, and began to yawn plaintively like a child just wakened from its first sleep.

'Where is the broomstick?' inquired Fan in threatening tones, and rattling the collection of Indian bows, arrows, and spears which stood behind the door.

'Ready!' cried Décamps, pointing to Tom, who, on hearing these well known sounds, had roused himself without more ado, and advanced towards his tutor with a perfectly innocent and unconscious air.

'That's right,' said Fan: 'now be a good fellow, particularly as one has come all this way on purpose to fetch you.'

TOM IS INVITED TO THE BALL

Tom waved his head up and down.

'So, so—now shake hands with your friends:—first rate!'

'Do you mean to take him with you?' asked Décamps.

'Rather!' replied Fan; 'and give him a good time into the bargain.'

'And where are you going?'

'To the Carnival Masked Ball, nothing less! Now then Tom, my friend, come along. We've got a cab outside waiting by the hour.'

As though fully appreciating the force of this argument, Tom trundled down stairs four steps at a time followed by his friend. The driver opened the cab door, and Tom, under Fan's guidance, stepped in as if he had done nothing else all his life.

'My eye! that's a queer sort of fancy dress,' said cabby; 'anyone might take him for a real bear. Where to, gentlemen?'

'Odéon Theatre,' said Fan.

'Grrrooonnn,' observed Tom.

'All right,' said the cabman. 'Keep your temper. It's a good step from here, but we shall get there all in good time.'

Half an hour later the cab drew up at the door of the theatre. Fan got down first, paid the driver, handed out Tom, took two tickets, and passed in without exciting any special attention.

At the second turn they made round the crush-room people began to follow Fan. The perfection with which the newcomer imitated the walk and movements of the animal whose skin he wore attracted the notice of some lovers of natural history. They pressed closer and closer, and anxious to find out whether he was equally clever in imitating the bear's voice, they began to pull his hairs and prick his ears—'Grrrooonnn,' said Tom.

A murmur of admiration ran through the crowd—nothing could be more lifelike.

Fan led Tom to the buffet and offered him some little cakes, to which he was very partial, and which he proceeded to swallow with so admirable a pretence of voracity that the bystanders burst out laughing. Then the mentor poured out a tumbler full of water, which Tom took gingerly between his paws, as he was accustomed to whenever Décamps did him the honour of permitting him to appear at table, and gulped down the contents at one draught. Enthusiasm knew no bounds! Indeed such was the delight and interest shown that when, at length, Fan wished to leave the buffet, he found they were hemmed in by so dense a crowd that he felt nervous lest Tom should think of clearing the road with claws and teeth. So he promptly led his bear to a corner, placed him with his back against the wall, and told him to stay there till further orders.

As has been already mentioned, this kind of drill was quite familiar to Tom, and was well suited to his natural indolence, and when a harlequin offered his hat to complete the picture, he settled himself comfortably, gravely laying one great paw on his wooden gun.

'Do you happen to know,' said Fan to the obliging harlequin, '*who* you have lent your hat to?'

'No,' replied harlequin.

'You mean to say you don't guess?'

'Not in the least.'

'Come, take a good look at him. From the grace of all his movements, from the manner in which he carries his head, slightly on one side, like Alexander the Great—from the admirable imitations of the bear's voice—you don't mean to say you don't recognise him?'

'Upon my word I don't.'

'Odry!'[1] whispered Fan mysteriously; 'Odry, in his costume from "The Bear and the Pacha"!'

[1] A well-known actor of the time.

' Oh, but he acts a *white* bear, you know.'

' Just so ; that's why he has chosen a brown bear's skin as a disguise.'

' Ho, ho ! You're a good one,' cried harlequin.

' Grrooonnn,' observed Tom.

' Well, now you mention it, I *do* recognise his voice. Really, I wonder it had not struck me before. Do ask him to disguise it better.'

' Yes, yes,' said Fan, moving towards the ball-room, ' but it will never do to worry him. However, I'll try to persuade him to dance a minuet presently.'

' Oh, could you really ? '

' He promised to do so. Just give a hint to your friends and try to prevent their teasing him.'

' All right.'

Tom made his way through the crowd, whilst the delighted harlequin moved from one mask to another, telling his news with warnings to be discreet, which were well received. Just then, too, the sounds of a lively galop were heard, and a general rush to the ball-room took place, harlequin only pausing to murmur in Tom's ear : ' I know you, my fine mask.'

' Grrooooonnn,' replied Tom.

' Ah, it's all very well to growl, but you'll dance a minuet, won't you, old fellow ? '

Tom waved his head up and down as his way was when anyone asked him a question, and harlequin, satisfied with this silent consent, ran off to find a columbine and to dance the galop.

Meanwhile, Tom remained alone with the waiters ; motionless at his post, but with longing eyes turned towards the counter on which the most tempting piles of cake were heaped on numerous dishes. The waiters, remarking his rapt attention, and pleased to tempt a customer, stretched out a dish, Tom extended his paw and gingerly took a cake—then a second—then a third : the waiters seemed never tired of offering, or Tom of

accepting these delicacies, and so, when the galop ended
and the dancers returned to the crush-room, he had
made short work of some dozens of little cakes.

Harlequin had recruited a columbine and a shepherdess,
and he introduced these ladies as partners for the promised
minuet.   With all the air of an old friend he whispered a
few words to Tom, who, in the best of humours after so
many cakes, replied with his most gracious growl.   The
harlequin, turning towards the gallery, announced that his
lordship had much pleasure in complying with the uni-
versal request, and amidst loud applause, the shepherdess
took one of Tom's paws and the columbine the other.
Tom, for his part, like an accomplished cavalier, walked
between his two partners, glancing at them by turns with
looks of some surprise, and soon found himself with them
in the middle of the pit of the theatre which was used as
a ball-room.   All took their places, some in the boxes,
others in the galleries, the greater number forming a
circle round the dancers.   The band struck up.

The minuet was Tom's greatest triumph and Fan's
masterpiece, and with the very first steps success was
assured and went on increasing with each movement,
till at the last figure the applause became delirious.   Tom
was swept off in triumph to a stage box where the
shepherdess, removing her wreath of roses, crowned him
with it, whilst the whole theatre resounded with the
applause of the spectators.

Tom leant over the front of the box with a grace all
his own; at the same time the strains of a fresh dance
were heard, and everyone hurried to secure partners
except a few courtiers of the new star who hovered round
in hope of extracting an order for the play from him, but
Tom only replied to their broadest hints with his perpetual
'Grroonnn.'

By degrees this became rather monotonous, and gradually Tom's court dwindled away, people murmuring that,
though his dancing powers were certainly unrivalled, his

conversation was a trifle insipid. An hour later Tom was alone ! So fleeting is public favour.

And now the hour of departure drew near. The pit

'THE MINUET WAS TOM'S GREATEST TRIUMPH'

was thinning and the boxes empty, and pale rays of morning light were glinting into the hall when the box-opener, who was going her rounds, heard sounds of snoring proceeding from one of the stage boxes. She opened the door, and there was Tom, who, tired out after his eventful night, had fallen fast asleep on the floor. The box-opener stepped in and politely hinted that it was six o'clock and time to go home.

'Grrooonnn,' said Tom.

'I hear you,' said the box-opener; 'you're asleep, my good man, but you'll sleep better still in your own bed. Come, come, your wife must be getting quite anxious! Upon my word I don't believe he hears a word I say. How heavily he sleeps!' And she shook him by the shoulder.

'Grrrooonnn!'

'All right, all right! This isn't a time to make believe. Besides, we all know you. There now, they're putting out the lights. Shall I send for a cab for you?'

'Grrroooonnn.'

'Come, come, the Odéon Theatre isn't an inn; come, be off! Oh, *that's* what you're after, is it? Fie, Monsieur Odry, fie! I shall call the guard; the inspector hasn't gone to bed yet. Ah, indeed! You won't obey rules! You are trying to beat me, are you? You would beat a woman—and a former artiste to M. Odry, would you? For shame! But we shall see. Here, help—police—inspector —help!'

'What's the matter?' cried the fireman on duty.

'Help!' screamed the box-opener, 'help!'

'What's the matter?' asked the sergeant commanding the patrol.

'Oh, it's old mother what's her name, shrieking for help in one of the stage boxes.'

'Coming!' shouted the sergeant.

'This way, Mr. Sergeant, this way,' cried the box-opener.

'All right, my dear, here I am. But where are you?'

'Don't be afraid; there are no steps—straight on this way—he's in the corner. Oh, the rascal, he's as strong as a Turk!'

' Grrrooonnn,' said Tom.

' There, do you hear him ? Is that to be called a Christian language ? '

' Come, come, my friend,' said the sergeant, who had at last managed to distinguish Tom in the faint twilight. ' We all know what it is to be young—no one likes a joke better than I do—but rules are rules, and the hour for going home has struck, so right about face, march! and quick step too.'

' Grrrooonnn '—

' Very pretty ; a first-rate imitation. But suppose we try something else now for a change. Come, old fellow, step out with a good will. Ah! you won't. You're going to cut up rough, are you ? Here, my man, lay hold and turn him out.'

' He won't walk, sergeant.'

' Well, what are the butt ends of your muskets for ? Come, a tap or two will do no harm.'

' Grrrooonnn—Grrrooonnn—Grrrooonnn—'

' Go on, give it him well ! '

' I say, sergeant,' said one of the men, ' it strikes me he's a *real* bear. I caught hold of him by the collar just now, and the skin seems to grow on the flesh.'

' Oh, if he's a real bear, treat him with every consideration. His owner might claim damages. Go and fetch the fireman's lantern.'

' Grrrooonnn.'

' Here's the lantern,' said a man; ' now then, throw some light on the prisoner.'

The soldier obeyed.

' It is certainly a real snout,' declared the sergeant.

' Goodness gracious me ! ' shrieked the box-opener as she took to her heels, ' a real live bear ! '

' Well, yes, a real live bear. Let's see if he has any name or address on him and take him home. I expect he has strayed, and being of a sociable disposition, came in to the Masked Ball.'

' Grrrooonnn.'

' There, you see, he agrees.'

' Hallo ! ' exclaimed one of the soldiers.

' What's the matter ? '

TOM DISCOVERED IN THE BOX

' He has a little bag hung round his neck.'

' Open the bag.'

' A card.'

' Read the card.'

The soldier took it and read :

'My name is Tom. I live at No. 109 Rue Faubourg St.-Denis. I have five francs in my purse. Two for a cab, and three for whoever takes me home.'

'True enough; there are the five francs,' cried the sergeant. 'Now then, two volunteers for escort duty.'

'Here!' cried the guard in chorus.

'Don't all speak at once! Let the two seniors have the benefit of the job; off with you, my lads.'

Two of the municipal guards advanced towards Tom, slipped a rope round his neck and, for precaution's sake, gave it a twist or two round his snout. Tom offered no resistance—the butt ends of the muskets had made him as supple as a glove. When they were fifty yards from the theatre, 'Bah!' said one of the soldiers, ''tis a fine morning. Suppose we don't take a cab. The walk will do him good.'

'Besides,' remarked the other, 'we should each have two and a half francs instead of only one and a half.'

'Agreed.'

Half an hour later they stood at the door of 109. After some knocking, a very sleepy portress looked out.

'Look here, Mother Wideawake,' said one of the guard; 'here's one of your lodgers. Do you recognise him?'

'Why, I should rather think so. It's Monsieur Décamps' bear!'

The same day, Odry the actor received a bill for little cakes, amounting to seven francs and a half.

SAÏ THE PANTHER [1]

ABOUT seventy or eighty years ago two little panthers were deserted by their mother in one of the forests of Ashantee. They were too young to get food for themselves, and would probably have died had they not been found by a passing traveller, and by him taken to the palace as a present to the king. Here they lived and played happily for several weeks, when one day the elder and larger, whose name was Saï, gave his brother, in fun, such a dreadful squeeze that, without meaning it, he suffocated him. This frightened the king, who did not care to keep such a powerful pet about him, and he gave him away to Mr. Hutchison, an English gentleman, who was a sort of governor for the English traders settled in that part of Africa.

Mr. Hutchison and Saï took a great fancy to each other, and spent a great deal of time together, and when, a few months later, Mr. Hutchison returned to Cape Coast he brought Saï with him. The two friends always had dinner at the same time, Saï sitting at his master's side and eating quietly whatever was given him. In general he was quite content with his portion, but once or twice, when he was hungrier than usual, he managed to steal a fowl out of the dish. For the sake of his manners the fowl was always taken from him, although he was invariably given some other food to satisfy his hunger.

At first the inhabitants of the castle and the children were much afraid of him, but he soon became very tame,

---

[1] From Loudon's *Magazine of Natural History*.

and his teeth and claws were filed so that he should not hurt anyone, even in play. When he got a little accustomed to the place, he was allowed to go where he liked within the castle grounds, and a boy was told off to look after him. Sometimes the boy would go to sleep when he ought to have been watching his charge, and then Saï, who knew perfectly well that this was not at all right, would steal quietly away and amuse himself till he thought his keeper would be awake again. One day, when he returned from his wanderings, he found the boy, as usual, comfortably curled up in a cool corner of the doorstep sound asleep. Saï looked at him for a moment, and then, thinking that it was full time for him to be taught his duty, he gave him one pat on his head, which sent the boy over like a ninepin and gave him a good fright, though it did not do him any harm.

Saï was very popular with everybody, but he had his own favourites, and the chief of these was the governor, whom he could not bear to let out of his sight. When his master went out he would station himself at the drawing-room window, where he could watch all that was going on, and catch the first sight of his returning friend. Being by this time nearly grown up, Saï's great body took up all the space, to the great disgust of the children, who could see nothing. They tried to make him move, first by coaxings and then by threats, but as Saï did not pay the smallest attention to either one or the other, they at last all took hold of his tail and pulled so hard that he was forced to move.

Strange to say, the black people were a great deal more afraid of Saï than any of the white ones, and one of his pranks nearly caused the death of an old woman who was the object of it. It was her business to sweep out and keep clean the great hall of the castle, and one morning she was crouching down on all fours with a short broom in her hand, thinking of nothing but how to get the dust out of the floor, when Saï, who had hidden him-

self under a sofa, and was biding his time, suddenly sprang
on to her back, where he stood triumphantly. The old

'THEY AT LAST ALL TOOK HOLD OF HIS TAIL'

woman believed her last hour had come, and the other
servants all ran away shrieking, lest it should be their

TERROR OF THE ORANG-OUTANG AT SAÏ

turn next. Saï would not budge from his position till the governor, who had been alarmed by the terrible noise, came to see what was the matter, and soon made Master Saï behave himself.

At this time it was settled that Saï was to travel to England under the care of one of his Cape Coast friends and be presented to the Duchess of York, who was very fond of animals. In those days, of course, journeys took much longer than they do now, and there were other dangers than any which might arise from storms and tempests. While the strong cage of wood and iron was being built which was to form Saï's house on the way to England, his lady keeper thought it would be a good opportunity to make friends with him, and used to spend part of every day talking to him and playing with him; for this, as everyone knows, is the only way to gain the affection of bird or beast. It was very easy to love Saï; he was so gentle and caressing, especially with children; and he was very handsome besides in his silky yellow coat with black spots, which, as the French say, does not spoil anything. Many creatures and many men might have made a great fuss at being shut into a cage instead of being allowed to walk about their own house and grounds, but everyone had always been kind to Saï, so he took for granted it was all right, and made himself as comfortable as he could, and was quite prepared to submit to anything disagreeable that he thought reasonable. But it very nearly happened that poor Saï had no voyage at all, for while he was being hauled from the canoe which had brought him from the shore into the ship, the men were so afraid to come near him that they let his cage fall into the sea, and if the sailors from the vessel had not been very quick in lowering a boat it would have been too late to save him. As it was, for many days he would not look up or eat or speak, and his friend was quite unhappy about him, although the same symptoms have sometimes been shown by human beings who have

only been *on* the sea instead of *in* it. At last he was
roused from his sad condition by hearing the lady's voice.
He raised his head and cocked his ears, first a little, then
more ; and when she came up to the cage he rolled over
and over with delight, and howled and cried and tried to
reach her. When he got a little calmer she told him to
put his paws through the bars and shake hands, and from
that moment Saï was himself again.

Now it was a very strange taste on the part of a
panther whose fathers and grandfathers had lived and
died in the heart of African forests, but Saï loved nothing
so much as lavender water, which white people use a
great deal in hot countries. If anyone took out a handkerchief which had been sprinkled with lavender water,
Saï would instantly snatch it away, and in his delight
would handle it so roughly that it was soon torn to atoms.
His friend in charge knew of this odd fancy, and on the
voyage she amused herself regularly twice a week with
making a little cup of paper, which she filled with the
scent and passed through the bars, taking care never to
give it him till he had drawn back his claws into their
sheaths. Directly he got hold of the cup Saï would roll
over and over it, and would pay no attention to anyone as
long as the smell lasted. It almost seemed as if he liked
it better than his food !

For some reason or other the vessel lay at anchor for
nearly two months in the river Gaboon, and Saï might
have been allowed to leave his cage if he had not been an
animal of such very strong prejudices. Black people he
could not endure, and, of course, they came daily in swarms
with food for the ship. Pigs, too, he hated, and they ran
constantly past his cage, while as for an orang-outang
monkey about three feet high, which a black trader once
tried to sell to the sailors, Saï showed such mad symptoms
at the very sight of it that the poor beast rushed in terror
to the other end of the vessel, knocking down everything
that came in its way. If the monkey took some time to

SAÏ HAS TO TAKE A PILL

recover from his fright, it was very long before Saï could
forget the shock he had received. Day and night he
watched and listened, and sometimes, when he fancied his
enemy was near, he would give a low growl and arch his
back and set up his tail; yet, as far as we know, he had
never from his babyhood killed anything.

But when at last the winds were favourable, and the
ship set sail for the open sea, other adventures were in
store for the passengers. Pirates infested the coast of
Africa in those days, and they came on board and carried
off everything of value, including the stores of provisions.
The only things they did not think worth removing were
the parrots, of which three hundred had been brought
by the sailors, and as these birds could not stand the cold,
and died off fast as the ship steered north, Saï was allowed
one a day, which just managed to keep him alive. Still,
there is very little nourishment to be got out of a parrot,
especially when you eat it with the feathers on, and Saï
soon became very ill and did not care even for parrots.
His keeper felt his nose and found it dry and feverish, so
she begged that she might take him out of his cage and
doctor him herself. A little while before, Saï would have
been enchanted to be free, but now he was too ill to
enjoy anything, and he just stretched himself out on deck,
with his head on his mistress's feet. Luckily she had
some fever medicine with her, good for panthers as well
as men and women, and she made up three large pills
which she hoped might cure Saï. Of course it was not to
be expected that he would take them of his own free will,
so she got the boy who looked after him to hold open his
mouth, while she pushed down the pills. Then he was
put back into his cage, the boy insisting on going with
him, and both slept comfortably together. In a few days,
with the help of better food than he had been having, he
got quite well, and on his arrival in England won the
admiration of the Duchess of York, his new mistress, by
his beauty and gentle ways. As his country house was

not quite ready for him, he was left for a few weeks with a man who understood animals, and seemed contented and happy, and was allowed to walk about as he liked. Here the Duchess of York used constantly to visit him and play with him, even going to see him the very day before he—and she—were to move into the country. He was in excellent spirits, and appeared perfectly well, but he must somehow have taken a chill, for when, on the following day, the Duchess's coachman came to fetch him, he found poor Saï had died after a few hours' illness from inflammation of the lungs.

After all he is not so much to be pitied. He had had a very happy life, with plenty of fun and plenty of kindness, and he had a very rapid and painless death.

THE BUZZARD AND THE PRIEST[1]

ABOUT one hundred and forty years ago a French priest received a present of a large brown and grey bird, which had been taken in a snare intended for some other creature, and was very wild and savage. The man who brought it was quite ignorant what kind of bird it was, but the priest knew it to be the common buzzard, and made up his mind to try to tame it. He began by keeping it shut up, and allowing it to take no food except out of his hand, and after about six weeks of this treatment it grew much quieter, and had learnt to know its master. The priest then thought it would be safe to give the buzzard a little more freedom, and after carefully tying its wings, so that it could not fly away, he turned it out into the garden. Of course it was highly delighted to find itself in the sun once more, and hopped about with joy, and the time passed quickly till it began to get hungry, when it was glad to hear its master calling it to come in to dinner. Indeed, the bird always seemed so fond of the priest, that in a few days he thought he might leave it quite free, so he unfastened its wings and left them loose, merely hanging a label with his own name round its neck, and putting a little bell round its leg. But what was the poor man's disgust, to see the buzzard instantly spread out its great wings and make for the neighbouring forest, deaf to all his calls! He naturally expected that, in spite of his trouble and precautions, the bird had flown away for ever, and sat sadly down to prepare his

[1] Bingley's *Animal Biography*.

next day's sermon.   Now sermons are things that take
up a great deal of attention, and he had almost forgotten
his lost favourite when he was startled by a tremendous
noise in the hall outside his study, and on opening the
door to see what was the matter, he saw his buzzard
rushing about, followed by five others, who were so
jealous of its copper plate and bell, that they had tried to
peck them off, and the poor thing had flown as fast as it
could to its master's house, where it knew it was safe.

After this it took care not to wander too far from
home, and came back every night to sleep on the priest's
window sill.   Soon it grew bolder still, and would sit on the
corner of the table when he was at dinner, and now and
then would rub its head against his shoulder, uttering
a low cry of affection and pleasure.   Sometimes it would
even do more, and follow him for several miles when he
happened to be riding.

But the buzzard was not the only pet the priest had
to look after.   There were ducks, and chickens, and dogs,
and four large cats.   The ducks and chickens it did not
mind, at least those that belonged to the house, and it
would even take its bath at the same time with the
ducklings, and never trod upon them when they got in
its way, or got cross and pecked them.   And if hawks or
any such birds tried to snap up the little ones who had
left their mother's wing to take a peep at the world,
the buzzard would instantly fly to their help, and never
once was beaten in the battle.   Curiously enough, however, it seemed to think it might do as it liked with the
fowls and ducks that belonged to other people, and so
many were the complaints of cocks and hens lamed and
killed, that the priest was obliged to let it be known that
he would pay for all such damage, in order to save his
favourite's life.   As to dogs and cats, it always got the
better of *them* ; in any experiment which it amused the
priest to make.   One day he threw a piece of raw meat
into the garden where the cats were collected, to be

scrambled for. A young and active puss instantly seized
it and ran away with her prize, with all the other cats
after her. But quick as she was, the buzzard, who had
been watching her movements from the bough of a tree,
was quicker still. Down it pounced on her back, squeezed
her sides with its claws, and bit her ears so sharply, that
she was forced to let go. In one moment another cat
had picked the morsel up in its teeth, but it did not hold

THE CATS NO MATCH FOR THE BUZZARD

it long. The process that had answered for one cat
would answer for a second, as the buzzard very well
knew. Down he swooped again, and even when the
whole four cats, who saw in him a common enemy,
attacked the bird at once, they proved no match for him,
and in the end they were clever enough to find that out.

It is not easy to know what buzzards in general think
about things, but this one hated scarlet as much as any
bull. Whenever he saw a red cap on any of the peasants'

heads, he would hide himself among the thick boughs overhanging the road where the man had to pass, and would nip it off so softly that the peasant never felt his loss. He would even manage to take off the wigs which every one wore then, and that was cleverer still, and off he would carry both wigs and

caps to a tall tree in a park near by, and hang them all over it, like a new kind of fruit.

As may be imagined, a bird so bold made many enemies, and was often shot at by the keepers, but for a long time it appeared to bear a charmed life, and nothing did it any harm. However, one unlucky day a keeper who was going his rounds in the forest, and who did not know what a strange and clever bird this buzzard was, saw him on the back of a fox which he had at-

THE BUZZARD CARRIES OFF HAT AND WIG tacked for want of something better to do, and fired two shots at them. One shot killed the fox; the other broke the wing of the buzzard, but he managed to fly out of reach of the keeper, and hid himself. Meanwhile the tinkling of the bell made the keeper guess that this must be the priest's pet, of which he had so often heard ; and being anxious to do what he could to repair the damage he had done, he at once told the priest what had happened. The priest went out directly to the forest, and gave his usual whistle, but neither on that evening nor on several others was there any reply. At last on the seventh night he heard a low answer, and on searching narrowly all through the wood, the priest found the poor buzzard, which had hopped nearly two miles towards its old home, dragging its broken wing after it. The bird was very thin, but was enchanted to see his old master, who carried him home and nursed him for six weeks, when he got quite well, and was able to fly about as boldly as ever.

COWPER AND HIS HARES [1]

No one was fonder of animals, or kinder to them, than
Cowper the poet, who lived towards the end of the last
century ; but of all creatures he loved hares best, perhaps because he, like them, was timid and easily frightened.
He has left a very interesting account of three hares that
were given to him when he was living in the country in
the year 1774, and as far as possible the poet shall tell
his own story of the friendship between himself and his
pets—Puss, Tiney, and Bess, as he called them.

Cowper was not at all a strong man, and suffered
terribly from fits of low spirits, and at these times he
could not read, and disliked the company of people, who
teased him by giving him advice or asking him questions.
It was during one of these seasons of solitude and
melancholy that he noticed a poor little hare belonging
to the children of one of his neighbours, who, without
meaning really to be unkind, had worried the little thing
almost to death. Soon they got tired even of playing
with it, and the poor hare was in danger of being starved
to death, when their father, whose heart was more tender
than theirs, proposed that it should be given to their
neighbour Mr. Cowper.

Now Cowper, besides feeling pity for the poor little
creature, felt that he should like to teach and train it,
and as just then he was too unhappy to care for his usual
occupations, he gladly accepted the present. In a very
short time Puss was given two companions, Tiney and

[1] From Bingley's *British Quadrupeds.*

Bess, and could have had dozens more if Cowper had wanted them, for the villagers offered to catch him enough to have filled the whole countryside if he would only give the order.

However, Cowper decided that three would be ample for his purposes, and as he wished them to learn nice clean habits, he began with his own hands to build them a house. The house contained a large hall and three bedrooms, each with a separate bed, and it was astonishing how soon every hare knew its own bedroom, and how careful he was (for in spite of their names they were all males) never to go into those of his friends.

Very soon all three made themselves much at home in their comfortable quarters, and Puss, the first comer, would jump on his master's lap and, standing up on his hind legs, would bite the hair on his temples. He enjoyed being carried about like a baby, and would even go to sleep in Cowper's arms, which is a very strange thing for a hare to do. Once Puss got ill, and then the poet took care to keep him apart from the other two, for animals have a horror of their sick companions, and are generally very unkind to them. So he nursed Puss himself, and gave him all sorts of herbs and grasses as medicine, and at last Puss began to get better, and took notice of what was going on round him. When he was strong enough to take his first little walk, his pleasure knew no bounds; and in token of his gratitude he licked his master's hand, first back, then front, and then between every finger. As soon as he felt himself quite strong again, he went with the poet every day, after breakfast, into the garden, where he lay all the morning under a trailing cucumber, sometimes asleep, but every now and then eating a leaf or two by way of luncheon. If the poet was ever later than usual in leaving the house, Puss would down on his knees and look up into his eyes with a pleading expression, or, if these means failed, he would seize his master's coat between his teeth, and pull as hard as he could towards the window. Puss was, perhaps, the pleasantest of all the hares, but Bess, who died young, was the cleverest and most amusing. He had his little tempers, and when he was not feeling very well, he was glad to be petted and made much of; but no sooner had he recovered than he resented any little attentions, and would growl and run away or even bite if you attempted to touch him. It was impossible really to tame Tiney, but there was something so serious and solemn in all he did, that it made you laugh even to watch him.

Bess, the third, was very different from the other two. He did not need taming, for he was tame from the beginning, as it never entered into his head that anyone could be unkind to him. In many things he had the same tastes as his friends. All three loved lettuces, dandelions, and oats; and every night little dishes were placed in their bedrooms, in case they might feel hungry. One day their master was clearing out a birdcage while his three hares were sitting by, and he placed on the floor a pot containing some white sand, such as birds use instead of a carpet. The moment they saw the sand, they made a rush for it and ate it up greedily. Cowper took the hint, and always saw, after that, that sand was placed where the hares could get at it.

After supper they all spent the evenings in the parlour, and would tumble over together, and jump over each other's backs, and see which could spring the farthest, just like a set of kittens. But the cleverest of them all was Bess, and he was also the strongest.

Poor Bess! he was the first to die, soon after he was grown up, and Tiney and Puss had to get on as best they could without him, which was not half as much fun. There was no one now to invent queer games, or to keep the cat in order when it tried to take liberties; and no one, too, to prevent Tiney from bullying Puss, as he was rather fond of doing. Tiney lived to be nine, quite a respectable age for a hare, and died at last from the effects of a fall. Puss went on for another three years, and showed no signs of decay, except that he was a little less playful, which was only to be expected. His last act was to make friends with a dog called Marquis, to whom he was introduced by his master; and though the spaniel could not take the place of Puss's early companions, he was better than nobody, and the two got on quite happily together, till the sad day (March 9, 1796) when Puss stretched himself at his master's feet and died peacefully and without pain, aged eleven years and eleven months.

A RAT TALE

HUGGY was an old rat when he died—very old indeed. He was born in the middle of a corn-rick, and there he might have lived his little life had not the farmer who owned the rick caused it to be pulled down. That was Huggy's first experience of flitting, and it was done in such a hurry that he had hardly time to be sorry. It was pitch dark when his mother shook him up roughly and told him to 'come along, or he would be killed by the farmer,' and poor Huggy, blinking his sleepy eyes, struggled out of his snug little bed into the cold black night.

Several old rats met him at the entrance, and sternly bade him stay where he was and make no noise, for the leader was about to speak. Huggy was wide-awake by this time. The rat spirit of adventure was roused within him by the scent of coming danger, and eagerly he listened to the shrill, clear voice of the leader:

'Friends, old and young, this is not a time for many words, but I want you all to know the cause of this sudden disturbance. Last night I was scavenging round the farmer's kitchen, seeking what I might devour, when in came the stable-boy tapping an empty corn-sieve which he had in his hand. He said a few words to the farmer, who rose hastily, and together they left the kitchen, I following at a convenient distance. They went straight to the stable, and talked for some time with their backs to the corn-bin, which was standing open in the window. After a while I managed to scramble up and

peer into it, only to confirm what I dreaded most—
the corn-bin was empty ! To-morrow they will pull down
this rick, thresh the corn, and replenish the empty bin.
So, my friends, unless we mean to die by dog, stick, or
fork, we had better be off as soon as it is daylight.'

There was a shuffle of feet all round, and a general
rush of anxious mothers into the rick to fetch out their
young. Huggy was waiting at the entrance ; so, as soon
as he caught sight of his mother, he raced off with her to
join the fast-assembling crowd at the back of the rick.
The leader ranged them in lines of ten abreast, and, after
walking up and down to see that all were in their places,
he gave a shrill squeak, and the column started. They
marched steadily for about two miles—slowly, of course,
because of the young ones. Nothing proved an obstacle
to them. Sometimes a high wall crossed their path, but
they merely ran up one side and down the other, as if it
was level road. Sometimes it was a broad river which
confronted them, but that they swam without hesitation
—rats will not stop at such trifles.

At length they came to a field where a man with a
pair of horses was ploughing. His coat, in which his
dinner was wrapt, lay on the wall some little distance
from him. Seeing such a number of rats, he left his horses
and ran for his life, and hid behind a knoll, whence he
could view the proceedings without himself being seen.
To his great disgust, he saw the creatures first crowd
round his coat, then run over it, and finally eat out of his
pocket the bread and cheese his wife had provided for his
dinner !

That was a stroke of luck for the rats. They had not
counted on so early a breakfast ; so it was with lightsome
hearts they performed the rest of their journey.

Huggy was very glad when it was over. He had never
been so far in his life—he was only three weeks old.
Their new home proved to be a cellar, which communicated on one side with sundry pipes running straight to

the kitchen, and on the other with a large ventilator opening to the outside air. A paradise for rats! and as to the inhabitants of the house—we shall see.

It was early in the afternoon when they arrived, so they had plenty of time to settle down before night. Huggy, having selected his corner, left his mother to make it comfortable for him, and scampered off for ' a poke round,' as he called it. First he went to the kitchen, peeped up through a hole in the floor, and, seeing no one about, cautiously crept out and sniffed into all the cupboards As he was emerging from the last he beheld a sight which made his little heart turn sick. There, in a corner which Huggy had not noticed before, lay a huge dog half asleep! And so great was Huggy's fright that he squeaked, very faintly indeed, yet loud enough to set Master Dog upon his feet. Next minute they were both tearing across the kitchen. Huggy was a wee bit in front, but so little that he could feel the dog's hot breath behind him. There was the hole—bump—scrabble, scrabble—Huggy was safe! Safe! yes—but oh, so frightened!—and what made him smart so dreadfully? Why, his tail . . . was gone—bitten off by the dog! Ah, Huggy, my poor little rat, if it had not been for that foolish little squeak of fright you might have been as other rats are—but now! Huggy almost squeaked again, it was so very sad—and painful. Slowly he crept back to the cellar, where he had to endure the jeers of his young companions and the good advice of his elders.

It was some weeks before Huggy fully recovered himself, and more weeks still before he could screw up his courage to appear among his companions as the 'tailless rat;' but at long and at last he did crawl out, and, because he looked so shy and frightened, the other rats were merciful, and let him alone. The old rat, too—the leader—took a great fancy to him, and used to allow Huggy to accompany him on his various exploits, which was considered a great privilege among the older rats,

'SEEING SUCH A NUMBER OF RATS, HE LEFT HIS HORSES AND RAN FOR HIS LIFE'

and Huggy was very proud of it. One night he and the leader were out together, when their walk happened to take them (as it generally did) round by the pantry. As a matter of course, they went in, and had a good meal off a loaf which the careless table-maid had left standing on the shelf. Beside the loaf was a box of matches, and Huggy could not be happy till he had found out what was inside. First he gnawed the box a little, then he dragged it up and down, then he gnawed a little more, and, finding it was not very good to eat, he began to play with it. Suddenly, without any warning, there was a splutter and a flare. Huggy and the leader were outside in a twinkling, leaving the pantry in a blaze. Luckily no great damage was done, for the flames were seen and put out in time.

So, little by little, Huggy was led on. In vain did his mother plead with him to be careful. He was ' a big rat now, and could look after himself,' he said. The following week the leader organised a party to invade the hen-house. Of course Huggy was among the number chosen. It required no little skill to creep noiselessly up the broken ladder, visiting the various nests ranged along each side of the walls; for laying hens are nervous ladies, and, if startled, make enough noise to waken a town. But the leader had selected his party well, and not a sound was made till the proper time came. Once up the ladder, each rat took it in turn to slip in behind the hen, and gently roll one egg at a time from under her. The poor birds rarely resisted; experience had taught them long since the futility of such conduct. It was the young and ignorant fowls who gave all the trouble; they fluttered about in a fright and disturbed the whole house. But the rats knew pretty well which to go to; so they worked on without interruption. When they had collected about a dozen eggs, the next move was to take them safely down the ladder into the cellar. This was very soon done. Huggy lay down on his back, nestled an egg cosily between himself and his two front paws; a feather was put through his mouth, by which means a rat on either side dragged him along. Huggy found it rather rough on his back going down the ladder, but, with a good supper in view, he could bear most things. The eggs having been brought thus to the level of the ground, the rats dragged them in the same way slowly and carefully down to the cellar.

So time went on. Night after night parties of rats went out, and each morning they returned with tales of adventure and cunning—all more or less daring. But the leader was getting old. Huggy had noticed for some time how grey and feeble he was becoming; nor was he much surprised when, one day, the leader told him that he (Huggy) would have to take his place as leader of the rats. Two days after this the old rat died, leaving Huggy to succeed him; and a fine lot of scrapes did that rat and his followers get into.

The larder was their favourite haunt, where joints of meat were hung on hooks ' quite out o' reach o' them rats,' as the cook said. But Huggy thought differently, and in a trice ten large rats had run up the wall and down the hook, and were gobbling the meat as fast as they could. But there was one hook in the centre of the ceiling which Huggy could not reach; from this hook a nice fat duck was suspended by a string. ' If only I could get on to that hook I should gnaw the string, and the duck would fall, and——'

Huggy got no further. An idea had come to him which he communicated quickly to the others. The plan seemed to be appreciated, for they all ran to an old chair, which was standing just under this difficult centre hook. The strongest rat went first, climbed up the back of the chair, and balanced himself on the top; Number 2 followed, and carefully balanced on Number 1; Number 1 then squeaked, which meant he could bear no more. It was a pity he could not stand *one* more; for, as they were, the topmost rat could just reach the prize, and though he nibbled all round as far as he could, it was not what might be called 'a square meal.' The cook was indeed amazed when, next morning, she found only three-fourths of her precious duck remaining. 'Ah!' she said, 'I'll be even with you yet, you cunning beasts!' And that night she sliced up part of a duck with some cheese, and put it in a plate on the larder floor. At his usual hour, when all was dark and quiet, Huggy and his followers arrived, and, seeing their much-coveted prize under their very noses, were cautious. But Huggy was up to the trick. 'To-night and to-morrow night you may eat it,' he said, 'but beware of the third.' So they partook of the duck, and enjoyed it that night and the next, but the third the dish was left untouched.

The cook was up betimes that morning, so that she might bury the corpses before breakfast. Her dog (the same who had robbed Huggy of his tail), according to his custom, followed her into the larder. On seeing the plate just as she had left it the

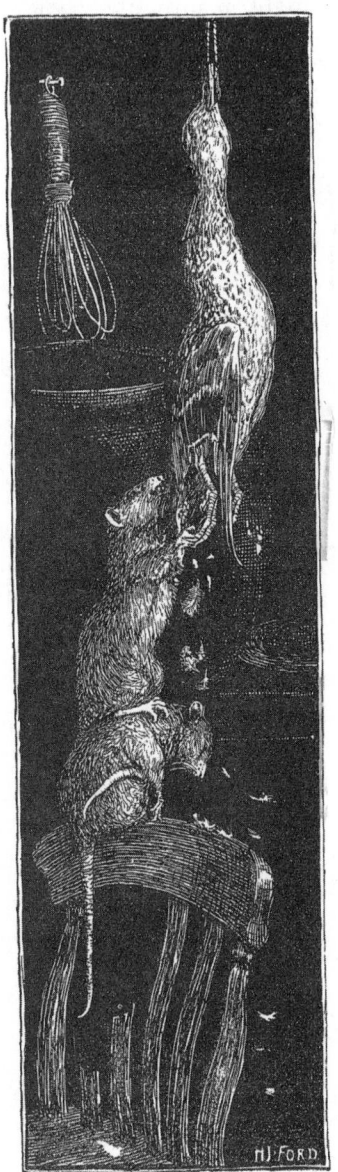

night before, the cook, in her astonishment, forgot the dog, who, finding no one gainsay him, licked the dish with infinite relish. Poor dog! In spite of all efforts to save him he died ten minutes afterwards; and the cook learnt her lesson also, for she never tried poisoning rats again.

Here end the chief events of Huggy's life—all, at least, that are worth recording.

Some years after the death of the dog I was sitting in the gloaming close to a steep path which led from the cellar down to the river, when what should I see but three large rats coming slowly towards me. The middle one was the largest, and evidently blind, for he had in his mouth a long straw, by which the other two led him carefully down the path. As the trio passed I recognised the centre one to be Huggy the Tailless.

Next morning my little Irish terrier, Jick, brought him to me in his mouth, dead; and I buried him under a Gloire de Dijon in a sunny corner of the garden.

.   .   .   .

Fantastic as some of the incidents may sound, they are, nevertheless, true, having been collected mainly from an old rat-catcher living in the town of Hawick.

SNAKE STORIES

In 1850 Baron de Wogan, a French gentleman, left his native land and set sail for North America, to seek his fortune and adventures. He was descended from two noble adventurers, the Wogan who led a cavalry troop from Dover to the Highlands, to fight for Charles II., and the Wogan who rescued Queen Clementina, wife of James III., from prison in Innspruck. In 1850 adventures, wild beasts, and Red Indians were more plentiful than now, and Wogan had some narrow escapes from snakes and bears. Soon after coming to North America he had his first adventure with a rattlesnake ; he was then camping at the gold fields of California, seeking for gold in order to have money enough to start on his voyages of discovery. His house was a log hut, built by himself, and his bed a sack filled with dry oak leaves.

One day, finding that his mattress required renewing, he went out with the sack and his gun. Having filled the sack with leaves, he went off with his gun in search of game for his larder, and only came home at nightfall. After having cooked and eaten his supper, he threw himself on his new mattress, and soon was asleep. He awoke about three, and would soon have fallen asleep again, but he felt something moving in the sack. His first thought was that it was a rat, but he soon felt by the way it moved that it was no quadruped, but a reptile, no rat, but a snake ! He must have put it in the sack with the leaves, as might easily happen in winter when these creatures are torpid from the cold, and sleep all curled

up. With one leap the Baron was out of its reach, but
wishing to examine it more closely, he took his gun to
protect him in case of danger, and came near the bed
again; but the ungrateful beast, forgetting that they had
been bedfellows, threw itself on the gun and began to bite
the muzzle. Fearing that it might turn and bite him next
the Baron pulled the trigger, and hitting the serpent,
literally cut it in two. It measured two feet long, and
when the Baron cut off its tail, he found a quantity of
scales which made the
rattling sound from
which this serpent gets
its name.

As soon as the Baron
had found enough gold,
he bought a mule whom
he called Cadi, and
whom he became very
fond of, and set off into
the backwoods in search
of sport and adventure.
Poor Cadi eventually

THE BARON KILLS THE SNAKE

met a terrible end, but that is a Bear story.) He soon added another companion, a young Indian girl, Calooa by name. She was the daughter of a chief of the Utah tribe, and had been taken prisoner, with several other women, by a tribe of hostile Indians whom the Baron fell in with. She would have been tortured and then burnt with the other prisoners had the Baron not saved her life by buying her for a silk handkerchief, a knife and fork, and some coloured pictures. She wandered with him and shared all his adventures, till she was found again by her tribe and taken back to them. One hot day they had been marching together about thirty miles through a country infested with panthers and pumas. The Baron was heading the little procession, when suddenly a cry from Calooa that she only used in moments of danger made him turn round. Then he saw that what he had taken to be a huge rotten branch of a tree, and had even thought of taking with him for their camp fire, that evening, was in reality an enormous serpent. It lay across the path asleep, its head resting on the trunk of a tree. The Baron raised his gun to his shoulder, and came nearer the monster to get a good aim. He fired, but missed. The horrid creature reared itself nearly on end and looked at him with that fixed stare by which the serpent fascinates and paralyses its victim. The Baron felt all the fascination, but conquering it, he fired a second time, and this time wounded the creature without killing it outright. Though mortally wounded, the snake's dying struggles were so violent that the young trees all round were levelled as if they had been cut with a scythe. As soon as they were sure that life was extinct, Calooa and the Baron came nearer to examine the snake's dead body. Though part of his tail was missing, he measured nevertheless five yards long and eighteen inches round. Thinking that it seemed of unusual girth, the Baron cut it open with an axe, and found inside the body of a young prairie wolf, probably about a week old. The peculiarity

of this snake was that it gave out a strong odour of musk, like the sea serpent in Mr. Kipling's book.

The most horrible serpent that the Baron encountered and slew was the horned snake; he learned afterwards from the Indians that it is the most deadly of all the snakes of North America, for not only is its bite venomous, but its tail has a sting which con-

tains the same poison. It crawls like other snakes, but when it attacks it forms itself into a circle, and then suddenly unbending itself flings itself like a lion on its victim, head forward and tail raised, thus attacking with both ends at once. If by chance it misses its aim and its tail strikes a young tree and penetrates the bark, that tree immediately begins to droop, and before long withers and dies. On the occasion when the Baron encountered it, Calooa and he had been fleeing all night fearing an attack of hostile Indians. About daylight they ventured to stop to take rest and food. While Calooa lit the fire the Baron took his gun and went in search of game. In about half an hour he returned with a wild turkey. When they had cooked and eaten it, he lay down and fell asleep, but had only slept two hours when he awoke, feeling his hand touched. It was Calooa, who woke him with a terror-stricken face. Looking in the direction she pointed, he saw about fifty yards away an enormous horned snake wound round a branch of sassafras. It was lying in wait for a poor little squirrel, that cowered in the hollow of an oak. As soon as the squirrel dared to show even the tip of its nose, the serpent flung itself at it, but in vain, as its great head could not get into the hole.

'Fortunately,' the Baron says, 'my gun was by my side. I rose and went to the rescue of the defenceless little creature. When the serpent saw me he knew he had another sort of enemy to deal with, and hissing furiously hurled himself in my direction, though without quitting his branch. I stopped and took aim. The serpent evidently understood my attitude perfectly, for unwinding himself he began to crawl with all his speed towards me. Between us there was fortunately an obstacle, a fallen chestnut tree ; to reach me he must either climb over it or go round, and he was too furious to put up with any delay. Ten paces from the tree I waited for him to appear, one knee on the ground, my gun at my shoulder, and the other elbow resting on my knee to steady my aim. At last I saw his horrid head appear above the fallen tree, at the same moment I fired, and the ball pierced his head through and through, though without instantly killing him. Quick as lightning he wound himself round a branch, lashing out with his tail in all directions. It was his dying struggle ; slowly his fury subsided, and uncoiling himself he fell dead alongside the tree. I measured him and found he was eight feet long, and seven or eight inches round. He was dark brown, and his head had two horns,

HOW THE INDIANS MAKE THE HORNED SNAKE DISGORGE HIS DINNER

or rather hard knobs. Wishing to carry away some souvenir to remember him by when I should be at home again in France, I tried to cut off his horns, but found it impossible. Out of curiosity I then took an axe and cut him open, when I found inside a little bird, dazed but living. Presently it revived and began to flutter about, and soon flew away among the bushes and was lost to sight. I did not then know that this is a common occurrence, and that when the Indians find a serpent asleep, as is generally the case after the creature has gorged itself, they hit it on the head with a stick, which makes it throw up what it has swallowed whole, and its victims are often still living.'

Calooa on one occasion had a narrow escape. She had put her hand into a hollow in a branch of a cherry-tree where was a blue jay's nest, to take eggs as she thought. Hardly had she put in her hand when she screamed with pain ; a rattlesnake that had taken possession of the nest had stung her. The Baron, much alarmed, expected to see Calooa die before his eyes. He did not know of the remedy the Indians use for snake bites. Calooa herself was quite undisturbed, and hunted about among the bushes till she found the plant she knew of, then crushing some of the leaves between two stones, she applied them to the bite, and in a couple of hours was completely cured.

Besides these snakes the Baron learned from the Indians that there is another even more dangerous, not from its sting, which is not poisonous, but because it winds itself round its victim, and strangles him to death. Fortunately the Baron never met one, or he would probably not have lived to tell his snake stories.

WHAT ELEPHANTS CAN DO

LONG, long ago the earth was very different from what it is now, and was covered with huge forests made up of enormous trees, and in these forests there roamed immense beasts, whose skeletons may sometimes be seen in our museums.

Of all these beasts there is only one remaining, and that is the elephant. Now the elephant is so big and shapeless that he makes one think he has been turned out by a child who did not know how to finish his work properly. He seems to need some feet badly and to want pinching about his body. He would also be the better for a more imposing tail; but such as he is, the elephant is more useful and interesting than many creatures of ten times his beauty. Large and clumsy though he may be, he alone of all animals has 'between his eyes a serpent for a hand,' and he turns his trunk to better account than most men do their two hands.

Ever since we first read about elephants in history they were just the same as they are now. They have not learnt, from associating with men, fresh habits which they hand down from father to son; each elephant, quick though he is to learn, has to be taught everything over again.

Yet there is no beast who has lived in such unbroken contact with man for so many thousands of years. We do not know when he first began to be distinguished for his qualities from the other wild animals, but as far back as we can trace the sculptures which adorn the Indian temples the elephant has a place. Several hundred years before Christ, the Greek traveller Herodotus was passing through Babylon and found a large number of elephants employed in the daily life of the city, and from time to time we catch glimpses of them in Eastern warfare, though it was not till the third century B.C. that they were introduced into Europe by Alexander the Great. The Mediterranean nations were quick to see the immense profit to which the elephant could be put, both in respect to the great weights he could carry, and also for his extraordinary teachableness. In India at the present day he performs all kinds of varied duties, and many are the stories told about his cleverness, for he is the only animal that can be taught to push as well as pull.

Most of us have seen elephants trained to perform in a circus, and there is something rather sad in watching their great clumsy bodies gambolling about in a way that is unnatural as well as ungraceful. But there is no question as to the amount that elephants can be taught, particularly by kindness, or how skilfully they will revenge themselves for any ill-treatment.

In the early part of this century an elephant was sent by a lady in India as a present to the Duke of Devonshire, who had a large villa at Chiswick.

This lucky captive had a roomy house of its own, built expressly for it in the park, a field to walk about in, and a keeper to look after it, and to do a little light gardening besides. This man treated the elephant (a female) with great kindness, and they soon became the best of friends. The moment he called out she stopped, and at his bidding would take a broom in her trunk and sweep the dead leaves off the grass ; after which she would carefully carry after him a large pail of water for him to re-fill his watering pot—for in those days the garden-hose was not invented. When the tidying up was all done, the elephant was given a carrot and some of the water, but very often the keeper would amuse himself with handing her a soda-water bottle tightly corked, and

telling her to empty it.   This she did by placing the
bottle in an inclined position on the ground and holding
it at the proper angle with her foot, while she twisted the
cork out with her trunk.   This accomplished, she would
empty all the water into her trunk without spilling a drop,
and then hand the bottle back to her keeper.

In India small children are often given into the
charge of an elephant, and it is wonderful to see what
care the animals take of them.   One elephant took such
a fancy to a small baby, that it used to stand over its
cradle, and drive away the flies that teased it while it
slept.   When it grew restless the elephant would rock the
cradle, or gently lift it to the floor and let it crawl about
between its legs, till the child at last declined to take any
food unless her friend was by to see her eat it.

Amazing tales have been told of what elephants can
be trained to do, but none is stranger than a story related
by a missionary named Caunter, about some wild
elephants in Ceylon.   Some native soldiers who had been
set to guard a large storehouse containing rice, were
suddenly ordered off to put down a rising in a village a
little distance away.   Hardly were their backs turned
when a wild elephant was seen advancing to the storehouse, which was situated in a lonely place, and after
walking carefully round it, he returned whence he came.
In a short time he was noticed advancing for the second
time, accompanied by a whole herd of elephants, all
marching in an orderly and military manner.

Now in order to secure the granary as much as possible, the only entrance had been made in the roof, and had
to be reached by a ladder.   This was soon found out by
the elephants, who examined the whole building atten-
tively, and being baffled in their designs, retired to con-
sult as to what they should do next.   Finally one of the
largest among them began to attack one of the corners
with his tusks, and some of the others followed his
example.   When the first relay was tired out, another set

THE ELEPHANT HELPS THE GARDENER

took its place, but all their efforts seemed useless ; the building was too strong for them. At length a third elephant came forward and attacked the place at which the others had laboured with such ill-success, and, by a prodigious effort, he managed to loosen one brick. After this it did not take long to dig a hole big enough to let the whole herd pass through, and soon the two spectators, hidden in a banyan-tree, saw little companies of three or four enter the granary and take their fill of rice until they all were satisfied. The last batch were still eating busily, when a shrill noise from the sentinel they had set on guard caused them to rush out. From afar they could perceive the white dress of the soldiers who had subdued the unruly villagers and were returning to their post, and the elephants, trunks in air, took refuge in the jungle, and only wagged their tails mockingly at the bullets sent after them by the discomfited soldiers.

THE DOG OF MONTARGIS

FOR three days Aubrey de Montdidier had not been seen by his friends and comrades in arms. On Sunday morning he had attended mass in the Church of Our Lady, but it was noticed that in the afternoon he was absent from the great tournament which was held at Saint Katherine's. This astonished his friend the young Sieur de Narsac, who had appointed to meet him there, that they might watch together the encounter between a Burgundian knight and a gentleman from Provence, both renowned in tilting, who were to meet together for the first time that day in Paris. It was unlike Aubrey to fail to be present on such an occasion, and when for three successive days he did not appear at his accustomed haunts, his friends grew anxious, and began to question among themselves whether some accident might not have befallen him. Early on the morning of the fourth day De Narsac was awakened by a continuous sound, as of something scratching against his door. Starting up to listen, he heard, in the intervals of the scratching, a low whine, as of a dog in pain. Thoroughly aroused, he got up and opened the door. Stretched before it, apparently too weak to stand, was a great, gaunt greyhound, spent with exhaustion and hunger. His ribs stood out like the bars of a gridiron beneath his smooth coat ; his tongue hung down between his jaws, parched and stiff ; his eyes were bloodshot, and he trembled in every limb.

On seeing De Narsac the poor creature struggled to his feet, feebly wagged his tail, and thrust his nose into

the young man's hands. Then only did De Narsac recognise in the half-starved skeleton before him the
favourite dog and constant companion of his friend,

DE NARSAC RECOGNISES HIS FRIEND'S DOG

Aubrey de Montdidier. It was clear from the poor
animal's emaciated appearance that it was in the last
stage of exhaustion. Summoning his servant, De Narsac

ordered food and water to be brought at once, and the
dog devoured the huge meal set before it. From his
starved appearance, and from the voracity with which he
devoured the food set before him, it was evident that
he had had nothing to eat for some days. No sooner
was his hunger appeased than he began to move uneasily
about the room. Uttering low howls of distress from
time to time, he approached the door; then, returning
to De Narsac's side, he looked up in his face and gently
tugged at his mantle, as if to attract his attention. There
was something at once so appealing and peculiar in the
dog's behaviour that De Narsac's curiosity was aroused,
and he became convinced that there was some connection
between the dog's starved appearance and strange manner
and the unaccountable disappearance of his master.
Perhaps the dog might supply the clue to Aubrey's place
of concealment. Watching the dog's behaviour closely,
De Narsac became aware that the dumb beast was in-
viting him to accompany him. Accordingly he yielded to
the dog's apparent wish, and, leaving the house, followed
him out into the streets of Paris.

Looking round from time to time to see that De
Narsac was coming after him, the greyhound pursued
its way through the narrow, tortuous streets of the
ancient city, over the Bridge, and out by the Porte St.-
Martin, into the open country outside the gates of the
town. Then, continuing on its track, the dog headed for
the Forest of Bondy, a place of evil fame in those far-off
days, as its solitudes were known to be infested by bands
of robbers. Stopping suddenly in a deep and densely
wooded glade of the wood, the dog uttered a succession
of low, angry growls; then, tugging at De Narsac's
mantle, it led him to some freshly turned-up earth, beneath
a wide-spreading oak-tree. With a piteous whine the
dog stretched himself on the spot, and could not be induced
by De Narsac to follow him back to Paris, where he
straightway betook himself, as he at once suspected foul

play. A few hours later a party of men, guided to the spot by the young Sieur de Narsac, removed the earth and dead leaves and ferns from the hole into which they had been hastily flung, and discovered the murdered body of Aubrey de Montdidier. Hurriedly a litter was constructed of boughs of trees, and, followed by the dog, the body was borne into Paris, where it was soon afterwards buried.

From that hour the greyhound attached himself to the Sieur de Narsac. It slept in his room, ate from his table, and followed close at his heels when he went out of doors. One morning, as the two were threading their way through the crowded Rue St.-Martin, De Narsac was startled by hearing a low, fierce growl from the greyhound. Looking down he saw that the creature was shaking in every limb; his smooth coat was bristling, his tail was straight and stiff, and he was showing his teeth. In another moment he had made a dart from De Narsac's side, and had sprung on a young gentleman named Macaire, in the uniform of the king's bodyguard, who, with several comrades in arms, was sauntering along on the opposite side of the street. There was something so sudden in the attack that the Chevalier Macaire was almost thrown on the ground. With their walking-canes he and his friends beat off the dog, and on De Narsac coming up, it was called away, and, still trembling and growling, followed its master down the street.

A few days later the same thing occurred. De Narsac and the Chevalier Macaire chanced to encounter each other walking in the royal park. In a moment the dog had rushed at Macaire, and, with a fierce spring at his throat, had tried to pull him to the ground. De Narsac and some officers of the king's bodyguard came to Macaire's assistance, and the dog was called off. The rumour of this attack reached the ears of the king, and mixed with the rumour were whisperings of a long-standing quarrel between Macaire and Aubrey de Montdidier.

Might not the dog's strange and unaccountable hatred for
the young officer be a clue to the mysterious murder of
his late master? Determined to sift the matter to the
bottom, the king summoned De Narsac and the dog to
his presence at the Hôtel St.-Pol. Following close on his
master's heels, the greyhound entered the audience-room,
where the king was seated, surrounded by his courtiers.
As De Narsac bowed low before his sovereign, a short,
fierce bark was heard from the dog, and, before he could
be held back, he had darted in among the startled courtiers,
and had sprung at the throat of the Chevalier Macaire,
who, with several other knights, formed a little group
behind the king's chair.

It was impossible longer to doubt that there was some
ground for the surmises that had rapidly grown to suspicion, and that had received sudden confirmation from
the fresh evidence of the dog's hatred.

The king decided that there should be a trial by the
judgment of God, and that a combat should take place
between man, the accused, and dog, the accuser. The
place chosen for the combat was a waste, uninhabited
plot of ground, frequently selected as a duelling-ground
by the young gallants of Paris.

In the presence of the king and his courtiers the
strange unnatural combat took place that afternoon. The
knight was armed with a short thick stick; the dog was
provided with an empty barrel, as a retreating ground
from the attacks of his adversary. At a given signal the
combatants entered the lists. The dog seemed quite to
understand the strange duel on which it was engaged.
Barking savagely, and darting round his opponent, he
made attempts to leap at his throat; now on this side,
now on that he sprang, jumping into the air, and then
bounding back out of reach of the stick. There was such
swiftness and determination about his movements, and
something so unnatural in the combat, that Macaire's
nerve failed him. His blows beat the air, without hitting

THE DOG FLIES AT MACAIRE IN THE PRESENCE OF THE KING

the dog; his breath came in quick short gasps; there
was a look of terror on his face, and for a moment, overcome by the horror of the situation, his eye quailed and
sought the ground. At that instant the dog sprang at his
throat and pinned him to the earth. In his terror, he
called out and acknowledged his crime, and implored the
king's mercy. But the judgment of God had decided.
The dog was called off before it had strangled its victim,
but the man was hurried away to the place of execution,
and atoned that evening for the murder of the faithful
greyhound's master.

The dog has been known to posterity as the Dog of
Montargis, as in the Castle of Montargis there stood for
many centuries a sculptured stone mantelpiece, on which
the combat was carved.

HOW A BEAVER BUILDS HIS HOUSE [1]

IF we could look back and see England and Wales as they were about a thousand years ago, we should most likely think that the best houses and most prosperous villages were the work not of the Saxon or British natives, but of the little beavers, which were then to be found in some of the rivers, though they have long ceased to exist there. Those who want to see what beavers can do, must cross over to America, and there, either in Canada or even as far south as Louisiana, they will find the little creatures as busy as ever and as clever at house-building as when they taught our forefathers a lesson in the time of Athelstan or Canute.

A beaver is a small animal measuring about three feet, and has fine glossy dark brown hair. Its tail, which is its trowel, and call bell, and many other things besides, is nearly a foot long, and has no hair at all, and is divided into little scales, something like a fish. Beavers cannot bear to live by themselves, and are never happy unless they have two or three hundred friends close at hand whom they can visit every day and all day, and they are the best and most kindly neighbours in the world, always ready to help each other either in building new villages or in repairing old ones.

Of course the first thing to be done when you wish to erect a house or a village is to fix on a suitable site, and the spot which every beaver of sense thinks most desirable is either a large pond or, if no pond is to be had, a flat

[1] Bingley's *Animal Biography*.

low plain with a stream running through, out of which a pond can be made.

It must be a very very long while since beavers first found out that the way to make a pond out of a stream was to build a dam across it so strong that the water could not break through. To begin with, they have to know which way the stream runs, and in this they never make a mistake. Then they gather together stakes about five feet long, and fix them in rows tight into the ground on each side of the stream ; and while the older and more experienced beavers are doing this—for the safety of the village depends on the strength of the foundation—the younger and more active ones are fetching and heaping up green branches of trees. These branches are plaited in and out of the rows of stakes, which by this time stretch right across the river, and form a dam often as much as a hundred feet from end to end. When the best workmen among them declare the foundation solid, the rest form a large wall over the whole, of stones, clay, and sand, which gradually tapers up from ten or twelve feet at the bottom, where it has to resist the pressure of the stream, to two or three at the top, so that the beavers can, if necessary, pass each other in comfort. And when the dam is pronounced finished, the overseer or head beaver goes carefully over every part, to see that it is the proper shape and exactly smooth and even, for beavers cannot bear bad work, and would punish any of their tribe who were lazy or careless.

The dam being ready and the pond made, they can now begin to think about their houses, and as all beavers have a great dislike to damp floors and wet beds, they have to raise their dwellings quite six or eight feet above the level of the stream, so that no sudden swelling of the river during the rainy season shall make them cold and uncomfortable. Beavers are always quite clear in their minds as to what they want, and how to get it, and they like to keep things distinct. When they are in the water they are perfectly happy, but when they are out of it they like to be dry, and in order to keep their houses warm and snug they wait till the water is low during the summer, and then they can drive piles into the bed of the stream with more safety and less trouble than if the river is running hard. It generally takes two or three months before the village is finished, and the bark and shoots of young trees, which is their favourite food, collected and stored up. But the little round huts, not unlike beehives, are only intended for winter homes, as no beaver would think of sleeping indoors during the summer, or, indeed, of staying two days in the same place. So every three or four years they spend the long days in making their village of earth, stones, and sticks, plastered together with some kind of mortar which they carry about on their tails, to spread neatly over the inside of their houses. All that a beaver does is beautifully finished as well as substantial. The walls of his house are usually about two feet thick, and sometimes he has as many as three stories to his house, when he has a large family or a number of friends to live with him. One thing is quite certain : no beaver will ever set up housekeeping alone; but sometimes he will be content with one companion, and sometimes he will have as many as thirty. But however full the hut may be, there is never any confusion; each beaver has his fixed place on the floor, which is covered with dried leaves and moss, and as they manage to keep open a door right below the surface of the stream, where their food is carefully stored up, there is no fear that they will ever be starved out. And there they lie all through the winter, and get very fat.

Once a French gentleman who was travelling through Louisiana, was very anxious to see the little beaver colony at work, so he hid himself with some other men close to a dam, and in the night they cut a channel about a foot wide right through, and very hard labour they found it.

The men had made no noise in breaking the dam, but the rush of the water aroused one beaver who slept more lightly than the rest, and he instantly left his hut and swam to the dam to examine what was wrong. He then struck four loud blows with his tail, and at the sound of his call every beaver left his bed and came rushing to see what was the matter. No sooner did they reach the dam and see the large hole made in it, than they took counsel, and then the one in whom they put the most trust gave orders to the rest, and they all went to the bank to make mortar. When they had collected as much as they could carry, they formed a procession, two and two, each pair loading each others' tails, and so travelling they arrived at the dam, where a relay of fresh labourers were ready to load. The mortar was then placed in the hole and bound tight by repeated blows from the beavers' tails. So hard did they work and so much sense did they show, that in a short time all was as firm as ever. Then one of the leading spirits clapped his tail twice, and in a moment all were in bed and asleep again.

Beavers are very hard-working, but they know how to make themselves comfortable too, and if they are content with bark and twigs at home, they appreciate nicer food if they can get it. A gentleman once took a beaver with him to New York, and it used to wander about the house like a dog, feeding chiefly upon bread, with fish now and then for a treat. Not being able to find any moss or leaves for a bed, it used to seize upon all the soft bits of stuff that came in its way, and carry them off to its sleeping corner. One day a cat discovered its hiding place, and thought it would be a nice comfortable place for her kittens to sleep, and when the beaver came back from his walk he found, like the three bears, that some-one was sleeping in his bed. He had never seen things of that kind before, but they were small and he was big, so he said nothing and lay down somewhere else. Only, if ever their mother was away, he would go and hold one of them to his breast to warm it, and keep it there till its mother came back.

THE WAR HORSE OF ALEXANDER [1]

THERE are not so many stories about horses as there are about dogs and cats, yet almost every great general has had his favourite horse, who has gone with him through many campaigns and borne him safe in many battle-fields. At a town in Sicily called Agrigentum, they set such store by their horses, that pyramids were raised over their burial-place, and the Emperor Augustus built a splendid monument over the grave of an old favourite.

The most famous horse, perhaps, who ever lived, was one belonging to Alexander the Great, and was called Bucephalus. When the king was a boy, Bucephalus was brought before Philip, King of Macedon, Alexander's father, by Philonicus the Thessalian, and offered for sale for the large sum of thirteen talents. Beautiful though he was, Philip wisely declined to buy him before knowing what manner of horse he was, and ordered him to be led into a neighbouring field, and a groom to mount him. But it was in vain that the best and most experienced riders approached the horse ; he reared up on his hind legs, and would suffer none to come near him. So Philonicus the Thessalian was told to take his horse back whence he came, for the king would have none of him.

Now the boy Alexander stood by, and his heart went out to the beautiful creature. And he cried out, 'What a good horse do we lose for lack of skill to mount him !' Philip the king heard these words, and his soul was vexed to see the horse depart, but yet he knew not what else to

[1] Part of the story of Bucephalus is taken from Plutarch.

do. Then he turned to Alexander and said: 'Do you think that you, young and untried, can ride this horse better than those who have grown old in the stables?' To which Alexander made answer, 'This horse I know I could ride better than they.' 'And if you fail,' asked Philip, 'what price will you pay for your good conceit of yourself?' And Alexander laughed out and said gaily, 'I will pay the price of the horse.' And thus it was settled.

So Alexander drew near to the horse, and took him by the bridle, turning his face to the sun so that he might not be frightened at the movements of his own shadow, for the prince had noticed that it scared him greatly. Then Alexander stroked his head and led him forwards, feeling his temper all the while, and when the horse began to get uneasy, the prince suddenly leapt on his back, and gradually curbed him with the bridle. Suddenly, as Bucephalus gave up trying to throw his rider, and only pawed the ground impatient to be off, Alexander shook the reins, and bidding him go, they flew like lightning round the course. This was Alexander's first conquest, and as he jumped down from the horse, his father exclaimed, 'Go, my son, and seek for a kingdom that is worthy, for Macedon is too small for such as thee.'

Henceforth Bucephalus made it clear that he served Alexander and no one else. He would submit quietly to having the gay trappings of a king's steed fastened on his head, and the royal saddle put on, but if any groom tried to mount him, back would go his ears and up would go his heels, and none dared come near him. For ten years after Alexander succeeded his father on the throne of Macedon (B.C. 336), Bucephalus bore him through all his battles, and was, says Pliny, 'of a passing good and memorable service in the wars,' and even when wounded, as he once was at the taking of Thebes, would not suffer his master to mount another horse. Together these two swam rivers, crossed mountains, penetrated into the dominions of the Great King, and farther still into the heart of Asia, beyond the Caspian and the river Oxus, where never European army had gone before. Then turning sharp south, he crossed the range of the Hindoo Koosh, and entering the country of the Five Rivers, he prepared to attack Porus, king of India. But age and the wanderings of ten years had worn Bucephalus out. One last victory near the Hydaspes or Jelum, and the old horse sank down and died, full of years and honours (B.C. 326). Bitter were the lamentations of the king for the friend of his childhood, but his grief did not show itself only in weeping. The most splendid funeral Alexander could devise was given to Bucephalus, and a gorgeous tomb erected over his body. And more than that, Alexander resolved that the memory of his old horse should be kept green in these burning Indian deserts, thousands of miles from the Thessalian plains where he was born, so round his tomb the king built a city, and it was called

'BUCEPHALIA.'

STORIES ABOUT BEARS

BARON de Wogan, a French gentleman, whose adventures
with snakes are also curious, was the hero of some en-
counters with the grizzly bear of North America. First,
I would have you understand what sort of a creature
he had for an opponent. Imagine a monster measuring
when standing upright eight or nine feet, weighing 900
lbs., of a most terrifying appearance, in agility and
strength surpassing all other animals, and cruel in proportion. Like his cousin the brown bear, whom he
resembles in shape, he is a hermit and lives alone in the
immense trackless forests which covered the Rocky Mountains, and indeed (at least in olden times) the greater part
of North America. During the day he sleeps in the
depths of some mountain cavern, and wakes up at dusk to
go out in search of prey. All the beasts of the forest live
in terror of him—even the white bear flies before him.
He would go down to the valleys and attack the immense
herds of buffaloes which grazed there, and which were
powerless against him, in spite of their numbers and
their great horns. They join themselves closely together
and form one compact rank, but the grizzly bear hurls
himself at them, breaks their ranks, scatters them, and
then pursuing them till he catches them up, flings himself on the back of one, hugs it in his iron embrace, breaks
its skull with his teeth, and so goes slaying right and left
before he eats one. Before the Baron's first, so to say,
hand-to-hand encounter with a grizzly, he had been long
enough in the country to know something of their ways,

and how worse than useless a shot is unless in a fatal spot.

After the return to her tribe of Calooa, a young Indian girl, who had been his one human companion in many days of wandering, the Baron was left with only his mule Cadi for friend and companion, and naturally felt very lonely. He set his heart on getting to the top of the Rocky Mountains, at the foot of which he then happened to be. Their glittering summits had so irresistible an attraction for him, that he did not stay to consider the difficulties which soon beset him at every step. No sooner did he conquer one than another arose, added to which the cold of these high regions was intense, and it constantly snowed. After three days he had to declare himself not only beaten, but so worn out that he must take a week's rest if he did not want to fall ill. First it was necessary to have some sort of a shelter, and by great good luck he found just at hand a cavern in the rock, which, without being exactly a palace, seemed as if it would answer his purpose.

Upon closer examination he found that it had more drawbacks than he cared about. All round were scattered gnawed bones of animals, and the prints of bear's claws on the ground left no doubt as to who the last inmate had been. The Baron, however, preferred to risk an invasion rather than seek another abode, and prepared for probable inroads by making across the entrance to the cave a barricade of branches of oak tied together with flax, a quantity of which grew near. He then lit a good fire inside the cave, but as the last tenant had not considered a chimney necessary, the dense smoke soon obliged him to beat a hasty retreat. Besides he had to go out to get supplies for his larder, at present as bare as Mother Hubbard's. With his usual good luck the Baron found, first, a large salmon flapping wildly in its effort to get out of a pool, where the fallen river had left it. This he killed, and next he shot a young deer about a mile away and carried it to camp on his back. In order to preserve these eatables he salted some of them with salt that he had previously found in a lake near, and had carefully preserved for future use. He then dug a hole in a corner of the cave, putting a thick layer of dry hay at the bottom, and buried his provisions Indian fashion, in order to preserve them.

As it was still only twelve o'clock, the Baron thought he would spend the rest of the day in exploring the neighbourhood; first he examined the cave, which he found to be formed of big blocks of rock firmly joined together; above the cave rose the cliff, and in front of it grew a fir-tree, which served at the same time to defend the entrance and as a ladder to enable him to mount the cliff. As he could not take Cadi with him, he fastened him to the fir-tree by his halter and girth joined together, so as to leave him plenty of room to graze. Then he put some eatables in his game bag, and set off on a tour of discovery. When he had walked about three hours, and had reached a rocky point from which he had a fine view of the surrounding country, he sat down to rest under an oak-tree. He knew nothing more till the cold awoke him—it was now six o'clock, and he had slept three hours. He started with all the haste he could to get back to his cave and Cadi before dark, but so tired and footsore was he that he was obliged to give in and camp where he was, for night was coming on fast. It was bitterly cold and snow fell constantly, so he lit a large fire, which at the same time warmed him, and kept away the bears whom he heard wandering round the camp most of the night. As soon as the sun was up in the morning, he set off with all his speed to see what had become of Cadi; but though fifteen miles is not much to bears balked of their prey, it is much to a weary and foot-sore man, and when he had hobbled to within half a mile of the camp, he saw that it was too late : the bears, whom he had driven away from his camp in the night with firebrands, had scented poor Cadi, and four of them were now devouring him—father, mother, and two cubs. Imagine his rage and grief at seeing his only friend and companion devoured piecemeal before his very eyes !

His first impulse was to fire, but he reflected in time that they were four to one, and that, instead of avenging Cadi, he would only share his fate. He decided to wait on a high rock till the meal was ended. It lasted an hour, and then he saw the whole family set off to climb the mountain, from the top of which he had been watching them. They seemed to be making straight for him, and as it would be certain death to sit and wait for them, he slipped into a cranny in the rock, hoping that he might not be perceived ; even if he was, he could only be attacked by one at a time. He had not long to wait : soon all four bears passed in single file, without smelling him or being aware of him ; for this he had to thank poor Cadi : their horrid snouts and jaws being smeared with his blood prevented their scenting fresh prey.

When he had seen them at a safe distance, he ventured to go down to the cave he could no longer call his own. Of Cadi, nothing remained but his head, still fastened to the tree by his halter. The barricade was gone, too, and from the cave came low but unmistakable growls. With one bound the Baron was up the tree, and from the tree on to the cliff. From there he threw stones down before the entrance to the cave, to induce the present inmate to come out, in order that he might take possession again. The bear soon came out, and, perceiving him, made for the fir-tree. By its slow and languid movements the Baron saw that it was curiosity more than anger that prompted it, and, moreover, it was evidently a very old bear, probably a grandfather, whose children and grandchildren had been to pay it a visit. Curiosity or not, the Baron had no wish to make a closer acquaintance, and fired a shot at the brute by way of a hint to that effect. This immediately turned his curiosity into wrath. Seizing the fir-tree, which he was

going to use as a ladder, he began to climb up. A second shot hit him in the shoulder. He fell mortally wounded, but even after a third shot, which took him in the flank, his dying struggles lasted twenty minutes, during which he tore at the roots of the fir-trees with his terrific claws. The Baron did not care to waste any of his bullets, now getting scarce, in putting out of his pain one of Cadi's murderers. When finally the bear was dead, the Baron came down to take possession of his cave, and at the same time of the bear's skin. On penetrating into the cave, he found that the rascal had paid him out in his own coin, and, in revenge for the Baron taking his cave, had eaten his provisions. The Baron was quits in the end, however, as the bear's carcase furnished him meat enough for several days. The Baron cut off pounds of steak, which he salted and dried over the fire. The useless remains he threw over the nearest precipice, so that they should not attract wild beasts, to keep him awake all night with their cries. Then, having made a huge fire in front of the entrance, which, moreover, he barricaded with branches, he threw himself on his bed of dry leaves to sleep the sleep of exhaustion.

Some time passed before the Baron's next encounter with a bear. He was camping one night in a dense forest, sleeping, as usual, with one eye and one ear open, and his weapon at hand, all ready loaded. His rest was broken by the usual nightly sounds of the forest, of leaves crunched and branches broken, showing that many of the inmates of the woods were astir ; but he did not let these usual sounds disturb him, till he heard in the distance the hoarse and unmistakable cry of the bear ; then he thought it time to change the shot in his gun for something more worthy of such a foe. This preparation made, he set off at dawn on his day's march, which up to midday led him along the bank of a large river. He thought no more of the blood-curdling howls of the night, till suddenly he heard from a distance terror-stricken cries. He put his ear to the ground, Indian fashion, to listen better, and as the danger, whatever it was, seemed to be coming nearer, he jumped into a thicket of wild cherry and willow trees, and waited there in ambush, gun in hand. In a few minutes, a band of Indians with their squaws appeared on the opposite bank of the river, and straightway leaped into the water, like so many frogs jumping into an undisturbed swamp. At first he thought he was being attacked, but soon saw it was the Indians who were being pursued, and that they all, men and women, were swimming for dear life; moreover, the women were laden with their children, one, and sometimes two, being strapped to their backs in a sort of cradle of birch bark. This additional weight made them swim slower than the men, who soon reached the opposite shore, and then took to their heels helter-skelter, except three, who remained behind to encourage the women.

The Baron at first thought it was an attack of other Indians, and that it would be prudent to beat a retreat, when suddenly the same terrible cry that had kept him awake in the latter part of the night resounded through the forest, and at the same time there appeared on a high bank on the other shore a huge mass of a dirty grey colour, which hurled itself downhill, plunged into the river, and began to swim across at a terrific speed. It was a grizzly bear of tremendous size. So fast did it swim, that in no time it had nearly caught up with the last of the squaws, a young woman with twin babies at her back, whose cries, often interrupted by the water getting into their mouths, would have melted the heart of a stone. The three Indians who had remained on the bank did their utmost to stop the bear by shooting their poisoned arrows at it; but the distance was too great, and the huge animal came on so fast that in another minute mother and children would be lost. The Baron could not remain a spectator of so terrible a scene. He came out of the thicket where he was hidden, and frightened the

Indians almost as much as if he had been another bear. Resting his gun on the trunk of a tree, he fired at the distance of 125 yards, and hit the animal right on the head. It dived several times, and the water all round was dyed red with blood ; but the wound was not mortal, and it continued on its way, only more slowly. After

urging the Indian, who seemed to be the unhappy woman's husband, to go into the water to help her—for, through terror and fatigue, she could no longer swim—the Baron took deliberate aim again and fired. The second shot, like the first, hit the bear on the head, but again without killing it. It stopped the brute, however, long enough to let the poor woman get to shore, where she fainted, and was carried away by the men to the forest, leaving the Baron and the bear to fight out their duel alone. The Baron had barely time to reload and climb to the top of one of the trees, when the bear was already at the foot of it. So near was he when he stood upright, that the Baron could feel his horrid breath. Up to then the Baron thought that all bears could climb like squirrels; fortunately for him he was mistaken. Expecting to be taken by storm, he fired straight in the creature's face. The two balls took a different course: one went through the jaw and came out by the neck, the other went into the chest. The bear uttered a terrific roar, stiffened itself in a last effort to reach him, and fell heavily on its back at the foot of the tree. The Baron might have thought him dead had he not already seen such wonderful resurrections on the part of bears; but the four shots, though at first they dazed and troubled the beast, seemed afterwards to act as spurs, and he rose furious and returned to the charge. The Baron tried to use his revolver, but, finding it impossible, he drew out his axe from his belt, and dealt a violent blow at the bear's head, which nearly split it in two, and sent the blood splashing in all directions. The bear again fell to the ground, this time to rise no more. The Baron being now convinced that the grizzly bear is no tree-climber, took his time to draw out his revolver, to take aim and fire. The shot put out one of the bear's eyes, the axe had already taken out the other. This finished him, but his death struggles lasted twenty minutes, during which the tree was nearly uprooted. When all was at an end the Baron came down; he cut off the formidable claws, and broke off the teeth with an axe to make a trophy in imitation of the Indians, and then proceeded to skin him and cut him up. The Indians, who had been watching the combat at a safe distance, now came back, enthusiastic. They surrounded them, the victor and the vanquished, and danced a war-dance, singing impromptu words. The Baron, seated on the bear's carcase, joined in the chorus ; but the Indians, not content with that, insisted on his joining in the dance as well. The rejoicing over, the Baron divided among the twenty Indians the flesh of the bear—about 15 lb. or 20 lb. fell to each. The skin he kept to himself, and the claws, of which the Indians made him a warrior's necklace, hanging it round his neck like an order of knighthood.[1]

[1] The young reader must no longer expect such adventures as the Baron de Wogan achieved.

STORIES ABOUT ANTS

IF any one will watch an ant-hill on a fine day in April, he will see the little inhabitants begin to rouse themselves from their winter's sleep, which lasts from the month of October, with the red ant at all events. Groups of them come out to the top of the ant-hill to warm and thaw themselves in the rays of the sun. Some, more active and robust, run in and out, waking up the lazy, hurrying the laggards, and rousing all the little community to begin their summer habits. But this activity does not last long; they are as yet only half awake, and still numb and torpid from the winter's cold, and the little throng increases or diminishes as the sun shines or disappears behind a cloud. As two, half-past two, and three o'clock arrive, they have nearly all disappeared inside the ant-heap, leaving only a few warriors, of a larger make and tried courage, to watch over the well-being of the little republic and to close up all openings with tiny chips of wood, dry leaves, and shreds of moss, so as to hide the entrances from human eye. Two or three sentinels wander round to see that all is secure. And then they enter, and all is still.

If we come back again in about a week, we shall find the ants in the middle of their regular migration to their summer quarters, not far from their winter ones. This takes place, with the red ant, at all events, with great regularity every April and October. The red ant is beyond doubt a slave-owner; the slaves may be easily recognised from their masters by being of a smaller make and light yellow colour. As soon as the masters

have fixed the day of their ' flitting,' they begin probably
to ensure the consent of the slaves by violently seizing
them, and rolling them into a ball, and then grasping them
firmly they set off towards the summer quarters at full
gallop, if an ant can be said to gallop. The master ant
is in a great hurry to get rid of his living burden ; he goes
straight ahead in spite of all obstacles, avoiding all in-
terruptions and delays, and as soon as he arrives at
the summer ant-heap, plunges in, deposits the slave all
breathless and terrified from his forced journey, and sets
off back for another.

Darwin, who closely studied the migrations of the
ant, says that they differ in their means of transport :
one sort is carried by the slaves ; the other, our friend the
red ant, scientifically called ' formica sanguinea,' carries
his property carefully in his mouth. It seems strange
to us that the master should carry the slave, but no
stranger than it would appear to the ants if they should
begin to study our habits, that some of us should sit in
a carriage and be driven by the coachman. The slave,
once installed in his summer quarters, seldom appears
again before the autumn exodus, unless in the event of
some disturbance in the camp, or its invasion by some ants
of a hostile tribe, when the slaves take part in the defence
and especially watch over the young ones. The slaves
seem to be carpenters and miners, and warriors when
necessary. They build the dwelling, repair it, of which
it has constant need, and defend it in case of attack with
dauntless courage. But their principal duties seem to be
to take charge of the development of the young, and to
feed the masters—no small task, as there seem to be ten
masters to one slave, and they seem incapable of eating
unless fed. Experiments have been tried of removing
the slaves from them, and though sugar and every sort of
tempting food is put down beside them, they will starve
rather than help themselves. In fact, one wonders what
the masters can be left for but to drive the slaves, which

they do with great ardour. A French gentleman who spent years studying the habits of the ants, tried one day, by way of experiment, to take a slave away from its master; he had great difficulty in removing it from its bearer, who struggled furiously and clung to its burden. When at last the slave was set free, instead of profiting by its liberty, it turned round and round in a circle as if dazed, then hid itself under a dead leaf. A master ant presently came along, an animated conversation took place, and the slave ant was seized upon and borne off again to bondage. The same gentleman another day observed a slave ant venture out to the entrance to the ant-hill to enjoy the warmth of the sun. A great master ant spied it and set to with blows of its horns (antennæ they are called) to persuade it that that was not its place. Finding the slave persisted in not understanding, the master resorted to force, and seizing it by its head, without taking the trouble to roll it up, as they are generally carried, he hurled it into the ant-hill, where no doubt it received the punishment it deserved.

If we came back to the ant-heap a week after our last visit, we should find the migration finished if the weather has been fine; but ants, especially after their first awaking, are extremely sensitive to wind and rain, and only work well in fine weather. They are equally affected by weather before a storm: even though the sun may be shining, they will remain in the ant-heap with closed doors. If it is shut before midday, the storm will burst before evening; if it is shut before eight or nine in the morning, the rain will fall before noon.

All this time we have been speaking only of the red ant; but there are any number of different kinds in Europe, not to mention the enormous ants of the tropics, who march in such armies that the people fly before them, deserting their villages. Different species differ totally in their habits and ways of building and living. The greater number of species live apart, and not in a community with an elaborately constructed house like the red ant. The little black ant is the commonest in this country, and the busiest and most active. She is the first to awake, in March, sometimes in February, and the last to sleep, sometimes not till November. Their instincts and habits of activity, however, are apt to deceive them, and they get up too soon. The French gentleman already mentioned observed an instance of the kind. On February 24, after an unusually mild winter, the sun shone as if it were already summer, and it was difficult to persuade oneself that it was not, except that there were no leaves on the trees, no birds singing in the branches, and no insects humming in the air. First our friend went to examine the red-ant-heap, which was closed as usual, all the inhabitants being still plunged in their winter sleep. The black ants, on the contrary, were all awake and lively, and seemed persuaded that the fine weather had come to stay. Their instincts deceived them, for that night it froze ; rain, snow, and fog succeeded each other in turn, and when next he visited the ant-heap he found them lying in masses, stiff and dead, before the entrance to their dwelling.

Between the red and black ants there is great enmity, and terrible combats take place. When they fight they grasp each other like men wrestling, and each tries to throw the other down, and break his back. The conquered remain on the battlefield, nearly broken in two, and feebly waving their paws, till they slowly expire in agonies. The conqueror, on the other hand, carries away his dead to burial and his wounded to the camp, and then, entering triumphantly himself, closes the doors after him. The gentleman already quoted witnessed the funeral of an ant. He had passed the ant-heap about a quarter of an hour, and left, as he thought, all the inhabitants behind him, when he saw what appeared to be an enormous red ant making for home. On stooping to look more closely, he saw that it was one ant carrying another.

He succeeded in separating them from each other, and then saw that the burden was neither a slave nor a prisoner, but a dead comrade being carried back to the ant-heap for a decent burial; for if ants fall into the hands of the enemy, they are subjected if alive to the most cruel tortures and if dead to mutilations. Usually, when an ant is relieved of anything it is carrying—whether it be a slave, a wounded ant, or some eatable—it will set off ·at full speed and let the burden be picked up by the next passing ant; but this one made no attempt to run away, and only turned round and round in a perplexed and irresolute way, till its dead friend was put down beside it, then it seized its precious burden and set off homewards with it. Travellers even tell that in Algeria there are ant cemeteries near the ant-heaps.

No lover of animals doubts that they have a language of their own, which we are too stupid or deaf to understand. Anyone who studies the ways of the ants sees, beyond a doubt, that they too have a way of communicating with each other. For instance, an ant was one day seen at some distance from the ant-hill, and evidently in no hurry to go back to it. In the middle of the path she perceived a large dead snail. She began by going round and round it, then climbed on its back, and walked all over it. Having satisfied herself that it was a choice morsel, but too large for her to carry home alone, she set off at once to seek help. On the way she met one of her companions; she ran at once to her; they rubbed their antennæ together, and evidently an animated conversation took place, for the second ant set off immediately in the direction of the snail. The first one continued on her way home, communicating with every ant she met in the same way; by the time she disappeared inside the ant-heap, an endless file of busy little ants were on their way to take their share of the spoil. In ten minutes the snail was completely covered by the little throng, and by the evening every trace of it had vanished.

Recent observations have proved that the time-honoured idea of the ant storing up provision for the winter is a delusion, a delusion which La Fontaine's famous fable, 'Le Fourmis et la Cigale,' has done much to spread and confirm. It is now known, as we'have already seen, that ants sleep all winter, and that the food which we constantly see them laden with is for immediate consumption in the camp. They eat all kinds of insects —hornets and cockchafers are favourite dishes—but the choicest morsel is a fine fat green caterpillar, caught alive. They seize it, some by its head, some by its tail; it struggles, it writhes, and sometimes succeeds in freeing itself from its enemies; but they do not consider themselves beaten, and attack it again. Little by little it becomes stupefied from the discharges of formic acid the ants throw out from their bodies, and presently it succumbs to their renewed forces. Finally, though the struggle may last an hour or more, it is borne to the ant-heap and disappears, to be devoured by the inmates. Perhaps these short ' Stories about Ants ' may induce some of you to follow the advice of the Preacher, and 'go to the ant ' yourselves for more.

THE TAMING OF AN OTTER [1]

OTTERS used once to be very common in England in the
neighbourhood of rivers, and even in some instances of
the sea, but in many places where they once lived in great
numbers they have now ceased to exist. They destroy
large quantities of fish, though they are so dainty that
they only care for the upper parts of the body. If the
rivers are frozen and no fish are to be had, they will eat
poultry, or even lambs ; and if these are not to be found,
they can get on quite well for a long time on the bark of
trees or on young branches.

Fierce though otters are when brought to bay, they
can easily be tamed if they are caught young enough.
More than a hundred years ago the monks of Autun, in
France, found a baby otter only a few weeks old, and took
it back to the convent, and fed it upon milk for nearly two
months, when it was promoted to soup and fish and
vegetables, the food of the good monks. It was not very
sociable with strange animals, but it made great friends
with a dog and cat who had known it from a baby, and
they would play together half the day. At night it had a
bed in one of the rooms, but in the day it always preferred a heap of straw when it was tired of running about.
Curious to say, this otter was not at all fond of the water,
and it was very seldom that it would go near a basin of
water that was always carefully left near its bed. When
it did, it was only to wash its face and front paws, after
which it would go for a run in the courtyard, or curl

[1] From Bingley's *British Quadrupeds.*

itself to sleep in the sun. Indeed it seemed to have such
an objection to water of all kinds, that the monks wondered whether it knew how to swim. So one day, when
they were not so busy as usual, some of the brothers took
it off to a good-sized pond, and waited to see what it would
do. The otter smelt about cautiously for a little, and then,
recognising that here was something it had seen before;
ducked its head and wetted its feet as it did in the mornings. This did not satisfy the monks, who threw it right
in, upon which it instantly swam to the other shore, and
came round again to its friends.

All tame otters are not, however, as forgetful of the
habits and manners of their race as this one was, and in
some parts they have even been taught to fish for their
masters instead of themselves. Careful directions are
given for their proper teaching, and a great deal of patience
is needful, because if an animal is once frightened or
made angry, there is not much hope of training it afterwards.
To begin with, it must be fed while it is very young on
milk or soup, and when it gets older, on bread and the
heads of fishes, and it must get its food from one person
only, to whom it will soon get accustomed and attached.
The next step is to have a sort of leather bag made, stuffed
with wool and shaped like a fish, large enough for the
animal to take in its mouth. Finally, he must wear a collar
formed on the principle of a slip noose, which can tighten
when a long string that is fastened to it, is pulled. This
is, of course, to teach the otter to drop the fish after he
has caught it.

The master then leads the otter slowly behind him,
till by this means he has learned how to follow, and then
he has to be made to understand the meanings of certain
words and tones. So the man says to him, 'Come here,'
and pulls the cord; and after this has been repeated
several times, the otter gradually begins to connect the
words with the action. Then the string is dropped, and
the otter trots up obediently without it. After that, the

sham fish is placed on the ground, and the collar, which
seems rather like a horse's bit, is pulled so as to force the
mouth open, while the master exclaims 'Take it!' and
when the otter is quite perfect in this (which most likely
will not happen for a long time) the collar is loosened,
and he is told to 'drop it.'

Last of all, he is led down to a river with clear shallow
water, where a small dead fish is thrown in. This he
catches at once, and then the cord which has been
fastened to his neck is gently pulled, and he gives up his
prize to his master. Then live fish are put in instead of
the dead one, and when they are killed, the otter is given
the heads as a reward.

Of course some masters have a special talent for
teaching these things, and some otters are specially apt
pupils. This must have been the case with the otter
belonging to a Mr. Campbell who lived near Inverness.
It would sometimes catch eight or ten salmon in a day,
and never attempted to eat them ; while a man in Sweden,
called Nilsson, and his family, lived entirely on the fish
that was caught for them by their otter. When he is in
his wild state, the otter lives in holes in the rocks, or among
the roots of trees, though occasionally he has been known
to burrow under ground, having his door in the water, and
only a very tiny window opening landwards, so that he
may not die of suffocation.

THE STORY OF ANDROCLES AND THE LION

MANY hundred years ago, there lived in the north of Africa a poor Roman slave called Androcles. His master held great power and authority in the country, but he was a hard, cruel man, and his slaves led a very unhappy life. They had little to eat, had to work hard, and were often punished and tortured if they failed to satisfy their master's caprices. For long Androcles had borne with the hardships of his life, but at last he could bear it no longer, and he made up his mind to run away. He knew that it was a great risk, for he had no friends in that foreign country with whom he could seek safety and protection ; and he was aware that if he was overtaken and caught he would be put to a cruel death. But even death, he thought, would not be so hard as the life he now led, and it was possible that he might escape to the sea-coast, and somehow some day get back to Rome and find a kinder master.

So he waited till the old moon had waned to a tiny gold thread in the skies, and then, one dark night, he slipped out of his master's house, and, creeping through the deserted forum and along the silent town, he passed out of the city into the vineyards and corn-fields lying outside the walls. In the cool night air he walked rapidly. From time to time he was startled by the sudden barking of a dog, or the sound of voices coming from some late revellers in the villas which stood beside the road along which he hurried. But as he got further into the country these sounds ceased, and there was silence and darkness

all round him. When the sun rose he had already
gone many miles away from the town in which he had
been so miserable. But now a new terror oppressed him
—the terror of great loneliness. He had got into a wild,
barren country, where there was no sign of human habi-
tation. A thick growth of low trees and thorny mimosa
bushes spread out before him, and as he tried to thread
his way through them he was severely scratched, and his
scant garments torn by the long thorns. Besides the
sun was very hot, and the trees were not high enough to
afford him any shade. He was worn out with hunger
and fatigue, and he longed to lie down and rest. But to
lie down in that fierce sun would have meant death, and
he struggled on, hoping to find some wild berries to eat,
and some water to quench his thirst. But when he came
out of the scrub-wood, he found he was as badly off as
before. A long, low line of rocky cliffs rose before him,
but there were no houses, and he saw no hope of finding
food. He was so tired that he could not wander further,
and seeing a cave which looked cool and dark in the side
of the cliffs, he crept into it, and, stretching his tired
limbs on the sandy floor, fell fast asleep.

Suddenly he was awakened by a noise that made his
blood run cold. The roar of a wild beast sounded in his
ears, and as he started trembling and in terror to his feet,
he beheld a huge, tawny lion, with great glistening white
teeth, standing in the entrance of the cave. It was impossible to fly, for the lion barred the way. Immovable
with fear, Androcles stood rooted to the spot, waiting for
the lion to spring on him and tear him limb from limb.

But the lion did not move. Making a low moan as if
in great pain, it stood licking its huge paw, from which
Androcles now saw that blood was flowing freely. Seeing
the poor animal in such pain, and noticing how gentle
it seemed, Androcles forgot his own terror, and slowly
approached the lion, who held up its paw as if asking
the man to help it. Then Androcles saw that a monster

ANDROCLES IN THE LION'S CAVE

thorn had entered the paw, making a deep cut, and causing great pain and swelling. Swiftly but firmly he drew the thorn out, and pressed the swelling to try to stop the flowing of the blood. Relieved of the pain, the lion quietly lay down at Androcles' feet, slowly moving his great bushy tail from side to side as a dog does when it feels happy and comfortable.

From that moment Androcles and the lion became devoted friends. After lying for a little while at his feet, licking the poor wounded paw, the lion got up and limped out of the cave. A few minutes later it returned with a little dead rabbit in its mouth, which it put down on the floor of the cave beside Androcles. The poor man, who was starving with hunger, cooked the rabbit somehow, and ate it. In the evening, led by the lion, he found a place where there was a spring, at which he quenched his dreadful thirst.

And so for three years Androcles and the lion lived together in the cave ; wandering about the woods together by day, sleeping together at night. For in summer the cave was cooler than the woods, and in winter it was warmer.

At last the longing in Androcles' heart to live once more with his fellow-men became so great that he felt he could remain in the woods no longer, but that he must return to a town, and take his chance of being caught and killed as a runaway slave. And so one morning he left the cave, and wandered away in the direction where he thought the sea and the large towns lay. But in a few days he was captured by a band of soldiers who were patrolling the country in search of fugitive slaves, and he was put in chains and sent as a prisoner to Rome.

Here he was cast into prison and tried for the crime of having run away from his master. He was condemned as a punishment to be torn to pieces by wild beasts on the first public holiday, in the great circus at Rome.

When the day arrived Androcles was brought out of his prison, dressed in a simple, short tunic, and with a scarf round his right arm. He was given a lance with which to defend himself—a forlorn hope, as he knew that he had to fight with a powerful lion which had been kept without food for some days to make it more savage and bloodthirsty. As he stepped into the arena of the huge circus, above the sound of the voices of thousands on thousands of spectators he could hear the savage roar of the wild beasts from their cages below the floor on which he stood.

Of a sudden the silence of expectation fell on the spectators, for a signal had been given, and the cage containing the lion with which Androcles had to fight had been shot up into the arena from the floor below. A moment later, with a fierce spring and a savage roar, the great animal had sprung out of its cage into the arena, and with a bound had rushed at the spot where Androcles stood trembling. But suddenly, as he saw Androcles, the lion stood still, wondering. Then quickly but quietly it approached him, and gently moved its tail and licked the man's hands, and fawned upon him like a great dog. And Androcles patted the lion's head, and gave a sob of recognition, for he knew that it was his own lion, with whom he had lived and lodged all those months and years.

And, seeing this strange and wonderful meeting between the man and the wild beast, all the people marvelled, and the emperor, from his high seat above the arena, sent for Androcles, and bade him tell his story and explain this mystery. And the emperor was so delighted with the story that he said Androcles was to be released and to be made a free man from that hour. And he rewarded him with money, and ordered that the lion was to belong to him, and to accompany him wherever he went.

And when the people in Rome met Androcles walking, followed by his faithful lion, they used to point at them and say, 'That is the lion, the guest of the man, and that is the man, the doctor of the lion.' [1]

---

[1] Apparently this nice lion did not bite anybody, when he took his walks abroad.. Or, possibly, he was muzzled.—ED.

ANDROCLES IN THE ARENA

MONSIEUR DUMAS AND HIS BEASTS

I

MOST people have heard of Alexandre Dumas, the great French novelist who wrote 'The Three Musketeers' and many other delightful historical romances. Besides being a great novelist, M. Dumas was a most kind and generous man—kind both to human beings and to animals. He had a great many pets, of which he gives us the history in one of his books. Here are some of the stories about them in his own words.

I was living, he says, at Monte Cristo (this was the name of his villa at St.-Germains); I lived there alone, except for the visitors I received. I love solitude, for solitude is necessary to anyone who works much. However, I do not like complete loneliness; what I love is that of the Garden of Eden, a solitude peopled with animals. Therefore, in my wilderness at Monte Cristo, without being quite like Adam in every way, I had a kind of small earthly paradise.

This is the list of my animals. I had a number of dogs, of which the chief was Pritchard. I had a vulture named Diogenes; three monkeys, one of which bore the name of a celebrated translator, another that of a famous novelist, and the third, which was a female, that of a charming actress. We will call the writer Potich, the novelist the Last of the Laidmanoirs, and the lady Mademoiselle Desgarcins. I had a great blue and yellow macaw called Buvat, a green and yellow parroquet called Papa Everard, a cat called Mysouff, a golden pheasant called

Lucullus, and finally, a cock called Cæsar. Let us give honour where honour is due, and begin with the history of Pritchard.

I had an acquaintance named M. Lerat, who having heard me say I had no dog to take out shooting, said, 'Ah! how glad I am to be able to give you something you will really like! A friend of mine who lives in Scotland has sent me a pointer of the very best breed. I will give him to you. Bring Pritchard,' he added to his two little girls.

How could I refuse a present offered so cordially? Pritchard was brought in.

He was an odd-looking dog to be called a pointer! He was long-haired, grey and white, with ears nearly erect, mustard-coloured eyes, and a beautifully feathered tail. Except for the tail, he could scarcely be called a handsome dog.

M. Lerat seemed even more delighted to give the present than I was to receive it, which showed what a good heart he had.

'The children call the dog Pritchard,' he said; 'but if you don't like the name, call him what you please.'

I had no objection to the name; my opinion was that if anyone had cause to complain, it was the dog himself. Pritchard, therefore, continued to be called Pritchard. He was at this time about nine or ten months old, and ought to begin his education, so I sent him to a gamekeeper named Vatrin to learn his duties. But, two hours after I had sent Pritchard to Vatrin, he was back again at my house. He was not made welcome; on the contrary, he received a good beating from Michel, who was my gardener, porter, butler, and confidential servant all in one, and who took Pritchard back to Vatrin. Vatrin was astonished; Pritchard had been shut up with the other dogs in the kennel, and he must have jumped over the enclosure, which was a high one. Early the next morning, when the housemaid had opened my front door, there was Pritchard sitting outside. Michel again beat the dog, and again took him back to Vatrin, who this time put a collar round his neck and chained him up. Michel came back and informed me of this severe but necessary measure. Vatrin sent a message to say that I should not see Pritchard again until his education was finished. The next day, while I was writing in a little summer-house in my garden, I heard a furious barking. It was Pritchard fighting with a great Pyrenean sheepdog which another of my friends had just given me. This dog was named Mouton, because of his white woolly hair like a sheep's, not on account of his disposition, which was remarkably savage. Pritchard was rescued by Michel from Mouton's enormous jaws, once more beaten, and for the third time taken back to Vatrin. Pritchard, it appears, had eaten his collar, though how he managed it Vatrin never knew. He was now shut up in a shed, and unless he ate the walls or the door, he could not possibly get out. He tried both, and finding the door the more digestible, he ate the door ; and the next day at dinner-time, Pritchard walked into the dining-room wagging his plumy tail, his yellow eyes shining with satisfaction. This time Pritchard was neither beaten nor taken back ; we waited till Vatrin should come to hold a council of war as to what was to be done with him. The next day Vatrin appeared.

'Did you *ever* see such a rascal?' he began. Vatrin was so excited that he had forgotten to say 'Good morning' or 'How do you do?'

'I tell you,' said he, 'that rascal Pritchard puts me in such a rage that I have crunched the stem of my pipe three times between my teeth and broken it, and my wife has had to tie it up with string. He'll ruin me in pipes, that brute—that vagabond!'

'Pritchard, do you hear what is said about you?' said I.

Pritchard heard, but perhaps did not think it mattered

much about Vatrin's pipes, for he only looked at me affectionately and beat upon the ground with his tail.

' I don't know what to do with him,' said Vatrin. ' If I keep him he'll eat holes in the house, I suppose; yet I don't like to give him up—he's only a dog. It's humiliating for a man, don't you know ? '

' I'll tell you what, Vatrin,' said I. ' We will take him down to Vésinet, and go for a walk through your preserves, and then we shall see whether it is worth while to take any more trouble with this vagabond, as you call him.'

' I call him by his name. It oughtn't to be Pritchard ; it should be Bluebeard, it should be Blunderbore, it should be Judas Iscariot ! '

Vatrin enumerated all the greatest villains he could think of at the moment.

I called Michel.

' Michel, give me my shooting shoes and gaiters; we will go to Vésinet to see what Pritchard can do.'

' You will see, sir,' said Michel, ' that you will be better pleased than you think.' For Michel always had a liking for Pritchard.

We went down a steep hill to Vésinet, Michel following with Pritchard on a leash. At the steepest place I turned round. ' Look there upon the bridge in front of us, Michel,' I said, ' there is a dog very like Pritchard.' Michel looked behind him. There was nothing but the leather straps in his hand; Pritchard had cut it through with his teeth, and was now standing on the bridge, amusing himself by looking at the water through the railing.

' He *is* a vagabond ! ' said Vatrin. ' Look ! where is he off to now ? '

' He has gone,' said I, ' to see what my neighbour Corrège has got for luncheon.' Sure enough, the next moment Pritchard was seen coming out of M. Corrège's back door, pursued by a maid servant with a broom. He had a veal cutlet in his mouth, which he had just taken out of the frying-pan.

'Monsieur Dumas!' cried the maid, 'Monsieur Dumas! stop your dog!'

We tried; but Pritchard passed between Michel and me like a flash of lightning.

'It seems,' said Michel, 'that he likes his veal under-done.'

'My good woman,' I said to the cook, who was still pursuing Pritchard, 'I fear that you are losing time, and that you will never see your cutlet again.'

'Well, then, let me tell you, sir, that you have no right to keep and feed a thief like that.'

'It is you, my good woman, who are feeding him to-day, not I.'

'Me!' said the cook, 'it's—it's M. Corrège. And what will M. Corrège say, I should like to know?'

'He will say, like Michel, that it seems Pritchard likes his veal underdone.'

'Well, but he'll not be pleased—he will think it's my fault.'

'Never mind, I will invite your master to luncheon with me.'

'All the same, if your dog goes on like that, he will come to a bad end. That is all I have to say—he will come to a bad end.' And she stretched out her broom in an attitude of malediction towards the spot where Pritchard had disappeared.

We three stood looking at one another. 'Well,' said I, 'we have lost Pritchard.'

'We'll soon find him,' said Michel.

We therefore set off to find Pritchard, whistling and calling to him, as we walked on towards Vatrin's shooting ground. This search lasted for a good half-hour, Pritchard not taking the slightest notice of our appeals. At last Michel stopped.

'Sir,' he said, 'look there! Just come and look.'

'Well, what?' said I, going to him.

'Look!.' said Michel, pointing. I followed the direction of Michel's finger, and saw Pritchard in a perfectly immovable attitude, as rigid as if carved in stone.

'Vatrin,' said I, 'come here.' Vatrin came. I showed him Pritchard.

'I think he is making a point,' said Vatrin. Michel thought so too.

'But what is he pointing at?' I asked. We cautiously came nearer to Pritchard, who never stirred.

'He certainly is pointing,' said Vatrin. Then making a sign to me—'Look there!' he said. 'Do you see anything?'

'Nothing.'

'What! you don't see a rabbit sitting? If I only had my stick, I'd knock it on the head, and it would make a nice stew for your dinner.'

'Oh!' said Michel, 'if that's all, I'll cut you a stick.'

'Well, but Pritchard might leave off pointing.'

'No fear of him—I'll answer for him—unless, indeed, the rabbit goes away.'

Vatrin proceeded to cut a stick. Pritchard never moved, only from time to time he turned his yellow eyes upon us, which shone like a topaz.

'Have patience,' said Michel. 'Can't you see that M. Vatrin is cutting a stick?' And Pritchard seemed to understand as he turned his eye on Vatrin.

'You have still time to take off the branches,' said Michel.

When the branches were taken off and the stick was quite finished, Vatrin approached cautiously, took a good aim, and struck with all his might into the middle of the tuft of grass where the rabbit was sitting. He had killed it!

Pritchard darted in upon the rabbit, but Vatrin took it from him, and Michel slipped it into the lining of his coat.

This pocket had already held a good many rabbits in its time!

Vatrin turned to congratulate Pritchard, but he had disappeared.

'He's off to find another rabbit,' said Michel.

And accordingly, after ten minutes or so, we came upon Pritchard making another point. This time Vatrin had a stick ready cut; and after a minute, plunging his hands into a brier bush, he pulled out by the ears a second rabbit.

'There, Michel,' he said, 'put that into your other pocket.'

'Oh,' said Michel, 'there's room for five more in this one.'

'Hallo, Michel! people don't say those things before a magistrate.' And turning to Vatrin I added, 'Let us try once more, Vatrin—the number three is approved by the gods.'

'May be,' said Vatrin, 'but perhaps it won't be approved by M. Guérin.'

M. Guérin was the police inspector.

Next time we came upon Pritchard pointing. Vatrin said, 'I wonder how long he would stay like that;' and he pulled out his watch.

'Well, Vatrin,' said I, 'you shall try the experiment, as it is in your own vocation; but I am afraid I have not the time to spare.'

Michel and I then returned home. Vatrin followed with Pritchard an hour afterwards.

'Five-and-twenty minutes!' he called out as soon as he was within hearing. 'And if the rabbit had not gone away, the dog would have been there now.'

'Well, Vatrin, what do you think of him?'

'Why, I say he is a good pointer; he has only to learn to retrieve, and that you can teach him yourself. I need not keep him any longer.'

'Do you hear, Michel?'

'Oh, sir,' said Michel, 'he can do that already. He retrieves like an angel!'

This failed to convey to me an exact idea of the way in which Pritchard retrieved. But Michel threw a handkerchief, and Pritchard brought it back. He then threw one of the rabbits that Vatrin carried, and Pritchard brought back the rabbit. Michel then fetched an egg and placed it on the ground. Pritchard retrieved the egg as he had done the rabbit and the handkerchief.

'Well,' said Vatrin, 'the animal knows all that human skill can teach him. He wants nothing now but practice. And when one thinks,' he added, 'that if the rascal would only come in to heel, he would be worth twenty pounds if he was worth a penny.'

'True,' said I with a sigh, 'but you may give up hope, Vatrin; that is a thing he will never consent to.'

II

I think that the time has now come to tell my readers a little about Mademoiselle Desgarcins, Potich, and the Last of the Laidmanoirs. Mademoiselle Desgarcins was a tiny monkey; I do not know the place of her birth, but I brought her from Havre, where I had gone—I don't know why—perhaps to look at the sea. But I thought I must bring something home with me from Havre. I was walking there on the quay, when at the door of a bird-fancier's shop I saw a green monkey and a blue and yellow macaw. The monkey put its paw through the bars of its cage and caught hold of my coat, while the blue parrot turned its head and looked at me in such an affectionate manner that I stopped, holding the monkey's paw with one hand, and scratching the parrot's head with the other. The little monkey gently drew my hand within reach of her mouth, the parrot half shut its eyes and made a little purring noise to express its pleasure.

'Monsieur Dumas,' said the shopman, coming out with the air of a man who was more decided to sell than

'MONSIEUR DUMAS, MAY I ACCOMMODATE YOU WITH MY MONKEY AND MY PARROT?'

I was to buy; 'Monsieur Dumas, may I accommodate you with my monkey and my parrot?' It would have been more to the purpose if he had said, 'Monsieur Dumas, may I *incommode* you with my monkey and my parrot?' However, after a little bargaining, I bought both animals, as well as a cage for the monkey and a perch for the parrot; and as soon as I arrived at home, I introduced them to Michel.

'This,' said Michel, 'is the green monkey of Senegal —*Cercopithecus sabœa.*'

I looked at Michel in the greatest astonishment. 'Do you know Latin, Michel?'

'I don't know Latin, but I know my "Dictionary of Natural History."'

'Oh, indeed! And do you know what bird this is?' I asked, showing him the parrot.

'To be sure I know it,' said Michel. 'It is the blue and yellow macaw—*Macrocercus arararanna.* Oh, sir, why did you not bring a female as well as a male?'

'What is the use, Michel, since parrots will not breed in this country?'

'There you make a mistake, sir; the blue macaw will breed in France.'

'In the south, perhaps?'

'It need not be in the south, sir.'

'Where then?'

'At Caen.'

'At Caen? I did not know Caen had a climate which permits parrots to rear their young. Go and fetch my gazetteer.'

· 'You will soon see,' said Michel as he brought it. I read: 'Caen, capital of the department of Calvados, upon the Orne and the Odon: 223 kilomètres west of Paris, 41,806 inhabitants.'

'You will see,' said Michel, 'the parrots are coming.'

'Great trade in plaster, salt, wood—taken by English in 1346—retaken by the French &c., &c.—never mind the date—That is all, Michel.'

'What! Your dictionary never says that the arararanna, otherwise called the blue macaw, produces young at Caen?'

'No, Michel, it does not say that here.'

'What a dictionary! Just wait till I fetch you mine and you will see.'

Michel returned in a few minutes with his book of Natural History.

'You will soon see, sir,' he said, opening his dictionary in his turn. 'Parrot—here it is—parrots are monogamous.'

'As you know Latin, Michel, of course you know what monogamous means.'

'That means that they can sing scales—gamut, I suppose?'

'Well, no, Michel, not exactly. It means that they have only one " wife." '

'Indeed, sir? That is because they talk like us most likely. Now, I have found the place: " It was long believed that parrots were incapable of breeding in Europe, but the contrary has been proved on a pair of blue macaws which lived at Caen. M. Lamouroux furnishes the details of these results." '

'Let us hear the details which M. Lamouroux furnishes.'

' " These macaws, from March 1818 until August 1822, including a period of four years and a half, laid, in all, sixty-two eggs." '

'Michel, I never said they did not lay eggs ; what I said was—'

' " Out of this number," ' continued Michel in a loud voice, ' " twenty-five young macaws were hatched, of which only ten died. The others lived and continued perfectly healthy." '

'Michel, I confess to having entertained false ideas on the subject of macaws.'

' " They laid at all seasons of the year, " ' continued Michel, ' " and more eggs were hatched in the latter than in the former years." '

'Michel, I have no more to say.'

'"The number of eggs in the nest varied. There have been as many as six at a time."'

'Michel, I yield, rescue or no rescue!'

'Only,' said Michel, shutting the book, 'you must be careful not to give them bitter almonds or parsley.'

'Not bitter almonds,' I answered, 'because they contain prussic acid; but why not parsley?'

Michel, who had kept his thumb in the page, reopened the book. '"Parsley and bitter almonds,"' he read, '"are a violent poison to parrots."'

'All right, Michel, I shall remember.'

I remembered so well, that some time after, hearing that M. Persil had died suddenly (persil being the French for parsley), I exclaimed, much shocked: 'Ah! poor man, how unfortunate! He must have been eating parrot!' However, the news was afterwards contradicted.

The next day I desired Michel to tell the carpenter to make a new cage for Mademoiselle Desgarcins, who would certainly die of cramp if left in her small travelling cage. But Michel, with a solemn face, said it was unnecessary. 'For,' said he, 'I am sorry to tell you, sir, that a misfortune has happened. A weasel has killed the golden pheasant. You will, however, have it for your dinner to-day.'

I did not refuse, though the prospect of this repast caused me no great pleasure. I am very fond of game, but somehow prefer pheasants which have been shot to those killed by weasels.

'Then,' said I, 'if the cage is empty, let us put in the monkey.' We brought the little cage close to the big cage, and opened both doors. The monkey sprang into her new abode, bounded from perch to perch, and then came and looked at me through the bars, making grimaces and uttering plaintive cries.

'She is unhappy without a companion,' said Michel.

'Suppose we give her the parrot?'

'You know that little boy, an Auvergnat, who comes here with his monkey asking for pennies. If I were you, sir, I would buy that monkey.'

'And why that monkey rather than another?'

'He has been so well educated and is so gentle. He has a cap with a feather, and he takes it off when you give him a nut or a bit of sugar.'

'Can he do anything else?'

'He can fight a duel.'

'Is that all?'

'No, he can also catch fleas on his master.'

'But, Michel, do you think that that youth would part with so useful an animal?'

We can but ask him, and there he is at this moment!'
And he called to the boy to come in. The monkey was
sitting on a box which the little boy carried on his back,
and when his master took off his cap, the monkey did the
same. It had a nice gentle little face, and I remarked to
Michel that it was very like a well-known translator of
my acquaintance.

'If I have the happiness to become the owner of this
charming animal,' I continued, 'we will call it Potich.'
And giving Michel forty francs, I left him to make his
bargain with the little Auvergnat.

III

I had not entered my study since my return from Havre,
and there is always a pleasure in coming home again
after an absence. I was glad to come back, and looked
about me with a pleased smile, feeling sure that the furniture and ornaments of the room, if they could speak,
would say they were glad to see me again. As I glanced
from one familiar object to another, I saw, upon a seat
by the fire, a thing like a black and white muff, which I
had never seen before. When I came closer, I saw that
the muff was a little cat, curled up, half asleep, and purring
loudly. I called the cook, whose name was Madame
Lamarque. She came in after a minute or two.

'So sorry to have kept you waiting, but you see, sir, I
was making a white sauce, and you, who can cook yourself, know how quickly those sauces curdle if you are not
looking after them.'

'Yes, I know that, Madame Lamarque; but what I
do not know is, where this new guest of mine comes
from.' And I pointed to the cat.

'Ah, sir!' said Madame Lamarque in a sentimental
tone, 'that is an antony.'

'An antony, Madame Lamarque! What is that?'

'In other words, an orphan—a foundling, sir.'

'Poor little beast!'

'I felt sure that would interest you, sir.'

'And where did you find it, Madame Lamarque?'

'In the cellar—I heard a little cry—miaow, miaow, miaow! and I said to myself, "That *must* be a cat!"'

'No! did you actually say that?'

'Yes, and I went down myself, sir, and found the poor little thing behind the sticks. Then I recollected how you had once said, "We ought to have a cat in the house."'

'Did I say so? I think you are making a mistake, Madame Lamarque.'

'Indeed, sir, you did say so. Then I said to myself, "Providence has sent us the cat which my master wishes for." And now there is one question I must ask you, sir. What shall we call the cat?'

'We will call it Mysouff, if you have no objection. And please be careful, Madame Lamarque, that it does not eat my quails and turtle-doves, or any of my little foreign birds.'

'If M. Dumas is afraid of that,' said Michel, coming in, 'there is a method of preventing cats from eating birds.'

'And what is the method, my good friend?'

'You have a bird in a cage. Very well. You cover three sides of the cage, you make a gridiron red-hot, you put it against the uncovered side of the cage, you let out the cat, and you leave the room. The cat, when it makes its spring, jumps against the hot gridiron. The hotter the gridiron is the better the cat is afterwards.'

'Thank you, Michel. And what of the troubadour and his monkey?'

'To be sure; I was coming to tell you about that. It is all right, sir; you are to have Potich for forty francs, only you must give the boy two white mice and a guinea-pig in return.'

'But where am I to find two white mice and a guinea-pig?'

'If you will leave the commission to me, I will see that they are found.'

I left the commission to Michel.

'If you won't think me impertinent, sir,' said Madame Lamarque, 'I should so like to know what *Mysouff* means.'

'Mysouff just means Mysouff, Madame Lamarque.'

'It is a cat's name, then?'

'Certainly, since Mysouff the First was so-called. It is true, Madame Lamarque, you never knew Mysouff.' And I became so thoughtful that Madame Lamarque was kind enough to withdraw quietly, without asking any questions about Mysouff the First.

That name had taken me back to fifteen years ago, when my mother was still living. I had then the great happiness of having a mother to scold me sometimes. At the time I speak of, I had a situation in the service of the Duc d'Orléans, with a salary of 1,500 francs. My work occupied me from ten in the morning until five in the afternoon. We had a cat in those days whose name was Mysouff. This cat had missed his vocation—he ought to have been a dog. Every morning I started for my office at half-past nine, and came back every evening at half-past five. Every morning Mysouff followed me to the corner of a particular street, and every evening I found him in the same street, at the same corner, waiting for me. Now the curious thing was that on the days when I had found some amusement elsewhere, and was not coming home to dinner, it was no use to open the door for Mysouff to go and meet me.[1] Mysouff, in the attitude of the serpent with its tail in its mouth, refused to stir from his cushion. On the other hand, the days I did come, Mysouff would scratch at the door until someone

---

[1] A remarkable instance of telepathy in the Cat.—A. L.

opened it for him. My mother was very fond of Mysouff; she used to call him her barometer.

'Mysouff marks my good and my bad weather,' my dear mother would say; 'the days you come in are my days of sunshine; my rainy days are when you stay away.'

When I came home, I used to see Mysouff at the street corner, sitting quite still and gazing into the distance. As soon as he caught sight of me, he began to move his tail; then as I drew nearer, he rose and walked backwards and forwards across the pavement with his back arched and his tail in the air. When I reached him, he jumped up upon me as a dog would have done, and bounded and played round me as I walked towards the house; but when I was close to it he dashed in at full speed. Two seconds after, I used to see my mother at the door.

Never again in this world, but in the next perhaps, I shall see her standing waiting for me at the door.

That is what I was thinking of, dear readers, when the name of Mysouff brought back all these recollections; so you understand why I did not answer Madame Lamarque's questions.

Henceforth Mysouff II. enjoyed the same privileges that Mysouff I. had done, although, as will be seen later, he was not distinguished by similar virtues, but was, in fact, a very different sort of cat.

IV

The following Sunday, when my son Alexandre and one or two intimate friends were assembled in my room, a second Auvergnat boy, with a second monkey, demanded admittance, and said that a friend having told him that M. Dumas had bought his monkey for forty francs, two white mice, and a guinea-pig, he was prepared to offer his for the same price. My friends urged me to buy the second monkey.

'Do buy this charming creature,' said my artist friend Giraud.

'Yes, do buy this ridiculous little beast,' said Alexandre.

'Buy him, indeed,' said I ; 'have I forty francs to give away every day, to say nothing of a guinea-pig and two white mice?'

'Gentlemen,' said Alexandre, 'I am sorry to tell you that my father is, without exception, the most avaricious man living.'

My guests exclaimed, but Alexandre said that one day he would prove the truth of his assertion. I was now called upon to admire the monkey, and to remark how like he was to a friend of ours. Giraud, who was painting a portrait of this gentleman, said that if I would let the monkey sit to him, it would help him very much in his work, and Maquet, another of my guests, offered, amidst general applause, to make me a present of it.[1] This decided me.

'You see,' said Alexandre, 'he accepts.'

'Come, young man,' said I to the Auvergnat, 'embrace your monkey for the last time, and if you have any tears to shed, shed them without delay.'

When the full price was paid, the boy made an attempt to do as I told him, but the Last of the Laidmanoirs refused to be embraced by his former master, and as soon as the latter had gone away, he seemed delighted and began to dance, while Mademoiselle Desgarcins in her cage danced, too, with all her might.

'Look!' said Maquet, 'they like each other. Let us complete the happiness of these interesting animals.'

We shut them up in the cage together, to the great delight of Mademoiselle Desgarcins, who did not care for Potich, and much preferred her new admirer. Potich, indeed, showed signs of jealousy, but, not being armed

---

[1] Maquet. The immortal Augustus MacKeat.

with the sword which he used to have when he fought
duels, he could not wash out his affronts in the blood
of his rival, but became a prey to silent melancholy and
wounded affection.

While we were still looking at the monkeys, a servant
came in bringing a tray with wine and seltzer water.

'I say,' said Alexandre, 'let us make Mademoiselle
Desgarcins open the seltzer-water bottle!' and he put the
bottle inside the cage on the floor. No sooner had he
done so, than all three monkeys surrounded it and looked
at it with the greatest curiosity. Mademoiselle Desgarcins
was the first to understand that something would happen
if she undid the four crossed wires which held down the
cork. She accordingly set to work, first with her fingers,
and then with her teeth, and it was not long before she
undid the first three. She next attacked the fourth,
while the whole company, both men and monkeys,
watched her proceedings with breathless attention. Presently a frightful explosion was heard: Mademoiselle
Desgarcins was knocked over by the cork and drenched
with seltzer water, while Potich and the Last of the
Laidmanoirs fled to the top of their cage, uttering piercing
cries.

'Oh!' cried Alexandre, 'I'll give my share of seltzer
water to see her open another bottle!' Mademoiselle
Desgarcins had got up, shaken herself, and gone to rejoin
her companions, who were still howling lamentably.

'You don't suppose she'll let herself be caught a second
time,' said Giraud.

'Do you know,' said Maquet, 'I should not wonder if
she would. I believe her curiosity would still be stronger
than her fear.'

'Monkeys,' said Michel, who had come in on hearing
their cries, 'are more obstinate than mules. The more
seltzer-water bottles you give them, the more they will
uncork.'

'Do you think so, Michel?'

' You know, of course, how they catch them in their own country.'

' No, Michel.'

' What! you don't know *that*, gentlemen?' said Michel, full of compassion for our ignorance. 'You know that monkeys are very fond of Indian corn. Well, you put some Indian corn into a bottle, the neck of which is just large enough to admit a monkey's paw. He sees the Indian corn through the glass——'

' Well, Michel?'

' He puts his hand inside, and takes a good handful of the Indian corn. At that moment the hunter shows himself. They are so obstinate—the monkeys, I mean—that they won't let go what they have in their hand, but as they can't draw their closed fist through the opening, there they are, you see, caught.'

' Well, then, Michel, if ever our monkeys get out, you will know how to catch them again.'

' Oh! no fear, sir, that is just what I shall do.'

The seltzer-water experiment was successfully repeated, to the triumph of Michel and the delight of Alexandre, who wished to go on doing it; but I forbade him, seeing that poor Mademoiselle Desgarcins's nose was bleeding from the blow of the cork.

' It is not that,' said Alexandre; ' it is because you grudge your seltzer water. I have already remarked, gentlemen, that my father is, I regret to say, an exceedingly avaricious man.'

V

It is now my painful duty to give my readers some account of the infamous conduct of Mysouff II. One morning, on waking rather late, I saw my bedroom door gently opened, and the head of Michel thrust in, wearing such a concerned expression that I knew at once that something was wrong.

'What has happened, Michel?'

'Why, sir, those villains of monkeys have managed to twist a bar of their cage, I don't know how, until they have made a great hole, and now they have escaped.'

'Well—but, Michel, we foresaw that that might occur, and now you have only to buy your Indian corn, and procure three bottles the right size.'

'Ah! you are laughing, sir,' said Michel, reproachfully, 'but you won't laugh when you know all. They have opened the door of the aviary——'

'And so my birds have flown away?'

'Sir, your six pairs of turtle doves, your fourteen quails, and all your little foreign birds, are eaten up!'[1]

'But monkeys won't eat birds!'

'No, but Master Mysouff will, and he has done it!'

'The deuce he has! I must see for myself.'

'Yes, go yourself, sir; you will see a sight—a field of battle—a massacre of St. Bartholomew!'

As I was coming out, Michel stopped me to point to Potich, who had hung himself by the tail to the branch of a maple, and was swinging gracefully to and fro. Mademoiselle Desgarcins was bounding gaily about in the aviary, while the Last of the Laidmanoirs was practising gymnastics on the top of the greenhouse. 'Well, Michel, we must catch them. I will manage the Last of the Laidmanoirs if you will get hold of Mademoiselle Desgarcins. As to poor little Potich, he will come of his own accord.'

'I wouldn't trust him, sir; he is a hypocrite. He has made it up with the other one—just think of that!'

'What! he has made friends with his rival in the affections of Mademoiselle Desgarcins?'

'Just so, sir.'

'That is sad indeed, Michel; I thought only human beings could be guilty of so mean an action.'

---

[1] Let the reader compare the conduct of Mr. Gully, later!

'You see, sir, these monkeys have frequented the society of human beings.'

I now advanced upon the Last of the Laidmanoirs with so much precaution that I contrived to shut him into the greenhouse, where he retreated into a corner and prepared to defend himself, while Potich, from the outside, encouraged his friend by making horrible faces at me through the glass. At this moment piercing shrieks were heard from Mademoiselle Desgarcins; Michel had just caught her. These cries so enraged the Last of the Laidmanoirs that he dashed out upon me; but I parried his attack with the palm of my hand; with which he came in contact so forcibly that he lost breath

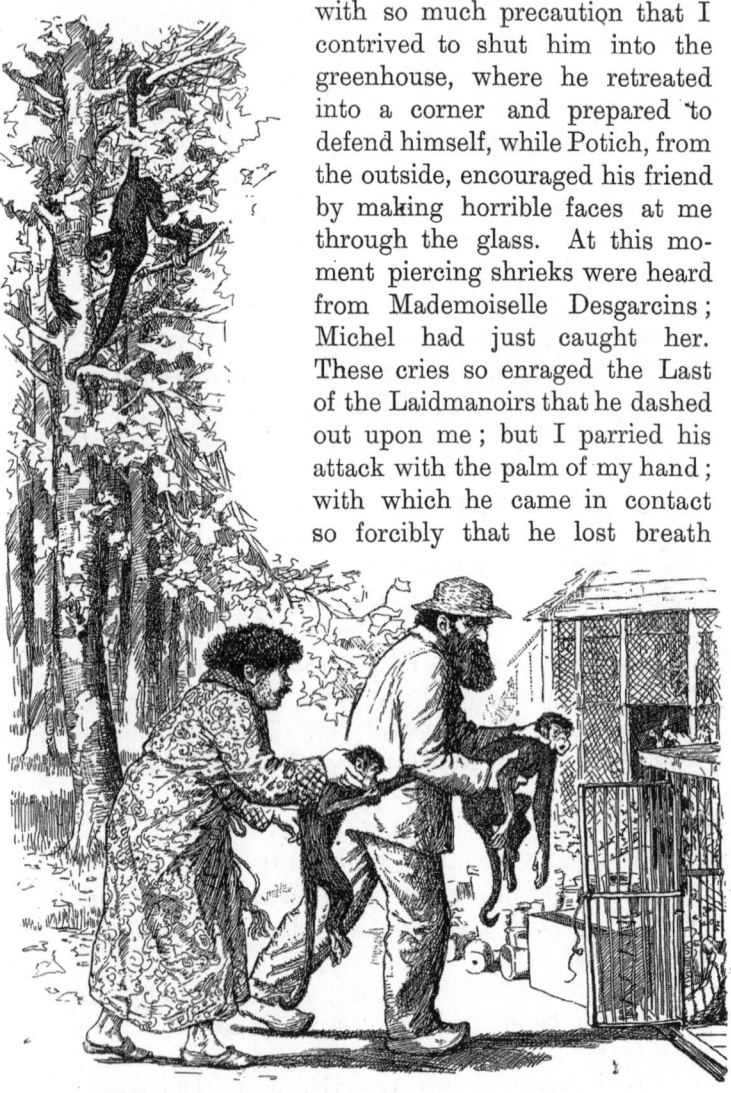

for a minute, and I then picked him up by the scruff
of the neck.

'Have you caught Mademoiselle Desgarcins?' I
shouted to Michel.

'Have you caught the Last of the Laidmanoirs?'
returned he.

'Yes!' we both replied in turn. And each bearing
his prisoner, we returned to the cage, which had in the
meantime been mended, and shut them up once more,
whilst Potich, with loud lamentations, fled to the top of
the highest tree in the garden. No sooner, however, did
he find that his two companions were unable to get out
of their cage, than he came down from his tree, approached
Michel in a timid and sidelong manner, and with clasped
hands and little plaintive cries, entreated to be shut up
again with his friends.

'Just see what a hypocrite he is!' said Michel.

But I was of opinion that the conduct of Potich was
prompted by devotion rather than hypocrisy; I compared
it to that of Regulus, who returned to Carthage to keep
his promised word, or to King John of France, who
voluntarily gave himself up to the English for the Countess
of Salisbury's sake.

Michel continued to think Potich a hypocrite, but on
account of his repentance he was forgiven. He was put
back into the cage, where Mademoiselle Desgarcins took
very little notice of him.

All this time Mysouff, having been forgotten, calmly
remained in the aviary, and continued to crunch the
bones of his victims with the most hardened indifference.
It was easy enough to catch *him*. We shut him into the
aviary, and held a council as to what should be his
punishment. Michel was of opinion that he should be
shot forthwith. I was, however, opposed to his immediate
execution, and resolved to wait until the following Sunday,
and then to cause Mysouff to be formally tried by my
assembled friends. The condemnation was therefore

postponed. In the meantime Mysouff remained a prisoner in the very spot where his crimes had been committed. He continued, however, to refresh himself with the remains of his victims without apparent remorse, but Michel removed all the bodies, and confined him to a diet of bread and water.

Next Sunday, having convoked a council of all·my friends, the trial was proceeded with. Michel was appointed Chief Justice and Nogent Saint-Laurent was counsel for the prisoner. I may remark that the jury were inclined to find a verdict of guilty, and after the first speech of the Judge, the capital sentence seemed almost certain. But the skilful advocate, in a long and eloquent speech, brought clearly before us the innocence of Mysouff, the malice of the monkeys, their quickness and incessant activity compared with the less inventive minds of cats. He showed us that Mysouff was incapable of contemplating such a crime; he described him wrapped in peaceful sleep, then, suddenly aroused from this innocent slumber by the abandoned creatures who, living as they did opposite the aviary, had doubtless long harboured their diabolical designs. We saw Mysouff but half awake, still purring innocently, stretching himself, opening his pink mouth, from which protruded a tongue like that of a heraldic lion. He shakes his ears, a proof that he rejects the infamous proposal that is being made to him; he listens; at first he refuses—the advocate insisted that the prisoner had begun by refusing—then, naturally yielding, hardly more than a kitten, corrupted as he had been by the cook, who instead of feeding him on milk or a little weak broth, as she had been told to do, had recklessly excited his carnivorous appetite by giving him pieces of liver and parings of raw chops; the unfortunate young cat yields little by little, prompted more by good nature and weakness of mind than by cruelty or greed, and, only half awake, he does the bidding of the villainous monkeys, the real instigators of the crime. The counsel here took the prisoner in his arms, showed us his paws, and defied any anatomist to say that with paws so made, an animal could possibly open a door that was bolted. Finally, he borrowed Michel's Dictionary of Natural History, opened it at the article 'Cat,' 'Domestic Cat,' 'Wild Cat'; he proved that Mysouff was no wild cat, seeing that nature had robed him in white, the colour of innocence; then smiting the book with vehemence, 'Cat!' he exclaimed, 'Cat! You shall now hear, gentlemen, what the illustrious Buffon, the man with lace sleeves, has to say about the cat.

'"The cat," says M. de Buffon, "is not to be trusted, but it is kept to rid the house of enemies which cannot otherwise be destroyed. Although the cat, especially when young, is pleasing, nature has given it perverse and untrustworthy qualities which increase with age, and which education may conceal, but will not eradicate." Well, then,' exclaimed the orator, after having read this passage, 'what more remains to be said? Did poor Mysouff come here with a false character seeking a situation? Was it not the cook herself who found him— who took him by force from the heap of sticks behind which he had sought refuge? It was merely to interest and touch the heart of her master that she described him mewing in the cellar. We must reflect also, that those unhappy birds, his victims—I allude especially to the quails, which are eaten by man—though their death is doubtless much to be deplored, yet they must have felt themselves liable to death at any moment, and are now released from the terrors they experienced every time they saw the cook approaching their retreat. Finally, gentlemen, I appeal to your justice, and I think you will now admit that the interesting and unfortunate Mysouff has but yielded, not only to incontrollable natural instincts, but also to foreign influence. I claim for my client the plea of extenuating circumstances.'

The counsel's pleading was received with cries of

applause, and Mysouff, found guilty of complicity in the murder of the quails, turtle-doves, and other birds of different species, but with extenuating circumstances, was sentenced only to five years of monkeys.

VI

The next winter, certain circumstances, with which I need not trouble my readers, led to my making a journey to Algiers. I seldom made any long journey without bringing home some animal to add to my collection, and accordingly I returned from Africa accompanied by a vulture, which I bought from a little boy who called himself a Beni-Mouffetard. I paid ten francs for the vulture, and made the Beni-Mouffetard a present of two more, in return for which he warned me that my vulture was excessively savage, and had already bitten off the thumb of an Arab and the tail of a dog. I promised to be very careful, and the next day I became the possessor of a magnificent vulture, whose only fault consisted in a strong desire to tear in pieces everybody who came near him. I bestowed on him the name of his compatriot, Jugurtha. He had a chain fastened to his leg, and had for further security been placed in a large cage made of spars. In this cage he travelled quite safely as far as Philippeville, without any other accident than that he nearly bit off the finger of a passenger who had tried to make friends with him. At Philippeville a difficulty arose. It was three miles from Stora, the port where we were to embark, and the diligence did not go on so far. I and several other gentlemen thought that we would like to walk to Stora, the scenery being beautiful and the distance not very great; but what was I to do about Jugurtha? I could not ask a porter to carry the cage; Jugurtha would certainly have eaten him through the spars. I thought of a plan: it was to lengthen his chain eight or ten feet by means of a cord; and then to drive him in front of me with a long pole. But the first difficulty was to induce Jugurtha to come out of his cage; none of us dared put our hands within reach of his beak. However, I managed to fasten the cord to his chain, then I made two men armed with pickaxes break away the spars. Jugurtha finding himself free, spread out his wings to fly away, but he could of course only fly as far as his cord would permit.

Now Jugurtha was a very intelligent creature; he saw that there was an obstacle in the way of his liberty, and that I was that obstacle; he therefore turned upon me with fury, in the hope of putting me to flight, or devouring me in case of resistance. I, however, was no less sagacious than Jugurtha; I had foreseen the attack, and provided myself with a good switch made of dogwood, as thick as one's forefinger, and eight feet long. With this switch I parried Jugurtha's attack, which astonished but did not stop him; however, a second blow, given with all my force, made him stop short, and a third caused him to fly in the opposite direction, that is, towards Stora. Once launched upon this road, I had only to use my switch adroitly to make Jugurtha proceed at about the same pace as we did ourselves, to the great admiration of my fellow-travellers, and of all the people whom we met on the road. On our arrival at Stora, Jugurtha made no difficulty about getting on board the steamer, and when tied to the mast, waited calmly while a new cage was made for him. He went into it of his own accord, received with gratitude the pieces of meat which the ship's cook gave him, and three days after his embarkation he became so tame that he used to present me with his head to scratch, as a parrot does. I brought Jugurtha home without further adventure, and committed him to the charge of Michel.

It was not until my return from Algiers on this occasion that I went to live at Monte Cristo, the building of which had been finished during my absence. Up to this time I had lived in a smaller house called the Villa Medicis, and while the other was building, Michel made arrangements for the proper lodging of all my animals, for he was much more occupied about their comfort than he was about mine or even his own. They had all plenty of room, particularly the dogs, who were not confined by any sort of enclosure, and Pritchard, who was naturally generous, kept open house with a truly Scottish hospitality. It was his custom to sit in the middle of the road and salute every dog that passed with a little not unfriendly growl; smelling him, and permitting himself to be smelt in a ceremonious manner. When a mutual sympathy had been produced by this means, a conversation something like this would begin :

'Have you a good master ?' asked the strange dog.

'Not bad,' Pritchard would reply.

'Does your master feed you well ?'

'Well, one has porridge twice a day, bones at breakfast and dinner, and anything one can pick up in the kitchen besides.'

The stranger licked his lips.

'You are not badly off,' said he.

'I do not complain,' replied Pritchard. Then, seeing the strange dog look pensive, he added, 'Would you like to dine with us ?'

The invitation was accepted at once, for dogs do not wait to be pressed, like some foolish human beings.

At dinner-time Pritchard came in, followed by an unknown dog, who, like Pritchard, placed himself beside my chair, and scratched my knee with his paw in such a confiding way that I felt sure that Pritchard must have been commending my benevolence. The dog, after spending a pleasant evening, found that it was rather too late to return home, so slept comfortably on the grass after his good supper. Next morning he took two or three steps as if to go away, then changing his mind, he inquired of Pritchard, 'Should I be much in the way if I stayed on here ?'

Pritchard replied, 'You could quite well, with manage-

DUMAS ARRIVES AT STORA WITH HIS VULTURE

ment, make them believe you are the neighbour's dog,
and after two or three days, nobody would know you did
not belong to the house. You might live here just as well
as those idle useless monkeys, who do nothing but amuse
themselves, or that greedy vulture, who eats tripe all day
long, or that idiot of a macaw, who is always screaming
about nothing.'

The dog stayed, keeping in the background at first,
but in a day or two he jumped up upon me and followed
me everywhere, and there was another guest to feed, that
was all. Michel asked me one day if I knew how many
dogs there were about the place. I answered that I did
not.

'Sir,' said Michel, 'there are thirteen.'

'That is an unlucky number, Michel; you must see
that they do not all dine together, else one of them is sure
to die first.'

'It is not that, though,' said Michel, 'it is the expense
I am thinking of. Why, they would eat an ox a day, all
those dogs; and if you will allow me, sir, I will just take
a whip and put the whole pack to the door, to-morrow
morning.'

'But, Michel, let us do it handsomely. These dogs,
after all, do honour to the house by staying here. So give
them a grand dinner to-morrow; tell them that it is the
farewell banquet, and then, at dessert, put them all to the
door.'

'But after all, sir, I cannot put them to the door,
because there isn't a door.'

'Michel,' said I, 'there are certain things in this world
that one must just put up with, to keep up one's character
and position. Since all these dogs have come to me, let
them stay with me. I don't think they will ruin me,
Michel. Only, on their own account, you should be careful
that there are not thirteen.'

'I will drive away one,' suggested Michel, 'and then
there will only be twelve.'

'On the contrary, let another come, and then there will be fourteen.'

Michel sighed.

'It's a regular kennel,' he murmured.

It was, in fact, a pack of hounds, though rather a mixed one. There was a Russian wolfhound, there was a poodle, a water spaniel, a spitz, a dachshund with crooked legs, a mongrel terrier, a mongrel King Charles, and a Turkish dog which had no hair on its body, only a tuft upon its head and a tassel at the end of its tail. Our next recruit was a little Maltese terrier, named Lisette, which raised the number to fourteen. After all, the expense of these fourteen amounted to rather over two pounds a month. A single dinner given to five or six of my own species would have cost me three times as much, and they would have gone away dissatisfied; for, even if they had liked my wine, they would certainly have found fault with my books. Out of this pack of hounds, one became Pritchard's particular friend and Michel's favourite. This was a dachshund with short crooked legs, a long body, and, as Michel said, the finest voice in the department of Seine-et-Oise. Portugo—that was his name—had in truth a most magnificent bass voice. I used to hear it sometimes in the night when I was writing, and think how that deep-toned majestic bark would please St. Hubert if he heard it in his grave. But what was Portugo doing at that hour, and why was he awake while the other dogs slumbered? This mystery was revealed one day, when a stewed rabbit was brought me for dinner. I inquired where the rabbit came from.

'You thought it good, sir?' Michel asked me with a pleased face.

'Excellent.'

'Well, then, you can have one just the same every day, sir, if you like.'

'Every day, Michel? Surely that is almost too much

'IT'S A REGULAR KENNEL'

to promise. Besides, I should like, before consuming so many rabbits, to know where they come from.'

' You shall know that this very night, if you don't mind coming out with me.'

' Ah! Michel, I have told you before that you are a poacher ! '

' Oh, sir, as to that, I am as innocent as a baby—and, as I was saying, if you will only come out with me to-night—'

' Must I go far, Michel? '

' Not a hundred yards, sir.'

' At what o'clock? '

' Just at the moment when you hear Portugo's first bark.'

' Very well, Michel, I will be with you.'

I had nearly forgotten this promise, and was writing as usual, when Michel came into my study. It was about eleven o'clock, and a fine moonlight night.

' Hallo! ' said I, ' Portugo hasn't barked yet, has he ? '

' No, but I was just thinking that if you waited for that, you would miss seeing something curious.'

' What should I miss, Michel? '

' The council of war which is held between Pritchard and Portugo.'

I followed Michel, and sure enough, among the fourteen dogs, which were mostly sleeping in different attitudes, Portugo and Pritchard were sitting up, and seemed to be gravely debating some important question. When the debate was ended, they separated; Portugo went out at the gate to the high road, turned the corner, and disappeared, while Pritchard began deliberately, as if he had plenty of time before him, to follow the little path which led up to a stone quarry. We followed Pritchard, who took no notice of us, though he evidently knew we were there. He went up to the top of the quarry, examined and smelt about over the ground with great care, and when he had found a scent and assured himself that it was fresh, he lay down flat and waited. Almost at the same moment, Portugo's first bark was heard some two hundred yards off. Now the plan the two dogs had laid was clear to us. The rabbits came out of their holes in the quarry every evening to go to their feeding ground ; Pritchard found the scent of one ; Portugo then made a wide circuit, found and chased the rabbit, and, as a rabbit or a hare always comes back upon its former track, Pritchard, lying in ambush, awaited its return. Accordingly, as the sound of Portugo's barking came closer, we saw Pritchard's yellow eyes light up and flame like a topaz ; then all of a sudden he made a spring, and we heard a cry of fright and distress.

'They've done it!' said Michel, and he went to Pritchard, took out of his mouth a nice plump rabbit, gave it a blow behind the ears to finish it, and, opening it on the spot, gave the inside to the two dogs, who shared their portion contentedly, although they probably regretted Michel's interference. As Michel told me, I could have eaten a stewed rabbit every day for dinner, if such had been my desire.

But after this, events of a different kind were taking place, which obliged me to leave my country pursuits, and I spent about two months in Paris. The day before I returned to St.-Germains I wrote and told Michel to expect me, and found him waiting for me on the road half way from the station.

'I must tell you, sir,' he said, as soon as I was within hearing, 'that two important events have happened at Monte Cristo since you went away.'

'Well, Michel, let me hear.'

'In the first place, Pritchard got his hind foot into a snare and instead of staying where he was as any other dog would have done, he bit off his foot with his teeth, and so he came home upon three legs.'

'But,' said I, much shocked, 'is the poor beast dead after such an accident ? '

' Dead, sir?   Was not I there to doctor him? '

' And what did you do to him then? '

' I cut off the foot properly at the joint with a pruning knife.   I then sewed the skin neatly over it, and now

JUGURTHA BECOMES DIOGENES

you would never know it was off!   Look there, the rascal has smelt you and is coming to meet you.'

And at that moment Pritchard appeared, coming at full gallop, so that, as Michel had said, one would hardly have noticed that he had only three feet.   My meeting with Pritchard was, as may be supposed, full of deep

emotion on both sides.   I was sorry for the poor animal.
When I had recovered a little, I asked Michel what his
other piece of news was.

'The latest news, sir, is that Jugurtha's name is no
longer Jugurtha.'

' What is it then ? '

' It is Diogenes.'

' And why ? '

' Look, sir ! '

We had now reached the little avenue of ash-trees
which formed the entrance to the villa.   To the left of
the avenue the vulture was seen walking proudly to and
fro in an immense tub, which Michel had made into a
house for him.

' Ah ! now I understand,' said I.   ' Of course, directly
he lives in a tub——'

' That's it ! ' said Michel.   ' Directly he lives in a tub,
he cannot be Jugurtha any more ; he *must* be Diogenes.'

I admired Michel's historical learning no less than I
did his surgical skill, just as the year before, I had bowed
before his superior knowledge of natural history.

VII

In order to lead to more incidents in the life of Pritchard,
I must now tell my readers that I had a friend called
Charpillon, who had a passion for poultry, and kept the
finest hens in the whole department of Yonne.   These
hens were chiefly Cochins and Brahmapootras ; they laid
the most beautiful brown eggs, and Charpillon surrounded
them with every luxury and never would allow them to be
killed.   He had the inside of his hen-house painted green,
in order that the hens, even when shut up, might fancy
themselves in a meadow.   In fact, the illusion was so
complete, that when the hen-house was first painted, the
hens refused to go in at night, fearing to catch cold ; but
after a short time even the least intelligent among them

understood that she had the good fortune to belong to a master who knew how to combine the useful with the beautiful. Whenever these hens ventured out upon the road, strangers would exclaim with delight, 'Oh! what beautiful hens!' to which some one better acquainted with the wonders of this fortunate village would reply, 'I should think so! These are M. Charpillon's hens.' Or, if the speaker were of an envious disposition, he might add, 'Yes indeed! hens that *nothing* is thought too good for!'

When my friend Charpillon heard that I had returned from Paris, he invited me to come and stay with him to shoot, adding as a further inducement that he would give me the best and freshest eggs I had ever eaten in my life. Though I did not share Charpillon's great love of poultry, I am very fond of fresh eggs, and the nankeen-coloured eggs laid by his Brahma hens had an especially delicate flavour. But all earthly pleasures are uncertain. The next morning Charpillon's hens were found to have only laid three eggs instead of eight. Such a thing had never happened before, and Charpillon did not know whom to suspect; however he suspected every one rather than his hens, and a sort of cloud began to obscure the confidence he had hitherto placed in the security of his enclosures. While these gloomy doubts were occupying us, I observed Michel hovering about as if he had something on his mind, and asked him if he wanted to speak to me.

'I should be glad to have a few words with you, sir.'

'In private?'

'It would be better so, for the honour of Pritchard.'

'Ah, indeed? What has the rascal been doing now?'

'You remember, sir, what your solicitor said to you one day when I was in the room?'

'What did he say, Michel? My solicitor is a clever man, and says many sensible things; still it is difficult for me to remember them all.'

'Well, sir,' he said, 'find out whom the crime benefits, and you will find the criminal.'

'I remember that axiom perfectly, Michel. Well?'

'Well, sir, whom can this crime of stolen eggs benefit more than Pritchard?'

'Pritchard? You think it is he who steals the eggs? Pritchard, who brings home eggs without breaking them!'

'You mean who *used* to bring them. Pritchard is an animal who has vicious instincts, sir, and if he does not come to a bad end some day, I shall be surprised, that's all.'

'Does Pritchard eat eggs, then?'

'He does; and it is only right to say, sir, that that is *your* fault.'

'What! my fault? My fault that Pritchard eats eggs?'

Michel shook his head sadly, but nothing could shake his opinion.

'Now really, Michel, this is too much! Is it not enough that critics tell me that I pervert everybody's mind with my corrupt literature, but you must join my detractors and say that my bad example corrupts Pritchard?'

'I beg pardon, sir, but do you remember how one day, at the Villa Medicis, while you were eating an egg, M. Rusconi who was there said something so ridiculous that you let the egg fall upon the floor?'

'I remember that quite well.'

'And do you remember calling in Pritchard, who was scraping up a bed of fuchsias in the garden, and making him lick up the egg?'

'I do not remember him scraping up a bed of fuchsias, but I do recollect that he licked up my egg.'

'Well, sir, it is that and nothing else that has been his ruin. Oh! he is quick enough to learn what is wrong; there is no need to show it him twice.'

'Michel, you are really extremely tedious. How have I shown Pritchard what is wrong?'

' By making him eat an egg. You see, sir, before that
he was as innocent as a new-born babe ; he didn't know
what an egg was—he thought it was a badly made golf
ball. But as soon as you make him eat an egg, he learns
what it is. Three days afterwards, M. Alexandre came
home, and was complaining to me of his dog—that he was
rough and tore things with his teeth in carrying them.
" Ah ! look at Pritchard," I said to him, " how gentle *he*
is ! you shall see the way he carries an egg." So I
fetched an egg from the kitchen, placed it on the ground,
and said, " Fetch, Pritchard ! " Pritchard didn't need
to be told twice, but what do you think the cunning rascal
did ? You remember, some days before, Monsieur ——
the gentleman who had such a bad toothache, you know.
You recollect his coming to see you ? '

' Yes, of course I remember.'

' Well, Pritchard pretended not to notice, but those
yellow eyes of his notice everything. Well, all of a
sudden he pretended to have the same toothache that
that gentleman had, and crack ! goes the egg. Then he
pretends to be ashamed of his awkwardness—he swallows
it in a hurry, shell and all ! I believed him—I thought
it was an accident and fetched another egg. Scarcely
did he make three steps with the egg in his mouth than
the toothache comes on again, and crack ! goes the second
egg. I began then to suspect something—I went and got
a third, but if I hadn't stopped then he'd have eaten
the whole basketful. So then M. Alexandre, who likes his
joke, said, " Michel, you may possibly make a good
musician of Pritchard, or a good astronomer, but he'll
never be a good incubator ! " ' '

' How is it that you never told me this before,
Michel ? '

' Because I was ashamed, sir ; for this is not the
worst.'

' What ! not the worst ? '

Michel shook his head.

'He has developed an unnatural craving for eggs; he got into M. Acoyer's poultry yard and stole all his. M. Acoyer came to complain to me. How do you suppose he lost his foot?'

'You told me yourself—in somebody's grounds where he had forgotten to read the notice about trespassing.'

'You are joking, sir—but I really believe he can read.'

'Oh! Michel, Pritchard is accused of enough sins without having *that* vice laid to his charge! But about his foot?'

'I think he caught it in some wire getting out of a poultry-yard.'

'But you know it happened at night, and the hens are shut up at night. How could he get into the hen-house?'

'He doesn't need to get into the hen-house after eggs; he can charm the hens. Pritchard is what one may call a charmer.'

'Michel, you astonish me more and more!'

'Yes, indeed, sir. I knew that he used to charm the hens at the Villa Medicis; only M. Charpillon has such wonderful hens, I did not think they would have allowed it. But I see now all hens are alike.'

'Then you think it is Pritchard who——'

'I think he charms M. Charpillon's hens, and that is the reason they don't lay—at least, that they only lay for Pritchard.'

'Indeed, Michel, I should much like to know how he does it!'

'If you are awake very early to-morrow, sir, just look out of your window--you can see the poultry-yard from it, and you will see a sight that you have never seen before!'

'I have seen many things, Michel, including sixteen changes of governments, and to see something I have never seen before I would gladly sit up the whole night!'

'There is no need for that—I can wake you at the right time.'

The next day at early dawn, Michel awoke me.

'I am ready, Michel,' said I, coming to the window.

'Wait, wait! let me open it very gently. If Pritchard suspects that he is watched, he won't stir; you have no idea how deceitful he is.'

Michel opened the window with every possible precaution. From where I stood, I could distinctly see the poultry-yard, and Pritchard lying in his couch, his head innocently resting upon his two fore-paws. At the slight noise which Michel made in opening the window, Pritchard pricked up his ears and half opened his yellow eye, but as the sound was not repeated he did not move. Ten minutes afterwards we heard the newly wakened hens begin to cluck. Pritchard immediately opened both eyes, stretched himself and stood upright upon his three feet. He then cast a glance all round him, and seeing that all was quiet, disappeared into a shed, and the next moment we saw him coming out of a sort of little window on the other side. From this window Pritchard easily got upon the sloping roof which overhung one side of the poultry-yard. He had now only to jump down about six feet, and having got into the inclosure he lay down flat in front of the hen-house, giving a little friendly bark. A hen looked out at Pritchard's call, and instead of seeming frightened she went to him at once and received his compliments with apparent complacency. Nor did she seem at all embarrassed, but proceeded to lay her egg, and that within such easy reach of Pritchard that we had not time to see the egg—it was swallowed the same instant. She then retired cackling triumphantly, and her place was taken by another hen.

'Well, now, sir,' said Michel, when Pritchard had swallowed his fourth egg, 'you see it is no wonder that Pritchard has such a clear voice. You know great singers always eat raw eggs the first thing in the morning.'

'I know that, Michel, but what I don't know is how Pritchard proposes to get out of the poultry-yard.'

'Just wait and see what the scoundrel will do.'

Pritchard having finished his breakfast, or being a little alarmed at some noise in the house, stood up on his hind leg, and slipping one of his fore-paws through the bars of the gate, he lifted the latch and went out.

'And when one thinks,' said Michel, 'that if anybody asked him why the yard door was left open, he would say it was because Pierre had forgotten to shut it last night!'

PRITCHARD AND THE HENS

'You think he would have the wickedness to say *that*, Michel?'

'Perhaps not to-day, nor yet to-morrow, because he is not come to his full growth, but some day, mind you, I should not be surprised to hear him speak.'

VIII

Before going out to shoot that day, I thought it only right to give M. Charpillon an account of Pritchard's proceedings. He regarded him, therefore with mingled feelings, in which admiration was more prominent than sympathy, and it was agreed that on our return the dog should be shut up in the stable, and that the stable door should be bolted and padlocked. Pritchard, unsuspicious of our designs, ran on in front with a proud step and with his tail in the air.

'You know,' said Charpillon, 'that neither men nor dogs are allowed to go into the vineyards. I ought as a magistrate to set an example, and Gaignez still more, as he is the mayor. So mind you keep in Pritchard.'

'All right,' said I, 'I will keep him in.'

But Michel approaching, suggested that I should send Pritchard home with him. 'It would be safer,' he said. 'We are quite near the house, and I have a notion that he might get us into some scrape by hunting in the vineyards.'

'Don't be afraid, Michel; I have thought of a plan to prevent him.'

Michel touched his hat. 'I know you are clever, sir—very clever; but I don't think you are as clever as that!'

'Wait till you see.'

'Indeed, sir, you will have to be quick, for there is Pritchard hunting already.'

We were just in time to see Pritchard disappear into a vineyard, and a moment afterwards he raised a covey of partridges.

'Call in your dog,' cried Gaignez.

I called Pritchard, who, however, turned a deaf ear.

'Catch him,' said I to Michel.

Michel went, and returned in a few minutes with Pritchard in a leash. In the meantime I had found a long stake, which I hung crosswise round his neck, and let him go loose with this ornament. Pritchard understood that he could no longer go through the vineyards, but the stake did not prevent his hunting, and he only went a good deal further off on the open ground.

From this moment there was only one shout all along the line.

'Hold in your dog, confound him!'

'Keep in your Pritchard, can't you! He's sending all the birds out of shot!'

'Look here! Would you mind my putting a few pellets into your brute of a dog? How can anybody shoot if he won't keep in?'

'Michel,' said I, 'catch Pritchard again.'

'I told you so, sir. Luckily we are not far from the house; I can still take him back.'

'Not at all. I have a second idea. Catch Pritchard.'

'After all,' said Michel, 'this is nearly as good fun as if we were shooting.'

And by-and-by he came back, dragging Pritchard by his stake. Pritchard had a partridge in his mouth.

'Look at him, the thief!' said Michel. 'He has carried off M. Gaignez's partridge—I see him looking for it.'

'Put the partridge in your game-bag, Michel; we will give him a surprise.'

Michel hesitated. 'But,' said he, 'think of the opinion this rascal will have of you!'

'What, Michel? do you think Pritchard has a bad opinion of me?'

'Oh, sir! a shocking opinion.'

'But what makes you think so?'

'Why, sir, do you not think that Pritchard knows in his soul and conscience that when he brings you a bird that another gentleman has shot, he is committing a theft?'

'I think he has an idea of it, certainly, Michel.'

'Well, then, sir, if he knows he is a thief, he must take you for a receiver of stolen goods. Look at the articles of the Code; it is said there that receivers are equally guilty with thieves, and should be similarly punished.'

'Michel, you open my eyes to a whole vista of terrors.

'PRITCHARD REAPPEARED NEXT MOMENT WITH A HARE IN HIS MOUTH'

But we are going to try to cure Pritchard of hunting. When he is cured of hunting, he will be cured of stealing.'

'Never, sir! You will never cure Pritchard of his vices.'

Still I pursued my plan, which was to put Pritchard's fore-leg through his collar. By this means, his right fore-foot being fastened to his neck, and his left hind-foot being cut off, he had only two to run with, the left fore-foot and the right hind-foot.

'Well, indeed,' said Michel, 'if he can hunt now, the devil is in it.'

He loosed Pritchard, who stood for a moment as if astonished, but once he had balanced himself he began to walk, then to trot; then, as he found his balance better, he succeeded in running quicker on his two legs than many dogs would have done on four.

'Where are we now, sir?' said Michel.

'It's that beast of a stake that balances him!' I replied, a little disappointed. 'We ought to teach him to dance upon the tight-rope—he would make our fortunes as an acrobat.'

'You are joking again, sir. But listen! do you hear that?'

The most terrible imprecations against Pritchard were resounding on all sides. The imprecations were followed by a shot, then by a howl of pain.

'That is Pritchard's voice,' said Michel. 'Well, it is no more than he deserves.'

Pritchard reappeared the next moment with a hare in his mouth.

'Michel, you said that was Pritchard that howled.'

'I would swear to it, sir.'

'But how could he howl with a hare in his mouth?'

Michel scratched his head. 'It was he all the same,' he said, and he went to look at Pritchard.

'Oh, sir!' he said, 'I was right. The gentleman he took the hare from has shot him. His hind-leg is all over blood. Look! there is M. Charpillon running after his hare.'

' You know that I have just put some pellets into your Pritchard?' Charpillon called out as soon as he saw me.

' You did quite right.'

' He carried off my hare.'

' There! You see,' said Michel, ' it is impossible to cure him.'

' But when he carried away your hare, he must have had it in his mouth?'

' Of course. Where else would he have it?'

' But how could he howl with a hare in his mouth?'

' He put it down to howl, then he took it up again and made off.'

' There's deceit for you, gentlemen!' exclaimed Michel.

Pritchard succeeded in bringing the hare to me, but when he reached me he had to lie down.

' I say,' said Charpillon, ' I hope I haven't hurt him more than I intended—it was a long shot.' And forgetting his hare, Charpillon knelt down to examine Pritchard's wound. It was a serious one; Pritchard had received five or six pellets about the region of his tail, and was bleeding profusely.

' Oh, poor beast!' cried Charpillon. ' I wouldn't have fired that shot for all the hares in creation if I had known.'

' Bah!' said Michel; ' he won't die of it.' And, in fact, Pritchard, after spending three weeks with the vet. at St.-Germains, returned to Monte Cristo perfectly cured, and with his tail in the air once more.

IX

Soon after the disastrous event which I have just related the revolution of 1848 occurred in France, in which King Louis Philippe was dethroned and a republic

established. You will ask what the change of government had to do with my beasts ? Well, although, happily,
they do not trouble their heads about politics, the revolution did affect them a good deal; for the French public,
being excited by these occurrences, would not buy my
books, preferring to read the ' Guillotine,' the ' Red
Republic,' and such like corrupt periodicals ; so that I
became for the time a very much poorer man. I was
obliged greatly to reduce my establishment. I sold my
three horses and two carriages for a quarter of their
value, and I presented the Last of the Laidmanoirs, Potich,
and Mademoiselle Desgarcins to the Jardin des Plantes
in Paris. I had to move into a smaller house, but my
monkeys were lodged in a palace ; this is a sort of thing
that sometimes happens after a revolution. Mysouff also
profited by it, for he regained his liberty on the departure
of the monkeys.

As to Diogenes, the vulture, I gave him to my worthy
neighbour Collinet, who keeps the restaurant Henri IV.,
and makes such good cutlets à la Béarnaise. There was
no fear of Diogenes dying of hunger under his new master's
care ; on the contrary, he improved greatly in health and
beauty, and, doubtless as a token of gratitude to Collinet,
he laid an egg for him every year, a thing he never
dreamt of doing for me. Lastly, we requested Pritchard
to cease to keep open house, and to discontinue his daily
invitations to strange dogs to dine and sleep. I was
obliged to give up all thoughts of shooting that year. It
is true that Pritchard still remained to me, but then
Pritchard, you must recollect, had only three feet ; he had
been badly hurt when he was shot by Charpillon, and the
revolution of February had occasioned the loss of one
eye.

It happened one day during that exciting period, that
Michel was so anxious to see what was going on that he
forgot to give Pritchard his dinner. Pritchard therefore
invited himself to dine with the vulture, but Diogenes,

being of a less sociable turn, and not in a humour to be trifled with, dealt poor Pritchard such a blow with his beak as to deprive him of one of his mustard-coloured eyes. Pritchard's courage was unabated; he might be compared to that brave field marshal of whom it was said that Mars had left nothing of him whole except his heart. But it was difficult, you see, to make much use of a dog with so many infirmities. If I had wished to sell him I could not have found a purchaser, nor would he have been considered a handsome present had I desired to give him away. I had no choice, then, but to make this old servant, badly as he had sometimes served me, a pensioner, a companion, in fact a friend. Some people told me that I might have tied a stone round his neck and flung him into the river; others, that it was easy enough to replace him by buying a good retriever from Vatrin; but although I was not yet poor enough to drown Pritchard, neither was I rich enough to buy another dog. However, later in that very year, I made an unexpected success in literature, and one of my plays brought me in a sufficient sum to take a shooting in the department of Yonne. I went to look at this shooting, taking Pritchard with me. In the meantime my daughter wrote to tell me that she had bought an excellent retriever for five pounds, named Catinat, and that she was keeping him in the stable until my return. As soon as I arrived, my first care was to make Catinat's acquaintance. He was a rough, vigorous dog of three or four years old, thoughtless, violent, and quarrelsome. He jumped upon me till he nearly knocked me down, upset my daughter's work-table, and dashed about the room to the great danger of my china vases and ornaments. I therefore called Michel and informed him that the superficial acquaintance which I had made with Catinat would suffice for the time, and that I would defer the pleasure of his further intimacy until the shooting season began at Auxerre.

Poor Michel, as soon as he saw Catinat, had been seized with a presentiment of evil.

'Sir,' he said, 'that dog will bring some misfortune upon us. I do not know yet what, but something will happen, I know it will!'

'In the meantime, Michel,' I said, 'you had better take Catinat back to the stable.' But Catinat had already left the room of his own accord and rushed downstairs to the dining-room, where I had left Pritchard. Now Pritchard never could endure Catinat from the first moment he saw him; the two dogs instantly flew at one another with so much fury that Michel was obliged to call me to his assistance before we could separate them. Catinat was once more shut up in the stable, and Pritchard conducted to his kennel in the stable-yard, which, in the absence of carriages and horses, was now a poultry-yard, inhabited by my eleven hens and my cock Cæsar. Pritchard's friendship with the hens continued to be as strong as ever, and the household suffered from a scarcity of eggs in consequence. That evening, while my daughter and I were walking in the garden, Michel came to meet us, twisting his straw hat between his fingers, a sure sign that he had something important to say.

'Well, what is it, Michel?' I asked.

'It came into my mind, sir,' he answered, 'while I was taking Pritchard to his kennel, that we never have any eggs because Pritchard eats them; and he eats them because he is in direct communication with the hens.'

'It is evident, Michel, that if Pritchard never went into the poultry-yard, he would not eat the eggs.'

'Then, do you not think, sir,' continued Michel, 'that if we shut up Pritchard in the stable and put Catinat into the poultry-yard, it would be better? Catinat is an animal without education, so far as I know; but he is not such a thief as Pritchard.'

'Do you know what will happen if you do that,

Michel?' I said. 'Catinat will not eat the eggs, perhaps, but he will eat the hens.'

'If a misfortune like that were to occur, I know a method of curing him of eating hens.'

'Well—but in the meantime the hens would be eaten.'

Scarcely had I uttered these words, when a frightful noise was heard in the stable-yard, as loud as that of a pack of hounds in full cry, but mingled with howls of rage and pain which indicated a deadly combat.

'Michel!' I cried, 'do you hear that?'

'Oh yes, I hear it,' he answered, 'but those must be the neighbours' dogs fighting.'

'Michel, those are Catinat and Pritchard killing each other!'

'Impossible, sir—I have separated them.'

'Well, then, they have met again.'

'It is true,' said Michel, 'that scoundrel Pritchard can open the stable-door as well as any one.'

'Then, you see, Pritchard is a dog of courage; he'll have opened the stable-door for Catinat on purpose to fight him. Be quick, Michel, I am really afraid one of them will be killed.'

Michel darted into the passage which led to the stable, and no sooner had he disappeared than I knew from the lamentations which I heard that some misfortune had happened. In a minute or two Michel reappeared sobbing bitterly and carrying Pritchard in his arms.

'Look, sir! just look!' he said; 'this is the last we shall see of Pritchard—look what your fine sporting dog has done to him. Catinat, indeed! it is Catilina he should be called!'

I ran up to Pritchard, full of concern—I had a great love for him, though he had often made me angry. He was a dog of much originality, and the unexpected things he did were only a proof of genius.

'What do you think is the matter?' I asked Michel.

'The matter?—the matter is that he is dead!'

' Oh no, surely not ! '

' Anyhow, he'll never be good for anything again.' And he laid him on the ground at my feet.

' Pritchard, my poor Pritchard ! ' I cried.

At the sound of my voice, Pritchard opened his yellow eye and looked sorrowfully at me, then stretched out his four legs, gave one sigh, and died. Catinat had bitten his throat quite through, so that his death was almost immediate.

' Well, Michel,' said I, ' it is not a good servant, it is a good friend that we have lost. You must wash him carefully—you shall have a towel to wrap him in—you shall dig his grave in the garden and we will have a tombstone made for him on which shall be engraved this epitaph :

Like conquering Rantzau, of courage undaunted,
Pritchard, to thee Mars honour has granted,
On each field of fight of a limb he bereft thee,
Till nought but thy gallant heart scatheless was left thee.

As my habit was, I sought consolation for my grief in literary labours. Michel endeavoured to assuage his with the help of two bottles of red wine, with which, mingled with his tears, he watered the grave of the departed. I know this because when I came out early next morning to see if my wishes with regard to Pritchard's burial had been carried out, I found Michel stretched upon the ground, still in tears, and the two bottles empty by his side.

THE ADVENTURES OF PYRAMUS

PYRAMUS was a large brown dog, born of a good family, who had been given, when a mere pup, to Alexandre Dumas, the great French novelist, then quite a young man. Now the keeper to whom Pyramus first belonged had also a tiny little fox cub without any relations about the place, so both fox-cub and dog-pup were handed over to the same mother, who brought them up side by side, until they were able to do for themselves. So when the keeper made young Dumas a present of Pyramus, he thought he had better bestow Cartouche on him as well.

Of course it is hardly necessary to say that these fine names were not invented by the keeper, who had never heard of either Pyramus or Cartouche, but were given to his pets by Dumas, after he had spent a little time in observing their characters.

Certainly it was a very curious study. Here were two animals, who had never been apart since they were born, and were now living together in two kennels side by side in the courtyard of the house, and yet after the first three or four months, when they were mere babies, every day showed some difference, and soon they ceased to be friends at all and became open enemies.

The earliest fight known to have taken place between them happened in this way. One day some bones were thrown by accident within the bounds of Cartouche's territory, and though if they belonged to anybody, it was clearly Cartouche, Pyramus resolved most unfairly to get hold of them. The first time Pyramus tried secretly to commit this act of piracy, Cartouche growled; the second time he showed his teeth; the third time he bit.

It must be owned that Cartouche had shown some excuse for his violent behaviour, because he always remained chained up, whereas Pyramus was allowed certain hours of liberty; and it was during one of these that he made up his mind to steal the bones from Cartouche, whose chain (he thought) would prevent any attempt at reprisals. Indeed, he even tried to make out to his conscience that probably the bones were not dainty enough for Cartouche, who loved delicate food, whereas anything was good enough for him, Pyramus. However, whether he wanted to eat the bones or not, Cartouche had no intention of letting them be stolen from him, and having managed to drive off Pyramus on the first occasion, he determined to get safely hold of the bones before his enemy was unchained again.

Now the chains of each were the same length, four feet, and in addition to that, Pyramus had a bigger head and longer nose than Cartouche, who was much smaller altogether. So it follows that when they were both chained up, Pyramus could stretch farther towards any object that lay at an equal distance between their kennels. Pyramus knew this, and so he counted on always getting the better of Cartouche.

But Cartouche had not been born a fox for nothing, and he watched with a scornful expression the great Pyramus straining at his chain with his eyes nearly jumping out of his head with greed and rage. 'Really,' said Cartouche to himself, 'if he goes on like that much longer, I shall have a mad dog for a neighbour before the day is out. Let me see if *I* can't manage better.' But as we know, being a much smaller animal than Pyramus, his nose did not come nearly so close to the bones; and after one or two efforts to reach the tempting morsel which was lying about six feet from each kennel, he gave it up, and retired to his warm bed, hoping that he might somehow hit upon some idea which would enable him to reach the ' bones of contention.'

All at once he jumped up, for after hard thought he had got what he wanted.   He trotted merrily to the length of his chain, and now it was Pyramus' turn to look on and to think with satisfaction : ' Well, if *I* can't get them, *you* can't either, which is a comfort.'

But gradually his grin of delight changed into a savage snarl, as Cartouche turned himself round when he

CARTOUCHE OUTWITS PYRAMUS

had got to the end of his chain, and stretching out his paw, hooked the bone which he gradually drew within reach, and before Pyramus had recovered from his astonishment, Cartouche had got possession of all the bones and was cracking them with great enjoyment inside his kennel.

It may seem very unjust that Cartouche was always kept chained up, while Pyramus was allowed to roam about freely, but the fact was that Pyramus only ate or stole when he was really hungry, while Cartouche was by nature the murderer of everything he came across. One day he broke his chain and ran off to the fowl-yard of Monsieur Mauprivez, who lived next door. In less than ten minutes he had strangled seventeen hens and two cocks : nineteen corpses in all ! It was impossible to find any ' extenuating circumstances ' in his favour. He was condemned to death and promptly executed.

Henceforth Pyramus reigned alone, and it is sad to think that he seemed to enjoy it, and even that his appetite grew bigger.

It is bad enough for any dog to have an appetite like Pyramus when he was at home, but when he was out shooting, and should have been doing his duty as a retriever, this fault became a positive vice. Whatever might be the first bird shot by his master, whether it happened to be partridge or pheasant, quail or snipe, down it would go into Pyramus's wide throat. It was seldom, indeed, that his master arrived in time to see even the last feathers.

A smart blow from a whip kept him in order all the rest of the day, and it was very rarely that he sinned twice in this way while on the same expedition, but un-luckily before the next day's shooting came round, he had entirely forgotten all about his previous caning, and justice had to be done again.

On two separate occasions, however, Pyramus's greedi-ness brought its own punishment. One day his master was shooting with a friend in a place where a small wood had been cut down early in the year, and after the low shrubs had been sawn in pieces and bound in bundles, the grass was left to grow into hay, and this hay was now in processs of cutting. The shooting party reached the spot just at the time that the reapers were having their dinner and taking their midday rest, and one of the reapers had laid his scythe against a little stack of wood about three feet high. At this moment a snipe got up, and M. Dumas fired and killed it. It fell on the other side of the stack of wood against which the scythe was leaning.

As it was the first bird he had killed that day, he knew of course that it would become the prey of Pyramus, so he did not hurry himself to go after it, but watched with amusement, Pyramus tearing along, even jumping over the stack in his haste.

But when after giving the dog the usual time to swallow his fat morsel, Monsieur did not see Pyramus coming back to him as usual in leaps and bounds, he began to wonder what could have happened, and made hastily for the stack of wood behind which he had disappeared. There he found the unlucky Pyramus lying on the ground, with the point of the scythe right through his neck. The blood was pouring from the wound, and he lay motionless, with the snipe dead on the ground about six inches from his nose.

The two men raised him as gently as possible, and carried him to the river, and here they bathed the wound with water. They then folded a pocket-handkerchief into a band, and tied it tightly round his neck to staunch the blood, and when this was done, and they were wondering how to get him home, a peasant fortunately passed driving a donkey with two panniers, and he was laid in one of the panniers and taken to the nearest village, where he was put safely into a carriage.

For eight days Pyramus lay between life and death. For a whole month his head hung on one side, and it was only after six weeks (which seems like six years to a dog) that he was able to run about as usual, and appeared to have forgotten his accident.

Only, whenever he saw a scythe he made a long round to avoid coming in contact with it.

Some time afterwards he returned to the house with his body as full of holes as a sieve. On this occasion he was taking a walk through the forest, and, seeing a goat feeding, jumped at its throat. The goat screamed loudly, and the keeper, who was smoking at a little distance off, ran to his help ; but before he could come up the goat was half dead. On hearing the steps of the keeper, and on listening to his strong language, Pyramus understood very well that this stout man dressed in blue would have something very serious to say to him, so he stretched his legs to their fullest extent, and started off like an arrow from a bow. But, as Man Friday long ago remarked, ' My little ball of lead can run faster than thou,' the keeper's little ball of lead ran faster than Pyramus, and that is how he came home with all the holes in his body.

There is no denying that Pyramus was a very bad dog, and as his master was fond of him, it is impossible to believe that he can *always* have been hungry, as, for instance, when he jumped up in a butcher's shop to steal a piece of meat and got the hook on which it was hung through his own jaws, so that someone had to come and unhook him. But hungry or not, Monsieur Dumas had no time to be perpetually getting him out of scrapes, and when a few months later an Englishman who wanted a sporting dog took a fancy to Pyramus, his master was not altogether sorry to say good-bye.

THE STORY OF A WEASEL [1]

WEASELS are so sharp and clever and untiring, that their activity has been made into a proverb ; and, like many other sharp and clever creatures, they are very mischievous, and fond of killing rabbits and chickens, and even of sucking their eggs, which they do so carefully that they hardly ever break one.

A French lady, called Mademoiselle de Laistre, a friend of the great naturalist, Monsieur de Buffon, once found a weasel when he was very young indeed, and, as she was fond of pets, she thought she would bring him up. Now a weasel is a little creature, and very pretty. It has short legs and a long tail, and its skin is reddish brown above and white below. Its eyes are black and its ears are small, and its body is about seven inches in length. But this weasel was much smaller than that when it went to live with Mademoiselle de Laistre.

Of course it had to be taught : all young things have, and this weasel knew nothing. The good lady first began with pouring some milk into the hollow of her hand and letting it drink from it. Very soon, being a weasel of polite instincts, it would not take milk in any other way. After its dinner, when a little fresh meat was added to the milk, it would run to a soft quilt that was spread in its mistress's bedroom, and, having soon discovered that it could get inside the quilt at a place where the stitches had given way, it proceeded to tuck itself up comfortably for an hour or two. This was all very well in the day,

[1] Bingley's *Animal Biography*.

but Mademoiselle de Laistre did not feel at all safe in leaving such a mischievous creature loose during the night,

MADEMOISELLE DE LAISTRE AND HER WEASEL

so whenever she went to bed, she shut the weasel up in a little cage that stood close by. If she happened to wake up early, she would unfasten the cage, and then the weasel would come into her bed, and, nestling up to her, go to sleep again. If she was already dressed when he was let out, he would jump all about her, and would never once miss alighting on her hands, even when they were held out three feet from him.

All his ways were pretty and gentle. He would sit on his mistress's shoulder and give little soft pats to her chin, or would run over a whole room full of people at the mere sound of her voice. He was very fond of the sun, too, and would tumble about and murmur with delight whenever it shone on him. The little weasel was rather a thirsty animal, but he would not drink much at a time, and, when he had once tasted milk, could not be persuaded to touch rain-water. Baths were quite new to him, too, and he could not make up his mind to them, even in the heat, from which he suffered a good deal. His nearest approach to bathing was a wet cloth wrapped round him, and this evidently gave him great pleasure.

Cats and dogs about the place condescended to make friends with him, and they never quarrelled nor hurt each other. Indeed, in many of their instincts and ways, weasels are not very unlike cats, and one quality they have in common is their curiosity. Nothing was dull or uninteresting to this little weasel. It was impossible to open a drawer or take out a paper without his little sharp nose being thrust round the corner, and he would even jump on his mistress's hands, the better to read her letters. He was also very fond of attracting attention, and in the midst of his play would always stop to see if anyone was watching. If he found that no one was troubling about him, he would at once leave off, and, curling himself up, go off into a sleep so sound that he might be taken up by the head and swung backwards and forwards quite a long time before he would wake up and be himself again.

STORIES ABOUT WOLVES

WOLVES are found in the colder and more northern parts of Asia and North America, and over the whole of Europe, except the British Isles, where they were exterminated long ago. Some say Lochiel killed the last wolf in Scotland, some say a gamekeeper was the hero. The wolf very much resembles the dog in appearance, except that his eyes are set in obliquely, and nearer his nose. His coat is commonly of a tawny grey colour, but sometimes black or white, and he varies in size according to the climate. Some wolves only measure two and a half feet in length, not counting the tail, others are much larger. They have remarkably keen sight, hearing, and sense of smell, and such a stealthy gait, that their way of slinking along has passed into a proverb in countries where wolves are common. They live in rocky caverns in the forest, sleep by day like other beasts of prey, and go out at night to forage for food. They eat small birds, reptiles, the smaller animals, such as rats and mice, some fruits, grapes among others, and rotten apples; they do not disdain even dead bodies, nor garbage of any sort. But in times of famine or prolonged snow, when all these provisions fail them, and they feel the pinch of hunger, then woe betide the flocks of sheep or the human beings they may encounter. In 1450 wolves actually came into Paris and attacked the citizens. Even so lately as the long and severe winter of 1894-5, the wolves came down into the plains of Piedmont and the lower Alpes Maritimes in such numbers that the soldiery had to be called out to destroy them. In such times a wolf in broad daylight will steal up to a flock of sheep peacefully feeding, seize on a fine fat one, and make away with it, unseen and unsuspected even by the watchful sheep dog. Should a first attempt prove successful, he will return again and again, till, finding he can no longer rob that flock unmolested, he will look out for another one still unsuspicious. If he once gets inside a sheep-fold at night, he massacres and mangles right and left. When he has slain to his heart's content, he goes off with a victim and devours it, then comes back for a second, a third, and a fourth carcase, which he carries away to hide under a heap of branches or dead leaves. When dawn breaks, he returns gorged with food to his lair, leaving the ground strewn with the bodies of the slain. The wolf even contrives to get the better of his natural enemy, the dog, using stratagem and cleverness in the place of strength. If he spies a gawky, long-legged puppy swaggering about his own farmyard, he will come closer and entice him out to play by means of every sort of caper and gambol. When the young simpleton has been induced to come out beyond the farmyard, the wolf, throwing off his disguise of amiable playfulness, falls upon the dog and carries him away to make a meal of. In the case of a dog stronger and more capable of making resistance the stratagem requires two wolves; one appears to the dog in its true character of wolf, and then disappears into an ambush, where the other lies hidden. The dog, following its natural instinct, pursues the wolf into the ambush, where the two conspirators soon make an end of it.

So numerous have wolves always been in the rural districts of France, that from the earliest times there has been an institution called the *Louveterie*, for their extermination. Since the French Revolution this has been very much modified, but there is still a reward of so much per head for every wolf killed. Under ordinary circumstances the wolf will not only not attack man, but will flee from him, for he is as cowardly as he is crafty. But if driven by hunger he will pursue, or rather he will follow a solitary traveller for miles, dogging his footsteps, and always keeping near, sometimes on one side, sometimes on the other, till the man, harassed and worn out by fatigue and fright, is compelled to halt; then the wolf, who has been waiting for this opportunity, springs on him and devours him.

Audubon, in his ' Quadrupeds of America,' tells a story of two young negroes who lived on a plantation on the banks of the Ohio in the State of Kentucky, about the year 1820. They each had a sweetheart, whom they used to go to visit every evening after their work was done. These negresses lived on another plantation about four miles away, but a short cut led across a large cane brake. When winter set in with its long dark nights no ray of light illuminated this dismal swamp. But the negroes continued their nightly expeditions notwithstanding, arming themselves by way of precaution with their axes. One dark night they set off over a thin crust of snow, the reflection from which afforded all the light they had to guide them on their way. Hardly a star appeared through the dense masses of cloud that nearly covered the sky, and menaced more snow. About half way to their destination the negroes' blood froze at the sound of a long and fearful howl that rent the air; they knew it could only come from a pack of hungry and perhaps desperate wolves. They paused to listen, and only a dismal silence succeeded. In the impenetrable darkness nothing was visible a few feet beyond them; grasping their axes they went on their way though with quaking hearts. Suddenly, in single file, out of the darkness sprang several wolves, who seized on the first man, inflicting terrible wounds with their fangs on his legs and arms; others as ravenous leapt on his companion, and dragged him to the ground. Both negroes fought manfully, but soon one had ceased to move, and the other, despairing of aiding his companion, threw down his axe and sprang on to the branch of a tree, where he found safety and shelter for the rest of that

'WHEN DAY BROKE'

miserable night. When day broke, only the bones of his friend lay scattered on the blood-stained, trampled snow; three dead wolves lay near, but the rest of the pack had betaken themselves to their lair, to sleep away the effects of their night's gorge.

A sledge journey through the plains of Siberia in winter is a perilous undertaking. If a pack of hungry wolves get on the track of a sledge, the travellers know, as soon as they hear the horrid howls and see the grey forms stealing swiftly across the snow, that their chances of escape are small. If the sledge stops one instant men and horses are lost ; the only safety is in flight at utmost speed. It is indeed a race for life ! The horses, mad with terror, seem to have wings ; the wolves, no less swift, pursue them, their cruel eyes gleaming with the lust for blood. From time to time a shot is fired, and a wolf falls dead in the snow ; bolder than the others, he has tried to climb into the sledge and has met his reward. This incident gives a momentary respite to the pursued, for the murderous pack will pause to tear in pieces and devour their dead comrade ; then, further inflamed with the taste of blood, they will continue the headlong pursuit with redoubled vigour.

Should the travellers be able to reach a village or friendly farmhouse before the horses are completely exhausted, the wolves, frightened by the lights, will slink away into the forest, balked this time of their prey. On the other hand, should no refuge be near, the wolves will keep up with the horses till the poor beasts stumble and fall from fatigue, when the whole pack will instantly spring upon men and horses, and in a few moments the bloodstained snow alone tells the tale.

There have been instances, but fortunately few, of wolves with a perfect craving for human flesh. Such was the notorious Bête (or beast) du Gévaudan, that from the year 1764 and onwards ravaged the district of that name, in Auvergne, to the south of the centre of France. This wolf was of enormous size, measuring six feet from the point of its nose to the tip of its tale. It devoured eighty-three persons, principally women and children, and seriously wounded twenty-five or thirty others. It was attacked from first to last by between *two and three hundred thousand* hunters, probably not all at once. With half a dozen wolves, each equal to 200,000 men, a country could afford to do without an army. But the wolf of Gévaudan was no common wolf. He never married, having no leisure, fortunately for the human race. The whole of France was in a state of alarm on its account; the peasants dared no longer go to their work in the fields alone and unarmed. Every day brought tidings of some fresh trouble; in the morning he would spread terror and confusion in some village in the plains, in the evening he would carry off some hapless victim from some mountain hamlet fifteen or twenty leagues away. Five little shepherd boys, feeding their flocks on the mountain-side, were attacked suddenly by the ferocious beast, who made off with the youngest of them; the others, armed only with sticks, pursued the wolf, and attacked it so valiantly that they compelled it to drop its prey and slink off into the wood. A poor woman was sitting at her cottage door with her three children, when the wolf came down on them and attempted to carry off each of the children in turn. The mother fought so courageously in defence of her little ones that she succeeded in putting the wolf to flight, but in so doing was terribly bitten herself, and the youngest child died of his wounds.

Sometimes twenty or thirty parishes joined forces to attack the beast, led by the most experienced huntsmen and the chief *louvetier* of the kingdom. On one occasion twenty thousand hunters surrounded the forest of Preinières, where it lay concealed; but on this, as well as every other occasion, the wolf escaped in the most surprising— one might almost say miraculous—manner, disappearing as if he had been turned into smoke. Some hunters declared that their bullets had rebounded off him, flattened and harmless. Others alleged that when he had been shot, like the great Dundee, with a silver bullet (a well-known charm against sorcery) at such close quarters that it appeared impossible he should not be mortally wounded, in a day or two some fresh horror would announce that the creature was still uninjured. The very dogs refused at length to go after him, and fled howling in the opposite direction. The belief became general that it was no ordinary wolf of flesh and blood, but the Fiend himself in beast shape. Prayers were put up in the churches, processions took place, and the Host remained exhibited as in the times of plague and public calamity.

The State offered a reward of 2,000 francs to whosoever should slay the monster; the syndics of two neighbouring towns added 500 francs, making a total of 100*l*. English money, a large sum in those days. The young Countess de Mercoire, an orphan, and châtelaine of one of the finest estates of the district, offered her hand and fortune in marriage to whoever should rid the country of the scourge. This inspired the young Count Léonce de Varinas, who, though no sportsman by nature, was so deeply in love with the Countess that he determined to gain the reward or perish in the attempt. Assisted by a small band of well-trained hunters, and by two formidable dogs, a bloodhound and a mastiff, he began a systematic attack on the wolf. After many fruitless attempts they succeeded one day in driving the creature into an abandoned quarry of vast size, the sides of which were twenty or thirty feet high and quite precipitous, and the only entrance a narrow cart track blasted out of the rock. The young Count, determined to do or die alone, sternly refused to allow his men to accompany him into the quarry, and left them posted at the entrance with orders only to fire on the beast should it attempt to force its way out. Taking only the dogs with him, and having carefully seen to the state of his weapons, he went bravely to the encounter. The narrow defile was so completely hemmed in on every side that, to the vanquished, there was no escape nor alternative but death. Here and there, on patches of half-melted snow, were footprints, evidently recent, of the huge beast; but the creature remained invisible, and for nearly ten minutes the Count had wandered among the rocks and bushes before the dogs began to give sign of the enemy's presence.

About a hundred yards from where he stood was a frozen pool, on the edge of which grew a clump of bulrushes. Among their dry and yellow stalks Léonce suddenly caught a glimpse of a pair of fiery eyes—nothing more; but it was enough to let him know that the longed-for moment had at length arrived. Léonce advanced cautiously, his gun cocked and ready to fire, and the dogs close at his heels, growling with rage and fear. Still the wolf did not stir, and Léonce, determining to try other tactics, stopped, raised his gun to his shoulder, and aimed between the gleaming eyes, nothing more being yet visible. Before he could fire the beast dashed from among the crackling reeds and sprang straight at him. Léonce, nothing daunted, waited till it was within ten paces and then fired. With a howl of anguish the wolf fell as if dead. Before Léonce had time to utter a shout of joy, it was on its feet again. Streaming with blood and terrible in its rage it fell on the young man. He attempted to defend himself with his bayonet, which, though of tempered steel, was broken as if it had been glass; his gun, too, was bent, and he himself was hurled to the ground. But for his faithful dogs it would soon have been all over with him. They flew at the wolf's throat, who quickly made an end of the bloodhound; one crunch broke his back, while one stroke of the ruthless paw disembowelled him. Castor, the mastiff, had, however, the wolf by the throat, and a fearful struggle ensued over the prostrate body of Léonce. They bit, they tore, they worried, they rolled over and over each other, the wolf, in spite of its wounds, having always the advantage. Half stunned by the fall, suffocated by the weight of the combatants, and blinded by the dust and snow they scattered in the fray, Léonce

THE DEATH OF THE FAMOUS WOLF OF GÉVAUDAN

had just sufficient strength to make one last effort in self-
defence. Drawing his hunting-knife, he plunged it to the
hilt in the shaggy mass above him. From a distance he
seemed to hear shouts of ' Courage, Monsieur! Courage,
Castor! We are coming!' then conscious only of an
overwhelming weight above him, and of iron claws tearing at his chest, he fainted away. When he came to
himself he was lying on the ground, surrounded by his
men. Starting up, he exclaimed, ' The beast! where is
the beast?'

' Dead, Monsieur! stone dead!' answered the head
keeper, showing him the horrid creature, all torn and
bloody, stretched out on the snow beside the dead bloodhound. Castor, a little way off, lay panting and bruised,
licking his wound. The Count's knife was firmly embedded in the beast's ribs; it had gone straight to the
heart and death had been instantaneous. A procession
was formed to carry the carcase of the wolf in triumph to
the castle of the Countess. The news had flown in advance,
and she was waiting on the steps to welcome the conquering hero. It was not long before the Countess and
the gallant champion were married; and, as the wolf left
no family, the country was at peace. Are you not rather
sorry for the poor wolf?

TWO HIGHLAND DOGS

I

RIGH and Speireag were two Highland dogs who lived in a beautiful valley not far from the west coast of Scotland, where high hills slope down to the shores of a blue loch, and the people talk a strange language quite different from English, or even from French, or German, or Latin, which is called Gaelic.

The name 'Righ' means a king, and 'Speireag' means a sparrow-hawk, but they are words no one, except a Highlander, can pronounce properly. However, the dogs had a great many friends who could not talk Gaelic, and when English-speaking people called them 'Ree' and 'Spearah,' they would always answer.

Righ was a great tawny deerhound, tall and slender, very stately, as a king should be, and as gentle as he was strong. He had a rough coat and soft brown eyes, set rather near together, and very bright and watchful. His chief business in life was to watch the faces of his friends, and to obey their wishes quickly, to take his long limbs away from the drawing-room hearth-rug when the butler came in to put on the coals, not to get in the way more than so big a dog could help, and not to get too much excited when anything in the conversation suggested the likelihood of a walk. But his father and all his ancestors had led very different lives; they had been trained to go out on the mountains with men who hunted the wild deer, and to help them in the chase, for the deerhounds run with long bounds and are as fleet as the stag himself.

Then, when the beautiful creature had been killed, it was their duty to guard the body, and to see that carrion crows, and eagles, and other wild birds should not molest it. But Righ's master was a Bishop, who, though he lived quite near to a great deer forest, and often took his dogs over the hills to where the deer lived, never killed anything, but loved to see all his fellow-creatures happy among the things they liked best.

Speireag was a very little dog, of the kind that is called a Skye terrier, though the island of Skye is one of the few places in which a long-haired terrier is very rare. He was quite small, what his Highland friends called ' a wee bit doggie; ' he was very full of life and courage, wonderfully plucky for his size, like the fierce little bird whose name he bore. Like a good many little people he lacked the dignity and repose of his big companion, and, though very good-tempered among his friends, was quite ready to bite if beaten, and did not take a scolding with half the gentleness and humility with which Righ would submit to punishment, perhaps because he needed it oftener, for he was so busy and active that he sometimes got into scrapes. He was only three years old at the time of this story and Righ was seven, so it was perhaps natural that Righ should be the wiser of the two.

They lived in a beautiful house quite near the loch, and they had a large garden to play in, and they could go in and out of the house and do just as they liked so long as they came when they were called and did as they were bid, and did not climb on the sofa cushions when their feet were muddy. There were very few houses on their side the water, and as their friends went about in boats as often as other people go out in carriages, the dogs were used to the water, and could swim as easily as walk, and what is more, knew how to sit still in a boat, so that they were allowed to go everywhere with their friends because they gave no trouble.

They had a very happy life, for there was always

something going on, which is what dogs like, and plenty
of people to go walks with. Their young masters sometimes went out with guns, and a dog, a country dog, loves
a gun better than anything in the world, because he
knows it means business in which he can help. Sometimes their mistress took them for a walk, and then they
knew that they must be on their best behaviour, and not
wander too far away from the road and have to be
whistled back, and not fight with the collies at the cottage
doors, nor chase cats, nor be tiresome in any way; they
generally kept close beside her, Righ walking very slowly
so as to accommodate his big strides to the progress of a
poor human thing with only two legs, and Speireag trotting along with tiny little footsteps that seemed to make
a great fuss and to be in a great hurry about nothing at all.

There was nothing, however, so delightful as going for
walks with their own master, the Bishop. For one thing,
they generally knew he really meant to do something
worth while. Pottering about with a gun or escorting a
lady is pleasant enough, but it generally means coming
home to lunch or tea, and the real joy of a dog's walk is
to feel that you are getting further and further away from
home, and that there are miles of heather and pine-wood
behind you, and yet you are still going on and on, with
chances of more hares and more squirrels to run after.
Sometimes the Bishop would stop at a shepherd's hut or
a lonely cottage under the lee of a hill, and sometimes he
would sit down to examine a flower he had gathered in
the wood, but they forgave him very good-temperedly, and
could always find something to interest them while they
waited.

Righ generally sat down beside his master and
stretched out his great limbs on the heather, for he liked
to think he was taking care of somebody or something.
Speireag would lie down for a minute, panting, with his
little red tongue hanging out and his hairy little paws all
wet and muddy; but he never rested for long, but would

dart off, pretending to have found a rat or a squirrel, even if none really existed.

It was in December 1887, the weather was raw and cold, there was ice floating about on the loch, and the sea gulls used to come up to the garden terrace to be fed. The young masters were away, and mistress could only take walks along the road, there was nothing to tempt her to a mountain scramble or a saunter in the woods. The Bishop was very busy, and day after day the dogs would start up from the rug at the sound of the opening of his study door upstairs, and after a minute's anxious listening, with ears cocked and heads erect, they would lie down again with a sigh of disappointment, for there was no sound of approach to the hat-stand nor of whistled invitation for a walk.

Finally came a sad day when the Bishop went away, and dog-life threatened to become monotonous. Then, one Saturday, hope revived, for a visitor came to the house, an old friend whom they loved and trusted as a good dog always loves what is trustworthy. He was a frequent visitor, and had, in fact, left the house but three weeks before. He was there for a holiday rest, and had leisure to bestow on dogs and on long walks, which they always shared.

He was very thoughtful for them, not the sort of man who would set off on a whole afternoon's ramble and say, when half a mile on his way, ' I wish I'd remembered Righ and Speireag ! ' He always remembered them, and thought for them ; and when he fed them after dinner, would always give big bits of biscuit to the big dog, and little bits to the little dog, and it is not every one who has the sense for that !

Every day, and often twice a day, he took them out, down to the church or the pier, or across the lake and up to the Pass of Glencoe, where stern grey hills and hovering eagles and a deep silent valley still seem to whisper together of a sad true story that happened there in just such weather as this two hundred years ago.

These were very happy days for dogs, for they did not mind the cold, it was only an excuse for wild scampering and racing, and they were very grateful for their friend's return. He had been ill, but was able to enjoy his walks, and though about sixty years of age he had all those qualities of youth which endear a man to a dog or a child. He was brave and unselfish, and strong to love and to endure, and they loved him without knowing why ; without knowing that he had lost his health from overwork in the service of the poor and suffering, and among outcasts so low as to be beyond the sympathy of any heart less loving than that of a dog or of a very good man. 'Father' Mackonochie he was always called, and though he had never had wife or children of his own, many a fatherless child, and many a lonely grown-up man or woman, felt that it was quite easy and natural to call him by a name so sacred.

On the Wednesday after he came, he took Righ and Speireag for a glorious walk through the shrubberies and out through a gate on to the road at the foot of the hills behind, a road that winds on and on for many miles, the mountains rising steeply above, the lake being cold and grey below ; the bank, that slopes away from the road to the water, in places covered with gorse and low bushes and heather, where an enterprising dog may hunt for rats and rabbits, or rush headlong after a pee-wit or moor-fowl as it rises with a scream at his approach and flutters off high into the air, and then descending to within a few feet of him, skims low before him, hopelessly far, yet tantalisingly near.

The way was familiar to them by land or by water. Often had they sailed up the loch in the same direction, further and further into the heart of the mountains, the valley becoming more and more narrow, the shores of the lake nearer and nearer to each other, till, had they gone far enough, they would have reached the Dog's Ferry, a spot where the water is so narrow that a dog may easily swim across. Righ, strong swimmer that he was, had often crossed the loch near his master's house, where the ferry boats ply, and needed no Dog's Ferry, but few dogs made such powerful strokes in the water as he.

This day, however, they did not reach the Dog's Ferry. The afternoon was closing in, there were streaks of gold in the dull grey sky, and it was, the good Father thought, time to return. 'Never mind, little man,' he said as Speireag looked reproachfully at him with wistful brown eyes gleaming through overhanging silvery locks, 'we'll do it to-morrow, only we must set off earlier.'

This was good news, and the little dog started home gaily, running, as little dogs will, ten miles, at least, to every one of the road, and tired enough when home was reached at last. Dinner was a welcome feast, and Righ and Speireag slept sound till it was time for evening service. They always attended chapel night and morning, and took their places at the foot of the steps, halfway, when both were present, between mistress in her seat and master at the place of his sacred office. To-night, as usual, they remained perfectly quiet and apparently indifferent to what was going on till, at the words 'Lighten our darkness,' bed-time came into immediate prospect, and they started into expectant attitudes, awaiting the final ' Amen.'

II

THE next morning, though cold, was fine and fairly bright, and the dogs watched eagerly for signs of the promised walk. The service in chapel was rather long this morning, for, as it was Advent, the ' Benedicite ' was read, and though Righ and Speireag noticed only that they had time for a longer nap than usual, there were some present who will never forget, as the season comes round again each year, the special significance of part of that song of praise—

> O ye frost and cold—O ye ice and snow—O ye nights and days,
> O ye light and darkness, O ye mountains and hills,
> O ye beasts and cattle, O ye holy and humble men of heart,
> Bless ye the Lord, piaise Him and magnify Him for ever!

But at last the service was over and the dogs trotted out into the hall, and followed mistress and their friend to the front door to see 'what the weather was like.' It was not a specially pleasant morning, but it would do for a walk, and after waiting a few minutes to have some sandwiches cut, the only detention that could be endured with patience, the three set out. After about six miles they were on new ground, but on they went, the lake to the right of the road getting narrower—on past the Dog's Ferry and still on, till the loch had become a river, and could be crossed by a bridge.

Righ and Speireag knew, by a more certain method than looking at clocks, that it was lunch time, half past one at least, and they never thought of doubting that they would cross the bridge and turn homewards along the other side the loch, and so get in about tea-time; or, for their friend was enterprising, by a longer way also on the further side, either of which would involve a delightful long walk, but with just that hint of a homeward turn which, even to dogs, is acceptable when breakfast has become a mere memory.

They accordingly followed the road on to the bridge, but as Father Mackonochie did not overtake them, Righ, ever watchful of his friends, turned to look back and saw him speaking to a girl, after which, to their surprise, he whistled them back, and instead of continuing along the road as it turned off to the right, kept straight on, though there was now only a rough track leading through a gate into the wood beyond.

When they had advanced a few paces into the wood, he

sat down under a tree and took out his packet of sandwiches. Righ and Speireag, sitting close beside him, had
their share, or perhaps more, for their wistful brown eyes
hungrily reminded him that they had multiplied the
distance many times over, and that an unexpected
luncheon out of doors is a joy in a dog's day, of a kind
for which a man may well sacrifice a part of his minor
pleasure.

Starting off again was a fresh delight. On they went,
further and further, always climbing higher and getting
deeper into the wood. To the left, the steep mountain-
side rose abruptly above them ; to the right, below the
path, the river tore its way between steep banks down,
down to its home in the lake. Now and then the trees
parted and made way for a wild mountain torrent leaping
from rock to rock down the hill side, and rushing across
their path to join the river below. As they climbed
further these became more frequent. Their friend could
stride across, setting an occasional foot upon a stepping-
stone, and Righ, too, could cross safely enough, long
limbed as he was, though now and then he had to swim,
and the streams were so rapid that it needed all his
strength to cross the current. Sometimes he helped
Speireag, for the brave little dog would always try to
follow his big companion, and sometimes, with an anxious
bark, would give warning that help was needed, and then
the kind Father would turn back to pick up the little dog
and carry him till they were in safety.

It was very hard work, they were always climbing,
and in many places the road was polished with a thin
coating of ice, but the dogs feared nothing and kept on
bravely.

The path dwindled to a mere track, and the climbing
became steeper still. The streams crossed their road still
oftener, and the stones were slippery with ice. The wood
became thinner, and as they had less shelter from the
trees, great flakes of half-frozen snow were driven against

their faces.   There was no thought now of hares or stags, Righ and Speireag had no energies left for anything but patient following.   Poor little Speireag's long coat was very wet, and as it dried a little, it became hard and crisp with frost.   The long hair falling over his eyes was matted together and tangled with briers, and his little feet were sore and heavy with the mud that had caked in the long tassels of silky hair.   Even Righ was very weary, and he followed soberly now instead of bounding along in front, his ears and tail drooped, and each time he crossed the ice-cold water he seemed more and more dejected.

As they left the wood behind them, the snow fell thick and blinding, but just at first, as they came out into the open, it seemed not quite so dark as under the trees. There was nothing to be seen but grey sky and grey moor, even the river had been left behind, and only blackened patches remained to show where, in summer, the ground was spread with a gay carpet of purple heather and sweet bog-myrtle.   They got deeper at each step into half-frozen marsh ; there was no sound or sign of life.   The dogs felt hungry and weary, and they ached with the cold and wet.   But they were following a friend, and they trusted him wholly.   Well they knew that each step was taking them farther from home, and farther into the cold and darkness.   But dog-wisdom never asserts itself, and in trustful humility they followed still, and the snow came down closer and closer around them, and even the grey sky and the grey moor were blotted out—and the darkness fell.

III

It was a disappointing home-coming for the Bishop that Thursday evening !   There was no hearty handshake from waiting friend, no rejoicing bay of big dog or extravagant excitement of little dog to welcome him.   The three had been out the whole day, he was told, and had not yet reappeared. A long walk had been projected, but they had been expected home long before this. When dinner-time came, and they did not appear, two servants had been sent out with lanterns to meet them, as the road, though not one to be missed, was dark, and some small accident might have happened. The men were not back yet, but doubtless the missing party would soon return.

The night was dark and stormy, and Father Mac-konochie had been for some time somewhat invalided, and as time passed the Bishop became increasingly anxious. At length he ordered a carriage, and with the gardener set off towards Kinloch, the head of the loch, thinking that accident or weariness might have detained his friend, and the carriage might be useful. On the way they met the first messengers returning with the news that nothing could be heard at Kinloch of the missing three, except that they had passed there between one and two o'clock in the afternoon. The Bishop and his men sought along the road, and inquired for tidings at the very few houses within reach, but in vain. The night was dark and little could be done, and there was always the hope that on their return they might find that some tidings had been heard, that the lost friends might have come back by the other side of the lake.

So at last they turned back, reaching home about four o'clock in the morning. No news had been heard, and all felt anxious and perplexed, but most believed that some place of shelter had been reached, as the dogs had not come home. They could find their way home from anywhere, and there seemed little doubt that, overtaken by darkness, all three had found shelter in a shepherd's or gamekeeper's hut, perhaps on the other side of the lake, as they had almost certainly crossed the bridge, no one having met them on the road by which they had started.

Nevertheless all that was possible must be done in case of the worst, and as soon as daylight returned four parties of men were despatched in different directions, the Bishop himself choosing that which his friend and his dogs were known to have taken the day before.

A whole day of search over miles and miles of the desolate wintry mountains revealed but one fact, that the party had eaten their luncheon under a tree in the wood, beyond the bridge. The squirrels had left the sandwich paper there to tell the tale, and for the first time it seemed likely that they had not turned homewards on reaching the head of the lake, either by the same road they had come, or by that on the other side of the water and through Glencoe.

One by one, the search parties came home with no tidings. No trace of the wanderers had been seen, no bark of dogs had been heard, no help had been found towards the discovery of the sad secret. Weary and heartsick as all felt, no time was to be lost, every hour made the anxiety greater, and all were ready in a very short time to start afresh.

Again, for the second time, all through the long night they wandered over the mountains, through the wood, and across the deer-forest beyond. It was an awful night. Again and again were their lights blown out; the snow lay deep in all the hollows; where the streams had overflowed their banks, the path was a sheet of solid ice; the rocks, polished and slippery, were climbed with utmost difficulty. At every opening in the hills an ice-cold wind whirled down glen and corrie, sleet and hail-stones beat against their faces, the frozen pools in the marshes gave way beneath their feet. The night was absolutely dark, not a star shone out to give them courage. The silence and the sounds were alike awful. Sometimes they could hear each other's laboured breathing as they tottered on the ice or waded through the snow, sometimes all other sounds were lost in the shrieking of the whirlwinds, the crackling of the ice, and the roaring of the swollen, angry streams.

What could have happened? Even if accident had occurred, either or both of the dogs would surely have returned, and how could even a Highland dog, hungry and shelterless, live through such a night as this?

Morning came again, and returning to the point, near the bridge at which the carriage had been left, two of the parties met, and drove home for food and dry clothing, and to learn what others might have to tell.

There was no news, and again the same earnest friends, with many more kind helpers, set out on their almost hopeless journey. The trackless wilds of the deer-forest seemed the most likely field for search, and all now, in various groups, set off in this direction.

Hour after hour passed without any gleam of hope, and even the Bishop began to feel that everything possible had been done, and was turning sadly homewards. A second party, a few hundred yards behind, had almost come to the same resolve, many of the men had been without rest since Thursday, and even the dog, who with one of the keepers of the deer-forest had joined the party, was limping wearily and was exhausted by the cold and the rough walking.

Suddenly he stopped, and, with ears pricked and head erect, listened. No one knows better than a Highlander the worth of a collie's opinion, and more than one stopped to listen too. Not far away, and yet faint, came the bark of a dog! Among the men was Sandy, one of the Bishop's stablemen, who knew and loved Righ and Speireag, and his heart leapt up as he recognised the deerhound's bay!

Away, to their left, the mountains were cleft by a narrow glen, the sound came from the bank on the hither side. The Bishop and his party had climbed to the further side, but a shout reached them, alert and watchful as they were.

They turned back wondering, scarcely daring to hope.

The men who had called to them were hastening to a given point, the dog, nose to ground, preceding them. There is no mistaking the air of a dog on business. The collie's intentness was as different from his late dejection as was the present haste of the men from the anxious watchful plodding of their long search.

In another moment they came in sight of something which made them hold back the dog, and which arrested their own footsteps. The Bishop himself must be the first to tread on what all felt was holy ground.

There, on the desolate hillside, lay the body of Father Mackonochie, wreathed about with the spotless snow, a peaceful expression on his face. One on either side sat the dogs, watching still, as they had watched through the two long nights of storm and darkness. Even the approach of friends did not tempt them to forsake their duty. With hungry, weary faces they looked towards the group which first came near them, but not till their own master knelt down beside all that remained of his old friend, did they yield up their trust, and rise, numbed and stiff, from the posts they had taken up, who knows how long before?

To say a few words of prayer and thanksgiving was the Bishop's first thought, his second to take from his pocket the sandwiches he carried, and to give all to Righ and Speireag.

A bier was contrived of sticks from a rough fence that marked the boundary of the deer-forest, and the body was lifted from the frozen ground on which it lay. The return to Kinloch, where the carriage waited, was very difficult, and the bearers had to change places very often.

Slow as was their progress, it was as rapid as Righ could manage, numbed with cold, and exhausted with hunger. The little dog was easily carried, and for once little Speireag was content to rest.

No one will ever know what those faithful dogs felt

'THE LONG VIGIL'

and endured during those two days and nights of storm and loneliness. Those who sought them in the darkness of that second awful night must have passed very near the spot where they lay, sleeping perhaps, or deafened by the storm, or even, possibly, listening anxiously with beating hearts to the footsteps which came so near, and yet turned away, leaving them, faithful to their post, in the night.

They in their degree, like the man whose last sleep they guarded, were ' true and faithful servants.'

It is pleasant to know that Righ and Speireag did not suffer permanently for all they had undergone! They lived for five years and a half after, and had many and many a happy ramble when the sun was bright and the woods were green, and squirrels and hares were merry. They could not be better cared for than they had always been, but, if possible, they were more indulged. If they contrived to get a dinner in the kitchen as well as in the dining-room, their friends remembered the days when they had none, and nobody told tales. If they lay in the sun quite across the front door, or took up the whole of the rug before the winter fire, everyone felt that there were arrears of warmth to be made up to them. Their portraits were painted, and in the sculpture which in his own church commemorates Father Mackonochie's death, the dogs have not been forgotten.

Righ was the elder of the two, and towards the end of his thirteen years showed signs of old age and became rheumatic and feeble, but Speireag, though three years younger, did not long survive him.

They rest now under a cairn in the beautiful garden they loved so well; dark green fir trees shelter their grave, a gentle stream goes merrily by on its way to the lake below, and in the crannies of the stones of which the cairn is built, fox-gloves and primroses and little ferns grow fresh and green.

On the cairn is this inscription :

IN MEMORY OF

15th December, 1887.

RIGH died 19th January, 1893.

SPEIREAG died 28th August, 1893.

MONKEY TRICKS AND SALLY AT THE ZOO[1]

Some monkeys are cleverer and more civilised than others, and the chiefs have their followers well in hand; every monkey having his own especial duties, which he is very careful to fulfil. When the stores of food which have been collected are getting low, the elders of the tribe—grey beards with long manes—meet together and decide where they shall go to lay in fresh supplies. This important point being settled, the whole body of monkeys, even down to the very little ones, leave the woods or mountain ravine where they live, and form into regular order. First scouts are posted; some being sent on to places in advance, others being left to guard the rear, while the main body, made up of the young and helpless monkeys, follow the chiefs, who march solemnly in front and carefully survey every precipice or doubtful place before they suffer anyone to pass over it.

It is not at all easy, even for an elderly and experienced monkey, to keep order among the host of lively chattering creatures for whose safety he is responsible, and indeed it would often be an impossible task if it were not for the help of the rear-guard. These much-tried animals have to make up quarrels which often break out by the way; to prevent the greedy ones from stopping to eat every scrap of fruit or berry that hangs from the trees as they pass, and to scold the mothers who try to linger behind in order to dress their children's hair and to make them smart for the day.

[1] *Naturalist's Note-book.*

Under these conditions, it takes a long time even for monkeys to reach their destination, which is generally a corn-field, but, once there, scouts are sent out to every rock or rising ground, so as to guard against any surprise. Then the whole tribe fall to, and after filling their cheek pouches with ears of corn, they make up bundles to tuck under their arms.   After the long march and the hasty picking, they begin to get thirsty as well as hungry, and the next thing is to find some water.   This is very soon done, as they seem able to detect it under the sand, however deep down it may be, and by dint of taking regular turns at digging, it does not take long before they have laid bare a well that is large enough for everybody.

Monkeys love by nature to imitate what they see, and have been known to smoke a pipe, and to pretend to read a book that they have seen other people reading.   But sometimes they can do a great deal more than this, and show that they can calculate and reason better than many men.   A large Abyssinian monkey was one day being taken round Khartoum by its master, and made to perform all sorts of tricks for the amusement of the bystanders. Among these was a date-seller, who was squatting on the ground beside his fruit.   Now the monkey was passionately fond of dates, but being very cunning was careful not to let this appear, and went on performing his tricks as usual, drawing little by little nearer to the date basket as he did so.   When he thought he was near enough for his purpose, he first pretended to die, slowly and naturally, and then, after lying for a moment on the sand as stiff as a corpse, suddenly bounded up with a scream straight in front of the date-seller's face, and stared at him with his wild eyes. The man looked back at him spell-bound, quite unaware that one of the monkey's hind feet was in the date basket, clawing up as much fruit as its long toes could hold. By some such trick as this the monkey managed to steal enough food daily to keep him fat and comfortable.

No cleverer monkey ever lived than the ugly old Sally,

who died at the Zoological Gardens of London only a few years ago. Her keeper had spent an immense deal of time and patience in training her up, and it was astonishing what she was able to do. 'Sally,' he would say, putting a tin cup full of milk into her hands, with a spoon hanging from it, 'show us how you used to drink when you were in the woods,' upon which Sally stuck all her. fingers into the milk and sucked them greedily. 'Now,' he continued, 'show us how you drink since you became a lady,' and then Sally took the spoon and drank her milk in dainty little sips. Next he picked up a handful of straw from the bottom of the cage, and remarked carelessly, 'Here, just tear those into six, will you, all the same length.' Sally took the straws, and in half a minute the thing was done. But she had not come to the end of her surprises yet. 'You're very fond of pear, I know,' said the keeper, producing one out of his pocket and cutting it with his knife ; 'well, I'm going to put some on my hand, but you're not to touch it until I've cut two short pieces and three long ones, and then you may take the second long one, but you aren't to touch any of the rest.' The man went on cutting his slices without stopping, and was quite ready to begin upon a sixth, when Sally stretched out her hand, and took the fourth lying along the row, which she had been told she might have. Very likely she might have accomplished even more wonderful things than this, but one cold day she caught a chill, and died in a few hours of bronchitis.

HOW THE CAYMAN WAS KILLED [1]

In the year 1782 there was born in the old house of Walton, near Pontefract, in Yorkshire, a boy named Charles Waterton, who afterwards became very famous as a traveller and a naturalist. As soon as he could walk, he was always to be found poking about among trees, or playing with animals, and both at home and at school he got into many a scrape through his love of adventure. He was only about ten when some other boys dared him to ride on a cow, and of course he was not going to be beaten. So up he got while the cow was only thinking how good the grass tasted, but the moment she felt a strange weight on her back, she flung her heels straight into the air, and off flew Master Waterton over her head.

Many years after this, Waterton was travelling in South America, seeing and doing many curious things. For a long time he had set his heart on catching a cayman, a kind of alligator that is found in the rivers of Guiana. For this purpose he took some Indians with him to the Essequibo, which falls into the sea not far from Demerara, and was known to be a famous place for caymans. It was no good attempting to go after them during the long, bright day. They were safely in hiding, and never thought of coming out till the sun was below the horizon.

So Waterton and his Indians waited in patience till the moon rose, and everything was still, except that now and then a huge fish would leap into the air and

[1] Waterton's *Wanderings in S. America.*

plunge again under water. Suddenly there broke forth
a fearful noise, unlike the cry of any other creature. As
one cayman called another answered ; and although
caymans are not very common anywhere, that night you
would have thought that the world was full of them.

The three men stopped eating their supper of turtle
and turned and looked over the river. Waterton could·
see nothing, but the Indian silently pointed to a black log
that lay in the stream, just over the place where they
had baited a hook with a large fish, and bound it on a
board. At the end of the board a rope was fastened, and
this was also made fast to a tree on the bank. By-and-
bye the black log began to move, and in the bright
moonlight he was clearly seen to open his long jaws and
to take the bait inside them. But the watchers on shore
pulled the rope too soon, and the cayman dropped the
bait at once. Then for an hour he lay quite still, thinking
what he should do next, but feeling cross at having lost
his supper, he made up his mind to try once more, and
cautiously took the bait in his mouth. Again the rope
was pulled, and again the bait was dropped into the river ;
but in the end the cayman proved more cunning than the
Indians, for after he had played this trick for three or
four times he managed to get the fish without the hook,
and when the sun rose again, Waterton knew that cayman hunting was over for that day.

For two or three nights they watched and waited, but
did not ever get so near success as before. Let them
conceal a hook in the bait ever so cleverly, the cayman
was sure to be cleverer than they, and when morning
came, the bait was always gone and the hook always left.
The Indians, however, had no intention of allowing the
cayman to beat them in the long run, and one of them
invented a new hook, which this time was destined to
better luck. He took four or five pieces of wood about a
foot long, barbed them at each end, and tied them firmly
to the end of a rope, thirty yards long. Above the barb

was baited the flesh of an acouri, a creature the size of a rabbit. The whole was then fastened to a post driven into the sand, and the attention of the cayman aroused to what was going on by some sharp blows on an empty tortoiseshell, which served as a drum.

About half-past five the Indian got up and stole out to look, and then he called triumphantly to the rest to come up at once, for on the hook was a cayman, ten feet and a half long.

But hard as it had been to secure him, it was nothing to the difficulty of getting him out alive, and with his scales uninjured, especially as the four Indians absolutely refused to help, and that left only two white men and a negro, to grapple with the huge monster. Of these, too, the negro showed himself very timid, and it was not easy to persuade him to be of any use.

The position was certainly puzzling. If the Indians refused their help, the cayman could not be taken alive at all, and if they gave it, it was only at the price of injuring the animal and spoiling its skin. At length a compromise occurred to Waterton. He would take the mast of the canoe, which was about eight feet long, and would thrust it down the cayman's throat, if it showed any signs of attacking him. On this condition, the Indians agreed to give their aid.

Matters being thus arranged, Waterton then placed his men—about seven in all—at the end of the rope, and told them to pull till the cayman rose to the surface, while he himself knelt down with the pole about four yards from the bank, ready for the cayman, should he appear, roaring. Then he gave the signal, and slowly the men began to pull. But the cayman was not to be caught without a struggle. He snorted and plunged violently, till the rope was slackened, when he instantly dived below. Then the men braced all their strength for another effort, and this time out he came and made straight for Waterton.

THE CAPTURE OF THE CAYMAN

The naturalist was so excited by his capture, that he lost all sense of the danger of his position. He waited till the cayman was within a few feet of him, when he flung away his pole, and with a flying leap, landed on the cayman's back, twisting up the creature's feet and holding tightly on to them. The cayman, very naturally, could not in the least understand what had happened, but he began to plunge and struggle, and to lash out behind with his thick scaly tail, while the Indians looked on from afar, and shouted in triumph.

To Waterton the only fear was, lest the rope should prove too weak for the strain, in which case he and the cayman would promptly disappear into the depths of the Essequibo. But happily the rope was strong, and after being dragged by the Indians for forty yards along the sand, the cayman gave in, and Waterton contrived to tie his jaws together, and to lash his feet on to his back. Then he was put to death, and so ended the chase of the cayman.

THE STORY OF FIDO

FIDO's master had to go a long journey across the country to a certain town, and he was carrying with him a large bag of gold to deposit at the bank there. This bag he carried on his saddle, for he was riding, as in those days there were no trains, and he had to travel as quickly as he could.

Fido scampered cheerfully along at the horse's heels, and every now and then the man would call out to him, and Fido would wag her tail and bark back an answer.

The sun was hot and the road dusty, and poor Fido's little legs grew more and more tired. At last they came to a cool, shady wood, and the master stopped, dismounted, and tied his horse to a tree, and took his heavy saddle-bags from the saddle.

He laid them down very carefully, and pointing to them, said to Fido, 'Watch them.'

Then he drew his cloak about him, lay down with his head on the bags, and soon was fast asleep.

Little Fido curled herself up close to her master's head, with her nose over one end of the bags, and went to sleep too. But she did not sleep very soundly, for her master had told her to watch, and every few moments she would open her eyes and prick up her ears, in case anyone were coming.

Her master was tired and slept soundly and long—much longer than he had intended. At last he was awakened by Fido's licking his face. The dog saw that

THE WOUNDING OF FIDO

the sun was nearly setting, and knew that it was time for her master to go on his journey.

The man patted Fido and then jumped up, much troubled to find he had slept so long. He snatched up his cloak, threw it over his horse, untied the bridle, sprang into the saddle, and calling Fido, started off in great haste. But Fido did not seem ready to follow him. She ran after the horse and bit at his heels, and then ran back again to the woods, all the time barking furiously. This she did several times, but her master had no time to heed her and galloped away, thinking she would follow him.

At last the little dog sat down by the roadside, and looked sorrowfully after her master, until he had turned a bend in the road. When he was no longer in sight she sprang up with a wild bark, and ran after him again. She overtook him just as he had stopped to water his horse at a brook that flowed across the road. She stood beside the brook and barked so savagely that her master rode back and called her to him; but instead of coming she darted off down the road still barking.

Her master did not know what to think, and began to fear that his dog was going mad. Mad dogs are afraid of water, and act in a strange way when they see it. While the man was thinking of this, Fido came running back again, and dashed at him furiously. She leapt at the legs of his horse, and even jumped up and bit the toe of her master's boot. Then she ran down the road again, barking with all her might.

Her master was now sure that she was mad, and, taking out his pistol he shot her. He rode away quickly, for he loved her dearly and could not bear to see her die.

He had not ridden very far when he stopped suddenly. He felt under his cloak for his saddle-bags. They were not there !

Could he have dropped them, or had he left them behind in the wood where he had rested ? He felt sure they must be in the wood, for he could not remember having picked them up or fastening them to his saddle.

. He turned his horse and rode back again as hard as he could.

When he came to the brook he sighed and said, ' Poor Fido ! ' but though he looked about he could see nothing of her. When he crossed the brook he saw some drops of blood on the ground, and all along the road he still saw drops of blood. Tears came into his eyes, and he felt very sad and guilty, for now he understood why little Fido had acted so strangely. She knew that her master had left behind his precious bags of gold, and so she had tried to tell him in the only way she could.

All the way to the wood lay the drops of blood. At last he reached the wood, and there, all safe, lay the bags of gold, and beside them, with her little nose lying over one end of them, lay faithful Fido, who, you will be pleased to hear, recovered from her wound, and lived to a great age.

BEASTS BESIEGED [1]

TWENTY-FIVE years ago (in the winter of 1870–1871) Paris was closely besieged by the Germans, who had beaten one French army after another on the frontier, and had now advanced into the very heart of the country. The cold was frightful, and no wood could be got, and as if this was not enough, food began to give out, and the people inside the city soon learned to know the tortures of hunger. There was no hay or corn for the horses; after sheep and oxen they were the first animals to be eaten, and then whispers were heard about elephants and camels and other beasts in the Jardin des Plantes, which is the French name for their Zoological Gardens.

Now it is quite bad enough to be taken from the forests and deserts where you never did anything but just what you chose, and to be shut up in a small cage behind bars; but it is still worse not to have enough food to eat, and worst of all to be made into food for other people. Luckily the animals did not know what was being talked about in the world outside, or they would have been more uncomfortable than they were already.

Any visitor to the Jardin des Plantes about Christmas time in 1870, and for many weeks later, would have seen a strange sight. Some parts of the Gardens were set aside for hospitals, and rows of beds occupied every sheltered building. Passing through these, the visitor found himself in the kingdom of the beasts, who were often much more gentle than their gaolers

[1] Adapted from Théophile Gautier.

After coming from the streets where nothing was the same as it had been six months before, and everything was topsy-turvy, it was almost soothing to watch the animals going on in their usual way, quite regardless of what men might be doing outside. There was the white bear swinging himself from side to side and rubbing his nose against the bars, just as he had done on the day that he had first taken up his abode there. There was a camel still asking for cakes, and an elephant trumpeting with fury because he didn't get any. Nobody had cakes for themselves, and it would have been far easier to place a gold piece in the twirling proboscis. An elephant who is badly fed is not a pretty spectacle. Its skin is so large that it seems as if it would take in at least three or four extra bodies, and having only one shrunken skeleton to cover, it shrivels up into huge wrinkles and looks like the earth after a dry summer. On the whole, certain kinds of bears come off best, for they can sleep all the winter through, and when they wake up, the world will seem the same as when they last shut their eyes, and unless their friend the white bear tells them in bear language all that has happened they will never be any the wiser.

Still it is not all the bears who are lucky enough to have the gift of sleep. Some remained broad awake, and stood idly about in the corners of their dens, not knowing how to get rid of the time that hung so heavily on their paws. What was the use for the big brown marten to go up to the top of his tree, when there was no one to tickle his nose with a piece of bread at the end of a string? Why should his brother take the trouble to stand up on his hind legs when there was nobody to laugh and clap him? Only one very young bear indeed, with bright eyes and a yellow skin, went on his own way, regardless of spectators, and he was busily engaged in looking at himself in a pail of water and putting on all sorts of little airs and graces, from sheer admiration of his own beauty.

Perhaps the most to be pitied of all were the lions, for they do not know how to play, and could only lie about and remember the days when towards sunset they crept towards the cool hill, and waited till the antelopes came down for their evening drink. And then, ah *then*! but that is only a memory, while stretched out close by is

THE DREAM OF THE HUNGRY LION

the poor lioness in the last stage of consumption, and looking more like those half-starved fighting lions you see on royal coats of arms than a real beast. At such times most children would give anything to catch up the Zoological Gardens and carry them right away into the centre of Africa, and let out the beasts and make them happy and comfortable once more. But that was not the feeling of the little boy who had been taken by his mother to see the beasts as a treat for his birthday. At each cage they passed he came to a standstill, and gazing at the animal with greedy eyes, he said, 'Mother, wouldn't you like to eat that?' Every time his mother answered him, 'No one eats these beasts, my boy; they are brought from countries a long way off, and cost a great deal of money.' The child was silent for a moment, but at the sight of the zebra, the elk, or the little hyæna, his face brightened again, and his voice might be heard piping forth its old question, 'Mother, wouldn't you like to eat that?'

It is a comfort to think that the horrid greedy boy was disappointed in his hopes. Whatever else he may have eaten, the taste of lions and of bears is still strange to him, for the siege of Paris came to an end at last, and the animals were made happy as of old with their daily portions.

MR. GULLY

HE was a herring gull, and one of the largest I have ever seen. He was beautiful to look at with his soft grey plumage, never a feather of which was out of place. Of his character I will say nothing; that can be best judged by reading the following truthful biography of my 'dove of the waters.'

I cannot begin at the beginning. Of his youth, which doubtless, in every sense of the word, was a stormy one, I know nothing. He had already acquired the wisdom, or perhaps in his case slyness is a better word, of years by the time that he came to us.

Gully was found one day in a field near our house in a very much exhausted condition. He had probably come a long distance, which he must have accomplished on foot, as he was unable to fly owing to his wing having been pinioned.

He was very hungry and greedily bolted a small fish that we offered him, and screamed for more. We then turned him into the garden, where he soon found a sheltered corner by our dining-room window and went to sleep standing on one leg. The other one he always kept tucked away so that it was quite invisible.

Next morning I came out to look for Gully and feed him. He had vanished! I thought of the pond where I kept my goldfish, forty beautiful goldfish. There sure enough was Mr. Gully swimming about contentedly, but where were the goldfish? Instead of the crystal clear pond, was a pool of muddy water; instead of forty gold-fish, all that I could make out, when Mr. Gully had been chased away and the water given time to settle, was one miserable little half-dead fish, the only survivor of the forty.

This was the first of Gully's misdeeds. To look at Gully, no one could believe him to be capable of hurting a fly. He had the most lovely gentle brown eyes you ever saw, and seemed more like a benevolent old professor than anything else. He generally appeared to be half asleep or else sunning himself with a contented smile on his thoughtful countenance.

Gully next took to killing the sparrows; he was very clever at this. When he had finished eating, the sparrows were in the habit of appropriating the remnants of the feast. This Gully strongly disapproved of, so when he had eaten as much as he wanted, he retired behind a chair and waited till the sparrows were busy feasting, then he would make a rush and seize the nearest offender. He sometimes used to kill as many as from two to four sparrows a day in this manner. The pigeons then took to coming too near his reach. At first he was afraid of them and left them alone; but the day came when a young fan-tail was foolish enough to take his airing on the terrace, close to Mr. Gully's nose. This was too much for Mr. Gully, who pounced upon the unfortunate 'squeaker' and slew him. *L'appétit vient en mangeant*, and after this Mr. Gully took the greatest delight in hunting these unfortunate birds and murdering them. No pigeon was too large for him to attack. I only just succeeded in saving the cock-pouter, a giant among pigeons, from an untimely death, by coming up in time to drive Mr. Gully away from his victim.

After this we decided to shut Mr. Gully up. We thought he would make a charming companion for the guinea-pigs. At that time I used to keep about fifty of various species in a hen-run. So to the guinea-pigs

Gully was banished. At first the arrangement answered admirably, Gully behaved as nicely as possible for about a month, and we were all congratulating ourselves on having found such a good way out of our difficulty, when all at once his thirst for blood was roused afresh. One day he murdered four guinea-pigs and the next day three more of these unfortunate little beasts.

We then let him join the hens and ducks. He at once constituted himself the leader of the latter; every morning he would lead them down to a pond at the bottom of the fields, a distance of about a quarter of a mile; and every evening he would summon them round him and lead them home. At his cry the ducks and drakes would come waddling up to him with loud quacks; he used always to march in the most stately manner about two yards ahead of them. Of the cocks and hens Gully deigned to take no notice. On two occasions he made an exception to this rule of conduct. On the first, he and a hen had a dispute over the possession of a worm. This dispute led to a fight of which Gully was getting the best when the combatants were separated. On the second occasion Gully was accused of decapitating a hen. No one saw him do it, but it looked only too like his work. He had a neat clean style.

One day he led his ducks to the pond as usual, but in the evening they returned by themselves. We came to the conclusion that the poor old bird must be dead. We quite gave him up for lost, and had mourned him for two or three weeks, when what should we see one day but Mr. Gully leading his ducks as usual to his favourite pond, as if he had never been away.

Where he had spent all the time he was absent remains a mystery to this day. After this he remained with us some time, during which he performed no new feat of valour with the exception of one fight which he had with a cat. In this fight he had some feathers pulled out, but ultimately succeeded in driving her off after giving her leg such a bite that she was lame for many a long day.

Since then he has again disappeared. Will he ever return? Mysterious was his coming and mysterious his going.

STORIES FROM PLINY

HOW DOGS LOVE

Now there was living at Rome, under the Emperors Vespasian and Titus (A.D. 69–81) a man called Pliny, who gave up his life to the study of animals and plants. He not only watched their habits for himself, but he listened eagerly to all that travellers would tell him, and sometimes happened to believe too much, and wrote in his book things that were not true. Still there were a great many facts which he had found out for himself, and the stories he tells about animals are of interest to every one, partly because it seems strange to think that dogs and horses and other creatures were just the same then as they are now.

The dogs that Pliny writes about lived in all parts of the Roman Empire, and were as faithful and devoted to their masters as our dogs are to us. One dog called Hyrcanus, belonging to King Lysimachus, one of the successors of Alexander the Great, jumped on to the funeral pyre on which lay burning the dead body of his master. And so did another dog at the burial of Hiero of Syracuse. But during the lifetime of Pliny himself, a dog's devotion in the heart of Rome had touched even the Roman citizens, ashamed though they generally were of showing their feelings. It had happened that a plot against the life of Nero had been discovered, and the chief conspirator, Titus Sabinus by name, was put to death, together with some of his servants. One of these men had a dog of which he was very fond, and from the moment the man was thrown into prison, the dog could not be persuaded to move away from the door. At last there came a day when the man suffered the cruel death common in Rome for such offences, and was thrown down a steep flight of stairs, where he broke his neck. A crowd of Romans had gathered round the place of execution, in order to see the sight, and in the midst of them all the dog managed to reach his master's side, and lay there, howling piteously. Then one of the crowd, moved with pity, threw the dog a piece of meat, but he only took it, and laid it across his master's mouth. By-and-bye, the men came for the body in order to throw it into the river Tiber, and even then the dog followed and swam after it, and held it up and tried to bring it to land, till the people came out in multitudes from the houses round about, to see what it was to be faithful unto death—and beyond it.

THE STRANGE HISTORY OF CAGNOTTE [1]

IN the early part of this century, a little boy of three years old, named Théophile Gautier, travelled with his parents from Tarbes, in the south of France, to Paris. He was so small that he could not speak any proper French, but talked like the country people; and he divided the world into those who spoke like him and were his friends, and those who did not, and were strangers.

But though he was only three, and a great baby in many ways, he loved his home dearly, and everything about it, and it nearly broke his heart to come away. His parents tried to comfort him by giving him the most beautiful chocolates and little cakes, and when that failed they tried what drums and trumpets would do. But drums and trumpets succeeded no better than cakes and chocolates, for the greater part of poor Théophile's tears were shed for the 'dog he had left behind him,' called Cagnotte, which his father had given away to a friend, as he did not think that any dog who had been accustomed to run along the hills and valleys above Tarbes, could ever make himself happy in Paris.

Théophile, however, did not understand this, but cried for Cagnotte all day long; and one morning he could bear it no longer. His nurse had put out all his tin soldiers neatly on the table, with a little German village surrounded by stiff green trees just in front of them, hoping Théophile might play at a battle or a siege, and she had also placed his fiddle (which was painted bright

[1] *Ménagerie Intime.*

scarlet) quite handy, so that he might play the triumphal march of the victor. Nothing was of any use. As soon as Josephine's back was turned Théophile threw soldiers and village and fiddle out of the window, and then prepared to jump after them, so that he might take the shortest way back to Tarbes and Cagnotte. Luckily, just as his foot was on the sill, Josephine came back from the next room, and saw what he was about. She rushed after him and caught him by the jacket, and then took him on her knee, and asked him why he was going to do anything so naughty and dangerous. When Théophile explained that it was Cagnotte whom he wanted and must have, and that nobody else mattered at all, Josephine was so afraid he would try to run away again, that she told him that if he would only have patience and wait a little Cagnotte would come to him.

All day long Théophile gave Josephine no peace. Every few minutes he came running to his nurse to know if Cagnotte had arrived, and he was only quieted when Josephine went out and returned carrying a little dog, which in some ways was very like his beloved Cagnotte. Théophile was not quite satisfied at first, till he remembered that Cagnotte had travelled a long long way, and it was not to be expected that he should look the same dog as when he started; so he put aside his doubts, and knelt down to give Cagnotte a great hug of welcome. The new Cagnotte, like the old, was a lovely black poodle, and had excellent manners, besides being full of fun. He licked Théophile on both cheeks, and was altogether so friendly that he was ready to eat bread and butter off the same plate as his little master.

The two got on beautifully, and were perfectly happy for some time, and then gradually Cagnotte began to lose his spirits, and instead of jumping and running about the world, he moved slowly, as if he was in pain. He breathed shortly and heavily, and refused to eat anything, and even Théophile could see he was feeling ill. One day Cagnotte was lying stretched out on his master's lap, and Théophile was softly stroking his skin, when suddenly his hand caught in what seemed to be string, or strong thread. In great surprise, Josephine was at once called, to explain the strange matter.   She stooped down, and peered closely at the dog's skin, then took her scissors and cut the thread. Cagnotte stretched himself, gave a shake, and jumped down from Théophile's lap, leaving a sort of black sheepskin behind him.

CAGNOTTE COMES OUT OF HIS SKIN

Some wicked men had sewn him up in this coat, so that they might get more money for him; and without it he was not a poodle at all, but just an ugly little street dog, without beauty of any kind.

After helping to eat Théophile's bread and butter and soup for some weeks, Cagnotte began to grow fatter, and his outside skin became too tight for him, and he was nearly suffocated. Once delivered from it, he shook his ears for joy, and danced a waltz of his own round the room, not caring a straw how ugly he might be as long as he was comfortable. A very few weeks spent in the society of Cagnotte made the memory of Tarbes and its mountains grow dim in the mind of Théophile. He learnt French, and forgot the way the country people talked, and soon he had become, thanks to Cagnotte, such a thorough little Parisian, that he would not have understood what his old friends said, if one of them had spoken to him.

STILL WATERS RUN DEEP; OR THE DANCING DOG [1]

WHEN Little Théophile became Big Théophile, he was as fond as ever of dogs and cats, and he knew more about them than anybody else. After the death of a large white spaniel called Luther, he filled the vacant place on his rug by another of the same breed, to whom he gave the name of Zamore. Zamore was a little dog, as black as ink, except for two yellow patches over his eyes, and a stray patch on his chest. He was not in the least handsome, and no stranger would ever have given him a second thought. But when you came to know him, you found Zamore was not a common dog at all. He despised all women, and absolutely refused to obey them or to follow them, and neither Théophile's mother nor his sisters could get the smallest sign of friendship from him. If they offered him cakes or sugar, he would accept them in a dignified manner, but never dreamed of saying 'thank you,' still less of wagging his tail on the floor, or giving little yaps of delight and gratitude, as well-brought-up dogs should do. Even to Théophile's father, whom he liked better than anyone else, he was cold and respectful, though he followed him everywhere, and never left his master's heels when they took a walk. And when they were fishing together, Zamore would sit silent on the bank for hours together, and only allowed himself one bark when the fish was safely hooked.

Now no one could possibly have guessed that a dog of

[1] *Ménagerie Intime.*

such very quiet and reserved manners was at heart as
gay and cheerful as the silliest kitten that ever was born,
but so he was, and this was how his family found it out.

One day he was walking as seriously as usual through
a broad square in the outskirts of Paris, when he was
surprised at meeting a large grey donkey, with two panniers on its back, and in the panniers a troop of dogs,
some dressed as Swiss shepherdesses, some as Turks,
some in full court costume. The owner of the animals
stopped the donkey close to where Zamore was standing,
and bade the dogs jump down. Then he cracked his
whip; the fife and drum struck up a merry tune, the
dogs steadied themselves on their hind legs, and the dance
began.

Zamore looked on as if he had been turned into stone.
The sight of these dogs, dressed in bright colours, this one
with his head covered by a feathered hat, and that one by
a turban, but all moving about in time to the music, and
making pirouettes and little bows ; were they really *dogs*
he was watching or some new kind of men ? Anyway he
had never seen anything so enchanting or so beautiful,
and if it was true that they were only dogs—well, *he* was
a dog too !

With that thought, all that had lain hidden in Zamore's
soul burst forth, and when the dancers filed gracefully
before him, he raised himself on his hind legs, and in spite
of staggering a little, prepared to join the ring, to the
great amusement of the spectators.

The dog-owner, however, whose name was Monsieur
Corri, did not see matters in the same light. He raised
his whip a second time, and brought it down with a crack
on the sides of Zamore, who ran out of the ring, and with
his tail between his legs and an air of deep thought, he
returned home.

All that day Zamore was more serious and more gloomy
than ever. Nothing would tempt him out, hardly even
his favourite dinner, and it was quite plain that he was

'AND WHAT DO YOU THINK SHE SAW?'

turning over something in his mind. But during the night his two young mistresses were awakened by a strange noise that seemed to come from an empty room next theirs, where Zamore usually slept. They both lay awake and listened, and thought it was like a measured stamping, and that the mice might be giving a ball. But could little mice feet tread so heavily as that? Supposing a thief had got in? So the bravest of the two girls got up, and stealing to the door softly opened it and looked into the room. And what do you think she saw? Why, Zamore, on his hind legs, his paws in the air, practising carefully the steps that he had been watching that morning!

This was not, as one might have expected, a mere fancy of the moment, which would be quite forgotten the next day. Zamore was too serious a dog for that, and by dint of hard study he became in time a beautiful dancer. As often as the fife and drum were heard in the streets, Zamore rushed out of the house, glided softly between the spectators, and watched with absorbed attention the dancing dogs who were doing their steps: but remembering the blow he had had from the whip, he took care not to join them. He noted their positions, the figures, and the way they held their bodies, and in the night he copied them, though by day he was just as solemn as ever. Soon he was not contented with merely copying what he saw, he invented for himself, and it is only just to say that, in stateliness of step, few dogs could come up to him. Often his dances were witnessed (unknown to himself) by Théophile and his sisters, who watched him through the crack of the door; and so earnest was he, that at length, worn out by dancing, he would drink up the whole of a large basin of water, which stood in the corner of the room.

When Zamore felt himself the equal of the best of the dancing dogs, he began to wish that like them he might have an audience.

Now in France the houses are not always built in a
row as they are in England, but sometimes have a square
court-yard in front, and in the house where Zamore lived,
this court was shut in on one side by an iron railing, which
was wide enough to let dogs of a slim figure squeeze
through.

One fine morning there met in this courtyard fifteen
or twenty dogs, friends of Zamore, to whom the night
before he had sent letters of invitation. The object of the
party was to see Zamore make his *début* in dancing, and
the ball-room was to be the court-yard, which Zamore had
carefully swept with his tail. The dance began, and the
spectators were so delighted, that they could not wait for
the end to applaud, as people ought always to do, but
uttered loud cries of ' Ouah, ouah,' that reminded you of
the noises you hear at a theatre. Except one old water
spaniel who was filled with envy at Zamore's talents, and
declared that no decent dog would ever make an exhibition
of himself like that, they all vowed that Zamore was the
king of dancers, and that nothing had ever been seen to
equal his minuet, jig, and waltz for grace and beauty.

It was only during his dancing moments that Zamore
unbent. At all other times he was as gloomy as ever, and
never cared to stir from the rug unless he saw his old
master take up his hat and stick for a walk. Of course,
if he had chosen, he might have joined Monsieur Corri's
troupe, of which he would have made the brightest ornament ; but the love of his master proved greater than his
love of his art, and he remained unknown, except of his
family. In the end he fell a victim to his passion for
dancing, and he died of brain fever, which is supposed to
have been caused by the fatigue of learning the schottische,
the fashionable dance of the day.

THEO AND HIS HORSES; JANE, BETSY, AND BLANCHE [1]

AFTER Théophile grew to be a man, he wrote a great many books, which are all delightful to read, and everybody bought them, and Théophile got rich and thought he might give himself a little carriage with two horses to draw it.

And first he fell in love with two dear little Shetland ponies who were so shaggy and hairy that they seemed all mane and tail, and whose eyes looked so affectionately at him, that he felt as if he should like to bring them into the drawing-room instead of sending them to the stable. They were charming little creatures, not a bit shy, and they would come and poke their noses into Théophile's pockets in search for sugar, which was always there. Indeed their only fault was, that they were so very, very small, and that, after all, was *not* their fault. Still, they looked more suited to an English child of eight years old, or to Tom Thumb, than to a French gentleman of forty, not so thin as he once was, and as they all passed through the streets, everybody laughed, and drew pictures of them, and declared that Théophile could easily have carried a pony on each arm, and the carriage on his back.

Now Théophile did not mind being laughed at, but still he did not always want to be stared at all through the streets, whenever he went out. So he sold his ponies and began to look out for something nearer his own

[1] From *Ménagerie Intime*.

size. After a short search he found two of a dapple grey colour, stout and strong, and as like each other as two peas, and he called them Jane and Betsy. But although, to look at, no one could ever tell one from the other, their characters were totally different, as Jane was very bold and spirited, and Betsy was terribly lazy. While Jane did all the pulling, Betsy was quite contented. just to run by her side, without troubling herself in the least, and, as was only natural, Jane did not think this at all fair, and took a great dislike to Betsy, which Betsy heartily returned. At last matters became so bad that, in their efforts to get at each other, they half kicked the stable to pieces, and would even rear themselves upon their hind legs in order to bite each other's faces. Théophile did all he could to make them friends, but nothing was of any use, and at last he was forced to sell Betsy. The horse he found to replace her was a shade lighter in colour, and therefore not quite so good a match, but luckily Jane took to her at once, and lost no time in doing the honours of the stable. Every day the affection between the two became greater: Jane would lay her head on Blanche's shoulder—she had been called Blanche because of her fair skin—and when they were turned out into the stable yard, after being rubbed down, they played together like two kittens. If one was taken out alone, the other became sad and gloomy, till the well-known tread of its friend's hoofs was heard from afar, when it would give a joyful neigh, which was instantly answered.

Never once was it necessary for the coachman to complain of any difficulty in harnessing them. They walked themselves into their proper places, and behaved in all ways as if they were well brought up, and ready to be friendly with everybody. They had all kinds of pretty little ways, and if they thought there was a chance of getting bread or sugar or melon rind, which they both loved, they would make themselves as caressing as a dog.

BLANCHE TELLING GHOST STORIES TO JANE IN THE STABLE

Nobody who has lived much with animals can doubt that they talk together in a language that man is too stupid to understand ; or, if anyone *had* doubted it, they would soon have been convinced of the fact by the conduct of Jane and Blanche when in harness. When Jane first made Blanche's acquaintance, she was afraid of nothing, but after they had been together a few months, her character gradually changed, and she had sudden panics and nervous fits, which puzzled her master greatly. The reason of this was that Blanche, who was very timid and easily frightened, passed most of the night in telling Jane ghost stories, till poor Jane learnt to tremble at every sound. Often, when they were driving in the lonely alleys of the Bois de Boulogne after dark, Blanche would come to a dead stop or shy to one side as if a ghost, which no one else could see, stood before her. She breathed loudly, trembled all over with fear, and broke out into a cold perspiration. No efforts of Jane, strong though she was, could drag her along. The only way to move her was for the coachman to dismount, and to lead her, with his hand over her eyes for a few steps, till the vision seemed to have melted into air. In the end, these terrors affected Jane just as if Blanche, on reaching the stable, had told her some terrible story of what she had seen, and even her master had been known to confess that when, driving by moonlight down some dark road, where the trees cast strange shadows, Blanche would suddenly come to a dead halt and begin to tremble, he did not half like it himself.

With this one drawback, never were animals so charming to drive. If Théophile held the reins, it was really only for the look of the thing, and not in the least because it was necessary. The smallest click of the tongue was enough to direct them, to quicken them, to make them go to the right or to the left, or even to stop them. They were so clever that in a very short time they had learned all their master's habits, and knew his daily haunts as well as he did himself. They would go of their own accord to the newspaper office, to the printing office, to the publisher's, to the Bois de Boulogne, to certain houses where he dined on certain days in the week, so very punctually that it was quite provoking; and if it ever happened that Théophile spent longer than usual at any particular place, they never failed to call his attention by loud neighs, or by pawing the ground, sounds of which he quite well knew the meaning.

But alas, the time came when a Revolution broke out in Paris. People had no time to buy books or to read them; they were far too busy in building barricades across the streets, or in tearing up the paving stones to throw at each other. The newspaper in which Théophile wrote, and which paid him enough money to keep his horses, did not appear any more, and sad though he was at parting, the poor man thought he was lucky to find some one to buy horses, carriage, and harness, for a fourth part of their worth. Tears stood in his eyes as they were led away to their new stable; but he never forgot them, and they never forgot him. Sometimes, as he sat writing at his table, he would hear from afar a light quick step, and then a sudden stop under the windows.

And their old master would look up and sigh and say to himself, 'Poor Jane, poor Blanche, I hope they are happy.'

MADAME THÉOPHILE AND THE PARROT[1]

AFTER the death of Cagnotte, whose story you may have read, Théophile was so unhappy that he would not have another dog, but instead, determined to fill the empty place in his heart with cats. One of those that he loved the best was a big yellowy-red puss, with a white chest, a pink nose, and blue eyes, that went by the name of Madame Théophile, because, when he was in the house, it never left his side for a single instant. It slept on his bed, dreamed while sitting on the arm of Théophile's chair while he was writing (for Théophile was by this time almost a grown-up man), walked after him when he went into the garden, sat by his side while he had his dinner, and sometimes took, gently and politely, the food he was conveying to his own mouth.

One day, a friend of Théophile's, who was leaving Paris for a few days, brought a parrot, which he begged Théophile to take care of while he was away. The bird not feeling at home in this strange place, climbed up to the top of his cage and looked round him with his funny eyes, that reminded you of the nails in a sofa. Now Madame Théophile had never seen a parrot, and it was plain that this curious creature gave her a shock. She sat quite still, staring quietly at the parrot, and trying to think if she had ever seen anything like it among the gardens and roofs of the houses, where she got all her ideas of the world. At last she seemed to make up her mind :

[1] *Ménagerie Intime.*

'Of course, it must be a kind of green chicken.'

Having set the question at rest, Madame Théophile jumped down from the table where she had been seated while she made her observations, and walked quickly to the corner of the room, where she laid herself flat down, with her head bent and her paws stretched out, like a panther watching his prey.

The parrot followed all her movements with his round eyes, and felt that they meant no good to him. He ruffled his feathers, pulled at his chain, lifted one of his paws in a nervous way, and rubbed his beak up and down his food tin. All the while the cat's blue eyes were talking in a language the parrot clearly understood, and they said: 'Although it is green, that fowl would make a nice dinner.'

But Madame Théophile had not lain still all this while. Slowly, without even appearing to move, she had drawn closer and closer. Her pink nostrils trembled, her eyes were half shut, her claws were pushed out and pulled into their sheaths, and little shivers ran down her back.

Suddenly her back rounded itself like a bent bow, and with one bound she leapt on the cage. The parrot knew his danger, and was too frightened to move ; then, calling up all his courage, he looked his enemy full in the face, and, in a low and deep voice he put the question : 'Jacky, did you have a good breakfast?'

This simple phrase struck terror into the heart of the cat, who made a spring backwards. If a cannon had been fired close to her ear, or a shopful of glass had been broken, she could not have been more alarmed. Never had she dreamed of anything like this.

'And what did you have—some of the king's roast beef?' continued the parrot.

'It is not a chicken, it is a man that is speaking,' thought the cat with amazement, and looking at her master, who was standing by, she retired under the bed. Madame Théophile knew when she was beaten.

THE BATTLE OF THE MULLETS AND
THE DOLPHINS

MANY singular stories may be found in Pliny, but
the most interesting is how men and dolphins combine
together on the coast of France, near Narbonne, to catch
the swarms of mullet that come into those waters at
certain seasons of the year.

‘ In Languedoc, within the province of Narbonne, there
is a standing pool or dead water called Laterra, wherein
men and dolphins together used to fish ; for at one certain
time of the year an infinite number of fishes called mullets,
taking the vantage of the tide when the water doth ebb,
at certain narrow weirs and passages with great force
break forth of the said pool into the sea ; and by reason
of that violence no nets can be set and pitched against
them strong enough to abide and bear their huge weight
and the stream of the water together, if so be men were
not cunning and crafty to wait and espie their time and
lay for them and to entrap them. In like manner the
mullets for their part immediately make speed to recover
the deep, which they do very soon by reason that the
Channel is near at hand ; and their only haste is for this,
to escape and pass that narrow place which affordeth
opportunities to the fishers to stretch out and spread their
nets. The fishermen being ware thereof and all the people
besides (for the multitude knowing when fishing time is
come, run thither, and the rather for to see the pleasant
sport), cry as loud as ever they can to the dolphins for
aid, and call “ Simo, Simo,” to help to make an end of this

their game and pastime of fishing. The dolphins soon
get the ear of their cry and know what they would have,

HOW THE DOLPHINS HELPED THE FISHERMEN TO CATCH THE MULLETS

and the better if the north winds blow and carry the
sound unto them; for if it be a southern wind it is later

ere the voice be heard, because it is against them. Howbeit, be the wind in what quarter soever, the dolphins resort thither flock-meal, sooner than a man would think, for to assist them in their fishing. And a wondrous pleasant sight it is to behold the squadrons as it were of those dolphins, how quickly they take their places and be arranged in battle array, even against the very mouth of the said pool, where the mullets are to shoot into the sea, to see (I say) how from the sea they oppose themselves and fight against them and drive the mullets (once affrighted and scared) from the deep on the shelves. Then come the fishers and beset them with net and toile, which they bear up and fortify with strong forks; howbeit, for all that, the mullets are so quick and nimble that a number of them whip over, get away, and escape the nets. But the dolphins are ready to receive them; who, contenting themselves for the present to kill only, make foul work and havoc among them, and put off the time of preying and feeding upon, until they have ended the battle and achieved the victory. And now the skirmish is hot, for the dolphins, perceiving also the men at work, are the more eager and courageous in fight, taking pleasure to be enclosed within the nets, and so most valiantly charging upon the mullets; but for fear lest the same should give an occasion unto the enemies and provoke them to retire and fly back between the boats, the nets, and the men there swimming, they glide by so gently and easily that it cannot be seen where they get out. And albeit they take great delight in leaping, and have the cast of it, yet none essayeth to get forth but where the nets lie under them, but no sooner are they out, but presently a man shall see brave pastime between them as they scuffle and skirmish as it were under the ramparts. And so the conflict being ended and all the fishing sport done, the dolphins fall to spoil and eat those which they killed in the first shock and encounter. But after this service performed, the dolphins retire not presently into the deep again, from whence they were called, but stay until to-morrow, as if they knew very well they had so carried themselves as that they deserved a better reward than one day's refection and victuals ; and therefore contented they are not and satisfied unless to their fish they have some sops and crumbs of bread given them soaked in wine, and had their bellies full.'

MONKEY STORIES

BEFORE telling you more stories about monkeys, we must tell you some dry facts about them, in order that you may understand the stories. There are three different kinds of monkeys—apes, baboons, and monkeys proper. The difference is principally in their tails, so that when you see them at the Zoo (for there are none wild in Europe, except at Gibraltar), you will know them by the apes having no tails and walking upright; baboons have short tails and go on all fours ; and monkeys have tails sometimes longer than their whole bodies, by which they can swing themselves from tree to tree. Apes and monkeys are so ready to imitate everything which men do, that the negroes believe that they are a lazy race of men, who will not be at the trouble to work. Baboons, on the contrary, can be taught almost nothing.

There are two kinds of apes, called oran otans and chimpanzees. They are both very wild and fierce, and difficult to catch, but, when caught, become not only tame, but very affectionate, and can be taught anything. Nearly two hundred years ago, in 1698, one was brought to London that had been caught in Angola. On board ship he became very fond of the people who took care of him, and was very gentle and affectionate, but would have nothing to do with some monkeys who were on the same ship. He had had a suit of clothes made for him, probably to keep him warm. As the ship got into colder regions he took great pleasure in dressing himself in them, and anything he could not put on for himself he used to bring in his paw to one of the sailors, and seem to ask him to dress him. He had a bed to sleep in, and at night used to put his head on the pillow and tuck himself in like a human being. His story is unfortunately a short one, for he died soon after coming to London. He could not long survive the change from his native forests to the cage of a menagerie.

TWO ORAN OTANS

Another, a female, was brought to Holland nearly a hundred years later, in 1776, but she, too, pined and died after seven months' captivity. She was very gentle and affectionate, and became so fond of her keeper that when they left her alone, she used to throw herself on the ground screaming, and tearing in pieces anything in her reach, just like a naughty child. She could behave as well as any lady in the land when she liked. When asked out to tea, she used to bring a cup and saucer, put sugar in the cup, pour out the tea, and leave it to cool; and at dinner her manners were just as good. She used her knife and fork, table napkin, and even toothpick, as if she had been accustomed to them all her life, which, of course, in her native forest was far from being the case. She learnt all her nice habits either from watching people at table, or from her keeper's orders. She was fond of strawberries, which she ate very daintily, on a fork, holding the plate in the other hand. She was particularly fond of wine, and drank it like a human being, holding the glass in her hand. She was better behaved than two other oran otans, who, though they could behave as well at table as any lady, and could use their knives and forks and glasses, and could make the cabin boy (for it was on board ship) understand what they wanted, yet, if he did not attend to them at once, they used to throw him down, seize him by the arm, and bite him.

A French priest had an oran otan that he had brought up from a baby, and who was so fond of his master that he used to follow him about like a dog. When the priest went to church he used to lock the oran otan up in a room; but one day he got out, and, as sometimes happens with dogs, who cannot get reconciled to Sunday, he followed his master to church. He managed, without the priest's seeing him, to climb on the sounding board above the pulpit, where he lay quite still till the sermon began. He then crept forward till he could see his master in the pulpit below, and imitated every one of his movements, till the congregation could not keep from laughing. The priest thought they were making fun of him, and was naturally very angry. The more angry he became the more gestures he used, every one of which the ape over-head repeated. At last a friend of the priest stood up in the congregation, and pointed out the real culprit. When the priest looked up and saw the imitation of himself, he could not keep from laughing either, and the service could not go on till the disturber had been taken down and locked up again at home.

Another kind is called the Barbary ape, because they are found in such numbers in Barbary that the trees in places seem nearly covered with them, though there are quantities as well in India and Arabia. They are very mischievous and great fighters. In India the natives sometimes amuse themselves by getting up a fight among them. They put down at a little distance from each other baskets of rice, with stout sticks by each basket, and then they go off and hide themselves among the trees to watch the fun. The apes come down from the trees in great numbers, and make as though they were going to attack the baskets, but lose courage and draw back grinning at each other. The females are generally the boldest, and the first to seize on the food; but as soon as they put their heads down to eat, some of the males set-to to drive them off. Others attack them in their turn. They all seize on the sticks, and soon a free fight begins, which ends in the weakest being driven off into the woods, and the conquerors enjoying the spoil. They are not only fierce but revengeful, and will punish severely any person who kills one of them. Some English people who were driving through country full of these apes in the East Indies, wished, out of sheer wantonness, to have one shot. The native servants, knowing what the consequences would be, were afraid; but, as their masters insisted, they had to obey, and shot a female whose little ones were clinging to her neck. She fell dead from the branches, and the little ones, falling with her, were killed too. Immediately all the other apes, to the number of about sixty, came down and attacked the carriage. They would certainly have killed the travellers if the servants, of whom there was fortunately a number, had not driven the apes off; and though the carriage set off as fast as the horses could lay legs to the ground, the apes followed for three miles.

Baboons are as ugly, revolting creatures as you could wish to see, and very fierce, so they can seldom be tamed nor even caught. There are, of course, few stories about

THE BABOONS WHO STOLE THE POOR MAN'S DINNER

them. When people try to catch them, they let their pursuers come so near that they think they have them, and then they bound away ten paces at once, and look down defiantly from the tree-top as much as to say, 'Don't you wish you may get me?' One baboon had so wearied his pursuers by his antics that they pointed a gun at him, though with no intention of firing. He had evidently seen a gun before, and knew its consequences, and was so frightened at the bare idea, that he fell down senseless and was easily captured. When he came to himself again he struggled so fiercely that they had to tie his paws together, and then he bit so that they had to tie his jaws up.

Baboons are great thieves, and come down from the mountains in great bodies to plunder gardens. They cram as much fruit as they possibly can into their cheek pouches to take away and eat afterwards at their leisure. They always set a sentinel to give the alarm. When he sees anyone coming, he gives a yell that lasts a minute, and then the whole troop sets off helter-skelter.

They will rob anyone they come upon alone in the most impudent way. They come softly up behind, snatch away anything they can lay their hands on, and then run off a little way and sit down. Very often it is the poor man's dinner that they devour before his eyes. Sometimes they will hold it out in their hands and pretend they are going to give it back, in such a comic way that I would defy you not to laugh, though it were your own dinner that had been snatched away and then offered to you.

Monkeys live in the tree-tops of the forests of India and South Africa, where they keep up a constant chattering and gambolling, all night as well as all day, playing games and swinging by their tails from tree to tree. One kind, the four-fingered monkey, can pass from one high tree-top to another, too far even for a monkey to jump, by making themselves into a chain, joined to each other by their tails.

They can even cross rivers in this way. There are any number of different kinds of monkeys, as you can see any day in the monkey house at the Zoo. One kind is well named the howling monkey, because they howl in chorus every morning two hours before daylight, and again at nightfall. The noise they make is so fearful that, if you did not know, you would think it was a forest full of fero-cious beasts quite near, thirsting for their prey, instead of harmless monkeys a mile or two away. There is always a leader of the chorus, who sits on a high branch above the others. He first howls a solo, and then gives a signal for the others to join in ; then they all howl together, till he gives another signal to stop.

The egret monkeys are great thieves. When they set to work to rob a field of millet, they put as many stalks as they can carry in their mouths, in each paw, and under each arm, and then go off home on their hind legs. If pursued, and obliged for greater speed to go on all their four legs, they drop what they carry in their paws, but never let go what they have in their mouths. The Chinese monkey is also a great thief, and even cleverer about carrying away his booty. They always set a sentinel on a high tree ; when he sees anyone coming, he screams 'Houp, houp, houp!' The others then seize as much as they can carry in their right arm, and set off on three legs. They are called Chinese, not because they come from China, but because the way the hair grows on their heads is like a Chinese cap. It is long and parts in the middle, spreading out all round.

In many parts of India monkeys are worshipped by the natives, and temples are erected for them. But mon-keys of one tribe are never allowed to come into any of these sanctuaries when another tribe is already in posses-sion. A large strong monkey was once seen by some travellers to steal into one of these temples ; as soon as the inhabitants saw that he did not belong to their tribe, they set on him to drive him out. As he was only one against many, though bigger and stronger than the others, he saw that he had no chance, and bounded up to the top, eleven stories high. As the temple ended in a little round dome just big enough for himself, he was master of the situation, and every monkey that ventured to climb up he flung down to the bottom. When this had happened three or four times, his enemies thought it best to let him alone, and he stayed there in peace till it was dark and he could slip away unseen.

ECCENTRIC BIRD BUILDERS [1]

EVERYBODY knows how fond birds are of building their
nests in church, and if we come to think of it, it is a very
reasonable and sensible proceeding. Churches are so
quiet, and have so many dark out-of-the-way corners,
where no one would dream of poking, certainly not the
woman whose business it is to keep the church clean.
So the birds have the satisfaction of feeling that their
young are kept safe and warm while they are collecting
food for them, and there is always some open door or
window to enable the parents to fly in or out.

But all birds have not the wisdom of the robins, and
swallows, and sparrows that have selected the church for
a home, and some of them have chosen very odd places
indeed wherein to build their nests and lay their eggs.
Hinges of doors, turning lathes, even the body of a dead
owl hung to a ring, have all been used as nurseries ; but
perhaps the oddest spot of all to fix upon for a nest is the
outside of a railway carriage, especially when we remember how often railway stations are the abode of cats, who
move safely about the big wheels, and even travel by
train when they think it necessary.

Yet, in spite of all the drawbacks, railway carriages
remain a favourite place for nesting birds, and there is a
curious story of a pair of water-wagtails which built a
snug home underneath a third-class carriage attached to
a train which ran four times daily between Cosham and
Havant. The father does not seem to have cared about

[1] From Jones' *Glimpses of Animal Life*.

railway travelling, which, to be sure, must appear a wretched way of getting about to anything that has wings ; for he never went with the family himself, but spent the time of their absence fluttering restlessly about the platform to which the train would return. He was so plainly anxious and unhappy about them, that one would have expected that he would have insisted on some quieter and safer place the following year when nesting time came round again ; but the mother apparently felt that the situation had some very distinct advantages, for she deliberately passed over every other spot that her mate pointed out, and went back to her third-class carriage.

Yet a railway carriage seems safety itself in comparison with a London street lamp, where a fly-catcher's nest was found a few years ago. Composed as it was of moss, hair, and dried grass, it is astonishing that it never caught fire, but no doubt the great heat of the gas was an immense help in hatching the five eggs which the birds had laid.

Those fly-catchers had built in a hollow iron ornament on the top of the lamp, but some tomtits are actually known to have chosen such a dangerous place as the spot close to the burner of a paraffin street lamp. And even when the paraffin was exchanged for gas, the birds did not seem to mind, and would sit quite calmly on the nest, while the lamplighter thrust his long stick past them to put out the light.

Birds reason in a different way from human beings, for a letter-box would not commend itself to us as being a very good place to bring up a family, with letters and packages tumbling on to their heads every instant. A pair of Scotch tomtits, however, thought otherwise, and they made a comfortable little nest at the back of a private letter-box, nailed on to the trunk of a tree in Dumfriesshire. The postman soon found out what was going on, but he took great pains not to disturb them, for he was fond of birds, and was very curious to see what the tomtits would do. What the tomtits did was to go peacefully on with their nest, minding their own business, and by-and-bye eight little eggs lay in the nest. By this time the mother had got so used to the postman, that she never even moved when he unlocked the door, only giving his hand a friendly peck when he put it in to take out the letters, and occasionally accepting some crumbs which he held out to it. But no sooner did the little birds break through their shells than the parents became more difficult to deal with. They did not mind knocks from letters for themselves, but they grew furiously angry if the young ones ever were touched by so much as a corner, and one day, when a letter happened to fall plump on top of the nest, they tore it right to pieces. In fact, it was in such a condition, that when the postman came as usual to make his collection, he was obliged to take the letter back to the people who had written it, for no Post Office would have sent it off in such a state.

THE SHIP OF THE DESERT[1]

OF all animals under the sun, perhaps the very ugliest is
the camel; but life in the deserts of Africa and Arabia
could not go on at all without the constant presence of this
clumsy-looking creature. Some African tribes keep camels
entirely for the use of their milk and flesh; and it is
noticeable that these animals are much shyer and more
timid than their brothers in Syria and Arabia, who will
instantly come trotting up to any fresh camel that appears
on the scene, or obey the call of any Bedouin, even if he
is a stranger.

In general, the camel is merely employed as a beast
of burden, and from this he gets his name of the ' ship of
the desert.' Like other ships, he sways from side to side,
and his awkward motion is apt to make his rider feel very
sick, till he gets accustomed to this way of travelling.
Camels are wonderfully strong and enduring animals,
and can stow up water within them for several days,
besides having an extraordinary power of smelling any
water or spring that is far beyond the reach of man's eyes.
These qualities are naturally very valuable in the burning
deserts which stretch unbroken for hundreds of miles,
where everything looks alike, and the sun as he passes
across the heavens is the traveller's only guide.

Partly from fear of warlike tribes, which wander
through the deserts of Arabia and Nubia, and partly from
the help and protection which a large body can give, the
one to the other, it is the custom for merchants and

[1] From Burckhardt's *Travels in Nubia.*

travellers to band together and travel in great caravans
of men and camels. They try, if possible, to find some
well by which they can encamp, and every man fills his
own skins with water before starting afresh on his journey.
More quarrels arise about water than people who live in
countries with plenty of streams and rivers can have any
idea of. One man will sell his skinful to another at a
very high price, while if a traveller thinks he will be very
prudent and lay in a large store, the rest are certain to
take it from him directly their own supply runs short.
Food they can do without on those burning plains, but
not water.

Some of these misfortunes befel a traveller of the name
of Burckhardt, who left Switzerland in the opening years
of this century, to pass several years in Africa and the
East. After going through Syria, he began to make his
way up the Nile, and even penetrated as far as Nubia,
joining for that purpose a caravan of traders under the
leadership of an Ababde—an Arab race who from the
earliest days have been acknowledged to be the best
guides across the desert.

Owing to the intense heat which prevails in those
countries, the marches always take place in the small
hours of the morning, and midnight seems to have been
the usual hour for the start. Very commonly the march
would continue for eleven hours, during which time the
men were only allowed to drink twice, while the asses,
who with the camels formed part of the caravan, were
put on half their allowance. Sometimes a detachment
was sent on to wells that were known to lie along the
route, to get everything ready for the rest when they
came up; but it often happened that the springs were so
choked up by drifting sand that no amount of digging
would free them. Then there was nothing for it but to
go on again.

It was in the month of March that Burckhardt and
his companions had their hardest experience of the dread-

ful desert thirst. The year had been drier than was common even in Nubia, and even in the little oases or fertile spots, most of the trees and acacias were withered and dead. Hour after hour the travellers toiled on, and soon the asses gave out, and their riders were forced to walk over the scorching sand. Burckhardt had been a little more careful of his stock of water than the other members of the caravan, and for some days had cooked no food or eaten anything but biscuits, so that he had been able to spare a draught every now and then for his own ass, and still had enough to last both of them for another day. However, it was quite clear that unless water was quickly found they must all die together, and a council was held as to what was best to be done. The Ababde chief's advice was—and always had been—to send out a company of ten or twelve of the strongest camels, to try to make their way secretly to the Nile, through the ranks of unfriendly Arab tribes encamped all along its eastern shore.

This was agreed upon; and about four in the afternoon the little band set out, loaded with all the skins in the caravan. The river was a ride of five or six hours distant; so that many hours of dreadful suspense must pass before the watchers left behind could know what was to be their fate. Soon after sunset a few stragglers came in, who had strayed from the principal band; but they had not reached the river, and could give no news of the rest. As the night wore on, several of the traders came to Burckhardt to beg for a taste of the water he was believed to have stored up; but he had carefully hidden what remained, and only showed them his skins which were empty. Then the camp gradually grew silent, and all sat and waited under the stars for the verdict of life or death. It was three in the morning when shouts were heard, and the camels, refreshed by deep draughts of the Nile water, came along at their utmost speed, bearing skins full enough for many days' journey. Only one man was missing; but traders are a cruel race, and these cared nothing about his fate, giving themselves up to feasting and song, and joy at their deliverance.

Yet only a year later, the fate that had almost over-taken them befel a small body of merchants who set out with their camels from Berber to Daraou. The direct road, which led past the wells of Nedjeym, was known to be haunted at that date by the celebrated robber Naym, who waylaid every caravan from Berber ; so the merchants hired an Ababde guide to take them by a longer and more easterly road, where there was another well at which they could water. Unluckily the guide knew nothing of the country that lay beyond, and the whole party soon lost themselves in the mountains. For five days they wandered about, not seeing a creature who could give them help, or even direct them to the right path. Then, their water being quite exhausted, they turned steadily westwards, hoping by this means soon to reach the Nile. But the river at this point takes a wide bend, and was, if they had known it, further from them than before ; and after two days of dreadful agony, fifteen slaves and one merchant died. In desperation, another merchant, who was an Ababde, and owner of ten camels, had himself lashed firmly on to the back of the strongest beast, lest in his weakness he should fall off, and then ordered the whole herd to be turned loose, thinking that perhaps the instinct of the animals would succeed where the knowledge of man had failed. But neither the Ababde nor his camels were ever seen again.

The merchants struggled forwards, and eight days after leaving the well of Owareyk they arrived in sight of some mountains which they knew ; but it was too late, and camels and merchants sank down helpless where they lay. They had just strength to gasp out orders for two of their servants to make their way on camels to the mountains where water would be found, but long before the mountains were reached, one of the men dropped off his camel and, unable to speak, waved his hands in farewell to his comrade. The other mechanically rode on, but his eyes grew dim and his head dizzy, and well though he knew the road, he suffered his camel to wander from it. After straying aimlessly about for some time, he dismounted and lay down in the shade of a tree to rest, first tying his camel to one of the branches. But a sudden puff of wind brought the smell of the water to the camel's nostrils, and with a furious bound, he broke the noose and galloped violently forward, and in half an hour was sucking in deep draughts from a clear spring. The man, understanding the meaning of the camel's rush, rose up and staggered a few steps after him, but fell to the ground from sheer weakness. Just at that moment a wandering Bedouin from a neighbouring camp happened to pass that way, and seeing that the man still breathed, dashed water in his face, and soon revived him. Then, laden with skins of water, the two men set out for those left behind, and hopeless though their search seemed to be, they found they had arrived in time, and were able to save them from a frightful death.

'*HAME, HAME, HAME, WHERE I FAIN WAD BE*'

NOTHING in nature is more curious or more difficult of explanation than the stories recorded of animals conveyed to one place, finding their way back to their old home, often many hundreds of miles away. Not very long ago, a lady at St. Andrews promised to make a present to a friend who lived somewhere north of Perth, of a fine cat which she wished to part with. When the day arrived, the cat was tied safely up in a hamper, put in charge of the guard, and sent on its way. It was met at the station by its new mistress, who drove it home, and gave it an excellent supper and a comfortable bed. This was on Friday. All Saturday it poked about, examining everything as cats will, but apparently quite happy and content with its quarters. About seven on Sunday morning, as the lady drew up her blind to let in the sunshine, she saw the new puss trotting down the avenue. She did not pay much attention to the fact till the day went on, and the cat, who generally had a good appetite, did not come in to its meals. When Monday came, but the puss did *not*, the lady wrote to her friend at St. Andrews saying she feared that the cat had wandered away, but she would make inquiries at all the houses round, and still hoped to find it. On Tuesday evening loud mews were heard outside the kitchen door of the St. Andrews house, and when it was opened, in walked the cat, rather dirty and very hungry, but otherwise not at all the worse for wear. Now as anybody can see if he looks at the map, it is a long way

from St. Andrews to Perth, even as the crow flies. There
are also two big rivers which *must* be crossed, the Tay
and the Eden, or if the cat preferred coming by train, at
least two changes have to be made. So you have to
consider whether, granting it an instinct of *direction*,
which is remarkable enough in itself, the animal was
sufficiently strong to swim such large streams; or whether
it was so clever that it managed to find out the proper
trains for it to take, and the places where it must get out.
Any way, home it came, and was only two days on the
journey, and there it is still in St. Andrews, for its mistress
had not the heart to give it away a second time.

Trains seem to have a special fascination for cats,
and they are often to be seen about stations. For a long
while one was regularly to be seen travelling on the
Metropolitan line, between St. James's Park and Charing
Cross, and a whole family of half-wild kittens are at this
moment making a play-ground of the lines and platforms
at Paddington. One will curl up quite comfortably on the
line right under the wheel of a carriage that is just going
to start, and on being disturbed bolts away and hides
itself in some recess underneath the platform. Occasionally you see one with part of its tail cut off, but as a rule
they take wonderfully good care of themselves. The
porters are very kind to them, and they somehow contrive to get along, for they all look fat and well-looking, and
quite happy in their strange quarters.

Of course cats are not the only animals who have what
is called the 'homing instinct.' Sheep have been known
to find their way back from Yorkshire to the moors north
of the Cheviots where they were born and bred, although
sheep are not clever beasts and they had come a round-
about journey by train. But there are many such stories
of dogs, and one of the most curious is told by an English
officer who was in Paris in the year 1815. One day, as
the officer was walking hastily over the bridge, he was
annoyed by a muddy poodle dog rubbing up against him,

and dirtying his beautifully polished boots. Now dirty
boots were his abhorrence, so he hastily looked round
for a shoe-black, and seeing one at a little distance off, at
once went up to him to have his boots re-blacked. A few
days later the officer was again crossing the bridge, when
a second time the poodle brushed against him and spoilt
his boots. Without thinking he made for the nearest
shoe-black, just as he had done before, and went on his
way; but when the same thing happened a third time, his
suspicions were aroused, and he resolved to watch. In a
few minutes he saw the dog run down to the riverside
and roll himself in the mud, and then come back to the
bridge and keep a sharp look-out for the first well-dressed
man who would be likely to repay his trouble. The officer
was so delighted with the poodle's cleverness, that he
went at once to the shoe-black, who confessed that the
dog was his and that he had taught him this trick for the
good of trade. The officer then proposed to buy the dog,
and offered the shoe-black such a large sum that he agreed
to part with his 'bread-winner.'

So the officer, who was returning at once to England,
carried the dog, by coach and steamer to London, where
he tied him up for some time, in order that he should
forget all about his old life, and be ready to make himself
happy in the new one. When he was set free, however,
the poodle seemed restless and ill at ease, and after two
or three days he disappeared entirely. What he did then,
nobody knows, but a fortnight after he had left the
London house, he was found, steadily plying his old trade,
on the Pont Henri Quatre.

A Northumbrian pointer showed a still more wonderful
instance of the same sagacity. He was the property of
one Mr. Edward Cook, who after paying a visit to his
brother, the owner of a large property in Northumberland,
set sail for America, taking the dog with him. They
travelled south together as far as Baltimore, where excellent shooting was to be got; but after one or two days'

sport the dog disappeared, and was supposed to have lost itself in the woods. Months went by without anything being known of the dog, when one night a dog was heard howling violently outside the quiet Northumberland house. It was admitted by the owner, Mr. Cook, who to his astonishment recognised it as the pointer which his brother had taken to America. They took care of him till his master came back, and then they tried to trace out his journey. But it was of no use. How the pointer made its way through the forest, from what port it started, and where it landed, remain a mystery to this day.

NESTS FOR DINNER

HOWEVER wonderful and beautiful nests may be, very few English people would like to eat them ; yet in China the nest of a particular variety of swallow is prized as a great delicacy.

These nests are chiefly gathered from Java, Sumatra, and other islands of the Malay Archipelago, and are carried thence to China, where they fetch a large price. Although, within certain limits, they are very plentiful, they are very difficult and dangerous to get, for the swallows build in the depths of large and deep caverns, mostly on the seashore, and the men have to be let down from above by ropes, or descend on ladders of bamboo. In Java, so many men have lost their lives in nest gathering, that in some parts a regular religious ceremony is held, twice or three times a year, before the expedition is undertaken ; prayers are said, and a bull is sacrificed.

It is not easy to know what the nests are really made of, because from the time that Europeans first noticed the trade—about two hundred years ago—they have differed among themselves in their accounts of the jelly-like substance used by the swallows. Some naturalists have thought it is the spawn of the fish, which floats thickly on the surface of these seas ; others, that it is a kind of deposit of dried sea foam gathered by the birds from the beach, while others again think that the substance is formed of sea plants chewed by the birds into a jelly; but, whatever it may be, the Chinese infinitely prefer nests to oysters or anything else, and are willing to pay highly for them.

The nests, which take about two months to build, are always found to be of two sorts : an oblong one just fitted to the body of the male bird, and a rounder one for the mother and her eggs. The most valuable nests are those which are whitest, and these generally belong to the male ; they are very thin, and finely worked. The birds are small and feed chiefly on insects, which are abundant on these islands ; their colour is grey, and they are wonderfully quick in their movements, like the humming birds, which are about their own size. They are sociable, and build in swarms, but they seldom lay more than two eggs, which take about a fortnight to hatch.

FIRE-EATING DJIJAM

SOME curious notes about walking unharmed through
fire, in the November (1894) number of 'Longman's
Magazine,' under the heading 'At the Sign of the Ship,'
suggested that a record might be kept of Djijam's
eccentricities, especially as they differed somewhat from
those of most other dogs.   Anyone accustomed to animals
knows, and anyone who is not can imagine, that dogs differ
as much in their behaviour and ways as human beings.
Djijam was as unlike any dog I have ever had, seen, or
heard of, as could be.   My wife, who is a patient and successful instructor of animals, never managed to teach him
anything, any attempt to impart usual or unusual accomplishments being met with the most absolute, impenetrable
idiocy, which no perseverance could conquer or diminish
in the least degree.   That this extreme stupidity was
really assumed is now pretty clear, though at the time it
was attributed to natural density.

   It was at Christmas-tide, about two years ago, that
my wife and I drove over to a village some few miles
away, to choose one of a litter of four fox-terrier pups,
which we heard were on sale at a livery stable.   We found
the mother of the lively litter almost overpowered by her
boisterous progeny, who though nearly three months old
had not yet found other homes.   Without any particular
objection on the part of the parent we examined the pups,
and selected and brought away one which seemed to have
better points than the rest, whom we left to continue their
gambols in the straw, unconscious probably that any other

means of warming themselves were possible. The journey home was accomplished with the customary puppish endeavours to escape restraint. The same evening, after the servants had retired to bed, Master Djijam was placed in the kitchen, out of harm's way as it was thought. The last thing at night we went to inspect the little animal, and could not at first discover his whereabouts. When a thing is lost it is customary to hunt about in unlikely places, so we looked into the high cinder-box under the kitchener, and found the object of our search comfortably curled up directly under the red-hot fire. It was fairly warm work fishing him out.

For another reason, not connected with heat, he was subsequently christened Djijam, a truly oriental name, which some of our friends think may have helped to develop his original taste for fire.

When Djijam was about six months old we observed that he frequently jumped up to people who were seated smoking. This induced a humorous friend one day to offer him the lighted end of a cigarette, which Djijam promptly seized in his mouth and extinguished. After that triumph Djijam usually watched for, and plainly demanded the lighted fag ends of cigarettes and cigars, so that his might be the satisfaction of finishing them off. This led to lighted matches being offered to him, which he eagerly took in his mouth, and if wax vestas, swallowed as a welcome addition to his ordinary diet. From matches to lighted candles was an easy step, and these he rapidly extinguished with great gusto as often as they were presented to him. He would also attack lighted oil lamps if placed on the floor, but they puzzled him, and defied his efforts to bite or breathe them out. A garden bonfire used to drive him wild with delight, and snatching brands from the fire, indoors or out, was a delirious joy. My wife discovered him once in the full enjoyment of a large lighted log on the dining-room carpet. Red-hot cinders he highly relished, though in obtaining them he frequently

'IN THE FULL ENJOYMENT OF A LARGE LIGHTED LOG ON THE DINING-ROOM CARPET'

singed off his moustaches. Perhaps the oddest of his fiery tricks was performed one day when he wished the cook to hand him some dainty morsel on which she chanced to be operating. This was against the rules, as he well knew, so she declined to accept the hint. Djijam was at once provoked to anger and cast round for some way of obtaining compensation, at the same time hoping, perhaps, to retaliate. He naturally went for the kitchen fire, out of which he drew a red-hot cinder and carried it in his mouth across the kitchen, through a small lobby into the scullery, to his box-bed, into the straw of which he must have speedily dropped the live coal, and jumped in after it. Soon after, the cook smelt wood burning and searched the lower part of the house lest anything were afire. Finding nothing wrong, she last of all visited the scullery, and found Djijam enjoying the warmth of his smouldering straw bed and wooden box.

Alas, Djijam grew snappish even to his best friends, and although it was suggested that he might be found an engagement on the Variety stage of the Westminster Aquarium, as a fire-eating hound, it was reluctantly decided that he should go the way of all flesh. I am sure if he had been asked, he would in some way have indicated that he preferred cremation to any other mode of disposal. But it was not to be, yet it was a melancholy satisfaction to learn that his end was peaceful though commonplace.

THE STORY OF THE DOG OSCAR

In the north-west of Scotland there is a very pretty loch which runs far up into the land. On one side great hills—almost mountains—slope down into the water, while on the opposite side there is a little village, with the road along which the houses straggle, almost part of the loch shore. At low tide, banks of beautiful golden seaweed are left at the edges of the water, and on this seaweed huge flocks of sea-gulls come and feed.

A few years ago there lived in this village a minister who had a collie-dog named Oscar. He lived all alone in his little cottage, and as Jean, the woman who looked after him, was a very talkative person, by no means congenial to him, Oscar was his constant companion and friend.

He seemed to understand all that was said to him, and in his long, lonely walks across the hills, it cheered him to have Oscar trotting quietly and contentedly beside him. And when he came home from visiting sick people, and going to places where he could not take Oscar, he would look forward to seeing the soft brown head thrust out of the door, peering into the darkness, ready to welcome him as soon as he should come in sight,

One of Oscar's favourite games was to go down to the shore when the tide was low, and with his head thrown up and his tail straight out, he would run at the flocks of gulls feeding on the seaweed, and scatter them in the air, making them look like a cloud of large white snow-flakes.

'OSCAR WOULD CHARGE AND ROUT THEM'

In a minute or two the gulls would settle down again to their meal, and again Oscar would charge and rout them.

This little manœuvre of his would be repeated many times, till a long clear whistle was heard from the road by the loch. Then the gulls might finish their supper in peace, for Oscar's master had called him, and now he was walking quietly along by his side, looking as if there were no such things in the world as gulls.

'No, Oscar, lad! Not to-day! not to-day!' said the minister one afternoon, as he put on his hat and coat and took his stick from the dog who always fetched it when he saw preparations being made for a walk.

'I can't take you with me; you must stay in the paddock. No run by the loch this afternoon, lad. 'Tis too long, and you are not so strong as you were. We are growing old together, Oscar.'

The dog watched his master till he disappeared over the little bridge and up the glen, and then he went and lay down by the paling which surrounded the bit of field. Jean soon went out to a friend's house to have a little gossip, and Oscar was left alone.

He felt rather forlorn. Across the road he heard the distant splashing of the waves as they ran angrily up the beach of the loch, and the whistling of the wind down the glen.

He watched the grey clouds scudding away overhead, and he envied the children he heard playing in the street, or racing after the tourist coach on its way up the Pass.

He began to feel drowsy.

'The gulls will be feeding on the banks now! How I wish . . .' and his eyes closed, and he dreamt a nice dream, that he was dashing along through shallow pools of water towards the white chattering flock, when—what was this in front of him? White feathers! Two gulls! Was he dreaming still? No, the gulls were real! What luck! He could not go to the gulls, so the gulls had come to him.

In a moment he was wide awake, and made a rush at the two birds who were gazing at him inquiringly with their heads on one side But after two or three rushes, 'What stupid gulls these are!' thought Oscar. 'They can scarcely fly.'

And, indeed, the birds seemed to have great difficulty in lifting themselves off the ground, and appeared to grow more and more feeble after each of Oscar's onslaughts. At last one of them fell.

'Lazy creature! you have had too much dinner! Up you get!'

But the gull lay down gasping.

Oscar made for the other. Why, that was lying down too! He went to the first one. It was quite still and motionless, and after one or two more gasps its companion was the same.

Oscar felt rather frightened. Was it possible that he had killed them? What would his master say? How was he to tell him it was quite a mistake? That he had only been in fun? He must put the gulls out of sight.

He dragged them to one side of the cottage where the minister used to try every year to grow a few cherished plants, and there in the loose earth he dug a grave for the birds.

Then he went back to his old place, and waited for his master's return.

When the minister came back, for the first time in his life, Oscar longed to be able to speak and tell him all that had happened. How could he without speech explain that the death of the birds was an accident—an unfortunate accident?

He felt that without an explanation it was no use unearthing the white forms in the border.

'Sir, sir!' cried Jean, putting her head in at the door. 'Here's Widow McInnes come to see you. She's in sore trouble.'

The minister rose and went to the door.

'Stay here, Oscar,' he said, for Widow McInnes was not fond of Oscar.

In a few minutes the minister came back.

He patted Oscar's soft head.

' OSCAR FELT RATHER FRIGHTENED '

'She wanted to accuse thee, Oscar lad, of killing the two white pigeons which her son sent her yesterday from the south, and which escaped this afternoon from their cage. As if you would touch the bairnies, as the poor woman calls them! Eh, lad?'

Oscar wagged his tail gratefully. Then in a sudden flash it came upon him that he *had* killed the pigeons. Now he saw the birds were pigeons, not gulls, and, worse than killing them, he had, all unknowingly, told his master a lie; and he could not undo it. He whined a little as if in pain, and moved slowly out of the room. The minister sat on, deep in thought, and then went outside the house to see the sunset. Great bands of thick grey cloud wrapped the hill-tops in their folds, and lay in long bands across the slopes, while here and there in the rifts were patches of pale lemon-coloured sky. The loch waters heaved sullenly against the shore. The minister looked away from the sunset, and his eye fell on a little mound in the bed by the cottage.

' What did I plant there ? ' he thought, and began poking it with his stick.

' Oscar, Oscar ! '

Oscar was bounding down the path. He had just determined to unbury the pigeons and bring them to his master, and, even if he received a beating, his master would know he had not meant to deceive.

But now, hearing the call, and the tone of the minister's voice, he knew it was too late. He stopped, and then crept slowly towards that tall black figure standing in the twilight, with the two white pigeons lying at his feet.

' Oh, Oscar, Oscar lad, what *have* you done ? '

At that moment a boy came running to the gate.

' Ye'll be the minister that Sandy Johnston is speiring after. He says, " Fetch the minister, and bid him come quick." '

The minister gave a few directions to Jean, and in a moment or two was ready to go with the boy. It was a long row to the head of the loch, and a long walk to reach the cottage where Sandy Johnston lay dying. The minister stayed with him for two nights, till he seemed to need his help no more, and then started off to come home. But while he was being rowed along the loch, a

'OH, OSCAR, OSCAR LAD, WHAT *HAVE* YOU DONE?'

fierce snowstorm came on. The boat made but little way, and they were delayed two or three hours. Cold and tired, the minister thought with satisfaction of his warm fireside, with Oscar lying down beside his cosy chair. Then, for the first time since it had happened, he thought of the pigeons, and he half smiled as he recalled Oscar's downcast face as he came up the path.

With quick steps he hurried along the street from the landing-place. The snow was being blown about round him, and the night was fast closing in. He was quite near his own gate now, and he looked up, expecting to see the familiar brown head peering out of the door for him ; but there was no sign of it.

He opened the gate and strode in. Still no Oscar to welcome him.

' Jean, Jean ! ' he called. Jean appeared from the kitchen, and even in the firelight he could see traces of tears on her rough face.

' Where is Oscar ? '

' Ah, sir, after ye were gone wi' the lad, he wouldna' come into the house, and wouldna' touch a morsel o' food. He lay quite still in the garden, and last night he died. An' it's my belief, sir, he died of a broken heart, because ye did na' beat him after killing the pigeons, and he couldna' make it up wi' ye.'

And the minister thought so, too ; and when Jean was gone, he sat down by his lonely fireside and buried his face in his hands.

DOLPHINS AT PLAY

For some reason or other, dolphins, those queer great fish that always seem to be at play, have been subjects for many stories. Pliny himself has told several, and his old translator's words are so strange, that, as far as possible, we will tell the tale as he tells it.

'In the days of Augustus Cæsar, the Emperor,' says Pliny, 'there was a dolphin entered the gulf or pool Lucrinus, which loved wondrous well a certain boy, a poor man's son; who using to go every day to school from Baianum to Puteoli, was wont also about noon-tide to stay at the water side and call unto the dolphin, "Simo, Simo," and many times would give him fragments of bread, which of purpose he ever brought with him, and by this means allured the dolphin to come ordinarily unto him at his call. Well, in process of time, at what hour soever of the day this boy lured for him and called "Simo," were the dolphin never so close hidden in any secret and blind corner, out he would and come abroad, yea, and scud amain to this lad, and taking bread and other victuals at his hand, would gently offer him his back to mount upon, and then down went the sharp-pointed prickles of his fins, which he would put up as it were within a sheath for fear of hurting the boy. Thus, when he once had him on his back, he would carry him over the broad arm of the sea as far as Puteoli to school, and in like manner convey him back again home; and thus he continued for many years together, so long as the

THE BOY GOES TO SCHOOL ON THE DOLPHIN'S BACK

child lived. But when the boy was fallen sick and dead
yet the dolphin gave not over his haunt, but usually came
to the wonted place, and missing the lad seemed to be
heavy and mourn again, until for very grief and sorrow
he also was found dead upon the shore.'

THE STARLING OF SEGRINGEN[1]

In a little German village in Suabia, there lived a barber, who combined the business of hair-cutting and shaving with that of an apothecary; he also sold good brandy, so that he had no lack of customers, not to speak of those who merely wished to pass an hour in gossiping.

Not the least of the attractions, however, was a tame starling, named Hansel, who had been taught to speak, and had learnt many sayings which he overheard, either from his master, the barber, or from the idlers who gathered about the shop. His master especially had some favourite sayings, or catchwords, such as, 'Truly, I am the barber of Segringen'—for this is the name of the village—'As heaven will,' 'By keeping bad company,' and the like; and these were most familiar to the starling.

Everybody for miles round had at least heard of Hansel, and many came on purpose to see him and hear him talk, for Hansel would often interpose a word into the conversation, which came in very aptly.

But it happened one day, Hansel's wings—which had been cut—having grown again, that he thought to himself: 'I have now learnt so much, I may go out and see the world.' And when nobody was looking, whirr!—away he went out of the window.

Seeing a flock of birds, he joined them, thinking: 'They know the country better than I.'

But alas! this knowledge availed them little, for all

---

[1] Translated from the German of Johann Peter Hebel.

of them, with Hansel, fell into a snare which had been laid by a fowler, who soon came to see what was in his net. Putting in his hand, he drew out one prisoner after another, callously wringing their necks one by one.

But suddenly, when he was stretching out his murderous fingers to seize another victim, this one cried out : ' I am the barber of Segringen ! '

The man almost fell backwards with astonishment and fright, believing he had to do with a sorcerer at least ; but presently recovering himself a little, he remembered the starling, and said : ' Eh, Hansel, is it you ! How did you come into the net ? '

' By keeping bad company,' replied Hansel.

' And shall I carry you home again ? '

' As heaven will,' replied the starling.

Then the fowler took him back to the barber, and related the manner of his capture, receiving a good reward.

The barber also reaped a fine harvest, for more people came to his shop on purpose to see the clever bird, who had saved his life by his ready tongue.

GRATEFUL DOGS [1]

A FARMER in Nebraska—one of the Western States of North America—possessed two dogs, a big one called Fanny, and a small one who was named Jolly. One winter day the farmer went for a walk and took with him his two pets ; they came to a brook that ran through the farm, and was now frozen up.

Fanny crossed it without much ado, but Jolly, who was always afraid of water, distrusted the ice, and refused to follow. Fanny paused at the other side, and barked loudly to induce her companion to come, but Jolly pretended not to understand.

Then Fanny ran back to him, and tried to explain that it was quite safe, but in vain, Jolly only looked after his master, and whimpered ; upon which, Fanny, losing patience, seized him by the collar, and dragged him over.

For this kindness Jolly showed himself grateful some time afterwards.

Fanny, greedy creature, was fond of fresh eggs. When she heard a hen cackle she always ran to look for the nest, and one day she discovered one under the fruit-shed. But, alas ! she could not get the beloved dainty because she was too large to go under the shed. Looking very pensive and thoughtful, she went away, and soon returned with Jolly, bringing him just before the hole.

---

[1] From ‘Das Echo,’ June 8, 1895. Letter to the editor, signed G. M., Mexico, purporting to be an extract from a letter of his brother in Nebraska. I have translated and recast it.

Jolly, however, was stupid and did not understand; Fanny put her head in, and then her paws, without being able, with all her efforts, to reach the egg; the smaller dog, seeing that there was something in the hole, went in to look, but not caring for eggs, came out empty-handed.

Thereupon Fanny looked at him in such a sad and imploring way, that her master, who was watching them, could scarcely suppress his laughter.

At last Jolly seemed to understand what was wanted; he went under the shed again, brought out the egg, and put it before Fanny, who ate it with great satisfaction, and then both dogs trotted off together.

GAZELLE

PASSAGES IN THE LIFE OF A TORTOISE

ALEXANDRE DUMAS, in whose book, as I told you, I read the story of Tom the Bear, as well as those of other animals, was one day walking past the shop of a large fishmonger in Paris. As he glanced through the window he saw an Englishman in the shop holding a tortoise, which he was turning about in his hands. Dumas felt an instant conviction that the Englishman proposed to make the tortoise into turtle soup, and he was so touched by the air of patient resignation of the supposed victim that he entered the shop, and with a sign to the shopwoman asked whether she had kept the tortoise for him which he had bespoken.

The shopwoman (who had known Dumas for many years) understood with half a word, and gently slipping the tortoise out of the Englishman's grasp, she handed it to Dumas, saying, 'Pardon, milord, the tortoise was sold to this gentleman this morning.'

The Englishman seemed surprised, but left the shop without remonstrating, and Dumas had nothing left for it but to pay for his tortoise and take it home.

As he carried his purchase up to his rooms on the third floor he wondered what could have possessed him to buy it, and what on earth he was to do with it now he had got it. It was certainly a remarkable tortoise, for the moment he put it down on the floor of his bedroom it started off for the fireplace at such a pace as to earn for itself the name of 'Gazelle.'

Once near the fire, Gazelle settled herself in the warmest corner she could find, and went to sleep.

Dumas, who wished to go out again and was afraid of his new possession coming to any harm, called his servant and said: 'Joseph, whilst I am out you must look after this creature.'

Joseph approached with some curiosity. 'Ah!' he remarked, 'why, it's a tortoise; that creature could bear a carriage on its back.'

'Yes, yes, no doubt it might, but I beg you won't try any experiments with it.'

'Oh, it wouldn't hurt it,' assured Joseph, who enjoyed showing off his information. 'The Lyons diligence might drive over it without hurting it.'

'Well,' replied his master, 'I believe the great sea turtle *might* bear such a weight, but I doubt whether this small variety——'

'Oh, *that's* of no consequence,' interrupted Joseph; 'it's as strong as a horse, and small though it is, a cartload of stones might pass——'

'Very good, very good; never mind that now. Just buy the creature a lettuce and some snails.'

'Snails! why, is its chest delicate?'

'No, why on earth do you ask such a thing?'

'Well, my last master used to take an infusion of snails for his chest—not that it prevented——'

Dumas left the room without waiting for the end. Before he was halfway downstairs he found that he had forgotten his handkerchief, and on returning surprised Joseph standing on Gazelle's back, gracefully poised on one leg, with the other out-stretched behind him in such a way that not an ounce of his eleven-stone weight was lost on the poor creature.

'Idiot! what are you about?'

'There, sir, didn't I say so?' rejoined Joseph, proudly.

'There, there, give me a handkerchief and mind you don't touch that creature again.'

'There, sir,' said the irrepressible Joseph, bringing the handkerchief. 'But indeed you need not be at all afraid ; a waggon could drive over——'

DUMAS FINDS JOSEPH STANDING ON GAZELLE'S BACK

Dumas fled.

He returned rather late at night, and no sooner took a step into his room than he felt something crack under his boot. He hastily raised his foot and took a further step with the same result : he thought he must be treading on eggs. He lowered his candlestick—the carpet was covered with snails.

Joseph had obeyed orders literally. He had bought the lettuces and the snails, had placed them all in a basket and Gazelle on the top, and then put the basket in the middle of his master's bedroom. Ten minutes later the warmth of the fire thawed the snails into animation, and the entire caravan set forth on a voyage of discovery round the room, leaving silvery tracks behind them on carpet and furniture.

As for Gazelle, she was quietly reposing at the bottom of the basket, where a few empty shells proved that all the fugitives had not been brisk enough to make their escape.

Dumas, feeling no fancy for a possible procession of snails over his bed, carefully picked up the stragglers one by one, popped them back into the basket, and shut down the lid. But in five minutes' time he realised that sleep would be out of the question with the noise going on, which sounded like a dozen mice in a bag of nuts. He decided to move the basket to the kitchen.

On the way there it occurred to him that if Gazelle went on at this rate she would certainly die of indigestion before morning. He remembered that the owner of the restaurant on the ground floor had a tank in the back yard where he often put fish to keep till wanted, and it struck him that the tank would be the very place for his tortoise. He at once put his idea into execution, got back to his room and to bed, and slept soundly till morning.

Joseph woke him early.

' Oh, sir, such a joke ! ' he exclaimed, standing at the foot of the bed.

' What joke ? '

' Why, what your tortoise has been up to ! '

' What on earth do you mean ? '

' Well, sir, could you believe that it got out of your room—goodness knows how—and walked downstairs and right into the tank ? '

' You owl! you might have guessed I put it there myself.'

' Did you indeed, sir ?   Well, you certainly *have* made a mess of it then.'

' How so ? '

' Why, the tortoise has eaten up a tench—a superb tench weighing three pounds—which the master of the restaurant put into the tank only last night.   The waiter has just been telling me about it.'

' Go at once and fetch me Gazelle and the scales.'

During Joseph's absence his master took down a volume of Buffon, and consulted that eminent authority on the subject of tortoises and turtles.   There seemed to be no doubt, according to the celebrated naturalist, that these creatures did eat fish voraciously when they got the chance.

' Dear, dear,' thought Dumas, ' I fear the owner of the tank has Buffon on his side.'

Just then Joseph returned with the accused in one hand and the kitchen scales in the other.

' You see,' began the irrepressible valet, ' these sort of creatures eat a lot.   They need it to keep up their strength, and fish is particularly nourishing.   Only see how strong sailors are, and they live so much on fish——'

His master cut him short.

' How much did you say that tench weighed ? '

' Three pounds.   The waiter asks nine francs for it.'

' And Gazelle ate it all ? '

' Every bit except the head, the back-bone, and the inside.'

' Quite correct, Monsieur Buffon had said as much.

Very well — but still — three pounds seems a good deal.'

He put Gazelle in the scale. She weighed exactly two pounds and a half! The deduction was simple. Either Gazelle had been falsely accused or the theft had been much smaller than was represented. Indeed the waiter readily took this view of the matter, and was quite satisfied with five francs as an indemnity.

The varied adventures of Gazelle had become rather a bore, and her owner felt that he must try to find some other home for her. She spent the following night in his room, but thanks to the absence of snails all went well. When Joseph came in next morning, his first act as usual was to roll up the hearthrug, and, opening the window, to shake it well out in the air. Suddenly he uttered an exclamation and flung himself half out of the window.

'What's the matter, Joseph?' asked his master, only half awake.

'Oh, sir—it's your tortoise. It was on the rug, and I never saw it—and——'

'Well! and——?'

'And I declare, before I knew what I was about, I shook it out of the window.'

'Imbecile!' shouted Dumas, springing out of bed.

'Ah!' cried Joseph with a sigh of relief. 'See, she's eating a cabbage!'

And so she was. Her fall had been broken by a rubbish heap, and after a few seconds in which to recover her equanimity, she had ventured to thrust her head out, when finding a piece of cabbage near, she at once began her breakfast.

'Didn't I say so, sir?' cried Joseph, delighted. 'Nothing hurts those creatures. There now, whilst she's eating that cabbage a coach-and-four might drive over her——'

'Never mind, never mind; just run down and fetch her up quick.'

Joseph obeyed, and as soon as his master was dressed he called a cab, and taking Gazelle with him, drove off to No. 109 in the Faubourg St.-Denis. Here he climbed to the fifth floor and walked straight into the studio of his friend, who was busy painting a delightful little picture of performing dogs. He was surrounded by a bear, who was playing with a log as he lay on his back,

DUMAS BRINGS GAZELLE TO NO. 109 FAUBOURG ST.-DENIS

a monkey, busy pulling a paint brush to pieces, and a frog, who was half-way up a little ladder in a glass jar. You will, I dare say, have guessed already that the painter's name was Décamps, the bear's Tom, the monkey's Jacko I., and the frog's Mademoiselle Camargo, and you will not wonder that Dumas felt that he could not better provide for Gazelle than by leaving her as an addition to the menagerie in his friend's studio.[1]

[1] See pp. 375.

COCKATOO STORIES [1]

ABOUT thirty years ago a gentleman, who was fond of birds and beasts, took into his head to try if parrots could not be persuaded to make themselves at home among the trees in his garden. For a little while everything seemed going beautifully, and the experimenter was full of hope. The parrots built their nests in the woods, and in course of time some young ones appeared, and gradually grew up to their full size. Then, unluckily, they became tired of the grounds which they knew by heart, and set off to see the world. The young parrots were strong upon the wing, and their beautiful bright bodies would be seen flashing in the sun, as much as fifteen miles away, and, then, of course, some boy or gamekeeper with a gun in his hand was certain to see them, and covet them for the kitchen mantel-shelf or a private collection.

The cockatoos however did not always care to choose trees for their building places. One little pair, whose grandparents had whisked about in the heat of a midsummer day in Australia, found the climate of England cold and foggy, and looked about for a warm cover for their new nest. They had many conversations on the subject, and perhaps one of these may have been overheard by a jackdaw, who put into their minds a brilliant idea, for the very next morning the cockatoos were seen carrying their materials to one of the chimneys, and trying to fasten them together half-way up. But cockatoos are not as clever as jackdaws about this kind of thing, and before

[1] *Naturalist's Note-Book.* Reeves & Turner: 1868.

the nest had grown to be more than a shapeless mass, down it came, and such a quantity of soot with it, that the poor cockatoos were quite buried, and lay for a day and night nearly smothered in soot, till they happened to be found by a housemaid who had entered the room. But in spite of this mishap they were not disheartened, and as soon as their eyes and noses had recovered from their soot bath, they began again to search for a more suitable spot. To the great delight of their master, they fixed upon a box which he had nailed for this very purpose under one of the gables, and this time they managed to build a nest that was as good as any nest in the garden. Still, they had no luck, for though the female laid two eggs, and sat upon them perseveringly, never allowing them to get cold for a single instant, it was all of no use, for the eggs turned out to be both bad !

Some cousins of theirs, a beautiful white cockatoo and his lovely rose-coloured wife, were more prosperous in their arrangements. They scooped out a most comfortable nest with their claws and bills in the rotten branch of an acacia tree, and there they brought up two young families, all of them white as snow, with flame-coloured crests. The eldest son, unhappily for himself, got weary of his brothers and sisters, and the little wood on the outskirts of the garden, where he was born, and one winter day took a flight towards the town. His parents never quite knew what occurred, but the poor young cockatoo came back severely wounded, to the great fury of all his family, who behaved very unkindly to him. It is a curious fact that no animals and very few birds can bear the sight of illness, and these cockatoos were no better than the rest. They did not absolutely ill-treat him, but they refused to let him enter their nest, and insisted that he should live by himself in a distant bush. At last his master took pity on him, and brought him into the garden, but this so enraged the cockatoos who were already in possession, that they secretly murdered him

However it is only just to the race of cockatoos to observe that they are not always so bad as this, for during the very same season an unlucky young bird, whose wing and leg were broken by an accident, was adopted by an elderly cockatoo who did not care for what her neighbours said, and treated him as her own son. The following year, when nesting time came round, the white cockatoos went back to their acacia branch, but were very much disgusted to find a pair of grey parrots there before them, and a little pair of bald round heads peeping over the edge. These little parrots grew up with such very bad tempers that no one would have anything to do with them, and as for their own relations, they looked upon them with the contempt that a cat often shows to a man. To be sure these relations were considered to be rather odd themselves, for they did not care to be troubled with a family of their own, so had taken under their protection two little kittens, who had been born in one of the boxes originally set apart for the parrots. The two birds could not endure to see the old cat looking after her little ones, and whenever she went out for a walk or to get her food, one of the parrots always took her place in the box. It would have been nice to know how long this went on, and if the kittens adopted any parrot-like ways. Luckily, there was one peculiarity of the parrots which it was beyond their power to imitate, and that was the horrible voice which renders the society of a parrot, and still more of a cockatoo, unendurable to most people.

THE OTTER WHO WAS REARED BY A CAT [1]

THERE is still living in the kingdom of Galloway a wonderful cat who is so completely above all the instincts
and prejudices of her race, that she can remain on friendly
terms with young rabbits, and wile away a spare hour
by having a game with a mouse. A *real* game, where
the fun is not all on one side, but which is enjoyed by
the mouse as much as by the cat.

Hardly less strange, from the opposite point of view,
is the friendship that existed between two cats and an
otter, which had been taken from its mother when only a
few hours old, to be brought up by hand by a gentleman.
This was not a very easy thing to manage. It was too
young to suck milk out of a spoon, which was the first
thing thought of, but a quill passed through a cork and
stuck into a baby's bottle proved a success, and through
this the little otter had its milk five times every day, until
he was more than five weeks old. Then he was introduced to a cat who had lately lost a kitten, and though
not naturally very good-tempered, the puss took to him
directly, evidently thinking it was her own kitten grown
a little bigger. In general this cat, which was partly
Persian and, as I have said, very cross, did not trouble
herself much about her young ones, which had to take
care of themselves as well as they could; but she could
not make enough of the little otter, and when he was as
big as herself she would walk with him every day to the
pond in the yard, where he had his bath, watching his

[1] *Naturalist's Note-Book.*

splashings and divings with great anxiety, and never happy till he got out safe.

But, like human children, the baby otter would have been very dull without someone to play with, and as there were no little otters handy, he made friends with a young cat called Tom.

All through the long winter, when the pond was frozen, and diving and swimming were no longer possible, he and Tom used to spend happy mornings playing hide and seek among the furniture in the dining-room, till Tom began to feel that the otter was getting rather rough, and that his teeth were very sharp, and that it would be a good thing to get out of his reach, on the top of a high cupboard or chimney piece.

But at last the snow melted, and the ice became water again, and the first day the sun shone, the otter and the old cat went out for a walk in the yard. After the little fellow had had his dive, which felt delicious after all the weeks that he had done without it, he wandered carelessly into a shed where he had never been before, and to his astonishment he suddenly heard a flutter of wings, and became conscious of a sharp pain in his neck. This was produced by the beak of a falcon, who always lived in the shed, and seeing the strange creature enter his door, at once made up his mind that it was its duty to kill it. The cat and the gentleman who happened to come in at the same moment rushed forward and beat off the bird, and then, blinded by excitement, like a great many other people, and not knowing friends from foes, the cat rushed at her master. In one moment she had severely bitten the calf of his leg, given his thigh a fearful scratch, and picked up the otter and carried him outside. Then, not daring to trust him out of her sight, she marched him sternly up the hill, keeping him all the while between her legs, so that no danger should come near him.

As the otter grew bigger the cats became rather afraid

of his claws and teeth, which grew bigger too, and inflicted bites and scratches without his knowing it. But if the cats tired of him, he never tired of the cats, and was always dull and unhappy when they were out of his way. Sometimes, when his spirits were unusually good (and his teeth unusually sharp), the poor playfellows were obliged to seek refuge in the bedrooms of the house, or even upon the roof, but the little otter had not lived so long with cats for nothing, and could climb nearly as well as they. When he had had enough of teasing, he told them so (for, of course, he knew the cat language), and they would come down, and he would stretch himself out lazily in front of the fire, with his arms round Tom's neck.

It would be nice to know what happened to him when he really grew up, whether the joys of living in a stream made him forget his old friends at the farm, or whether he would leave the chase of the finest trout at the sound of a mew or a whistle. But we are not told anything about it, so everybody can settle it as they like.

STORIES ABOUT LIONS

THE lion in its wild state is a very different animal from the lion of menageries and wild-beast shows. The latter has probably been born in captivity, reared by hand, and kept a prisoner in a narrow cage all its life, deprived not only of liberty and exercise, but of its proper food. The result is a weak, thin, miserable creature, with an unhappy furtive expression, and a meagre mane, more like a poodle than the king of beasts in a savage state.

The lion of South Africa differs in many points from that of Algeria, of whom we are going to speak. In Algeria there are three kinds of lions—the black, the tawny, and the grey. The black lion, more rarely met with than the two others, is rather smaller, but stronger in build. He is so called from the colour of his mane, which falls to his shoulder in a heavy black mass. The rest of his coat is the colour of a bay horse. Instead of wandering like the other two kinds, he makes himself a comfortable dwelling, and remains there probably all his life, which may last thirty or forty years, unless he falls a victim to the hunter. He rarely goes down to the plains in search of prey, but lies in ambush in the evening and attacks the cattle on their way down from the mountain, killing four or five to drink their blood. In the long summer twilights he waits on the edge of a forest-path for some belated traveller, who seldom escapes to tell the tale.

The tawny and grey lion differ from each other only in the colour of their mane ; all three have the same habits and characteristics, except those peculiar to the black lion

just described. They all turn night into day, and go out
at dusk to forage for prey, returning to their lair at dawn
to sleep and digest in peace and quiet. Should a lion, for
any reason, shift his camp during the day, it is most
unlikely that he will attack, unprovoked, any creature,
whether human or otherwise, whom he may chance to
meet ; for during the day he is 'full inside,' and the lion
kills not for the sake of killing, but to satisfy his hunger.
The lion is a devoted husband ; when a couple go out on
their nightly prowl, it is always the lioness who leads the
way ; when she stops he stops too, and when they arrive at
the fold where they hope to procure their supper, she lies
down, while he leaps into the midst of the enclosure, and
brings back to her the pick of the flock. He watches her
eat with great anxiety lest anything should disturb her,
and never begins his own meal till she has finished hers.
As a father he is less devoted ; the old lion being of a
serious disposition, the cubs weary him with their games,
and while the family is young the father lives by himself,
but at a short distance, so as to be at hand in case of
danger. When the cubs are about three months old, and
have finished teething (a process which often proves fatal
to little lionesses), their mother begins to accustom them
to eat meat by bringing them mutton to eat, which she
carefully skins, and chews up small before giving to them.
Between three and four months old they begin to follow
their mother at night to the edge of the forest, where their
father brings them their supper. At six months the whole
family change their abode, choosing for the purpose a very
dark night. Between eight months and a year old they
begin to attack the flocks of sheep and goats that feed by
day in the neighbourhood of their lair, and sometimes
venture to attack oxen, but being still young and awkward,
they often wound ten for one killed, and the father lion is
obliged to interfere. At the age of two years they can slay
with one blow an ox, horse, or camel, and can leap the
hedges two yards high that surround the folds for protec-

tion. This period in the history of the lion is the most disastrous to the shepherds and their flocks, for then the

lion goes about killing for the sake of learning to kill. At three years they leave their parents and set up families of

THE LION CAUGHT IN THE PIT

their own, but it is only at the age of eight that they attain their full size and strength, and, in the case of the male, his full mane.

The question is sometimes asked, why does the lion roar? The answer is, for the same reason that the bird sings. When a lion and lioness go out together at night, the lioness begins the duet by roaring when she leaves her den, then the lion roars in answer, and they roar in turn every quarter of an hour, till they have found their supper; while they are eating they are silent, and begin roaring as soon as satisfied, and roar till morning. In summer they roar less and sometimes not at all. The Arabs, who have good reason to know and dread this fearsome sound, have the same word for it as for the thunder. The herds being constantly exposed to the ravages of the lion, the natives are obliged to take measures to protect them, but, the gun in their unskilled hands proving often as fatal to themselves as to their enemy, they are forced to resort to other means. Some tribes dig a pit, about ten yards deep, four or five wide, and narrower at the mouth than the base. The tents of the little camp surround it, and round them again is a hedge two or three yards high, made of branches of trees interlaced; a second smaller hedge divides the tents from the pit in order to prevent the flocks from falling into it. The lion prowling in search of food scents his prey, leaps both hedges at one bound, and falls roaring with anger into the pit digged for him. The whole camp is aroused, and so great is the rejoicing that no one sleeps all night. Guns are let off and fires lit to inform the whole district, and in the morning all the neighbours arrive, not only men, but women, children, and even dogs. When it is light enough to see, the hedge surrounding the pit is removed in order to look at the lion, and to judge by its age and sex what treatment it is to receive, according to what harm it may have done. If it is a young lion or a lioness the first spectators retire from the sight disgusted, to make room for others whose raptures are equally soon calmed. But if it is a full-grown lion with abundant mane, then it is a very different scene; frenzied gestures and appropriate cries spread the joyful news from one to another, and the spectators crowd in such numbers that they nearly edge each other into the pit. When everyone has thrown his stone and hurled his imprecation, men armed with guns come to put an end to the noble animal's torture; but often ten shots have been fired before, raising his majestic head to look contemptuously on his tormentors, he falls dead. Not till long after this last sign of life do the bravest venture to let themselves down into the pit, by means of ropes, to pass a net under the body of the lion, and to hoist it up to the surface by means of a stake planted there for the purpose. When the lion is cut up, the mothers of the tribe receive each a small piece of his heart, which they give to their sons to eat to make them strong and courageous; with the same object they make themselves amulets of hairs dragged out from his mane.

Other tribes make use of the ambush, which may be either constructed underground or on a tree. If underground a hole is dug, about one yard deep, and three or four wide, near a path frequented by the lion; it is covered with branches weighted down by heavy stones, and loose earth is thrown over all. Four or five little openings are left to shoot through, and a larger one to serve as a doorway, which may be closed from within by a block of stone. In order to ensure a good aim the Arabs kill a boar and lay it on the path opposite the ambush; the lion inevitably stops to sniff this bait, and then they all fire at once. Nevertheless he is rarely killed on the spot, but frantically seeking his unseen enemies, who are beneath his feet, he makes with frenzied bounds for the nearest forest, there sometimes to recover from his wounds, sometimes to die in solitude. The ambush in a tree is conducted on the same lines as the other, except that the hunters are above instead of below their quarry, from whom they are screened by the branches.

There are, however, in the province of Constantine some tribes of Arabs who hunt the lion in a more sports-

manlike manner. When a lion has made his presence
known, either by frequent depredations or by roarings,
a hunting party is formed. Some men are sent in advance
to reconnoitre the woods, and when they return with
such information as they have been able to gather as to
the age, sex, and whereabouts of the animal, a council
of war is held, and a plan of campaign formed. Each

THE AMBUSH

hunter is armed with a gun, a pistol, and a yataghan, and
then five or six of the younger men are chosen to ascend
the mountain, there to take their stand on different commanding points, in order to watch every movement of
the lion, and to communicate them to their companions
below by a pre-arranged code of signals. When they are
posted the general advance begins; the lion, whose hear-

ing is extremely acute, is soon aware of the approach of
enemies, who in their turn are warned by the young men
on the look-out. Finally, when the lion turns to meet the
hunters the watchers shout with all their might ' Aou
likoum ! ' ' Look out ! ' At this signal the Arabs draw
themselves up in battle array, if possible with their backs
to a rock, and remain motionless till the lion has
approached to within twenty or thirty paces ; then the
word of command is given, and each man taking the best
aim he can, fires, and then throws down his rifle to seize
his pistol or yataghan. The lion is generally brought to
the ground by this hail of bullets, but unless the heart
or the brain have been pierced he will not be mortally
wounded ; the hunters therefore throw themselves upon
him before he can rise, firing, stabbing right and left,
blindly, madly, without aim, in the rage to kill. Sometimes in his mortal agony the lion will seize one of the
hunters, and, drawing him under his own body, will
torture him, almost as a cat does a mouse before killing
it. Should this happen, the nearest relation present
of the unhappy man will risk his own life in the
attempt to rescue him, and at the same time to put an
end to the lion. This is a perilous moment ; when the
lion sees the muzzle of the avenger's rifle pointed at his
ear he will certainly crush in the head of his victim,
even if he has not the strength left to spring on his assailant before the latter gives him the *coup de grâce*.

The Arabs in the neighbourhood of Constantine used,
about fifty years ago, to send there for a famous French
lion-hunter, Jules Gérard by name, to rid them of some
unusually formidable foe. They never could understand
his way of going to work—alone and by night—which
certainly presented a great contrast to their methods.
On one occasion a family of five—father, mother, and three
young lions—were the aggressors. The Arab sheik, leading Monsieur Gérard to the river, showed him by their
footprints on the banks where this fearful family were in

the habit of coming to drink at night, but begged him not
to sacrifice himself to such fearful odds, and either to
return to the camp, or to take some of the tribe with him.
Gérard declining both suggestions, the sheik was obliged
to leave, as night was at hand, and the lions might appear
at any moment. First he came near the hunter, and
spoke these words low : 'Listen, I have a counsel to give
thee. Be on thy guard against the Lord of the Mighty
Head ; he will lead the way. If thy hour has come, he
will kill thee, and the others will eat thee.' Coming still
nearer the sheik whispered : ' *He* has stolen my best mare
and ten oxen.' 'Who? who has stolen them?' asked
Monsieur Gérard. '*He*,' and the sheik pointed for
further answer to the mountain. 'But name him, name
the thief.' The answer was so low as to be barely audible :
'The Lord of the Mighty Head,' and with this ominous
counsel the sheik departed, leaving Gérard to his vigil.

As the night advanced the moon appeared, and lit up
the narrow ravine. Judging by its position in the
heavens it might be eleven o'clock, when the tramp of
many feet was heard approaching, and several luminous
points of reddish light were seen glittering through the
thicket. The lions were advancing in single file, and the
lights were their gleaming eyes. Instead of five there
were only three, and the leader, though of formidable
dimensions, did not come up to the description of the
Lord of the Mighty Head. All three stopped to gaze in
wonder at the man who dared to put himself in their path.
Gérard took aim at the shoulder of the leader and fired.
A fearful roar announced that the shot had told, and the
wounded lion began painfully dragging himself towards
his assailant, while the other two slunk away into the
wood. He had got to within three paces when a second
shot sent him rolling down into the bed of the stream.
Again he returned to the charge, but a third ball right in
the eye laid him dead. It was a fine, large, young lion of
three years, with formidable teeth and claws. As agreed

'ALL THREE STOPPED TO GAZE AT THE MAN WHO DARED TO PUT HIMSELF IN THEIR PATH'

upon with the sheik, Monsieur Gérard immediately lit a
bonfire in token of his victory, in answer to which shots were
fired to communicate the good news to all the surrounding district. At break of day two hundred Arabs arrived
to insult their fallen enemy, the sheik being the first to
appear, with his congratulations, but also with the information that at the same hour that the young lion had been
shot, the Lord of the Mighty Head had come down and
taken away an ox. These devastations went on unchecked
for more than a year, one man alone, Lakdar by name,
being robbed of forty-five sheep, a mare, and twenty-nine
oxen. Finally he lost heart, and sent to beg Monsieur
Gérard to come back and deliver him if possible of his
tormentor. For some nights the lion made no sign, but
on the thirteenth evening Lakdar arrived at the lion-
hunter's camp, saying : ' The black bull is missing from
the herd ; to-morrow morning I shall find his remains and
thou wilt slay the lion for me.'

Accordingly next morning at dawn Lakdar returned
to announce that he had found the dead bull. Gérard
rose and, taking his gun, followed the Arab. Through
the densest of the forest they went, till at the foot of a
narrow rocky ravine, close to some large olive trees, they
found the partially devoured carcase. Monsieur Gérard
cut some branches the better to conceal himself, and took
up his position under one of the olive trees, there to await
the approach of night, and with it the return of the lion
to the spoil. Towards eight o'clock, when the feeble light
of the new moon barely penetrated into the little glade, a
branch was heard to crack at some distance. The lion-
hunter rose and, shouldering his weapon, prepared to do
battle. From about thirty paces distant came a low growl,
and then a guttural sound, a sign of hunger with the lion,
then silence, and presently an enormous lion stalked from
the thicket straight towards the bull, and began licking
it. At this moment Monsieur Gérard fired, and struck
the lion within about an inch of his left eye. Roaring

with pain, he reared himself up on end, when a second bullet right in the chest laid him on his back, frantically waving his huge paws in the air. Quickly reloading, Monsieur Gérard came close to the helpless monster, and while he was raising his great head from the ground fired two more shots, which laid the lion stone dead, and thus brought to an end the career of the 'Lord of the Mighty Head.'

BUILDERS AND WEAVERS

No one can examine birds and their ways for long together without being struck by the wonderful neatness and cleverness of their proceedings. They make use of a great many different kinds of materials for their nests, and manage somehow to turn out a nest which not only will hold eggs, but is strong and of a pretty shape. Rotten twigs are, curiously enough, what they love best for the outside, and upon the twigs various substances are laid, according to the species and taste of the builder. The jay, for instance, collects roots and twists them into a firm mass, which he lays upon the twigs ; the American starling uses tough wet rushes and coarse grass, and after they are matted together, somehow ties the nest on to reeds or a bush ; while the missel thrush lines the casing of twigs with tree moss, or even hay. To these they often add tufts of wool, and lichen, and the whole is fastened together by a kind of clay. The favourite spot chosen by the missel thrush is the fork of a tree in an orchard, where lichens are large and plentiful enough to serve as a covering for the nests.

Still, if the account given by Vaillant and Paterson is true, the sociable grosbeaks surpass all the other birds in skill and invention. They have been known to cover the trunks of trees with a huge kind of fluted umbrella, made of dry, fine grass, with the boughs of the trees poking through in various places. No doubt in the beginning the nest was not so large, but it is the custom of these

birds to live together in clans, and each year fresh 'rooms'
have to be added. When examined, the bird city was
found to have many gates and regular streets of nests,
each about two inches distant from the other. The
structure was made of ' Boshman's ' grass alone, but so
tightly woven together that no rain could get through.
The nests were all tucked in under the roof, which, by
projecting, formed eaves, thus keeping the birds warm and
dry. Sometimes the umbrella has been known to contain
as many as three hundred separate nests, so it is no
wonder that the tree at last breaks down with the weight,
and the city has to be founded again elsewhere.

Now in the nests of all these birds there has been a
good deal of what we called ' building ' and ' carpentry '
when we are talking of our own houses and our own
trades. But there are a whole quantity of birds spread
over the world, who are almost exclusively weavers, and
can form nests which hang down from the branch of a
tree without any support. To this class belongs the
Indian sparrow, which prefers to build in the tops of the
very highest trees (especially on the Indian fig) and particularly on those growing by the river-side. He weaves
together tough grass in the form of a bottle, and hangs it
from a branch, so that it rocks to and fro, like a hammock.
The Indian sparrow, which is easily tamed, does not
like always to live with his family, so he divides his nest
into two or three parts, and is careful to place its entrance
underneath, so that it may not attract the notice of the
birds of prey. In these nests glow-worms have frequently
been found, carefully fastened into a piece of fresh clay,
but whether the bird deliberately tries in this way to light
up his dark nest, or whether he has some other use for
the glow-worm, has never been found out. But it seems
quite certain that he does not *eat* it, as Sir William Jones
once supposed.

The Indian sparrow is a very clever little bird, and
can be taught to do all sorts of tricks. He will catch a

ring that is dropped into one of the deep Indian wells.
before it reaches the water. He can pick the gold ornament
neatly off the forehead of a young Hindu woman, or carry
a note to a given place like a carrier pigeon. At least so
it is said; but then very few people have even a bowing
acquaintance with the Indian sparrow.

'MORE FAITHFUL THAN FAVOURED'

THERE never was a more faithful watch-dog than the
great big-limbed, heavy-headed mastiff that guarded Sir
Harry Lee's Manor-house, Ditchley, in Oxfordshire.[1] The
sound of his deep growl was the terror of all the gipsies
and vagrants in the county, and there was a superstition
among the country people, that he was never known to
sleep. Even if he was seen stretched out on the stone
steps leading up to the front entrance of the house, with
his massive head resting on his great fore-paws, at the
sound of a footfall, however distant, his head would be
raised, his ears fiercely cocked, and an ominous stiffening
of the tail would warn a stranger that his movements
were being closely watched, and that on the least suspicion
of anything strange or abnormal in his behaviour, he
would be called to account by Leo. Strangely enough,
the mastiff had never been a favourite of his master's.
The fact that dogs of his breed are useless for purposes of
sport, owing to their unwieldy size and defective sense
of smell, had prevented Sir Harry from taking much notice of him. He looked upon the mastiff merely as a
watch-dog. The dog would look after him, longing to be
allowed to join him in his walk, or to follow him when
he rode out, through the lanes and fields round his house,
but poor Leo's affection received little encouragement.
So long as he guarded the house faithfully by day and

[1] More about this gentleman and his dog may be read in *Wood-
stock*, by Sir Walter Scott.

night, that was all that was expected of him: and as in doing this he was only doing his duty, and fulfilling the purpose for which he was there, little notice was taken of him by any of the inmates of the house. His meals were supplied to him with unfailing regularity, for his services as insuring the safety of the house were fully recognised; but as Sir Harry had not shown him any signs of favour, the servants did not think fit to bestow unnecessary attention on him. So he lived his solitary neglected life, in summer and winter, by night and day, zealous in his master's interests, but earning little reward in the way of notice or affection.

One night, however, something occurred that suddenly altered the mastiff's position in the household, and from being a faithful slave, he all at once became the beloved friend and constant companion of Sir Harry Lee. It was in winter, and Sir Harry was going up to his bedroom as usual, about eleven o'clock. Great was his astonishment on opening the library door, to find the mastiff stretched in front of it. At sight of his master Leo rose, and, wagging his tail and rubbing his great head against Sir Harry's hand, he looked up at him as if anxious to attract his attention. With an impatient word Sir Harry turned away, and went up the oak-panelled staircase, Leo following closely behind him. When he reached his bedroom door, the dog tried to follow him into the room, and if Sir Harry had been a more observant man, he must have noticed a curious look of appeal in the dog's eyes, as he slammed the door in his face, ordering him in commanding tones to 'Go away!' an order which Leo did not obey. Curling himself up on the mat outside the door, he lay with his small deep-sunk eyes in eager watchfulness, fixed on the door, while his heavy tail from time to time beat an impatient tattoo upon the stone floor of the passage.

Antonio, the Italian valet, whom Sir Harry had brought home with him from his travels, and whom he trusted absolutely, was waiting for his master, and was engaged in spreading out his things on the toilet table.

'That dog is getting troublesome, Antonio,' said Sir Harry. 'I must speak to the keeper to-morrow, and tell him to chain him up at night outside the hall. I cannot have him disturbing me, prowling about the corridors and passages all night. See that you drive him away, when you go downstairs.'

'Yes, signor,' replied Antonio, and began to help his master to undress. Then, having put fresh logs of wood on the fire, he wished Sir Harry good-night, and left the room. Finding Leo outside the door, the valet whistled and called gently to him to follow him; and, as the dog took no notice, he put out his hand to take hold of him by the collar. But a low growl and a sudden flash of the mastiff's teeth, warned the Italian of the danger of resorting to force. With a muttered curse he turned away, determined to try bribery where threats had failed. He thought that if he could secure a piece of raw meat from the kitchen, he would have no difficulty in inducing the dog to follow him to the lower regions of the house, where he could shut him up, and prevent him from further importuning his master.

Scarcely had Antonio's figure disappeared down the passage, when the mastiff began to whine in an uneasy manner, and to scratch against his master's door. Disturbed by the noise, and astonished that his faithful valet had disregarded his injunctions, Sir Harry got up and opened the door, on which the mastiff pushed past him into the room, with so resolute a movement that his master could not prevent his entrance. The instant he got into the room, the dog's uneasiness seemed to disappear. Ceasing to whine, he made for the corner of the room where the bed stood in a deep alcove, and, crouching down, he slunk beneath it, with an evident determination to pass the night there. Much astonished, Sir Harry was too sleepy to contest the point with the dog, and allowed him to remain under the bed, without making any further attempt to dislodge him from the strange and unfamiliar resting-place he had chosen.

When the valet returned shortly after with the piece of meat with which he hoped to tempt the mastiff downstairs, he found the mat deserted. He assumed that the dog had abandoned his caprice of being outside his master's door, and had betaken himself to his usual haunts in the basement rooms and passages of the house.

Whether from the unaccustomed presence of the dog in his room, or from some other cause, Sir Harry Lee was a long time in going to sleep that night. He heard the different clocks in the house strike midnight, and then one o'clock; and as he lay awake watching the flickering light of the fire playing on the old furniture and on the dark panels of the wainscot, he felt an increasing sense of irritation against the dog, whose low, regular breathing showed that he, at any rate, was sleeping soundly. Towards two in the morning Sir Harry must have fallen into a deep sleep, for he was quite unconscious of the sound of stealthy steps creeping along the stone corridor and pausing a moment on the mat outside his room. Then the handle of the door was softly turned, and the door itself, moving on its well-oiled hinges, was gently pushed inward. In another moment there was a tremendous scuffle beneath the bed, and with a great bound the mastiff flung himself on the intruder, and pinned him to the floor. Startled by the unexpected sounds, and thoroughly aroused, Sir Harry jumped up, and hastily lit a candle. Before him on the floor lay Antonio, with the mastiff standing over him, uttering his fierce growls, and showing his teeth in a dangerous manner. Stealthily the Italian stole out his hand along the floor, to conceal something sharp and gleaming that had fallen from him, on the dog's unexpected onslaught, but a savage snarl from Leo warned him to keep perfectly still. Calling off the mastiff, who instantly obeyed the sound of his master's voice, though with bristling hair and stiffened tail he still kept his eyes fixed on the Italian, Sir Harry demanded from the valet the cause of his unexpected intrusion into his bedroom at that hour, and in that way. There was so much embarrassment and hesitation in Antonio's reply,

'AND PINNED HIM TO THE GROUND'

that Sir Harry's suspicions were aroused. In the meantime the unusual sounds at that hour of the night had awakened the household. Servants came hurrying along the passage to their master's room. Confronted by so many witnesses, the Italian became terrified and abject, and stammered out such contradictory statements, that it was impossible to get at the truth of his story, and Sir Harry saw that the only course open to him was to have the man examined and tried by the magistrate.

At the examination the wretched valet confessed that he had entered his master's room with the intention of murdering and robbing him, and had only been prevented by the unexpected attack of the mastiff.

Among the family pictures in the possession of the family of the Earls of Lichfield, the descendants of Sir Harry Lee, there is a full-length portrait of the knight with his hand on the head of the mastiff, and beneath this legend, 'More faithful than favoured.'

DOLPHINS, TURTLES, AND COD

STORIES FROM AUDUBON [1]

IN the excellent life of Mr. Audubon, the American naturalist (published in 1868 by Sampson Low, Marston &
Co.), some curious stories are to be found respecting the
kinds of fish that he met with in his voyages both through
the Atlantic and the Gulf of Mexico.   Audubon's remarks
about the habits of dolphins are specially interesting, and
will be read with pleasure by everybody who cares for
' the sea and all that in them is.'

Dolphins abound in the Gulf of Mexico and the neighbouring seas, and are constantly to be seen chasing flying
fish, which are their food.   Flying fish can swim more
rapidly than the dolphins, which of course are far larger
creatures ; but if they find themselves much outnumbered,
and in danger of being surrounded, they spread the fins
that serve them for wings, and fly through the air for a
short distance.   At first this movement throws out the
dolphins, who are unable to follow the example of their
prey, but they soon contrive to keep up with the flying
fish by giving great bounds into the air ; and as the flying
fish's powers are soon exhausted, it is not long before the
hunt comes to an end and the dolphins seize the fish as
they tumble into the sea.

Sailors are fond of catching dolphins, and generally
bait their hooks with a piece of shark's flesh.   When the
fish is taken, its friends stay round it till the last moment,

[1] From *Audubon's Life*, by Robert Buchanan. Sampson Low & Co.

only swimming away as the dolphin is hauled on board. For its size, which is generally about three feet long and has rarely been known to exceed four feet, the dolphin has a remarkably good appetite, and sometimes he eats so much that he is unable to escape from his enemy, the bottle-nosed porpoise. A dolphin that was caught in the Gulf of Mexico was opened by the sailors, and inside him were counted twenty-two flying fish, each one six or seven inches long, and all arranged quite neatly with their tails foremost. Before they have their dinner they are full of fun, and their beautiful blue and gold bodies may often be seen leaping and bounding and diving about the ship—a sight which the sailors always declare portends a gale. Indeed, the stories to which dolphins give rise are many and strange. The negroes believe that a silver coin fried or boiled in the same water as the fish, will turn into copper if the dolphin is in a state unfit for food ; but as no one can swear that he has ever seen the transmutation of the metal, it may be suspected that the tale was invented by the cook for the sake of getting an extra dollar.

About eighty miles from the Peninsula of Florida are a set of low, sandy banks known as the *Tortuga* or *Turtle Islands*, from the swarms of turtles which lay their eggs in the sand, and are eagerly sought for by traders.

Turtles are of many sorts, but the green turtle is considered the best, and is boiled down into soup, which is both rich and strengthening. They are cautious creatures, and never approach the shore in the daylight, or without watching carefully for some time to see if the coast is indeed clear. They may be seen on quiet moonlight nights in the months of May and June, lying thirty or forty yards from the beach, listening intently, and every now and then making a loud hissing noise intended to frighten any enemies that may be lurking near. If their quick ears detect any sound,

however faint, they instantly dive and swim to some
other place; but if nothing is stirring, they land on the
shore, and crawl slowly about with the aid of their flappers,
until they find a spot that seems suitable for the hatching
of their eggs, which often number two hundred, laid at
one time. The operations are begun by the turtle scoop-
ing out a hole in the burning sand by means of her hind
flappers, using them each by turns, and throwing up the
sand into a kind of rampart behind her. This is done so
quickly that in less than ten minutes she will often have
dug a hole varying from eighteen inches to two feet.
When the eggs are carefully placed in separate layers,
the loose sand is laid over them, and the hole not only
completely hidden but made to look exactly like the rest
of the beach, so that no one could ever tell that the surface
had been disturbed at all. Then the turtle goes away and
leaves the hot sand to do the rest.

In course of time the young turtles, hardly bigger
than a five-shilling piece, leave their shells, and make
their way to the water, unless, before they are hatched,
their nest has been discovered by men, or by the
cougars and other wild animals, who feed greedily on
them. If they belong to the tribe of the green turtles,
they will at once begin to seek for sea plants, and
especially a kind of grass, which they bite off near the
roots, so as to get the tenderest parts. If they are young
hawk-bills, they will nibble the seaweed, and soon go on to
crabs and shell-fish, and even little fishes. The logger-
heads grow a sharp beak, which enables them to crack the
great conch shells, and dig out the fish that lives inside,
while the trunk turtle, which is often of an immense size
but with a very soft body, loves sea-urchins and shell-fish.
All of them can swim so fast that they often seem to be
flying, and it needs much quickness of eye and hand to
spear them in the water. Even to catch them on shore
is a matter of great difficulty, and in general more than
one man is required for the service. The turtle is raised

up from behind by a man on his knee, pushing with all his might against her shoulder; but this has to be done with great caution, or else the hunter may get badly bitten. When the turtle is fully raised up, she is thrown over on her back, and, like a sheep in a similar position, can seldom recover herself without help. The turtles, when caught, are put into an enclosure of logs with a sandy or muddy bottom through which the tide flows, and here they are kept and fed by their captors till they are ready for the market. Unlike most creatures, their price is out of all proportion to their weight, and a loggerhead turtle weighing seven hundred pounds has been known to cost no more than a green turtle of thirty.

Early in May, and well into June, the seas extending northwards from Maine to Labrador are alive with ships just starting for the cod fishing. Their vessels are mostly small but well stocked, and a large part of the space below is filled with casks, some full of salt and others empty. These empty ones are reserved for the oil that is procured from the cod.

Every morning, as soon as it is light, some of the crew of each ship enters a small boat, which can be sailed or rowed as is found necessary. When they reach the cod banks every man boards up part of his boat for the fish when caught, and then takes his stand at the end with two lines, baited at the opening of the season with salted mussels, and later with gannets or capelings. These lines are dropped into the sea on either side of the boat, and when the gunwale is almost touching the water and it is dangerous to put in any more fish, they give up work for the morning and return to the harbour. In general, fishing is a silent occupation, but cod fishers are rather a talkative race, and have bets with each other as to the amount of the 'takes' of the respective crews. When they get back to their vessels, often anchored eight or ten miles away, they find that the men who have been left behind have set up long tables on deck, carried the salt barrels on shore, placed all ready the casks for the livers, and cleared the hold of everything but a huge wedge of salt for the salting. Then, after dinner, some of the men row back to the cod banks, while the others set about cleaning, salting, and packing the fish, so as to be quite finished when the men return from their second journey. It is almost always midnight before the work is done, and the men can turn in for their three hours' sleep.

If, as often happens, the hauls have been very large, the supply soon threatens to become exhausted, so on Sunday the captain sails off for a fresh bank. Then, the men who are the laziest or most unskilful in the matter of fishing take out the cargo that has been already salted, and lay it out on scaffolds which have been set up on the rocks. When the sun has dried the fish for some time, they are turned over ; and this process is repeated several times in the day. In the evening they are piled up into large stacks, and protected from the rain and wind. In July the men's work is in one way less hard than before, for this is the season when the capelings arrive to spawn upon the shores, and where capelings are, cod are sure to follow. Now great nets are used, with one end fastened to the land, and these nets will sometimes produce twenty or thirty thousand fish at a haul.

With so many men engaged in the cod fishing, and considering the number of diseases to which cod are subject, it is perhaps quite as well that each fish should lay such a vast supply of eggs, though out of the eight million laid by one fish which have been counted, it is calculated that, from various causes, only about a hundred thousand come to maturity.

MORE ABOUT ELEPHANTS [1]

LONG, long ago, when the moon was still young, and
some of the stars that we know best were only gradually
coming into sight, the earth was covered all over with a
tangle of huge trees and gigantic ferns, which formed the
homes of all sorts of enormous beasts. There were no
men, only great animals and immense lizards, whose
skeletons may still be found embedded in rocks or frozen
deep down among the Siberian marshes; for, after the
period of fearful heat, when everything grew rampant,
even in the very north, there came a time of equally intense cold, when every living creature perished in many
parts of the world.

When the ice which crushed down life on the earth
began to melt, and the sun once more had power to pierce
the thick cold mists that had shrouded the world, animals
might have been seen slowly creeping about the young
trees and fresh green pastures, but their forms were
no longer the same as they once were. The enormous
frames of all sorts of huge monsters, and the great
lizard called the ichthyosaurus, had been replaced by
smaller and more graceful creatures, who could move
lightly and easily through this new world. But changed
though it seemed to be, one beast still remained to tell the
story of those strange old times, and that was the elephant.

Now anybody who has ever stood behind a big, clumsy
cart-horse going up a hill cannot fail to have been struck
with its likeness to an elephant; and it is quite true that

[1] From *The Wild Elephant.* Sir J. Emerson Tennent.

elephants and horses are nearly related.   Of course in the
East, where countries are so big and marches are so long,
it is necessary to have an animal to ride of more strength
and endurance than a horse, and so elephants, who are,
when well treated, as gentle as they are strong, were very
early trained as beasts of burden, or even as ' men-of-war.'

In their wild condition they have a great many curious habits.   They roam about the forests of India or
Africa in herds, and each herd is a real family, who have
had a common grandfather.   The elephants are very
particular as to the number of their herd; it is never less
than ten, or more than twenty-one, but being very sociable
they easily get on terms of civility with other herds, and
several of these groups may be seen moving together towards some special pond or feeding ground.   But friendly
as they often are, each clan keeps itself as proudly distinct from the rest as if they were all Highlanders.   Any
unlucky elephant who has lost his own herd, and tries to
attach himself to a new one, is scouted and beaten away
by every member of the tribe, till, like a man who is
punished and scorned for misfortunes he cannot help, the
poor animal grows desperate, and takes to evil courses,
and is hunted down under the name of ' a rogue.'

Elephants have a great idea of law and order, and
carefully choose a leader who is either strong enough or
clever enough to protect the herd against its enemies.
Even a female has sometimes been chosen, if her wisdom
has been superior to that of the rest; but male or female,
the leader once fixed upon, the herd never fails to give
him absolute obedience, and will suffer themselves to be
killed in their efforts to save his life.

As everyone knows, during the dry season in India
water becomes very scarce, and even the artificial tanks
that have been built for reservoirs are very soon empty.
About the middle of this century, an English officer,
Major Skinner by name, had drawn up to rest on the em-
bankment of a small Indian tank, which, low though it

'LONG, LONG AGO,' THE ELEPHANT DREAMS OF HIS OLD COMPANIONS

was, contained the only water to be found for a great distance. On three sides of the tank there was a clearing, but on the fourth lay a very thick wood, where the herd lay encamped all day, waiting for darkness to fall, so that they might all go to drink. Major Skinner knew the habits of elephants well, and what to expect of them, so he sent all his natives to sleep, and climbed himself into a large tree that sheltered the tank at one corner. However, it appeared that the elephants were unusually cautious that night, for he sat in his tree for two hours before a sound was heard, though they had been lively enough as long as the sun was shining.

Suddenly a huge elephant forced his way through the thickest part of the forest, and advanced slowly to the tank, his ears at full cock, and his eyes glancing stealthily round. He gazed longingly at the water for some minutes, but did not attempt to drink—perhaps he felt it would be a mean advantage to take of his comrades—and then he quietly retraced his steps backwards till he had put about a hundred yards between himself and the water, when five elephants came out of the jungle and joined him. These he led forward, listening carefully as before, and placed them at certain spots where they could command a view both of the open country and the forest. This done, and the safety of the others provided for, he went to fetch the main body of the herd, which happened to be four or five times as large as usual. Silently, as if preparing for an assault, the whole of this immense body marched up to where the scouts were standing, when a halt was signalled, so that the leader might for the last time make sure that no hidden danger, in the shape of man, lion, or tiger, awaited them. Then permission was given, and with a joyful toss of their trunks in the air, in they dashed, drinking, wallowing, and rolling over with delight, till one would have thought it had been years since they had tasted a drop of water, or known the pleasures of a bath.

From his perch in the tree Major Skinner had been

watching with interest the movements of the herd, and when he saw that they had really had their fill, he gently broke a little twig and threw it on the ground. It seemed hardly possible that such a tiny sound could reach the ears of those great tumbling, sucking bodies, but in one instant they were all out of the tank, and tearing towards the forest, almost carrying the little ones between them.

Of course it is not always that elephants can find tanks without travelling many hundreds of miles after them, and on these occasions their wonderful sagacity comes to their aid. They will pause on the banks of some dried-up river, now nothing but a sandy tract, and feel instinctively that underneath that sand is the water for which they thirst. But then, how to get at it? The elephants know as well as any engineer that if they tried to dig a hole straight down, the weight of their bodies would pull down the whole side of the pit with them, so that is of no use. In order to get round this difficulty, long experience has taught them that they must make one side to their well a gentle slope, and when this is done they can wait with perfect comfort for the water, whose appearance on the surface is only a question of time.

Much might be written about the likes and dislikes of elephants, which seem as a rule to be as motiveless as the likes and dislikes of human beings. Till they are tamed and treated kindly by some particular person, elephants show a decided objection to human beings, and in Ceylon have a greater repugnance to a white skin than to a brown one. In fact, they are shy of anything new or strange, but will put up with any animal to which they are accustomed. Elks, pigs, deer, and buffaloes are their feeding companions, and the elephants take no more notice of their presence than if they were so many canaries. Indeed, as far as can be gathered, the elephant is much more afraid of the little domestic animals with which it is quite unacquainted than of the huge vegetable-eating beasts with which both it and its forefathers were on

intimate terms.   Goats and sheep it eyes with annoyance ;
they are new creatures, and were never seen in jungles or
forests ; but, bad as they might be, dogs, the shadows of

THE ELEPHANT FALLS ON HIS KNEES BEFORE THE LITTLE SCOTCH TERRIER

men, were worse still.   They were so quick, so lively, and had such hideous high voices, which they were always using, not keeping them for special occasions like any self-respecting quadruped.   Really they might almost as well be parrots with their incessant chatter.   But of all kinds of dogs, surely the one called a Scotch terrier was the most alarming and detestable.   One day an animal of this species actually seized the trunk of an elephant in its teeth, and the elephant was so surprised and frightened that it fell on its knees at once.   At this the dog was a little frightened too, and let go, but recovered itself again as the elephant rose slowly to its feet, and prepared to charge afresh.   The elephant, not knowing what to make of it, backed in alarm, hitting out at the dog with its front paws, but taking care to keep his wounded trunk well beyond its reach.   At last, between fright and annoyance he lost his head completely, and would have fairly run away if the keeper had not come in and put a stop to the dog's fun.

If Æsop had known elephants—or Scotch terriers—he might have made a fable out of this; but they had not visited Greece in his day.

BUNGEY [1]

DURING the reigns of Queen Elizabeth and James, there lived a brave and accomplished knight called Sir John Harington, who had been knighted on the field of battle by the famous Earl of Essex, and had translated into English a long poem, by an Italian called Ariosto. But busy though he was in so many ways, Sir John still had time to spare for his 'raw dogge' Bungey, and in the year 1608 he writes a long letter to Prince Henry, elder brother of Charles I., full of the strange doings of his favourite. Bungey seems to have been used by Sir John as a sort of carrier pigeon, and he tells how he would go from Bath to Greenwich Palace, to 'deliver up to the cowrte there such matters as were entrusted to his care.' The nobles of the court made much of him, and sometimes gave him errands of their own, and it was never told to their 'Ladie Queen, that this messenger did ever blab ought concerning his highe truste, as others have done in more special matters.' More wonderful even than this was his behaviour concerning two sacks of wheat which Bungey had been commissioned by Sir John's servant Combe, to carry from Bath to his own house at Kelston, a few miles distant. The sacks were tied round the dog's body by cords, but on the way the cords got loose, and Bungey, clever though he was, could not tie them up again. However he was not to be beaten, and hiding one 'flasket' in some bushes that grew near by, he bore the other in his teeth to Kelston, and then returning, fetched the hidden one out of the rushes and

' From Jesse's *British Dogs*.

arrived with it in good time for dinner. Sir John is plainly rather afraid that Prince Henry may not quite believe this instance of sagacity, for he adds, ' Hereat your Highnesse may perchance marvell and doubte ; but we have living testimonie of those who wroughte in the fields, and espied his work, and now live to tell they did muche long to plaie the dogge, and give stowage to the wine themselves, but they did refraine, and watchede the passinge of this whole business.'

As may well be guessed, the fame of Bungey's talents soon spread, and then, as now, there were many dog stealers in the country. On one occasion, as Sir John was riding from Bath to London, Bungey was tempted to leave his side by the sight of a pond swarming with wild duck or mallard. Unluckily other people besides Bungey thought it good sport to hunt wild fowl, and did not mind seizing valuable dogs, so poor Bungey was caught and bound, till it could be settled who would give the highest price for him.

At last his captors decided that they would take him to London, which was not very far off, and trust to chance for finding a buyer. As it happened, the Spanish Ambassador was on the look out for a dog of that very kind, and he was so pleased with Bungey, that he readily agreed to give the large sum asked by the men who brought him. Now Bungey was a dog who always made the best of things, and as Sir John tells the Prince, ' suche was the courte he did pay to the Don, that he was no lesse in good likinge there than at home.' In fact, everybody grew so fond of him, that when after six weeks Sir John discovered where he was and laid claim to him, no one in the house could be prevailed on to give him up. Poor Sir John, who, as we know, was very much attached to Bungey, was at his wit's end what to do, when it suddenly occurred to him to let the dog himself prove who was his real master. So, having the Ambassador's leave to what he wished in the matter, he called all the company together at dinner-time,

and bade Bungey go into the hall where dinner was already
served, and bring a pheasant from the dish. This, as Sir
John says, ' created much mirthe ; but much more, when
he returned at my commandment to the table, and put it
again in the same cover.' After such a proof there was
no more to be said, and Sir John was allowed to be the
dog's master. But Bungey's life was not destined to be
a very long one, and his death was strange and sudden.
As he and his master were once more on the road from

BUNGEY AT THE SPANISH AMBASSADOR'S HOUSE

London to Bath on their return journey, he began jumping
up on the horse's neck, and ' was more earneste in fawn-
inge and courtinge my notice, than what I had observed
for time backe ; and after my chidinge his disturbing my
passinge forwardes, he gave me some glances of such
affection as moved me to cajole him ; but alas ! he crept
suddenly into a thorny brake, and died in a short time.'
    It is impossible to guess what kind of illness caused
the death of poor Bungey, but it is pleasant to think that

Sir John never forgot him, and also loved to talk of him to his friends. ' Now let Ulysses praise his dogge Argus,' he writes to Prince Henry, ' or Tobit be led by that dogge whose name doth not appear ; yet could I say such things of my Bungey as might shame them both, either for good faith, clear wit, or wonderful deedes ; to say no more than I have said of his bearing letters to London and Green-wich, more than a hundred miles. As I doubt not but your Highness would love my dogge, if not myselfe, I have been thus tedious in his storie ; and again saie, that of all the dogges near your father's courte, not one hathe more love, more diligence to please, or less paye for pleasinge, than him I write of.'

LIONS AND THEIR WAYS

ALTHOUGH it would not be safe to put one's self into the power of a lion, trusting to its generosity to make friends, there are a great many stories of the kindness of lions to other creatures which are perfectly true. One day, more than a hundred years ago, a lion cub only three months old was caught in one of the great forests near the river Senegal, and brought to a Frenchman as a gift. The Frenchman, who was fond of animals, undertook to train it, and as the cub was very gentle and quiet this was easily done. He soon grew very fond of his master, and enjoyed being petted both by him and his friends, and what was more strange in a beast whose forefathers had passed all their lives in solitude, the lion hated being by himself. The more the merrier was clearly *his* motto, and whether the company consisted of dogs, cats, ducks, sheep, geese, or monkeys (which were his bedfellows), or men and women, did not matter to him ; and you may imagine his joy, when one night as he went to bed he found two little new-born pups in his straw. He was quite as pleased as if he had been their mother ; indeed he would hardly let the mother go near them, and when one of them died, he showed his grief in every possible way, and became still more attached to its brother.

After six months the lion, now more than a year old, was sent off to France, still with the little pup for company. At first his keepers thought that the strangeness of everything would make him frightened and savage,

¹ Bingley's *Animal Biography.*

but he took it all quite calmly and was soon allowed to roam about the ship as he pleased. Even when he landed at Havre, he only had a rope attached to his collar, and so he was brought to Versailles, the pup trotting happily by his side. Unfortunately, however, the climate of Europe did not agree with the dog as with the lion, for he gradually wasted away and died, to the terrible grief of his friend. Indeed he was so unhappy that another dog was put into the cage to make up for the lost one, but this dog was not used to lions, and only knew that they were said to be savage beasts, so he tried to hide himself. The lion, whose sorrow, as often happens, only made him irritable and cross, was provoked by the dog's want of confidence in his kindness, and just gave him one pat with his paw which killed him on the spot. But he still continued so sad, that the keepers made another effort, and this time the dog behaved with more sense, and coaxed the lion into making friends. The two lived happily together for many years, and the lion recovered some of his spirits, but he never forgot his first companion, or was quite the same lion again.

Many hundreds of miles south of Senegal a Hottentot who lived in Namaqualand was one evening driving down a herd of his master's cattle, to drink in a pool of water, which was fenced in by two steep walls of rock. It had been a particularly hot summer, and water was scarce, so the pool was lower than usual, and it was not until the whole herd got close to the brink, that the Hottentot noticed a huge lion, lying right in the water, preparing to spring. The Hottentot, thinking as well as his fright would let him think at all, that anything would serve as supper for the lion, dashed straight through the herd, and made as fast as he could for some trees at a little distance. But a low roar behind him told him that he had been wrong in his calculations, and that the lion was of opinion that man was nicer than bull. So he fled along as quickly as his trembling legs would let him, and just reached one of

'THE HOTTENTOT NOTICED A HUGE LION LYING IN THE WATER'

the tree aloes in which some steps had been cut by the
natives, as the lion bounded into the air. However the
man swung himself out of his enemy's range, and the lion
fell flat upon the ground. Now the branches of the tree
were covered with hundreds of nests of a kind of bird
called the Sociable Grosbeak, and it was to get these nests
that the natives had cut in the smooth trunk the steps
which had proved the salvation of the Hottentot. Behind
the shelter of the nests the Hottentot cowered, hoping
that when he was no longer seen, the lion would forget
him and go in search of other prey. But the lion seemed
inclined to do nothing of the sort. For a long while he
walked round and round the tree, and when he got tired
of that he lay down, resolved to tire the man out. The
Hottentot hearing no sound, peeped cautiously out, to see
if his foe was still there, and almost tumbled down in
terror to meet the eyes of the lion glaring into his. So
the two remained all through the night and through the
next day, but when sunset came again the lion could bear
his dreadful thirst no longer, and trotted off to the nearest
spring to drink. Then the Hottentot saw his chance,
and leaving his hiding place he ran like lightning to his
home, which was only a mile distant. But the lion did
not yield without a struggle ; and traces were afterwards
found of his having returned to the tree, and then scented
the man to within three hundred yards of his hut.

THE HISTORY OF JACKO I.

THE ship 'Roxalana' of Marseilles lay anchored in the Bay of Loando, which as we all know is situated in South Guinea. The 'Roxalana' was a merchant vessel, and a brisk traffic had been going on for some time with the exchange of the European goods with which the ship had been laden, for ivory and other native produce. All hands were very busy getting on board the various provisions and other stores needed for a long voyage, for it was in the days of sailing vessels only, and it would be some time before they could hope to return to Marseilles.

Now the captain of the 'Roxalana' was a mighty hunter, and seeing that all was going on well under the first officer's direction, he took his gun and a holiday and went up country for one more day's sport.

He was as successful as he was brave, and he had the great good luck to meet a tiger, a young hippopotamus, and a boa constrictor. All these terrible creatures fell before the unerring aim of the Provençal Nimrod, and after so adventurous a morning's work the captain naturally began to feel tired and hungry, so he sat down under the shade of some trees to rest and have some lunch.

He drew a flask of rum out of one pocket, and having uncorked it placed it on his right side; from his other pocket he produced a huge guava, which he laid on his left side, and finally he drew a great wedge of ship biscuit from his game bag and put it between his knees. Then he took out his tobacco pouch and began to fill his pipe

ANNOYANCE OF THE CAPTAIN ON FINDING HIS FLASK OF RUM UPSET

so as to have it ready at hand when he had finished his meal.

Imagine his surprise when, having filled his pipe, he found the flask had been upset and the guava had disappeared!

I am afraid the captain made use of some very strong language, but there was nothing for it but to make the best of the biscuit, the sole relic of his feast. As he munched it he warily turned his head from side to side, watching for the thief, when all of a sudden something fell upon his head. The captain put up his hand and found—the skin of his guava. Then he raised his eyes and saw a monkey dancing for joy at his own pranks in the tree just above him.

As I have already shown the captain was an excellent shot. Without stirring from his seat, he took up his gun and with a shot snapped the end of the branch on which his persecutor was sitting.

Down came branch and monkey, and the captain at once captured the latter before it had time to recover from the surprise of its rapid fall.

He was small and quite young, only half grown, but of a rather rare kind, as the captain, who had an ever-ready eye to the main chance, at once perceived.

'Ah ha!' said he, 'this little fellow will be worth fifty francs if he's worth a farthing by the time we get back to Marseilles.'

So saying he popped the monkey into his game-bag and buttoned it carefully up. Then, feeling that a piece of biscuit was not quite a sufficient lunch after the fatigues of his morning's sports, he retraced his steps and returned to his ship in company with his monkey, whom he named 'Jacko.'

Before leaving Loando the captain, who was fond of pets, bought a beautiful white cockatoo with a saffron crest and jet black beak. 'Cataqua' (that was his harmonious name) was indeed a lovely creature and extremely accomplished into the bargain. He spoke French, English, and Spanish equally well, and sang 'God save the King,' the 'Marseillaise,' and the Spanish National Anthem with great perfection.

The aptitude for languages made him a ready pupil, and his vocabulary was largely increased by daily association with the crew of the 'Roxalana,' so that before they had been very long at sea Cataqua swore freely in the purest Provençal, to the delight and admiration of his captain.

The captain was very fond of his two pets, and every morning, after inspecting the crew and giving each man his orders for the day, he would go up to Cataqua's cage, followed by Jacko, and give the cockatoo a lesson. When this was well said he would reward his pupil by sticking a lump of sugar between the wires of the cage, a reward which delighted Cataqua whilst it filled Jacko with jealousy.

He too loved sugar, and the moment the captain's back was turned he would draw near the cage and pull and pinch till the lump of sugar generally changed its destination, to the despair of Cataqua, who, crest erect and with brandished claw, rent the air with shrieks of rage mingled with angry oaths.

Jacko meanwhile stood by affecting an innocent air and gently sucking the sugar which he had stowed away in one of his pouches. Unluckily none of Cataqua's owners had taught him to cry 'stop thief' and he soon realised that if Jacko were to be punished he must see to it himself.

So one day, when the monkey after safely abstracting the sugar pushed a paw between the bars of the cage to gather up some remaining crumbs, Cataqua, who was gently swinging, head down, and apparently unconscious of what was going on, suddenly caught Jacko's thumb in his beak and bit it to the bone.

Jacko uttered a piercing shriek, rushed to the rigging

and climbed as far as he could, when he paused, clinging on by three paws and piteously brandishing the fourth in the air.

Dinner-time came, and the captain whistled for Jacko, but contrary to all customs no Jacko came. The captain whistled again, and this time he thought he heard an answering sound which seemed to come from the sky. He raised his eyes and beheld Jacko still waving his injured paw. Then began an exchange of signals, with the result that Jacko firmly refused to come down. Now the captain had trained his crew to habits of implicit obedience and had no notion of having his orders resisted by a monkey, so he took his speaking trumpet and called for Double Mouth.

Double Mouth was the cook's boy, and he had well earned his nickname by the manner in which he took advantage of his culinary position to make one meal before the usual dinner hour without its interfering in the least with his enjoyment of a second at the proper time. At the captain's call Double Mouth climbed on deck from the cook's galley and timidly approached his chief.

The captain, who never wasted words on his subordinates, pointed to Jacko, and Double Mouth at once began to give chase with an activity which proved that the captain had chosen well. As a matter of fact Jacko and Double Mouth were dear friends, the bond of sympathy which united them being one of greediness, for many a nice morsel Jacko had to thank the cook's boy for. So when the monkey saw who was coming, instead of trying to escape him he ran to meet him, and in a few minutes the two friends, one in the other's arms, returned to the deck where the captain awaited them.

The captain's one treatment for wounds of all kinds consisted of a *compress* steeped in some spirit, so he at once dipped a piece of rag in rum and bandaged the patient's thumb with it. The sting of the alcohol on the wound made Jacko dance with pain, but noticing that the moment the captain's back was turned Double Mouth rapidly swallowed the remains of the liquid in which the rag had been dipped, he realised that however painful as a dressing it might possibly be agreeable to the palate. He stretched out his tongue and very delicately touched the bandage with its tip. It was certainly rather nice, and he licked more boldly. By degrees the taste grew on him, and he ended by putting his thumb, bandage and all, into his mouth and sucking it bodily.

The result was that (the captain having ordered the bandage to be wetted every ten minutes) by the end of a couple of hours Jacko began to blink and to roll his head, and as the treatment continued he had at length to be carried off by Double Mouth, who laid him on his own bed.

Jacko slept without stirring for some hours. When he woke the first thing which met his eyes was Double Mouth busy plucking a fowl. This was a new sight, but Jacko seemed to be particularly struck by it on this occasion. He got up from the bed and came near, his eyes steadily fixed on the fowl, and carefully watched how the whole operation proceeded. When it was ended, feeling his head a little heavy still, he went on deck to take the air.

The weather was so settled and the wind so favourable that the captain thought it only a waste to keep the poultry on board alive too long, so he gave orders that a bird should be served daily for his dinner in addition to his usual rations. Soon after a great cackling was heard amongst the hencoops and Jacko climbed down from the yard where he was perched at such a rate that one might have thought he was hastening to the rescue. He tore into the kitchen, where he found Double Mouth already plucking a newly killed fowl, till not an atom of down was left on it.

Jacko showed the deepest interest in the process, and on returning to deck he, for the first time since his accident, approached Cataqua's cage, carefully keeping beyond range of his beak however. After strolling several times round, he at last seized a favourable moment and clutching hold of one of Cataqua's tail feathers, pulled hard till it came out regardless of the cockatoo's screams and flappings. This trifling experiment caused Jacko the greatest delight, and he fell to dancing on all fours, jumping up and falling back on the same spot which all his life was the way in which he showed his supreme content about anything.

Meantime the ship had long lost sight of land and was in full sail in mid ocean. It appeared unnecessary to the captain, therefore, to keep his cockatoo shut up in a cage, so he opened the door and released the prisoner, there being no means of escaping beyond the ship. Cataqua instantly took advantage of his freedom to climb to the top of one of the masts, where, with every appearance of rapture, he proceeded to regale the ship's company with his entire large and varied vocabulary, making quite as much noise by himself as all the five-and-twenty sailors who formed his audience.

Whilst this exhibition was taking place on deck a different scene was being enacted below. Jacko had as usual approached Double Mouth at plucking time, but this time the lad, who had noticed the extreme attention with which the monkey watched him, thought that possibly there might be some latent talent in him which it was a pity not to develop.

Double Mouth was one of those prompt and energetic persons who waste no time between an idea and its execution. Accordingly he quietly closed the door, put a whip into his pocket in case of need, and handed Jacko the duck he was about to pluck, adding a significant touch to the handle of the whip as a hint.

But Jacko needed neither hint nor urging. Without more ado he took the duck, placed it between his knees as he had seen his tutor do, and fell to with a will. As he found the feathers giving place to down and the down to skin, he became quite enthusiastic, so much so that when his task was done he fell to dancing for joy exactly as he had done the day before by Cataqua's cage.

Double Mouth was overjoyed for his part. He only regretted not having utilised Jacko's talents sooner, but he determined to do so regularly in the future. Next day the same operation took place, and on the third day, Double Mouth, recognising Jacko's genius, took off his own apron and tied it round his pupil, to whom from that moment he resigned the charge of preparing the poultry for the spit. Jacko showed himself worthy of the confidence placed in him, and by the end of a week he had quite distanced his teacher in skill and quickness.

Meantime the ship was nearing the Equator. It was a peculiarly sultry day, when the very sky seemed to sink beneath its own weight; not a creature was on deck but the man at the helm and Cataqua in the shrouds. The captain had flung himself into his hammock and was smoking his pipe whilst Double Mouth fanned him with a peacock's tail. Even Jacko seemed overcome by the heat, and instead of plucking his fowl as usual, he had placed it on a chair, taken off his apron, and appeared lost in slumber or meditation.

His reverie, however, did not last long. He opened his eyes, glanced round him, picked up a feather which he first stuck carelessly in his mouth and then dropped, and at length began to slowly climb the ladder leading on deck, pausing and loitering at each step. He found the deck deserted, which apparently pleased him, as he gave two or three little jumps whilst he glanced about to look for Cataqua, who with much gesticulation was singing ' God save the King ' at the top of his voice.

Then Jacko seemed to forget his rival's existence altogether, and began lazily to climb the rigging on the opposite side, where he indulged in various exercises, swinging by his tail head down, and generally appearing to have only come with a view to gymnastics. At length, seeing that Cataqua took no notice of him, he quietly sidled that way, and at the very moment that the performance of the English National Anthem was at its height, he seized the singer firmly with his left hand just where the wings join the body.

Cataqua uttered a wild note of terror, but no one was sufficiently awake to hear it.

'By all the winds of heaven!' exclaimed the captain suddenly. 'Here's a phenomenon—snow under the Equator!'

'No,' said Double Mouth, 'that's not snow, that's—ah, you rascal!' and he rushed towards the companion.

'Well, what is it then?' asked the captain, rising in his hammock.

'What is it?' cried Double Mouth from the top of the ladder. 'It's Jacko plucking Cataqua!'

The captain was on deck in two bounds, and with a shout of rage roused the whole crew from their slumbers.

'Well!' he roared to Double Mouth, 'what are you about, standing there? Come, be quick!'

Double Mouth did not wait to be told twice, but was up the rigging like a squirrel, only the faster he climbed the faster Jacko plucked, until when the rescuer reached the spot it was a sadly bare bird which he tore from Jacko's vindictive hands and carried back to his master.

Needless to say that Jacko was in dire disgrace after this exploit. However, in time he was forgiven and often amused the captain and crew with his pranks.

When the 'Roxalana' reached Marseilles after a quick and prosperous voyage, he was sold for seventy-five francs to Eugène Isabey the painter, who gave him to Flero for a Turkish hookah, who in his turn exchanged him for a Greek gun with Décamps.

SIGNORA AND LORI [1]

A GENTLEMAN living at Güstrow, in Mecklenburg, who
was very fond of animals, possessed a fine parrot, which
had beautiful plumage, and could talk better than most
of his kind. Besides the parrot, he had a poodle, called
Signora Patti, after the great singer, whom the gentleman
had once heard when he was upon a visit to Rostock;
after his return home he bestowed the name upon his
dear poodle.

Under the tuition of her master, the poodle began to
be an artist in her way. There was no trick performed
by dogs too difficult for her to learn. The parrot, whose
name was Lori, paid the greatest attention whilst the
Signora's lessons were going on, and he soon had all the
vocabulary, which the Signora carried in her head, not
only in his memory, but on his tongue.

When the dog was told by her master to ' go to the
baker,' then Lori could croak out the words also. Signora
Patti would hasten to fetch the little basket, seat herself
before her master, and, looking up at him with her wise
eyes, scrape gently upon the floor with her paw, which
signified: ' Please put in the money.' Her master
dropped in a few coins, the Signora ran quickly to the
baker with the basket, and brought it back filled with
little cakes; placing it before her master, she awaited her
reward, a good share of the dainties.

Often, for a variety in the lessons, she had to go to
the baker without money; then her master simply gave

[1] Translated from *Deutsche Blätter*, 1867. No. 10.

the order, 'on tick!' and the Signora, who knew that the
cakes would be sent, obeyed the command at once.

The parrot made a droll use of these practisings,
turning to account his knowledge of speech in the slyest
way. If he found himself alone with the poodle, who
was perhaps comfortably stretched on her cushion, Lori
would cry—imitating his master's voice—as if he quite
understood the joke: 'Go out!' Poor Patti would get

LORI REFUSES TO SHARE WITH THE SIGNORA

up in obedience to the order and slink out of the door
with her ears drooping. And immediately Lori would
whistle, just in the tone used by his master, and the
Signora then returned joyfully into the room.

But it was not only for pastime that Lori exercised
his gift; the cunning bird used it for the benefit of his
greedy beak. It began to happen often to the master to
find that his private account-book, carefully kept in the
smallest details, did not agree well with that of his

neighbour the baker. The Signora, declared the baker, had become most accomplished in the art of running up a long bill, and always, of course, at her master's orders. Only he, the master, when he looked over the reckoning, growled to himself : ' My neighbour is a rogue ; he chalks up the amount double.'

How very much was he astonished, then, and how quickly were his suspicions turned into laughter, when he beheld, through a half-open door, the following absurd scene.

It was one fine morning, and Lori sat upon the top of his cage, calling out in his shrillest tones : ' Signora, Signora ! ' The poodle hastened to present herself before him, wagging her tail, and Lori continued, ' Go to the baker.' The Signora fetched the little basket from its place, and put it before her tyrant, scratching her paw on the floor to ask for money.

' On tick ! ' was Lori's prompt and brief remark ; the Signora seized the basket, and rushed out of the door. Before long she returned, laid the basket, full of the little cakes, before the parrot, and looked with a beseeching air for the reward of her toil.

But the wicked Lori received her with a sharp ' get out,' putting her to flight, and proceeded to enjoy his ill-gotten gains in solitude.

OF THE LINNET, POPINJAY OR PARROT, AND OTHER BIRDS THAT CAN SPEAK

THE linnets be in manner the best birds of all others, howbeit, they be very docible. Do they will whatsoever they are taught and bidden, not only with their voice, but also with their feet and bills, as if they were hands. In the territory about Arelate (Arles) there is a bird called Taurus (because it loweth like a bull or cow, for otherwise a small bird it is). There is another also named Anthus, which likewise resembleth the neighing of horses; and if haply by the approach of horses they be driven from their grass whereof they feed, they will seem to neigh, and flying unto them, chase them away, and to be revenged of them again. But above all other birds of the air, the parrots pass for counterfeiting a man's voice, insomuch as they will seem to parle and prate our very speech. This fowl cometh out of the Indies; it is all the body over green, only it hath a collar about the neck of vermilion red, different from the rest of her feathers. The parrot can skill to salute emperors, and bid good-morrow: yea, and to pronounce what words she heareth. She loveth wine well, and when she hath drunk freely, is very pleasant and playful. She hath an head as hard as is her beak. When she learns to speak, she must be beaten about the head with a rod of iron; for otherwise she careth for no blows. When she taketh her flight down from any place, she lighteth upon her bill, and resteth thereupon, and by that means saveth her feet, which by nature are but weak and feeble, and so carrieth her own weight more lightly.

There is a certain pie, of nothing so great reckoning and account as the parrot, because she is not far set, but here by near at hand : howbeit, she pronounces that which is taught her more plainly and distinctly than the other. These take a love to the words that they speak ; for they not only learn them as a lesson, but they learn them with a delight and pleasure, insomuch that a man shall find them studying thereupon, and conning the said lesson ; and by their careful thinking upon that which they learn they show plainly how mindful and intentive they be thereto. It is for certain known that they have died for very anger and grief that they could not learn to pronounce some hard words ; as also unless they hear the same words repeated often unto them, their memory is so shittle, they will soon forget the same again. If they miss a word and have lost it, they will seek to call it again to remembrance ; and if they fortune to hear the same word in the meantime, they will wonderfully joy thereat. As for their beauty, it is not ordinary, although it be not very lovely. But surely amiable enough are they in this, that they can so well resemble man's speech. It is said that none of their kind are good to be made scholars, but such only as feed upon mast ; and among them, those that have five toes to their feet. But even these also are not fit for that purpose, after the first two years of their age. And their tongue is broader than ordinary ; like as they be all that counterfeit man's voice, each one in their kind, although it be in manner general to birds whatsoever to be broad-tongued.

Agrippina the Empress, wife to Claudius Cæsar, had a black-bird or a throstle at what time I compiled this book, which could counterfeit man's speech ; a thing never seen or known before. The two Cæsars also, the young princes (to wit, Germanicus and Drusus,) had one stare, and sundry nightingales, taught to parle Greek and Latin.

Moreover, they would study upon their lessons, and meditate all day long; and from day to day come out with new words still, yea, and are now able to continue a long speech and discourse.   Now for to teach them the better, these birds must be in a secret place apart by themselves, when they can hear no other voice; and one is to sit over them, who must repeat often that which he would have them to learn; yea, and please them also with giving them such meat as they best love.

PATCH AND THE CHICKENS

On a farm up in Durham, there were six little chickens who were deserted by the mother hen as soon as they were hatched. So the farmer's wife put them in a basket and carried them into the cottage to keep them warm by the fire.

There they were discovered by a smooth-coated terrier, named Patch, who was at that time very sad because her little puppy had just died, and she began to look after the chickens as if they were her own children. The little chicks also turned to her quite naturally for care and protection.

She used to treat them very gently, and would sit and watch them feed with the greatest interest. She would curl herself up, and then let them climb about her, and go to sleep between her paws. Sometimes she did not seem to consider the floor comfortable enough for her adopted family, and would jump on to a wooden settle which stood in the kitchen, and then with her feet she would pat the cushions into a cosy bed, and very carefully would take one chicken after another in her mouth, and place them on the softest part.

Soon the time came for the chickens to be sent out into the world.

One day when Patch was out for a walk they were taken to the farmyard.

When the poor little dog returned she was quite broken-hearted, and ran whining about the cottage. Then, as if seized with a sudden thought, she walked out of the door, and in a very short time she reappeared, followed by her feathered family, and again they took up their abode in the cottage. Every morning Patch used to take them out for a walk, and it was a most amusing sight to see the little terrier followed by a procession of six stately hens.

At last their living in the house became such an inconvenience to the farmer's wife that poor Patch's children had to be killed.

For some time Patch was very unhappy, and would still go into the farmyard to look for her six chickens.

THE FIERCE FALCON [1]

THERE are not nearly so many stories about birds as about dogs and cats, because birds can fly away, and it is more difficult to know what becomes of them. Perhaps, properly speaking, stories about birds have no business in a 'Beast Book,' but as long as the story is interesting, it does not do to be too particular.

A good many years ago, a gentleman named St. John was exploring the high hills near the source of the Findhorn, in Invernessshire, when he found a young falcon which was being reared as a pet by a shepherd boy, who gave her trout to eat. There was not much beauty about the falcon when Mr. St. John first saw her, for her plumage was dark-brown, with long-shaped spots on the breast, but in spite of that he took a fancy to her, and persuaded her master to sell her to him. When, however, she had passed her second birthday, and might be considered grown up, she put on all her finest feathers, and was very much admired by everyone. Her throat became a lovely soft cream colour, and the brown on her back changed into a lovely dark grey, while on her bosom, each little feather was crossed by a bar. But lovely though she was, Mr. St. John felt her to be a great care, for she was very strong as well as very brave, and would never think twice about attacking dogs or even people, if they offended her. As for the fowls, she soon made such short work of *them*, that her master was obliged to chain her up in the kitchen garden, which had hitherto formed the

[1] From *Wild Sports of the Highlands.* By C. St. John.

property of a tame owl. Luckily for the owl, the falcon at once made friends with him, and he was even allowed to finish up any of the falcon's dinner which she did not want herself.

Matters went quite smoothly for some weeks, and Mr. St. John was beginning to flatter himself that his pet was quieting down, and becoming quite a home bird, when one day a duck, tempted by the sight of the garden, whose gate had been carelessly left open, advanced a few steps along the path. Seeing nothing and nobody (for being daylight, the owl was asleep and the falcon too cunning to move) the duck became bolder, and walked merrily on, pecking at anything that took her fancy, and making funny little noises of satisfaction, unconscious of a pair of bright eyes that were watching her from behind a bush. Indeed, so absorbed was the duck in her afternoon tea, that she never even saw the falcon steal softly out and soar a little way up into the air, and suddenly swoop down with great force, and before the victim had time to be frightened she was dead, and her body was carried away in the falcon's claws, to serve for her supper.

Now the duck was the mother of a large family, all newly hatched, and it would have fared very badly with them in their babyhood, had it not been for the kindness of a guinea-fowl, who adopted them as her own, directly she heard that they were left orphans and helpless. The guinea-fowl, indeed, was quite glad of the chance, because she had a warm heart, and had mourned sadly for her husband, who had been lately condemned to death on account of a series of horrible murders he had committed among the young chickens. So the good creature thought the duck's sad accident quite providential, and at once set about filling her place. Like many other mothers, instead of making the little ducklings fall into *her* ways, *she* fell into theirs, and never left their sides, except on urgent business. And they had, even then, only to call to her if they saw great clumsy animals such as dogs or children coming their way, and down she would rush in a frightful hurry, half scrambling, half flying over bushes and palings, and making furious pecks at the children's legs, if they ventured too close to her little ones.

Still, not all her love nor all her courage would have prevented the guinea-fowl falling a victim to the falcon, if once the bird had got loose, and as it was, the falcon continued to do a good deal of damage to the creatures about the farmyard. A cock, who had hitherto crowed very loudly and declared himself king of the birds, was foolish enough to give battle to our falcon. An hour after, a few feathers were all that remained of *him*, and as to the pigeons, if they ever happened to get within the length of her chain, their doom was certain. At last the gaps in the poultry yard became so serious that Mr. St. John made up his mind that the falcon must be fastened up in a still more out-of-the-way place, and while he was altering her chain away she flew. Of course he thought she was gone for ever, and he watched her circling about the house with a very sad heart, for he still was fond of her, though she was such a very bad bird, and gave him so much trouble ; but as it was getting dark, he had to go in, and stealing a last look at her as he entered the house, he saw her settling down for the night, in the top of a tall tree.

For five days no more was seen or heard of the wanderer, and it was not until the fifth morning that Mr. St. John observed her, high in the air, fighting fiercely with some hooded crows. He stood out on the grass, where there was nothing to hide him, and whistled loudly. In an instant the falcon heard him, busily engaged though she was, and wheeled down to her old master, perching on his arm, and rubbing her beak against him. She did not seem to have been softened or improved by her taste of liberty, for she showed herself quite as ready as of old to attack everything within reach of her chain, first killing them, and then pulling off their hair or plucking out their feathers, before she began her meal. The only animal which she could not swallow was a mole, and one day she swooped down on a Skye terrier, and it would certainly not have escaped alive, had not its master come to the rescue. But it is time we thought of something nicer than this dreadful bird.

MR. BOLT, THE SCOTCH TERRIER [1]

ALL children who know anything of dogs or cats will have found out very soon that the ugly ones are generally far cleverer and more sensible than the pretty ones, who are very apt to think too much of themselves, and will spend a long time admiring themselves in the glass, just as if they were vain men and women. Perhaps it is not altogether their fault if they are stupid, for when they are shaped well, and have fine glossy coats, their masters and mistresses spoil them, and give them too much to eat, so they grow lazy and greedy and disobedient, and like better to lie on the hearth-rug than to do tricks or jump over fences.

Now, luckily for himself, Mr. Bolt, the hero of this story, was quite a plain dog. There could be no doubt about it; and those who loved him did so because he was useful and good company, and not because he was elegant or graceful. Bolt was a large Scotch terrier, rough and hairy, with a thick sort of grey fringe, and great dark eyes looking out from underneath the fringe. His tail and his legs were very short, and his back was very long, so long that he reminded one of a furniture van more than anything else.

But, clever though he was, Bolt had his faults, and the worst of them was that he was very apt to take offence when none was intended, and was far too ready to pick a quarrel, and to hit out with all his might. He probably owed some of this love of fighting to the country in which

[1] Jesse's *British Dogs.*

he was born; for, although a Scotch dog by descent, he was Irish by birth, and his earliest home was near Dublin. As everybody knows, the happiest moment of an Irishman's life is when he is fighting something or somebody, and Bolt in his youth was as reckless as any Irishman of them all. He was hardly a year old when he turned upon his own mother, who had done something to displease him when they were chained together in a stable, and never let her throat go until she was stone dead. Cats, too, were his natural enemies, whom he fought and conquered when no dogs were at hand, and sometimes he would steal out at night from his master's bed, where he always slept, and go for a chase by the light of the moon. Early one morning a fearful noise was heard in the house, and when his master, unable to bear it any longer, got out of bed to see what had happened, he found a strange cat lying on the stairs quite dead, and the house-cat, with which Bolt was barely on speaking terms, sitting in a friendly manner by the side of the conqueror. It is supposed that the strange cat had been led either by motives of curiosity or robbery to enter by some open window, and that the house-cat, unable to drive him out, had welcomed Bolt's ready help for the purpose. Fighter though he was by nature, Bolt had inherited enough Scotch caution not to begin a quarrel unless he had a fair chance of victory; but he was generous, and seldom attacked dogs smaller than himself, unless he was forced into it, or really had nothing better to do. He always began by seizing his enemy's hind leg, which no other dog had been known to do before, and he had such a dislike to dogs whose skins were yellow, that not even the company of ladies, and the responsibility weighing upon him as their escort, would stop Bolt's wild rush at his yellow foe. He hated being shut up too, and showed amazing cleverness in escaping from prison. If that was *quite* impossible, he did the next best thing, which was to gnaw and destroy every article he could in any way reach.

One day when he had behaved so oddly that his family feared he must be going mad (children have been known to frighten their parents in a similar way), he was chained up in a little room, and, feeling too angry to sleep, he amused himself all night with tearing a Bible, several shoes, and a rug, while he gnawed a hole through the door, and bit through the leg of a table. In the morning, when his master came to look at him, he seemed quite recovered, and very well pleased with himself.

As you will see, Bolt had plenty of faults, but he also had some very good qualities, and when he did not think himself insulted by somebody's behaviour, he could show a great deal of sense. One night the cook had been sitting up very late, baking bread for the next day, and being very tired, she fell asleep by the kitchen fire, and a spark fell out on her woollen dress. As there was no blaze, and the girl was a heavy sleeper, she would most likely never have waked at all till it was too late, only luckily for her, the smell reached Bolt's nose as he was lying curled up on his master's bed, near the door which always stood open. Before rousing the house, and giving them all a great fright, he thought he had better make sure exactly what was wrong, so he ran first down to the kitchen from which the smell seemed to come, and finding the cook half stupefied by the smoke, he rushed back to call his master. This he managed to do by tearing up and down the room, leaping on the bed, and pulling off all the clothes, so that the poor man was quite cold. His master was much astonished at the state of excitement Bolt was in, and feared at first that he had gone mad, but after a few minutes he decided that he would get up and see what was the matter. Bolt went carefully before him into the kitchen and sat down by the side of the sleeping girl, turning his face anxiously to the door, to make sure that his master should make no mistake. So in a few seconds the fire was put out, and the girl escaped with nothing worse than a slight scorching.

I might tell you many stories of Bolt and his funny ways, but I have only room for one now. After some time his mistress and her daughter left the house in which Bolt had spent so many years, and took lodgings in Dublin. Bolt went with them, but when they all arrived, the landlady declared she did not like dogs, and Bolt must be placed elsewhere. Now this was very awkward; of course it was out of the question that Bolt could be left behind, yet it was too late to make other arrangements, so after some consideration he was sent back to some lodgings near by, where his master had formerly lived, and where they promised to take great care of him. His young mistress called every day to carry him off for a walk, and she often tried to get him to enter the house she herself was living in, but nothing would persuade the offended Bolt to go inside the door. He would sit on the step for some time, hoping she would be persuaded to return with *him*, but when he found *that* was hopeless, he walked proudly back to his own rooms. His mistresses stayed in that house for nearly a year, and in all that time Bolt never forgot or forgave the slight put upon him, or could be induced to enter the house. Indeed, his feelings were so bitterly hurt, that even when they all set up house again, it was months before Bolt could be got to do anything more than pay his family a call now and then, and sometimes dine with them. So you see it is a serious thing to offend a dog, and he needs to be as delicately handled as a human being.

A RAVEN'S FUNERAL

IN the days of Tiberius the Emperor, there was a young raven hatched in a nest upon the church of Castor and Pollux ; which to make a trial how he could fly, took his first flight into a shoemaker's shop just over against the said church. The master of the shop was well enough content to receive this bird, as commended to him from so sacred a place, and in that regard set great store by it. This raven in short time being acquainted to man's speech, began to speak, and every morning would fly up to the top of the Rostra, or public pulpit for orations, when, turning to the open Forum or market place, he would salute and bid good-morrow to Tiberius Cæsar, and after him to Germanicus and Drusus, the young princes, every one by their names : and anon the people of Rome also that passed by. And when he had so done, afterwards would fly again to the shoemaker's shop aforesaid. This duty practised, yea and continued for many years together, to the great wonder and admiration of all men.

Now it fell out so, that another shoemaker who had taken the next shop unto him, either upon a malicious envy or some sudden spleen and passion of anger, killed the raven. Whereat the people took such indignation, that they, rising in an uproar, first drove him out of that street, and made that quarter of the city too hot for him ; and not long after murdered him for it. But contrariwise, the carcase of this raven was solemnly interred, and the funeral performed with all the ceremonial obsequies that could be devised. For the corpse of this bird was bestowed

A RAVEN'S FUNERAL

in a coffin, couch, or bed, and the same bedecked with
chaplets of fresh flowers of all sorts, carried upon the
shoulders of two blackamoors, with minstrels before,
sounding the haut-boys, and playing on the fife, as far as
the funeral fire, which was piled and made in the right
hand of the causey Appia, in a certain plain or open
field.

So highly reputed the people of Rome that ready wit
and apt disposition in a bird, as they thought it a sufficient
cause to ordain a sumptuous burial therefore.

A STRANGE TIGER [1]

In the year 1790, a baby tiger only six weeks old, whose skin was most beautifully marked in black and yellow, and whose figure was as perfectly modelled as the figure of any tiger could be, was put on board a large East India Company's ship called the ' Pitt,' to be brought to London as a present to George III. Of course, in those days, no one ever thought of coming through the Red Sea, but all vessels sailed all the way round by the Atlantic, so the voyage naturally took many months, especially if the winds were unfavourable. Under these circumstances it was as well to choose your fellow-passengers carefully, as you had to live such a long time with them.

Unlike most of its tribe, the little tiger soon made itself at home on board ship, and as it was too small to do much harm, it was allowed to run about loose and played with anybody who had time for a game. It generally liked to sleep with the sailors in their hammocks, and they would often pretend to use it for a pillow, as it lay at full length on the deck. Partly out of fun, and partly because it was its nature so to do, the tiger would every now and then steal a piece of meat, if it found one handy. One day it was caught red-handed by the carpenter, who took the beef right out of its mouth, and gave it a good beating, but instead of the man getting bitten for his pains, as he might have expected, the tiger

[1] Bingley's *Animal Biography*.

THE TIGER AND HIS FRIEND

took his punishment quite meekly, and bore the carpenter no grudge after. One of its favourite tricks was to run out to the very end of the bowsprit, and stand there looking over the sea, and there was no place in the whole ship to which it would not climb when the fancy took it. But on the whole, the little tiger preferred to have company in its gambols, and was especially fond of dogs, of which there were several on board. They would chase each other and roll over together just like two puppies, and during the ten months or so that the voyage from China lasted, they had time enough to become fast friends. When the vessel reached London, the tiger was at once taken to the Tower, which was the Zoological Gardens of those days. The little fellow did not mind, for he was always ready to take what came and make the best of it, and all the keepers grew as fond of him as the sailors had been.

No more is known about him for eleven years, when he was quite grown up, and then one day, just after he had had his dinner, a black rough-haired terrier pup was put into his cage. Most tigers would have eaten it at once, but not this one, who still remembered his early friends on board ship. He used to watch for the pup every day, and lick it all over, taking care never to hurt it with his rough tongue. In general, the terrier had its food outside the cage, but sometimes it was forgotten, and then it would try to snatch a bit of the tiger's meat; but this the tiger thought impertinent, and made the dog understand that it was the one thing he would not stand.

After several months of close companionship, the terrier was for some reason taken away, and one day, when the tiger awakened from his after-dinner nap, he found the terrier gone, and a tiny Dutch mastiff in its place. He was surprised, but as usual made no fuss, and proceeded to give it a good lick, much to the alarm of the little mastiff. However, its fright soon wore off, and in a day or two it might be seen barking round him and even biting his feet, which the tiger never objected to, perhaps because he could hardly have felt it.

Two years after the tiger had been settled in the Tower, the very same carpenter who had beaten him for stealing the beef came back to England and at once paid a visit to his old friend. The tiger was enchanted to see him, and rushing to the grating, began rubbing himself against it with delight. The carpenter begged to be let into the cage, and though the keepers did not like it, he declared there was no danger, and at last they opened the door. In a moment the tiger was by his side, nearly knocking him down with joy and affection, licking his hands and rubbing his head on his shoulders, and when, after two or three hours, the carpenter got up to go, the tiger would hardly let him leave the den, for he wanted to keep him there for ever.

But all tigers cannot be judged by this tiger.

HALCYONS AND THEIR BIOGRAPHERS

SOME of the old writers, such as Pliny, Plutarch, Ovid, and Aristotle, tell a pretty story about a bird called the halcyon, which flew sporting over the seas, and in mid-winter, when the days were shortest, sat on its nest and brooded over its eggs. And Neptune, who loved these small, gay-plumaged creatures, took pity on them, and kept the waves still during the time of their sitting, so that by-and-bye the days in a man's life that were free from storm and tempest became known as his 'halcyon days,' by which name you will still hear them called.

Now after a careful comparison of the descriptions of the ancient writers, modern naturalists have come to the conclusion that the 'halcyon' of Pliny and the rest was no other than our beautiful kingfisher, which flashes its lovely green and blue along the rivers and cascades both of the Old World and the New. It is now known that the kingfisher is one of the burrowing birds, and that it scoops out in the sand or soft earth of the river banks a passage which is often as much as four feet long and grows wider as it recedes from the water. It feeds upon fish, and fish bones may be found in large numbers on the floor of the kingfisher's house, which, either from laziness or a dislike to change, he inhabits for years together. His eyes are wonderfully quick, and he can detect a fish even in tur-bulent waters from the bough of a tree. Then he makes a rapid dart, and rarely misses his prey. No bird has been the subject of so many superstitions and false stories as the kingfisher, which attracted much attention from its great beauty. Ovid changes the king of Magnesia and his wife Alcyone into kingfishers, Pliny talks of the bird's sweet voice (whereas its note is particularly harsh and ugly), and Plutarch mistakes the sea-urchin's shell for that of the halcyon. Even the Tartars have a story to tell of this bird, and assure us that a feather plucked from a kingfisher and then cast into the water will gain the love of every woman it afterwards touches, while the Ostiacs held that the possession of the skin, bill, and claws of the kingfisher will ensure the owner a life made up of 'halcyon days.'

THE STORY OF A FROG

PART I

EVERYONE knows what excitement the approach of the shooting season causes to a certain class of people in Paris. One is perpetually meeting some of them on their way back from the canal where they have been 'getting their hands in' by popping at larks and sparrows, dragging a dog after them, and stopping each acquaintance to ask: 'Do you like quails and partridges?' 'Certainly.' 'Ah, well, I'll send you some about the second or third of next month.' 'Many thanks.' 'By the way I hit five sparrows out of eight shots just now. Not bad, was it?' 'First rate indeed!'

Well, towards the end of August 1830, one of these sportsmen called at No. 109 in the Faubourg St.-Denis, and on being told that Décamps was at home, climbed to the fifth floor, dragging his dog up step by step, and knocking his gun against every corner till he reached the studio of that eminent painter. However, he only found his brother Alexandre, one of those brilliant and original persons whose inherent laziness alone prevented his bringing his great natural gifts to perfection.

He was universally voted a very good fellow, for his easy good nature made him ready to do or give whatever anyone asked. It was not surprising, therefore, that the new comer soon managed to persuade Alexandre that nothing could be more delightful than to attend the opening of the shooting season on the plains of St.-Denis, where, according to general report, there were swarms of quails, clouds of partridges, and troops of hares.

As a result of this visit, Alexandre Décamps ordered a shooting coat from his tailor, a gun from the first gun-maker's in Paris, and a pair of gaiters from an equally celebrated firm ; all of which cost him 660 francs, not to mention the price of his licence.

On August 31 Alexandre discovered that one important item was still wanting to his outfit—a dog. He went at once to a man who had supplied various models to his brother Eugène's well-known picture of 'performing dogs,' and asked if he happened to have any sporting dogs.

The man declared he had the very thing, and going to the kennel promptly whipped off the three-cornered hat and little coat worn by a black and white mongrel whom he hastened to present to his customer as a dog of the purest breed. Alexandre hinted that it was not usual for a pointer to have such sharp-pointed ears, but the dealer replied that 'Love' was an English dog, and that it was considered the very best form for English dogs to have pointed ears. As this statement *might* be true, Alexandre made no further objections, but paid for the dog and took Love home with him.

At five o'clock next morning Alexandre was roused up by his sporting friend, who, scolding him well for not being ready earlier, hurried him off as fast as possible, declaring the whole plain would be shot before they could get there.

It was certainly a curious sight ; not a swallow, not even the meanest little sparrow, could rise without a volley of shots after it, and everyone was anxiously on the look-out for any and every sort of bird that could possibly be called game.

Alexandre's friend was soon bitten by the general fever and threw himself energetically amidst the excited crowd, whilst Alexandre strolled along more calmly, dutifully followed by Love. Now everyone knows that the first duty of any sporting dog is to scour the field and

LOVE'S DISGRACEFUL BEHAVIOUR OUT SHOOTING

not to count the nails in his master's boots. This thought naturally occurred to Alexandre, and he accordingly made a sign to Love and said: ' Seek ! '

Love promptly stood up on his hind legs and began to dance.

'Dear me,' said Alexandre, as he lowered his gun and contemplated his dog: 'It appears that Love unites the lighter accomplishments to his more serious education. I seem to have made rather a good bargain.' However, having bought Love to point and not to dance, he waited till the dance was over and repeated in firm tones: 'Seek!'

Love stretched himself out at full length and appeared to be dead.

Alexandre put his glass into his eye and inspected Love. The intelligent creature was perfectly immovable; not a hair on his body stirred, he might have been dead for twenty-four hours.

'This is all very pretty,' said Alexandre, 'but, my friend, this is not the time for these jokes. We are here to shoot—let us shoot. Come! get up.'

Love did not stir an inch.

'Wait a bit,' remarked Alexandre, as he picked up a stick from the ground and took a step towards Love, intending to stir him up with it: 'Wait a bit.' But no sooner did Love see the stick in his master's hand than he sprang to his feet and eagerly watched his movements. Alexandre thinking the dog was at last going to obey, held the stick towards him, and for the third time ordered him to 'seek.'

Love took a run and sprang gracefully over the stick.

Love could do three things to perfection—dance on his hind legs, sham dead, and jump for the king!

Alexandre, however, who did not appreciate the third accomplishment any more than he had done the two others, broke the stick over Love's back, which sent him off howling to his master's friend.

As fate would have it the friend fired at that very moment, and an unfortunate lark fell right into Love's jaws. Love thankfully accepted this windfall, and made but one mouthful of the lark. The infuriated sportsman threw himself on the dog, and seizing him by the throat to force open his jaws, thrust in his hand and drew out—three tail feathers: the bird itself was not to be thought of.

Bestowing a vicious kick on the unhappy Love, he turned on Alexandre, exclaiming : ' Never again do you catch me shooting with you. Your brute of a dog has just devoured a superb quail. Ah ! come here if you dare, you rascal ! '

Poor Love had not the least wish to go near him. He ran as fast as he could to his master, a sure proof that he preferred blows to kicks.

However, the lark seemed to have whetted Love's appetite : and perceiving creatures of apparently the same kind rise now and then from the ground, he took to scampering about in hopes of some second piece of good luck.

Alexandre had some difficulty in keeping up with him, for Love hunted his game after a fashion of his own, that is to say with his head up and his tail down. This would seem to prove that his sight was better than his scent, but it was particularly objectionable to his master, for he put up the birds before they were within reach, and then ran barking after them. This went on nearly all day.

Towards five o'clock Alexandre had walked about fifteen miles and Love at least fifty ; the former was exhausted with calling and the latter with barking, when, all of a sudden Love began to point, so firmly and steadily that he seemed changed to stone.

At this surprising sight Alexandre, forgetful of all his fatigues and disappointments, hurried up, trembling lest Love should break off before he could get within reach. No fear ; Love might have been glued to the spot. Alexandre came up to him, noted the direction of his eyes and saw that they were fixed on a tuft of grass, and that under this grass there appeared to be some greyish object.

Thinking it must be a young bird which had strayed from its covey, he laid down his gun, took his cap in his hand, and cautiously creeping near, like a child about to catch a butterfly, he flung the cap over the unknown object, put in his hand and drew out—a frog !

Anyone else would have flung the frog away, but Alexandre philosophically reflected that there must certainly be some great future in store for this, the sole result of his day's sport ; so he accordingly put the frog carefully into his game bag and brought it home, where he

THE SOLE RESULT OF HIS DAY'S SPORT

transferred it to an empty glass jam jar and poured the contents of his water-bottle on its head.

So much care and trouble for a frog may appear excessive ; but Alexandre knew what this particular frog had cost him, and he treated it accordingly.

It had cost him 660 francs, without counting his licence.

PART II

' Ah, ah ! ' cried Dr. Thierry as he entered the studio next day, ' so you've got a new inmate.' And without paying any attention to Tom's friendly growls or to Jacko's engaging grimaces, he walked straight up to the

jar which contained Mademoiselle Camargo—as she had
already been named.[1]

Mademoiselle Camargo, unaware that Thierry was not
only a learned doctor, but also a most intellectual and
delightful person, fell to swimming round and round her
jar as fast as she could go, which however did not prevent
her being seized by one of her hind legs.

MADEMOISELLE CAMARGO BECOMES A BAROMETER

' Dear me,' said Thierry, as he turned the little creature about, ' a specimen of the *Rana temporaria*. See,
there are the two black spots near the eyes which give it
the name. Now if you only had a few dozens of this
species, I should advise you to have a fricassée made of
their hind legs, to send for a couple of bottles of good

[1] A fashionable dancer in Paris.

claret, and to ask me to dinner. But as you only happen
to have one, we will, with your leave, content ourselves
with making a barometer.'

'Now,' said Thierry, opening a drawer, 'let us attend
to the prisoner's furniture.' Saying which he took out
two cartridges, a gimlet, a penknife, two paint-brushes,
and four matches. Décamps watched him without in the
least understanding the object of all these preparations,
which the doctor was making with as much care as though
for some surgical operation.

First he emptied the powder out of the cartridges into
a tray and kept the bullets. Then he threw the brushes
and ties to Jacko and kept the handles.

'What the deuce are you about?' cried Décamps,
snatching his two best paint-brushes from Jacko. 'Why
you're ruining my establishment!'

'I'm making a ladder,' gravely replied Thierry.

And true enough, having bored holes in the bullets,
he fixed the brush handles into them so as to form the
sides of the ladder, using the matches to make the rungs.
Five minutes later the ladder was completed and placed
in the jar, where the weight of the bullets kept it firmly
down.

No sooner did Mademoiselle Camargo find herself the
owner of this article of furniture than she prepared to test
it by climbing up to the top rung.

'We shall have rain,' said Thierry.

'You don't say so,' replied Décamps, 'and there's my
brother who wanted to go out shooting again to-day.'

'Mademoiselle Camargo does not advise his doing so,'
remarked the doctor.

'How so?'

'My dear friend, I have been providing you with an
inexpensive but reliable barometer. Each time you see
Mademoiselle Camargo climb to the top of her ladder it's
'a sure sign of rain; when she remains at the bottom you
may count on fine weather, and if she goes up half-way,

don't venture out without your umbrella; changeable, changeable.'

' Dear me, dear me,' said Décamps.

During the next six months Mademoiselle Camargo continued to foretell the weather with perfect and un-erring regularity. But for painful reasons into which we need not inquire too closely, Mademoiselle's useful career soon closed, and she left a blank in the ménagerie.

THE WOODPECKER TAPPING ON THE HOLLOW OAK TREE

MOST children who were taught music forty or fifty years ago, learnt as one of their first tunes an air called ' The Woodpecker Tapping on the Hollow Oak Tree.' Oak trees are not the only ones that woodpeckers, and especially American woodpeckers, 'tap' on. There is hardly any old tree which they disdain to work upon, sometimes for food, sometimes for nesting purposes, sometimes it would seem merely for the sake of employment and of keeping their bills in order.

For the woodpecker's bill is a very powerful instrument, and can get through a great deal of work. In the case of the ' ivory-billed woodpecker,' it is not only white, and hard, and strong, but it has a ribbed surface, which tends to prevent its breaking, and even if he does not form one of this class, the woodpecker is as clever in his own line as any carpenter, and more industrious than many. The moment that he notices symptoms of decay in any tree, he flies off to make a careful examination of it, and when he has decided on the best mode of attack, he loses no time, and has even been known to strip all the bark off a dead pine tree of thirty feet long in less than twenty minutes. And this not in little bits, but in sheets five or six feet long, and as whole as the fleece of a sheep when it is sheared.

Of course different varieties of woodpeckers have little differences in their habits, in the same way that habits

differ in different families; but certain customs and ways
of digging are common to them all. Every woodpecker,
for instance, when placed in a wooden cage, will instantly
set to work to dig himself out of it, and to keep him safe,
he needs to be surrounded by wire, against which his bill
is utterly useless. In general the male and female work
by turns at the hole, which is always begun by the male,
and is as perfectly round as if it had been measured and
drawn from one point to another. For a while the boring
is quite straight, and then it takes a sloping direction, so
as to provide a partial shelter against the rain. Sometimes the bird will begin by a slope, and end in a direct
line, but the hole is never straight all through, and the
depth varies from two to five feet, according to the kind
of woodpecker that is digging. The inside of the nest and
the passage to it are as smooth as if they had been
polished wlth a plane, and the chips of wood are often
thrown down in a careless manner, at some distance, in
order that attention may not be attracted to the spot.
Often the bird's labours have to begin, especially in
orchards, which are favourite nesting places with them,
with having to turn out swarms of insects, nestling comfortably between the bark and the tree. These he either
kills or eats; anyhow he never rests until they are safely
got rid of.

The woodpecker, is never still, and, in many respects,
is like a mischievous boy; so, as can be imagined, he is
not very easy to make a pet of. One adventurous person,
however, captured a woodpecker in America, and has
left us a history of its performances during the three
days it lived in captivity. The poor bird was very
miserable in its prison, and cried so like a child that many
persons were completely taken in. Left alone for a short
time in the room while his captor had gone to look after
his horse, he examined the room carefully to see where
lay his best chance of escape. His quick eye soon
detected the plaster between the window and the ceiling,

and he began at once to attack the weak place. He worked so hard that when his master returned he had laid bare the laths, and had bored a hole bigger than his own head, while the bed was strewn with big fragments of plaster. A very little while longer and he would have been free, and what a pity that he was disturbed in his work! But his master was most anxious to keep him a little longer, to observe his ways, so he tied him to the leg of the table, and went off to get him some food. By the time the man came back the mahogany table was lying in bits about the floor, and the woodpecker was looking eagerly round to see what other mischief he could do. He would not eat food of any kind, and died in three days, to the great regret of his captor.

DOGS OVER THE WATER

No animal, not even the horse, has made itself so many friends as the dog. A whole library might be filled with stories about what dogs have done, and men could learn a great deal from the sufferings dogs have gone through for masters that they love.

Whatever differences there may be between foreigners and Englishmen, there is at any rate none in the behaviour of British and foreign dogs. 'Love me, love my dog,' the proverb runs, but in general it would be much more to the point to say 'love my dog, love me.' We do not know anything of the Austrian officer of whose death I am going to tell you, but after hearing what his dog did, we should all have been pleased to make the master's acquaintance.

In the early years of this century, when nearly every country in Europe was turned into a battlefield by Napoleon, there was a tremendous fight between the French and the Austrians at Castiglione in Lombardy, which was then under the Austrian yoke. The battle was hard fought and lasted several hours, but at length the Austrian ranks were broken and they had to retreat, after frightful losses on both sides. After the field had been won, Napoleon, as his custom was, walked round among the dead and dying, to see for himself how the day had gone. Not often had he performed this duty amidst a greater scene of blood and horror, and as he came to a spot where the dead were lying thickest, he saw to his surprise a small long-eared spaniel standing with his feet on the breast of an Austrian officer, and his eyes fixed on his face, waiting to detect the slightest movement. Absorbed in his watch, the dog never heard the approach of the Emperor and his staff, but Napoleon called to one of his attendants and pointed out the spaniel. At the sound of his voice the spaniel turned round, and looked at the Emperor, as if he knew that to him only he must appeal for help. And the prayer was not in vain, for Napoleon was very seldom needlessly cruel. The officer was dead and beyond any aid from him, but the Emperor did what he could, and gave orders that the dog should be looked after by one of his own men, and the wounded Austrians carefully tended. *He* knew what it was to be loved as blindly by men as that officer was loved by his dog.

Nearly two years before this time, France was trembling in the power of a set of bloody ruffians, and in Paris especially no man felt his head to be safe from one hour to the other. Hundreds of harmless people were clapped into prison on the most paltry charges, and if they were not torn to pieces by infuriated crowds, they ended their lives on the guillotine.

Among the last of the victims before the fall of Robespierre, which finished the Reign of Terror, was a magistrate in one of the departments in the North of France whom everyone looked up to and respected. It may be thought that it would not have been easy to find a pretext for throwing into prison a man of such an open and honourable life, but when other things failed, a vague accusation of conspiracy against the Government was always possible, and accordingly the magistrate was arrested in his own house. No one was there to help him or to share his confinement. He had long sent away his children to places of safety; some of his relations were in gaol like himself, and his friends dared not come forward. They could have done him no good, and would only have shared his fate. In those dark days every man had to suffer alone, and nobly they did it. Only one friend the magistrate had who ventured openly to show his affection, and

The Faithful Spaniel

even *he* might go no farther than the prison doors, namely his spaniel, who for twelve years had scarcely left his side; but though dogs were not yet proscribed, the spaniel's whinings availed nothing, and the gates were shut against him. At first he refused to believe that his master would never come back, and returned again and again with the hopes of meeting the magistrate on his way home. At last the dog's spirits gave way, and he went to the house of a friend of the family who knew him well, and received him kindly. Even here, however, he had to be carefully hidden lest his protector should be charged with sheltering the dog of an accused person, and have to pay the penalty on the guillotine. The animal seemed to know what was expected of him, and never barked or growled as dogs love to do; and indeed he was too sad to take any interest in what was going on around him. The only bright spot in his day was towards evening when he was secretly let out, and he made straight for the gate of the prison. The gate was never opened, but he always hoped that *this* time it would be, and sat on and on till he felt that his chance was gone for that day. All the prison officials knew him by sight, and were sorry for him, and one day the gaoler's heart was softened, and he opened the doors, and led him to his master's cell. It would be difficult to say which of the two was the happier, and when the time came for the prisoners to be locked up for the night, the man could scarcely tear away the dog, so closely did he cling to his master. However, there was no help for it, he had to be put outside, lest it should occur to some one in authority to make a visit of inspection to the prison. Next evening the dog returned at the same hour and was again admitted, and when his time was up, he went home with a light heart, sure that by sunset next day he would be with his beloved master.

This went on for several weeks, and the dog, at any rate, would have been quite satisfied if it had gone on for ever. But one morning the magistrate was told that he was to be brought before his judges to make answer to his charge and receive his sentence. In the midst of a vast crowd, which dared not show sympathy even if it felt it, the magistrate pleaded for the last time, without a friend to give him courage except his dog, which had somehow forced himself through guards and crowd, and lay crouched between his legs, happy at this unexpected chance of seeing his master.

Sentence of death was pronounced, as was inevitable, and the hour of execution was not long delayed. In the wonderful way that animals always *do* know when something out of the common is passing, the spaniel was sitting outside the door when his master walked out for the last time, although it was long before the hour of his daily visit. Alone, of all the friends that he had known and loved, his dog went with him, and stood beside him on the steps of the guillotine, and sat at his feet when his head fell. Vaguely the spaniel was aware that something terrible had happened; his master, who had never failed him before, would not speak to him now. It was in vain to lick his hand: he got no pat in answer. But if his master was asleep, and his bed was underground, then he too must sleep by his side till the morning came and the world awoke again.

So two nights passed, and three. Then his friend, who had sheltered him during these long weeks, came to look for him, and, after much coaxing and caressing, persuaded him to return to his old hiding-place. With great difficulty he was induced to swallow some food, but the moment his protector's back was turned, he rushed out and fought his way to his master's grave.

This lasted for three months, and every day the dog looked sadder and thinner than the day before. At length his friend thought he would try a new plan with him, and tied him firmly up. But in the morning he found that the dog had, like Samson, broken through his bonds, and was lying on the grave, which he never left again.

Food was brought to him—he never came to seek it himself, and in time he refused even what was lying there before him. One day his friends found him trying to scratch up the earth where his master lay ; and all at once his strength gave way, and with one howl he died, showing the two men who stood around of love that was stronger than death, and fidelity that lasted beyond the grave.[1]

One more story of a little dog—this time an English one—and I have done.

It was on February 8, 1587, that Mary Queen of Scots ended her eighteen years of weary captivity upon a scaffold at Fotheringay. Carefully dressed in a robe of black velvet, with a long mantle of satin floating above it, and her head covered with a white crape veil, Mary ascended the platform, where the executioner was awaiting her. Some English nobles, sent by Queen Elizabeth to see that her orders were carried out, were standing by, and some of Queen Mary's faithful women. But besides these was one whose love for her was hardly less—the Queen's little dog, who had been her constant companion in the prison. ' He was sitting there the whole time,' says an eye-witness, ' keeping very quiet, and never stirring from her side ; but as soon as the head was stricken off and placed upon the seat, he began to bestir himself and cry out ; afterwards he took up a position between the body and the head, which he kept until some one came and removed him, and this had to be done by violence.' We are not told who took him away and tenderly washed off the blood of Mary which was staining his coat, but we may be sure that it was one of the Queen's ladies who cherished everything that belonged to her, and in memory of her mistress would care for her little dog to the end of its days.

[1] From *Observations in Natural History*.

THE CAPOCIER AND HIS MATE

WHEN Vaillant the traveller was in Africa, he made the acquaintance of a bird to which he gave the name of capocier. It was a small creature, which was in the habit of coming with its mate several times a day into Vaillant's tent; a proceeding which he thought arose from pure friendship, but which he soon found sprang from interested motives. Vaillant was making a collection of birds, and his table was strewn about with moss, wool, and such things as he used for stuffing. The capocier, with more sense than might have been expected of him, found out very soon that it was much easier to steal Vaillant's soft material than to collect it laboriously for himself, and the naturalist used to shut his eyes with amusement while the birds flew off with a parcel of stuffing as big as themselves.

He followed them, and tracked them to a bush which grew by a spring in the corner of a deserted garden. Here they had placed a thick layer of moss, in a fork of one of the branches, and were now engaged in weaving in grass, cotton, and flax. The whole of the second day the little pair worked hard, the male making in all forty-six journeys to Vaillant's room, for thieving purposes. The spoil was always laid either on the nest itself, or within the reach of the female, and when enough had been collected, they both trampled it in, and pressed it down with their bodies.

At last the male got tired, and tried to prevail on his wife to play a game. She declined, and said she had no time for such things; so, to revenge himself, the male proceeded to pull to pieces her work. Seeing that he would have his own way, the female at length consented to play for a little, and fluttered from bush to bush, while her mate flew after her, but she always managed to keep just out of his reach. When he had had enough, he let her go back to her work, while he sang a song for a little, and then made ready to help build the nest. He found, or stole, the materials necessary, and carried them back to his wife, who packed them firmly in and made all tidy. But her husband was much more idle than she, and he soon tired of steady labour. He complained of the heat, and laughed at her for being in such a hurry, and said there was plenty of time before them, and he wanted a little fun. So eight times during that one morning the poor wife had to leave off her building, and hide her impatience, and pretend to play, when she would much rather have been doing something else, and it was three days before the bottom was finished and the sides begun.

Certainly the making of the bottom *was* rather a troublesome business; for the birds had to roll over every part of it, so as to get it firm and hard. Then, when all was right, they made a border, which they first trimmed round, and next overlaid with cotton, pressing it all together with their breasts and shoulders. The twigs of the bush in which the nest was built were interlaced into the sides to prevent the whole structure being blown down, and particular care was taken that none of them should stick out in the inside of the nest, which was absolutely smooth and solid. After seven days it was done, and very pretty it was. It was perfectly white in colour, and about nine inches high on the outside where it had been made very thick, and not more than five inches within. However that was quite big enough for two such little people.

OWLS AND MARMOTS

IT is curious, when we come to think of it, how very few of the creatures that live upon the earth, ever take the trouble to build any kind of house to live in. For the most part, they are contented to find out some cave or hole or convenient place where they can be hidden, and from which they can steal forth to get their food, but as for collecting materials from the outside to make their dwelling place stronger or more beautiful, as do the beavers, for instance, why, we might all look for many years before we should find a horse or a tiger employing himself like that!

Yet we all know that all the birds that live (the cuckoo excepted) manage to build some kind of a nest, and so do some fishes and many insects. It would take too long to write about them all, but we will just see how some of the cleverest among them go to work.

One of the first things that struck Europeans travelling sixty or seventy years ago in the wild country beyond the great Mississippi, was the fact that whole districts, sometimes several acres in extent and sometimes several miles, were covered with little mounds of the shape of a pyramid, about two feet wide at the bottom, and at the most eighteen inches high. These are the houses of the marmots or prairie dogs, and when deserted as they often are by their original inhabitants, they become the homes of burrowing owls.

Now a neat, comfortable, well-built house is really quite

necessary for the marmot, as he goes fast to sleep when the weather begins to get cold, and does not wake up till the sun is shining warmly again on the earth above him. Then he sets to work, either to repair the walls of his house which have been damaged by the heavy rains and hard frosts, or if that seems useless labour, to dig a fresh one somewhere else. But industrious as he is, the hard work does not make the marmot at all a ' dull boy,' and he can still spare time for a good game now and then.

Of course, as we are talking about birds, perhaps we ought not to be describing marmots, which are naturally not birds at all; but as they build for the burrowing owls to inhabit, a description of the houses may not be out of place.

The entrance to the marmot's house is either at the top or on the side of the little mound above ground. Then he hollows out a passage straight down for one, or sometimes two feet, and this passage is continued in a sloping direction for some distance further, when it leads, like a story in the ' Arabian Nights,' into a large warm room, built of soft dry grass, which has been packed into a tight, firm mass. In general the outside of the little mounds is covered with small plants and grasses, so that the marmot always has his food near at hand, but occasionally they prefer to make their villages in barren spots, as being safer from enemies. Still, wherever they are, the sociable little colony of marmots are said to be haunted by at least one burrowing owl, a bird about nine inches long, and from a distance not very unlike the marmot itself, when it is sitting up, listening for the approach of danger. If no burrow seems likely to be vacant at the time he wants one, the owl does not scruple to turn out the owner, who has to begin all his labour over again. Sometimes, when affairs above ground are more than usually disturbed, and foes of all kinds are prowling about, seeking whom they may devour, owls and marmots and rattlesnakes, and lizards rush helter-skelter into the underground city, taking refuge from the dangers of the upper world. It would be a strange sight if we could see it, and it would be stranger still if the fugitives manage to separate without some of the party having gone to make the dinners of the rest.

EAGLES' NESTS

EAGLES, as a rule, build their nests on the shelves of rocks, high out of reach of any but the boldest climbers. There are, however, some species among them who prefer the tops of trees, at a height varying from fifteen to fifty feet. These nests are constructed of long sticks, grass, and even reeds, and are often as much as five or six feet high, and at least four broad. Soft pine tops form the lining, and a bed for the young. Many eagles are clever divers, and like the excitement of catching their own fish, instead of merely forcing the fish-hawks to give up their prey, and an American naturalist gives an interesting account of the sporting proceedings of two eagles on the Green River in Kentucky. The naturalist had been lying hidden among the rocks on the bank of the river for about two hours, when suddenly far above his head where the eagle had built his nest, he heard a loud hissing, and on looking up, saw that the little eaglets had crawled to the edge of the nest, and were dancing with hope and excitement at the idea of a good dinner. In a few moments the parent eagle reached the rock and balancing himself on the edge by the help of his wings and tail, handed over his spoil to the young ones. The little eagles seemed in luck that day, for soon their mother appeared in sight carrying in her claws a perch. But either the watcher below made some movement, or else her eyes were far sharper than her mate's, for with a loud cry she dropped her fish, and hovered over the nest to protect it in case of an attack. When all was quiet again, the naturalist went out cautiously to examine the perch, which he found to weigh as much as $5\frac{1}{2}$ lbs. You do not catch such big perch in England.